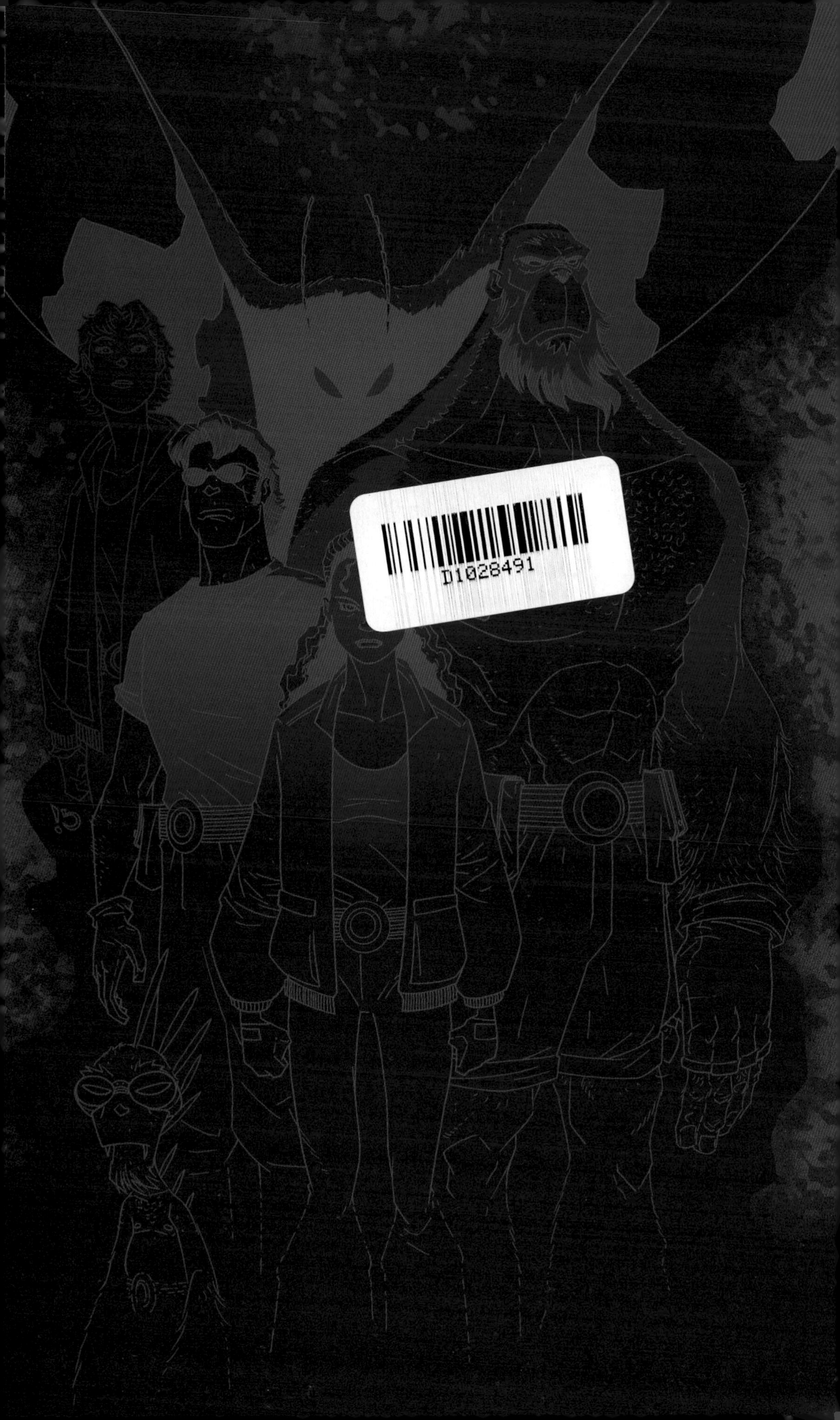

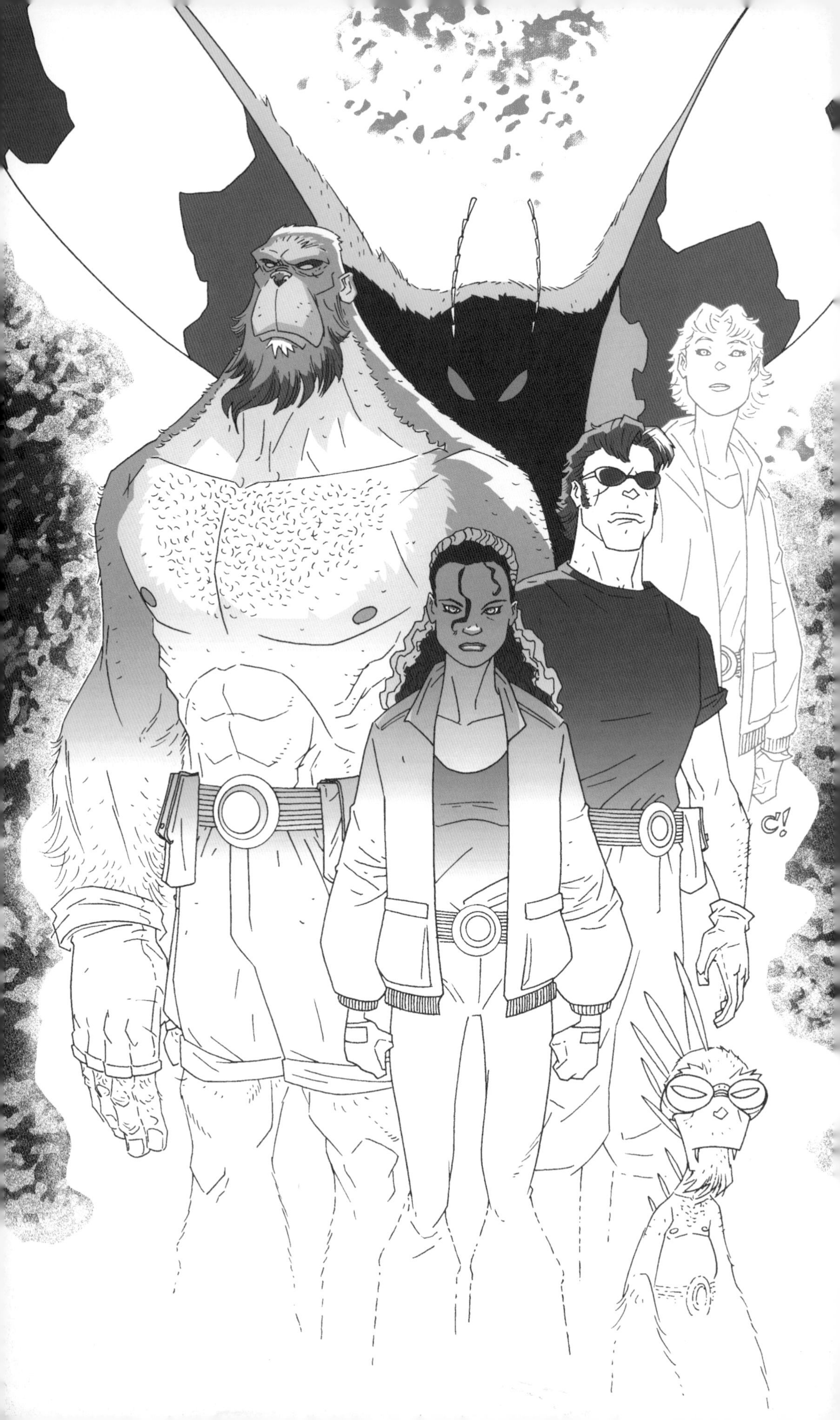

TODD AND CRAIG'S

THE Perhapanauts™

SECOND CHANCES

WORDS · **TODD DEZAGO**
PICTURES · **CRAIG ROUSSEAU**
COLORS · **RICO RENZI**
LETTERS · **DEZAGO & ROUSSEAU**

COVER · **ROUSSEAU**
INTRODUCTION · **CRAIG ROUSSEAU**
WITH ILLUSTRATION BY **TODD DEZAGO**

DARK HORSE BOOKS®

PUBLISHER · **MIKE RICHARDSON**

EDITOR · **DAVE LAND**

ASSISTANT EDITOR · **KATIE MOODY**

COLLECTION DESIGNER · **TINA ALESSI**

ART DIRECTOR · **LIA RIBACCHI**

THE PERHAPANAUTS: SECOND CHANCES

This book collects issues one through four of the Dark Horse comic-book series *The Perhapanauts: Second Chances.*

Published by
Dark Horse Books
A division of Dark Horse Comics, Inc.
10956 SE Main Street
Milwaukie, OR 97222

darkhorse.com

To find a comic shop in your area, call the Comic Shop Locator Service toll-free at 1-888-266-4226.

First edition: May 2007
ISBN-10: 1-59307-797-1
ISBN-13: 978-1-59307-797-6

10 9 8 7 6 5 4 3 2 1
Printed in China

HAPA-DUCTION

As is often the case in life—and especially so in the creation of *The Perhapanauts*—this was not our original intent. (Me writing this introduction, I mean, not this book itself.)

With our wildly successful first trade paperback, we were able to cajole our good friend and comics superstar Mike Wieringo into contributing not only a sweet pinup of the 'Haps, but also a great introduction singing our praises and whatnot. It put us in a bit of a bind, actually, since he was our ace in the hole. As great as that intro was, we still would've felt a bit weird asking him for one for the second volume as well . . . and while just cutting and pasting that first one in crossed our minds, we decided against it.

So, after Mike awkwardly said "no," we started to think about who else we could ask to write glowing things about us, and it finally dawned on me . . . it really didn't matter. Sure, we could have asked/begged another A-list artist/writer or celebrity to throw us a bone, but really . . . who decides to buy a book based on the introduction? Yes, it certainly strokes the ego when somebody tells you how much they've enjoyed your work (and make no mistake, we—especially Todd—would never turn down compliments or good reviews), but I don't think it really helps sell a book. I know I've never bought a book just because _____ _____ wrote the introduction . . . Have you? (And if you have, we probably don't know _____ _____ well enough anyway.)

If you're reading this, you've already bought this book, so thanks—and if by some odd chance you haven't yet, put down the latté, head on over to the register, and help us out, willya? Now sit back, relax, and enjoy one helluva fun book, if I do say so myself . . .

Craig

PS: Oh, but if someone DOES know _____ _____, couldya get 'em to write a nice introduction for the next trade?

PPS: When putting together this trade collection, we lined up more than a few friends and artists we dig to contribute pinups. Turns out we lined up more than we originally had room for, so instead of an introduction page to thank everybody and sing their praises, we opted to run another pinup just like we did in the First Blood *trade (honestly, wouldn't you rather see another great pinup than read about them?). On that note, we'd like to thank everybody who contributed to both this trade and the first one as well . . .*

PPPS: Oh, and since I wound up writing this introduction, I thought it only fair that Todd should haveta draw the accompanying pinup . . . after 'Ringo said "no" again.

todd '07

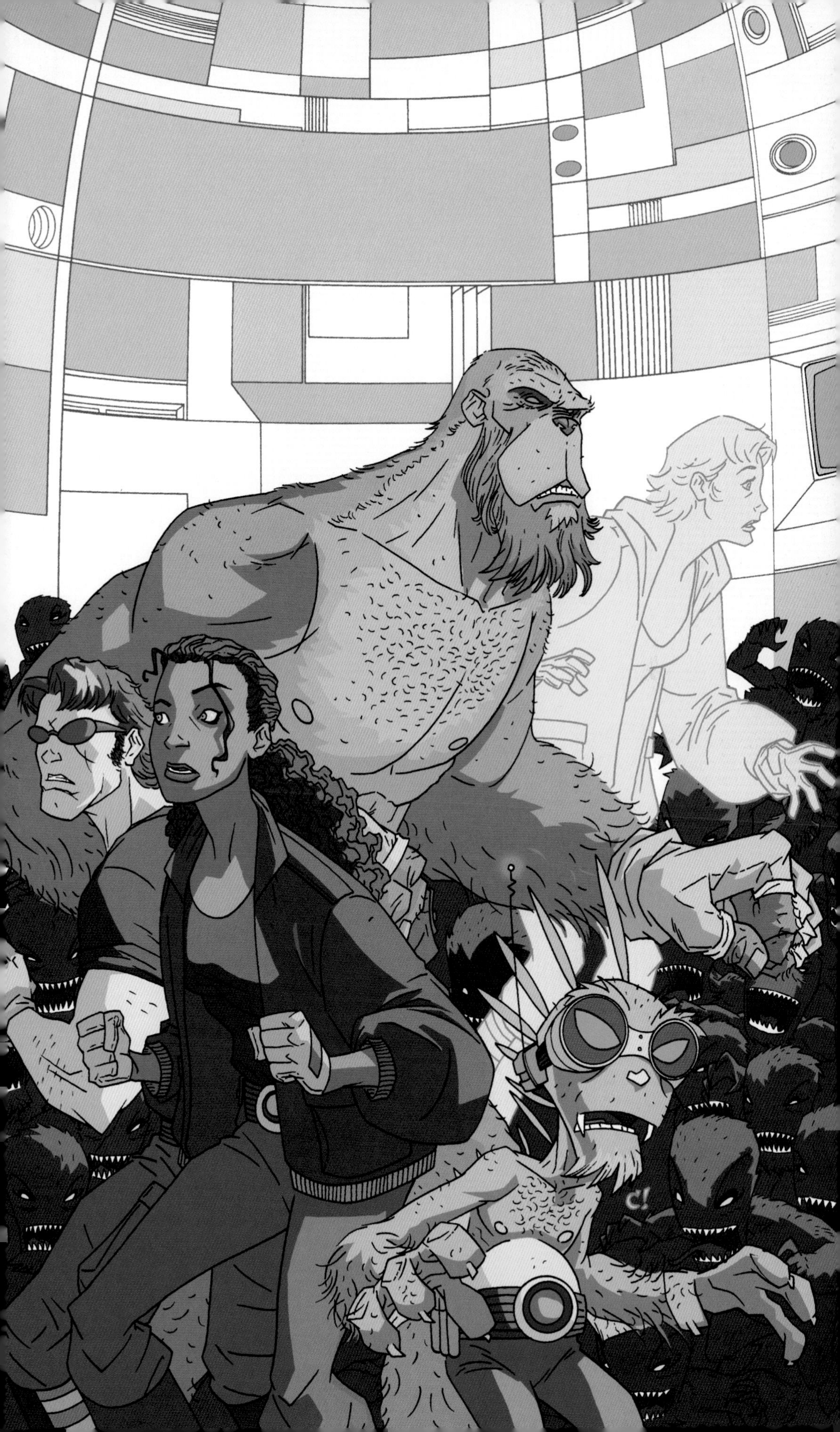

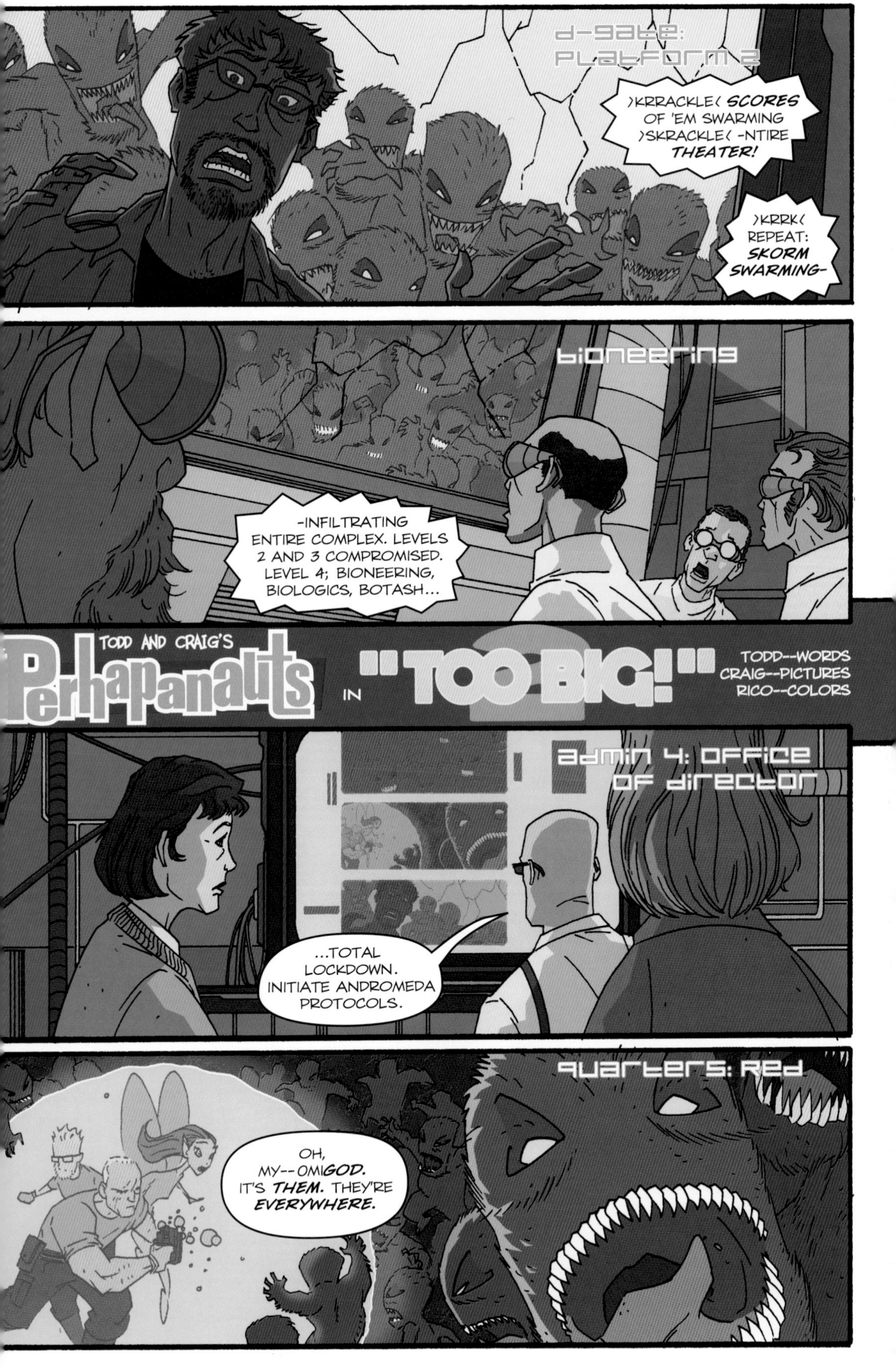

D-GATE: PLATFORM 2
)KRRACKLE(SCORES OF 'EM SWARMING)SKRACKLE(-NTIRE THEATER!
)KRRK(REPEAT: SKORM SWARMING-
BIONEERING
-INFILTRATING ENTIRE COMPLEX. LEVELS 2 AND 3 COMPROMISED. LEVEL 4; BIONEERING, BIOLOGICS, BOTASH...
TODD AND CRAIG'S
Perhapanauts
IN "TOO BIG!"
TODD--WORDS
CRAIG--PICTURES
RICO--COLORS
ADMIN 4: OFFICE OF DIRECTOR
...TOTAL LOCKDOWN. INITIATE ANDROMEDA PROTOCOLS.
QUARTERS: RED
OH, MY--OMIGOD. IT'S THEM. THEY'RE EVERYWHERE.

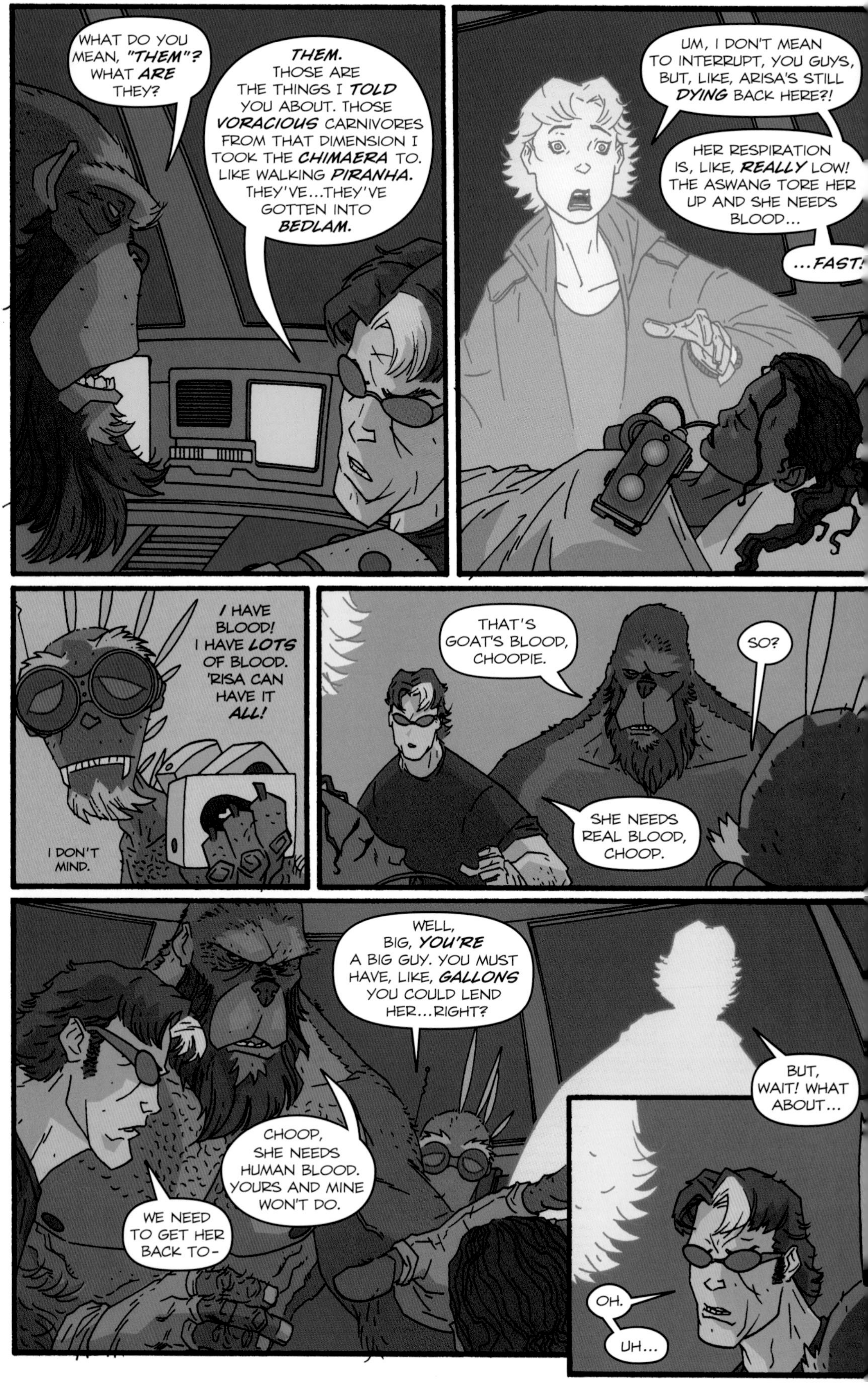
WHAT DO YOU MEAN, "THEM"? WHAT ARE THEY?
THEM. THOSE ARE THE THINGS I TOLD YOU ABOUT. THOSE VORACIOUS CARNIVORES FROM THAT DIMENSION I TOOK THE CHIMAERA TO. LIKE WALKING PIRANHA. THEY'VE...THEY'VE GOTTEN INTO BEDLAM.
UM, I DON'T MEAN TO INTERRUPT, YOU GUYS, BUT, LIKE, ARISA'S STILL DYING BACK HERE?!
HER RESPIRATION IS, LIKE, REALLY LOW! THE ASWANG TORE HER UP AND SHE NEEDS BLOOD...
...FAST!
I HAVE BLOOD! I HAVE LOTS OF BLOOD. 'RISA CAN HAVE IT ALL!
I DON'T MIND.
THAT'S GOAT'S BLOOD, CHOOPIE.
SO?
SHE NEEDS REAL BLOOD, CHOOP.
WELL, BIG, YOU'RE A BIG GUY. YOU MUST HAVE, LIKE, GALLONS YOU COULD LEND HER...RIGHT?
CHOOP, SHE NEEDS HUMAN BLOOD. YOURS AND MINE WON'T DO.
WE NEED TO GET HER BACK TO-
BUT, WAIT! WHAT ABOUT...
OH.
UH...

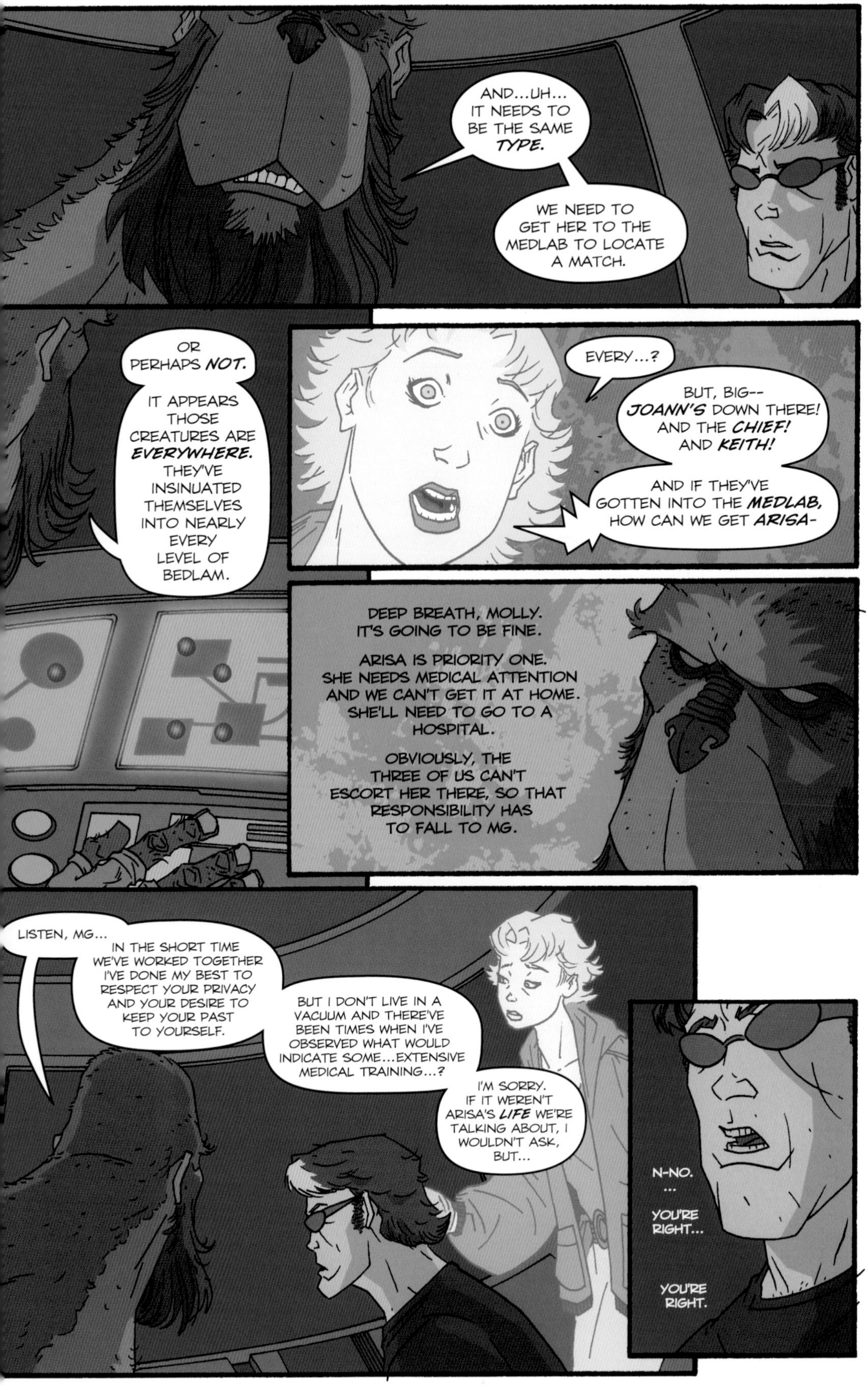
AND...UH... IT NEEDS TO BE THE SAME TYPE.
WE NEED TO GET HER TO THE MEDLAB TO LOCATE A MATCH.
OR PERHAPS NOT.
IT APPEARS THOSE CREATURES ARE EVERYWHERE. THEY'VE INSINUATED THEMSELVES INTO NEARLY EVERY LEVEL OF BEDLAM.
EVERY...?
BUT, BIG-- JOANN'S DOWN THERE! AND THE CHIEF! AND KEITH!
AND IF THEY'VE GOTTEN INTO THE MEDLAB, HOW CAN WE GET ARISA-
DEEP BREATH, MOLLY. IT'S GOING TO BE FINE.
ARISA IS PRIORITY ONE. SHE NEEDS MEDICAL ATTENTION AND WE CAN'T GET IT AT HOME. SHE'LL NEED TO GO TO A HOSPITAL.
OBVIOUSLY, THE THREE OF US CAN'T ESCORT HER THERE, SO THAT RESPONSIBILITY HAS TO FALL TO MG.
LISTEN, MG...
IN THE SHORT TIME WE'VE WORKED TOGETHER I'VE DONE MY BEST TO RESPECT YOUR PRIVACY AND YOUR DESIRE TO KEEP YOUR PAST TO YOURSELF.
BUT I DON'T LIVE IN A VACUUM AND THERE'VE BEEN TIMES WHEN I'VE OBSERVED WHAT WOULD INDICATE SOME...EXTENSIVE MEDICAL TRAINING...?
I'M SORRY. IF IT WEREN'T ARISA'S LIFE WE'RE TALKING ABOUT, I WOULDN'T ASK, BUT...
N-NO.
...
YOU'RE RIGHT...
YOU'RE RIGHT.

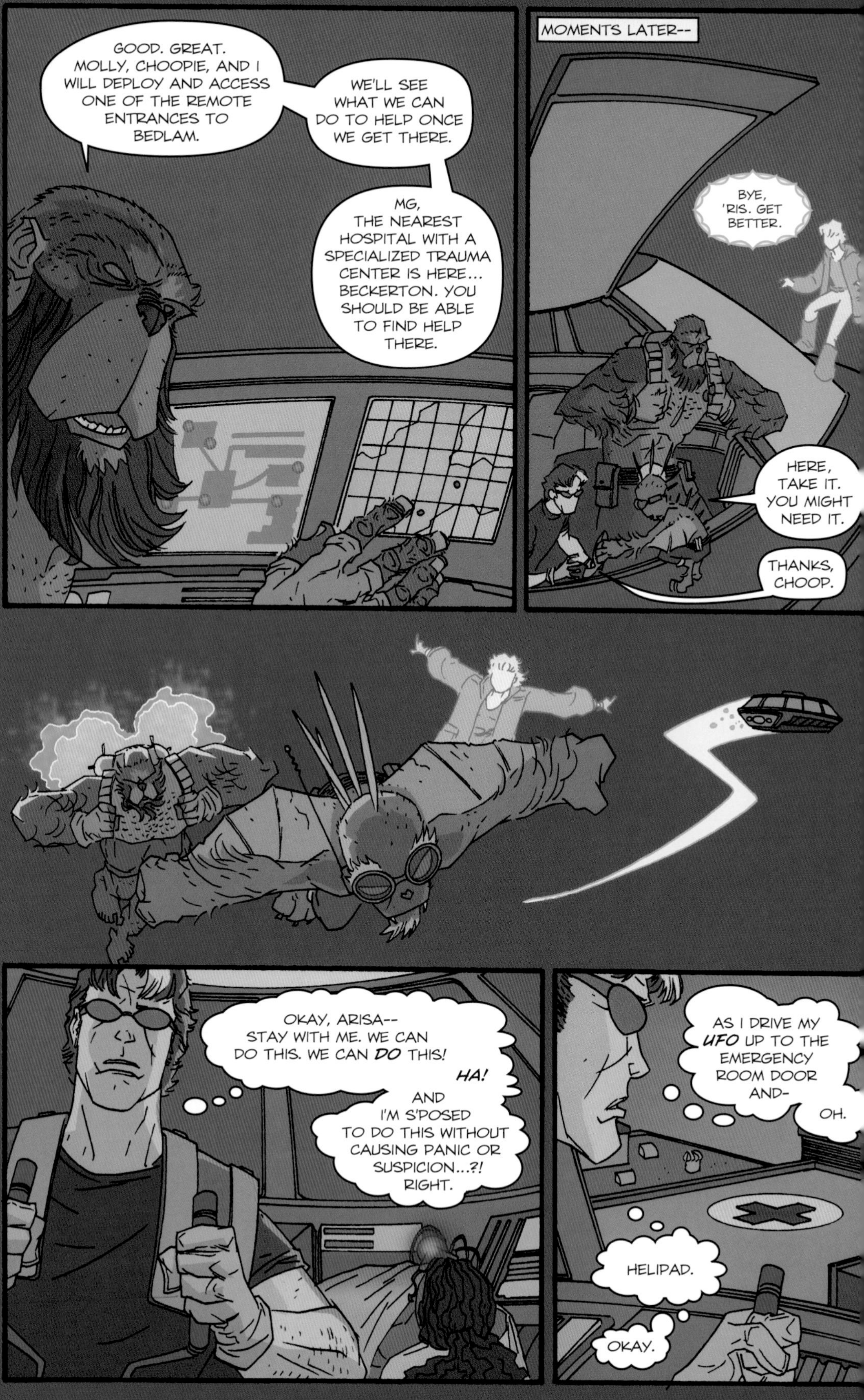
GOOD. GREAT. MOLLY, CHOOPIE, AND I WILL DEPLOY AND ACCESS ONE OF THE REMOTE ENTRANCES TO BEDLAM.
WE'LL SEE WHAT WE CAN DO TO HELP ONCE WE GET THERE.
MG, THE NEAREST HOSPITAL WITH A SPECIALIZED TRAUMA CENTER IS HERE... BECKERTON. YOU SHOULD BE ABLE TO FIND HELP THERE.
MOMENTS LATER--
BYE, 'RIS. GET BETTER.
HERE, TAKE IT. YOU MIGHT NEED IT.
THANKS, CHOOP.
OKAY, ARISA-- STAY WITH ME. WE CAN DO THIS. WE CAN *DO* THIS!
HA!
AND I'M S'POSED TO DO THIS WITHOUT CAUSING PANIC OR SUSPICION...?! RIGHT.
AS I DRIVE MY *UFO* UP TO THE EMERGENCY ROOM DOOR AND-
OH.
HELIPAD.
OKAY.

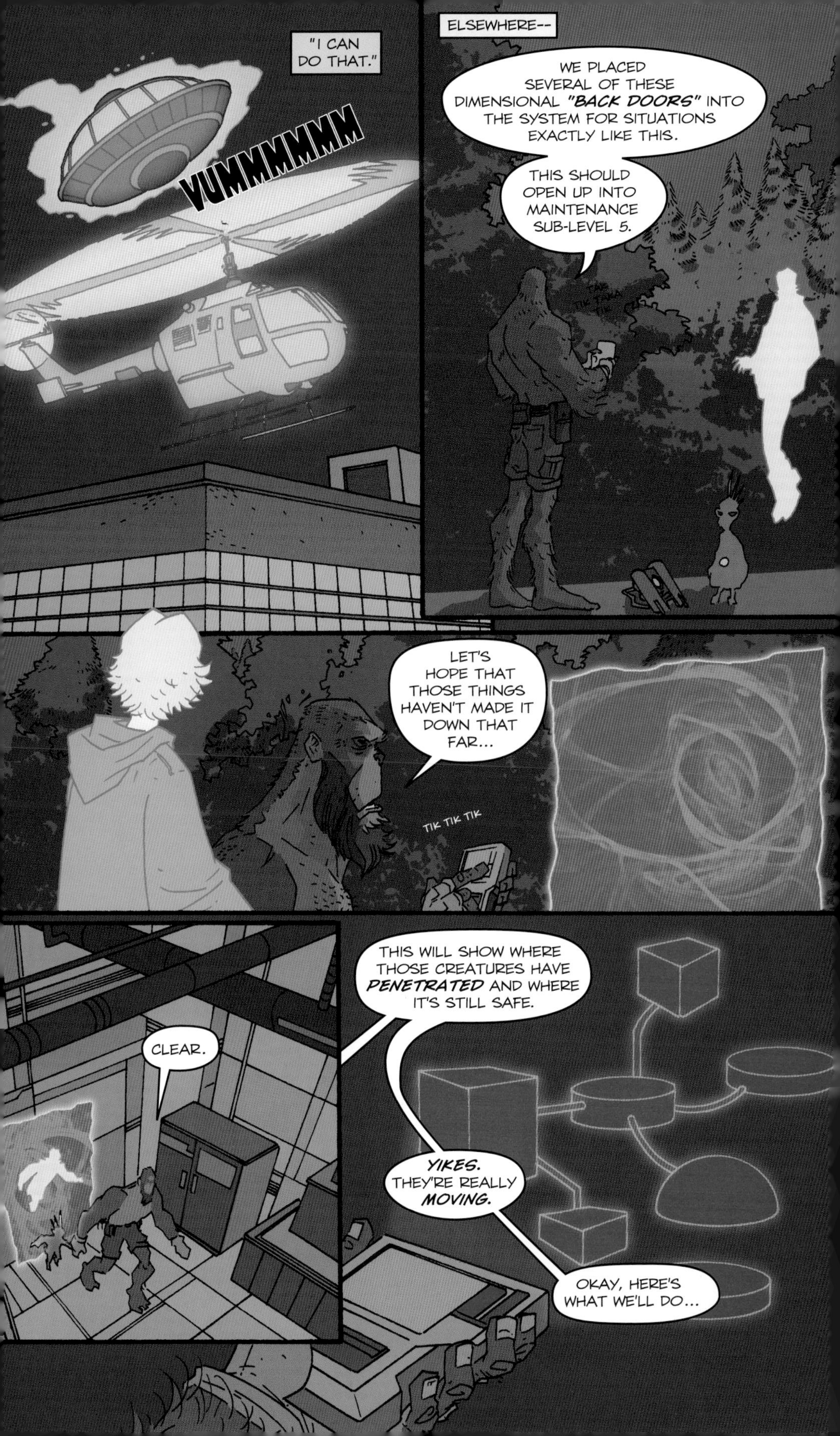
"I CAN DO THAT."
VUMMMMMM
ELSEWHERE--
WE PLACED SEVERAL OF THESE DIMENSIONAL "BACK DOORS" INTO THE SYSTEM FOR SITUATIONS EXACTLY LIKE THIS.
THIS SHOULD OPEN UP INTO MAINTENANCE SUB-LEVEL 5.
LET'S HOPE THAT THOSE THINGS HAVEN'T MADE IT DOWN THAT FAR...
TIK TIK TIK
CLEAR.
THIS WILL SHOW WHERE THOSE CREATURES HAVE PENETRATED AND WHERE IT'S STILL SAFE.
YIKES. THEY'RE REALLY MOVING.
OKAY, HERE'S WHAT WE'LL DO...

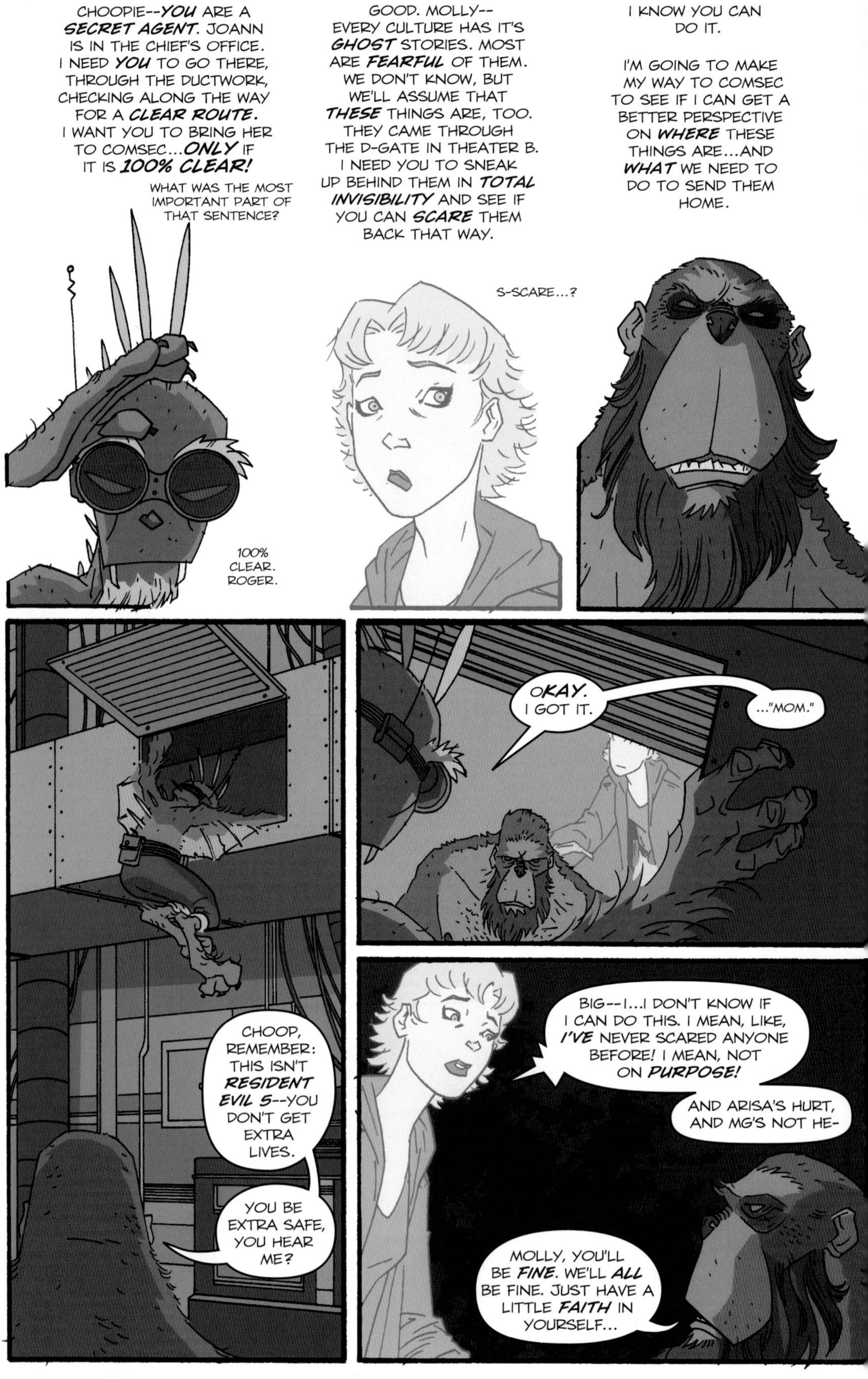
CHOOPIE--YOU ARE A SECRET AGENT. JOANN IS IN THE CHIEF'S OFFICE. I NEED YOU TO GO THERE, THROUGH THE DUCTWORK, CHECKING ALONG THE WAY FOR A CLEAR ROUTE. I WANT YOU TO BRING HER TO COMSEC...ONLY IF IT IS 100% CLEAR!
WHAT WAS THE MOST IMPORTANT PART OF THAT SENTENCE?
100% CLEAR. ROGER.
GOOD. MOLLY-- EVERY CULTURE HAS IT'S GHOST STORIES. MOST ARE FEARFUL OF THEM. WE DON'T KNOW, BUT WE'LL ASSUME THAT THESE THINGS ARE, TOO. THEY CAME THROUGH THE D-GATE IN THEATER B. I NEED YOU TO SNEAK UP BEHIND THEM IN TOTAL INVISIBILITY AND SEE IF YOU CAN SCARE THEM BACK THAT WAY.
S-SCARE...?
I KNOW YOU CAN DO IT.
I'M GOING TO MAKE MY WAY TO COMSEC TO SEE IF I CAN GET A BETTER PERSPECTIVE ON WHERE THESE THINGS ARE...AND WHAT WE NEED TO DO TO SEND THEM HOME.
CHOOP, REMEMBER: THIS ISN'T RESIDENT EVIL 5--YOU DON'T GET EXTRA LIVES.
YOU BE EXTRA SAFE, YOU HEAR ME?
OKAY. I GOT IT.
..."MOM."
BIG--I...I DON'T KNOW IF I CAN DO THIS. I MEAN, LIKE, I'VE NEVER SCARED ANYONE BEFORE! I MEAN, NOT ON PURPOSE!
AND ARISA'S HURT, AND MG'S NOT HE-
MOLLY, YOU'LL BE FINE. WE'LL ALL BE FINE. JUST HAVE A LITTLE FAITH IN YOURSELF...

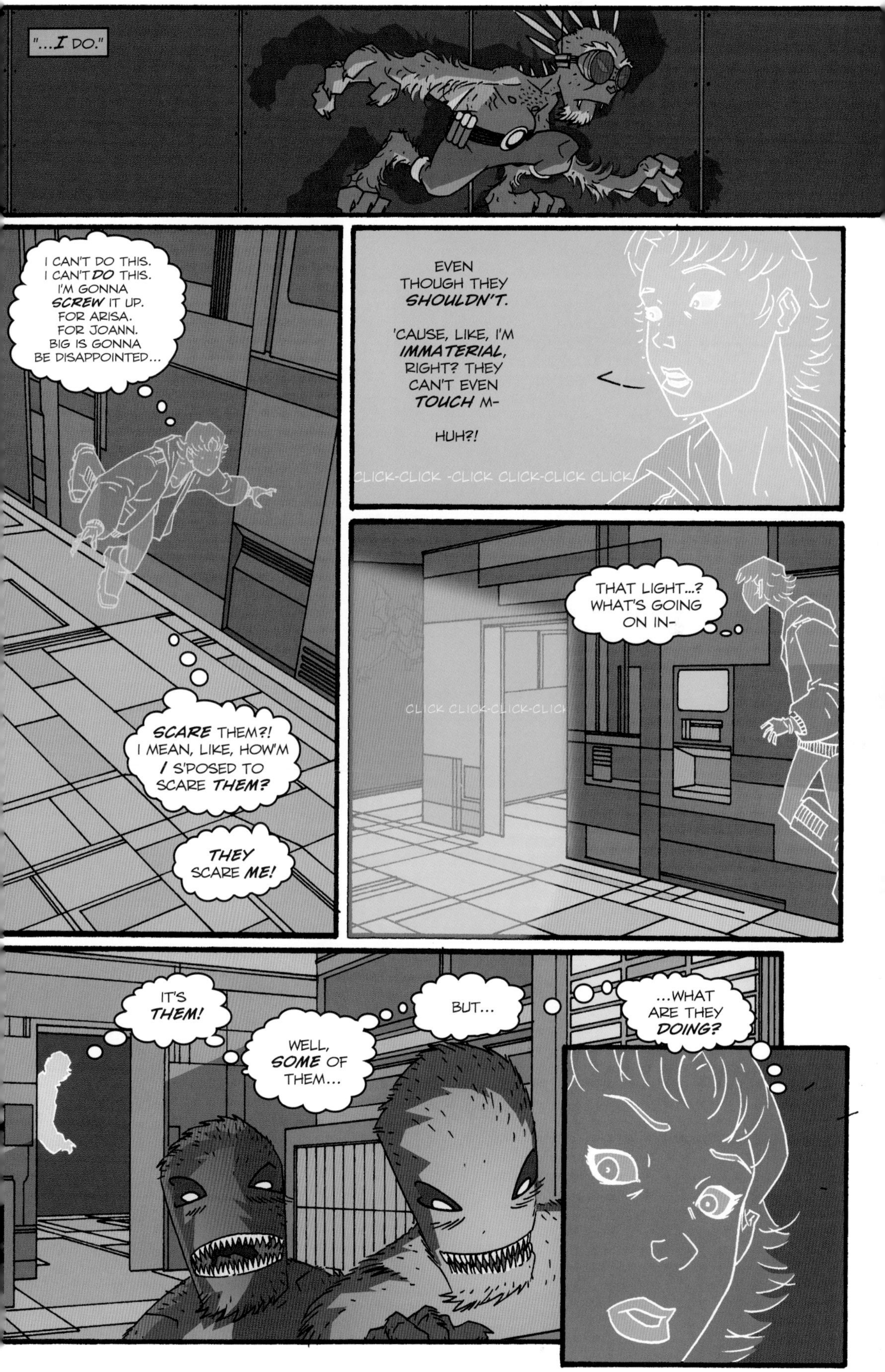
"...I DO."
I CAN'T DO THIS. I CAN'T DO THIS. I'M GONNA SCREW IT UP. FOR ARISA. FOR JOANN. BIG IS GONNA BE DISAPPOINTED...
SCARE THEM?! I MEAN, LIKE, HOW'M I S'POSED TO SCARE THEM?
THEY SCARE ME!
EVEN THOUGH THEY SHOULDN'T.
'CAUSE, LIKE, I'M IMMATERIAL, RIGHT? THEY CAN'T EVEN TOUCH M-
HUH?!
CLICK-CLICK -CLICK CLICK-CLICK CLICK
THAT LIGHT...? WHAT'S GOING ON IN-
CLICK CLICK-CLICK-CLICK
IT'S THEM!
WELL, SOME OF THEM...
BUT...
...WHAT ARE THEY DOING?

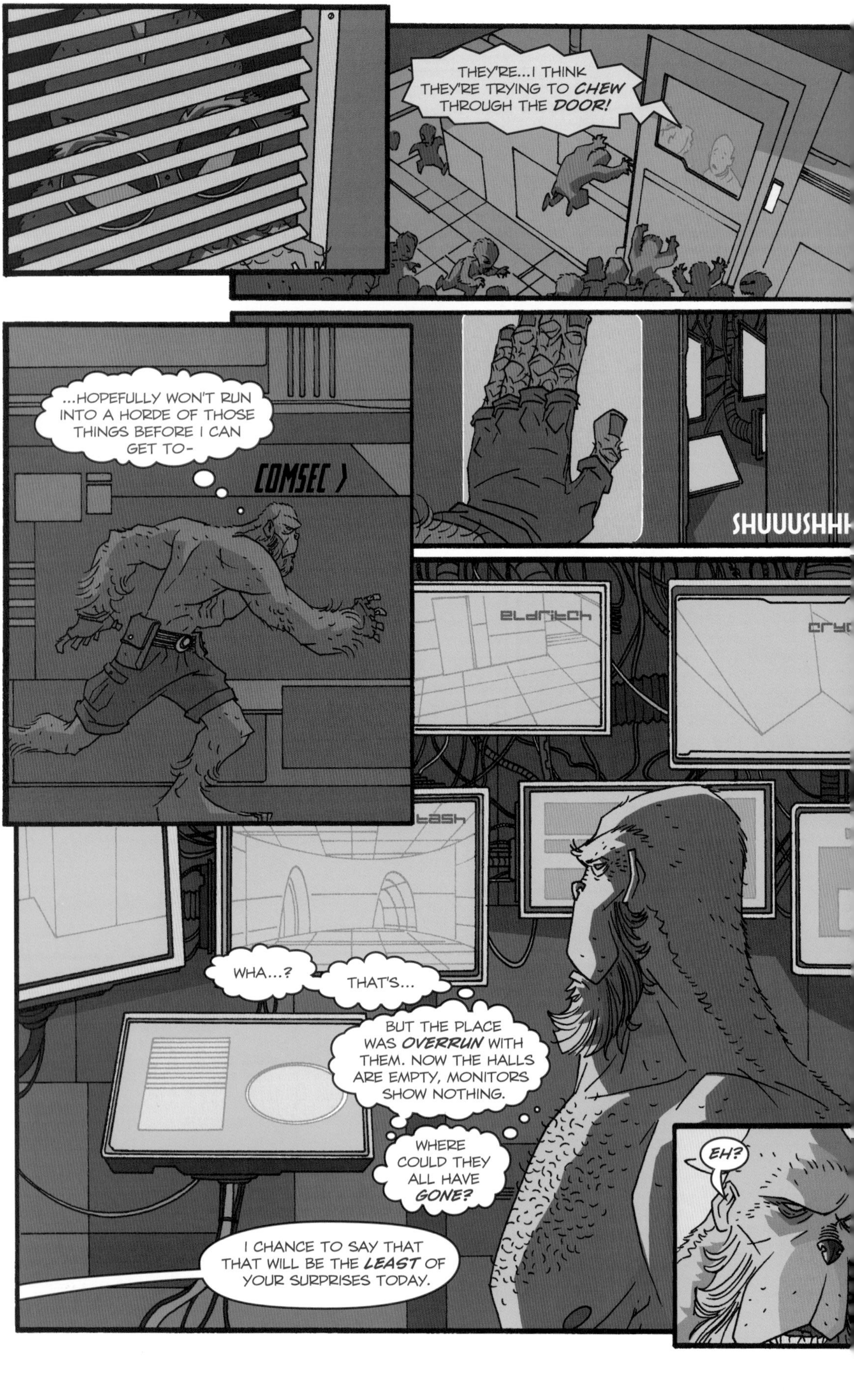
THEY'RE...I THINK THEY'RE TRYING TO CHEW THROUGH THE DOOR!
...HOPEFULLY WON'T RUN INTO A HORDE OF THOSE THINGS BEFORE I CAN GET TO-
COMSEC
SHUUUSHHH
ELDRITCH
WHA...?
THAT'S...
BUT THE PLACE WAS OVERRUN WITH THEM. NOW THE HALLS ARE EMPTY, MONITORS SHOW NOTHING.
WHERE COULD THEY ALL HAVE GONE?
I CHANCE TO SAY THAT THAT WILL BE THE LEAST OF YOUR SURPRISES TODAY.
EH?

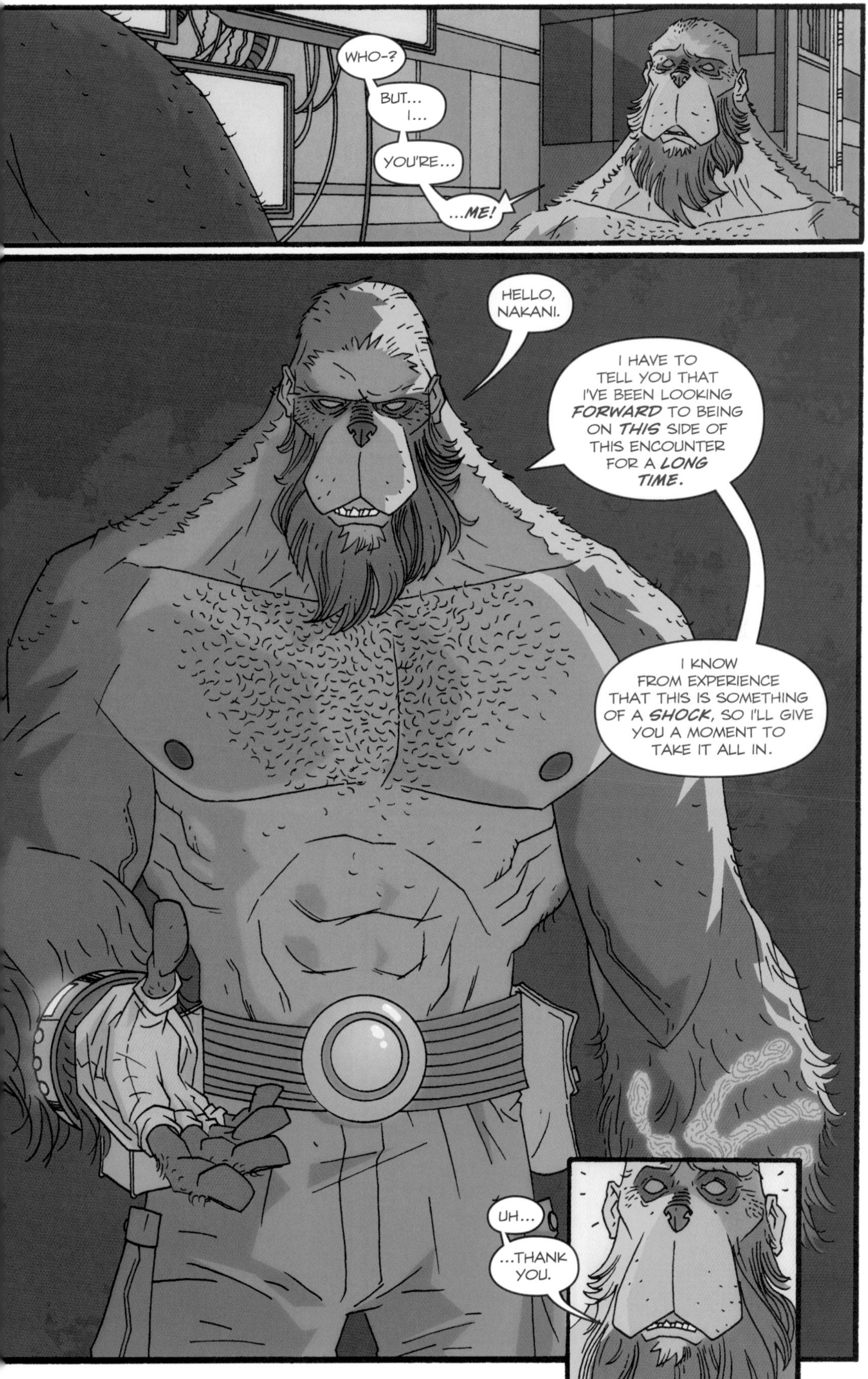
WHO-?
BUT... I...
YOU'RE...
...ME!
HELLO, NAKANI.
I HAVE TO TELL YOU THAT I'VE BEEN LOOKING FORWARD TO BEING ON THIS SIDE OF THIS ENCOUNTER FOR A LONG TIME.
I KNOW FROM EXPERIENCE THAT THIS IS SOMETHING OF A SHOCK, SO I'LL GIVE YOU A MOMENT TO TAKE IT ALL IN.
UH...
...THANK YOU.

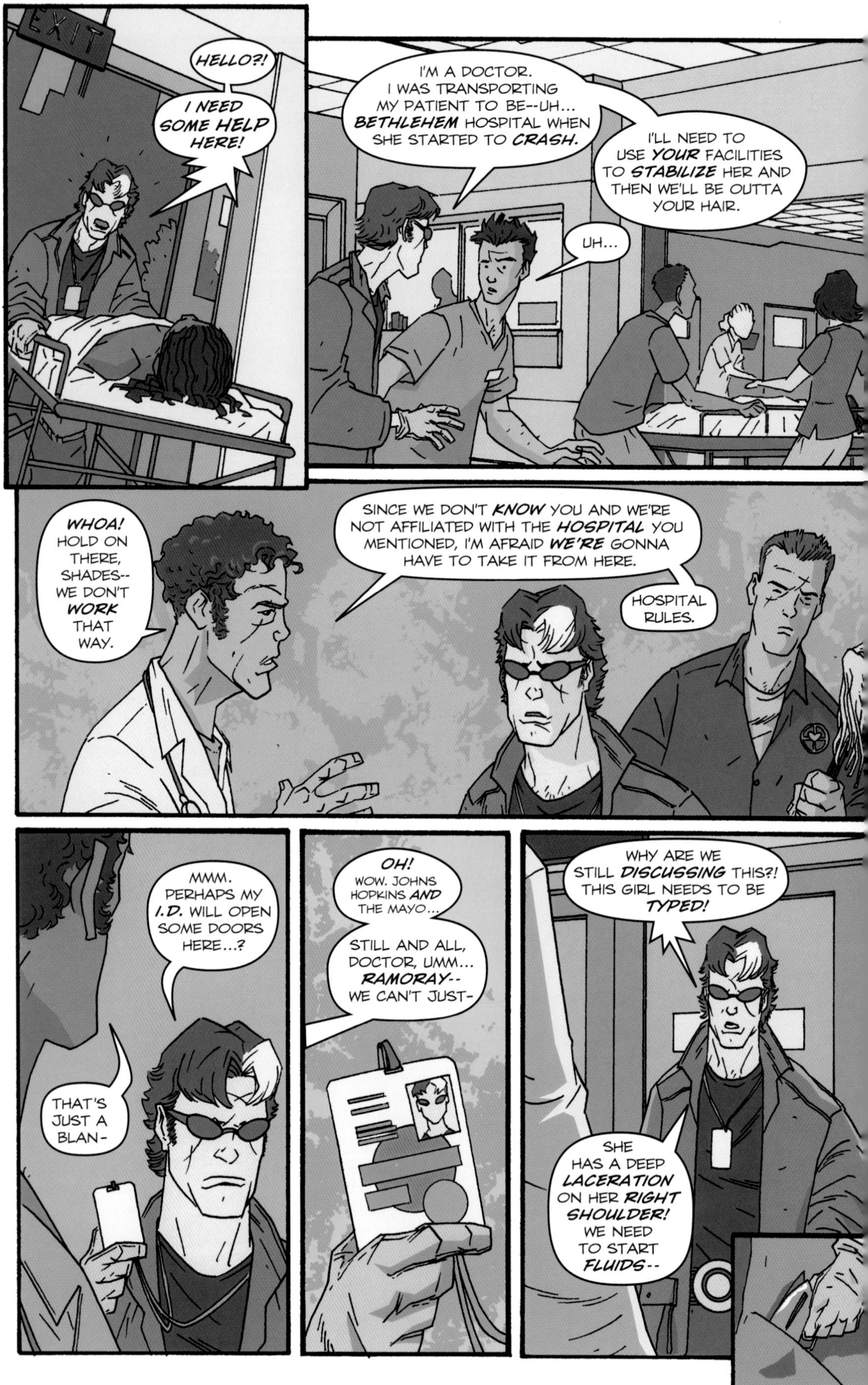

EXIT
HELLO?!
I NEED SOME HELP HERE!
I'M A DOCTOR. I WAS TRANSPORTING MY PATIENT TO BE--UH... BETHLEHEM HOSPITAL WHEN SHE STARTED TO CRASH.
I'LL NEED TO USE YOUR FACILITIES TO STABILIZE HER AND THEN WE'LL BE OUTTA YOUR HAIR.
UH...
WHOA! HOLD ON THERE, SHADES-- WE DON'T WORK THAT WAY.
SINCE WE DON'T KNOW YOU AND WE'RE NOT AFFILIATED WITH THE HOSPITAL YOU MENTIONED, I'M AFRAID WE'RE GONNA HAVE TO TAKE IT FROM HERE.
HOSPITAL RULES.
MMM. PERHAPS MY I.D. WILL OPEN SOME DOORS HERE...?
THAT'S JUST A BLAN-
OH! WOW. JOHNS HOPKINS AND THE MAYO...
STILL AND ALL, DOCTOR, UMM... RAMORAY-- WE CAN'T JUST-
WHY ARE WE STILL DISCUSSING THIS?! THIS GIRL NEEDS TO BE TYPED!
SHE HAS A DEEP LACERATION ON HER RIGHT SHOULDER! WE NEED TO START FLUIDS--

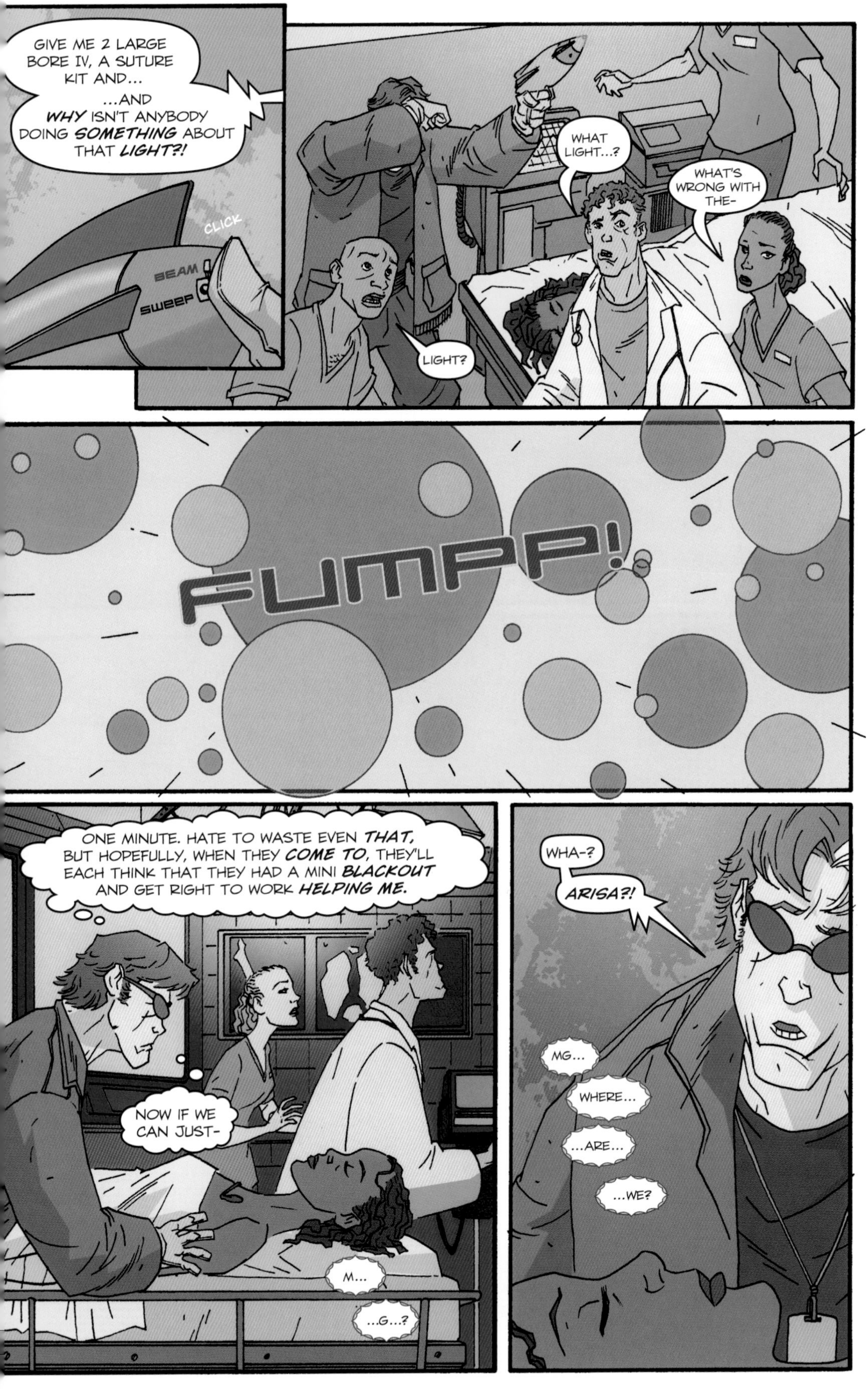
GIVE ME 2 LARGE BORE IV, A SUTURE KIT AND...
...AND *WHY* ISN'T ANYBODY DOING *SOMETHING* ABOUT THAT *LIGHT?!*
CLICK
BEAM
SWEEP
WHAT LIGHT...?
WHAT'S WRONG WITH THE-
LIGHT?
FUMPP!
ONE MINUTE. HATE TO WASTE EVEN *THAT,* BUT HOPEFULLY, WHEN THEY *COME TO,* THEY'LL EACH THINK THAT THEY HAD A MINI *BLACKOUT* AND GET RIGHT TO WORK *HELPING ME.*
NOW IF WE CAN JUST-
M...
...G...?
WHA-?
ARISA?!
MG...
WHERE...
...ARE...
...WE?

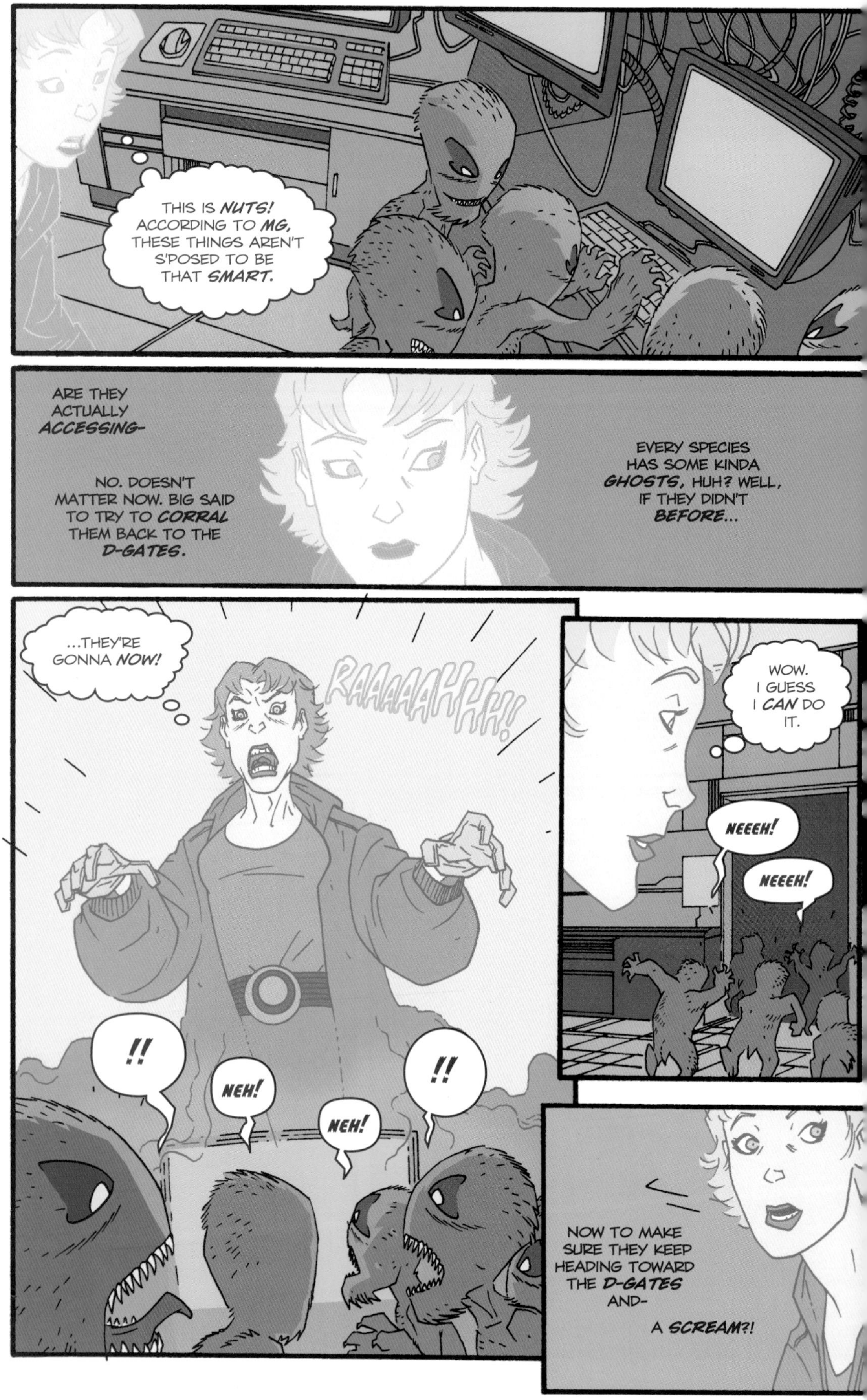
THIS IS NUTS! ACCORDING TO MG, THESE THINGS AREN'T S'POSED TO BE THAT SMART.
ARE THEY ACTUALLY ACCESSING-
NO. DOESN'T MATTER NOW. BIG SAID TO TRY TO CORRAL THEM BACK TO THE D-GATES.
EVERY SPECIES HAS SOME KINDA GHOSTS, HUH? WELL, IF THEY DIDN'T BEFORE...
...THEY'RE GONNA NOW!
RAAAAAAHHH!!
!!
NEH!
NEH!
!!
WOW. I GUESS I CAN DO IT.
NEEEH!
NEEEH!
NOW TO MAKE SURE THEY KEEP HEADING TOWARD THE D-GATES AND-
A SCREAM?!

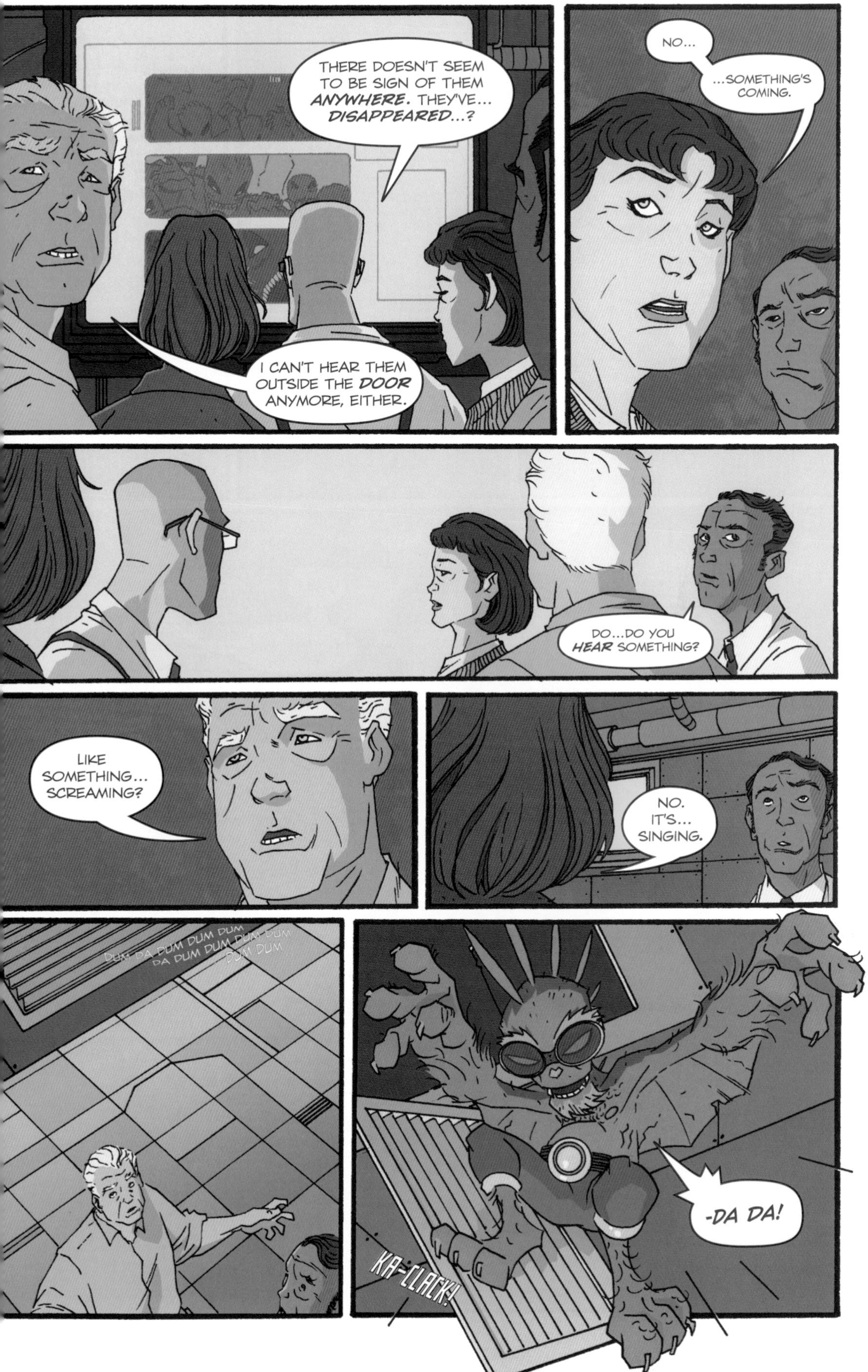
THERE DOESN'T SEEM TO BE SIGN OF THEM *ANYWHERE.* THEY'VE... *DISAPPEARED*...?
I CAN'T HEAR THEM OUTSIDE THE *DOOR* ANYMORE, EITHER.
NO...
...SOMETHING'S COMING.
DO...DO YOU *HEAR* SOMETHING?
LIKE SOMETHING... SCREAMING?
NO. IT'S... SINGING.
DUM DA DUM DUM DUM DUM
DA DUM DUM DUM DUM
DUM DUM
-DA DA!
KA-CLACK!

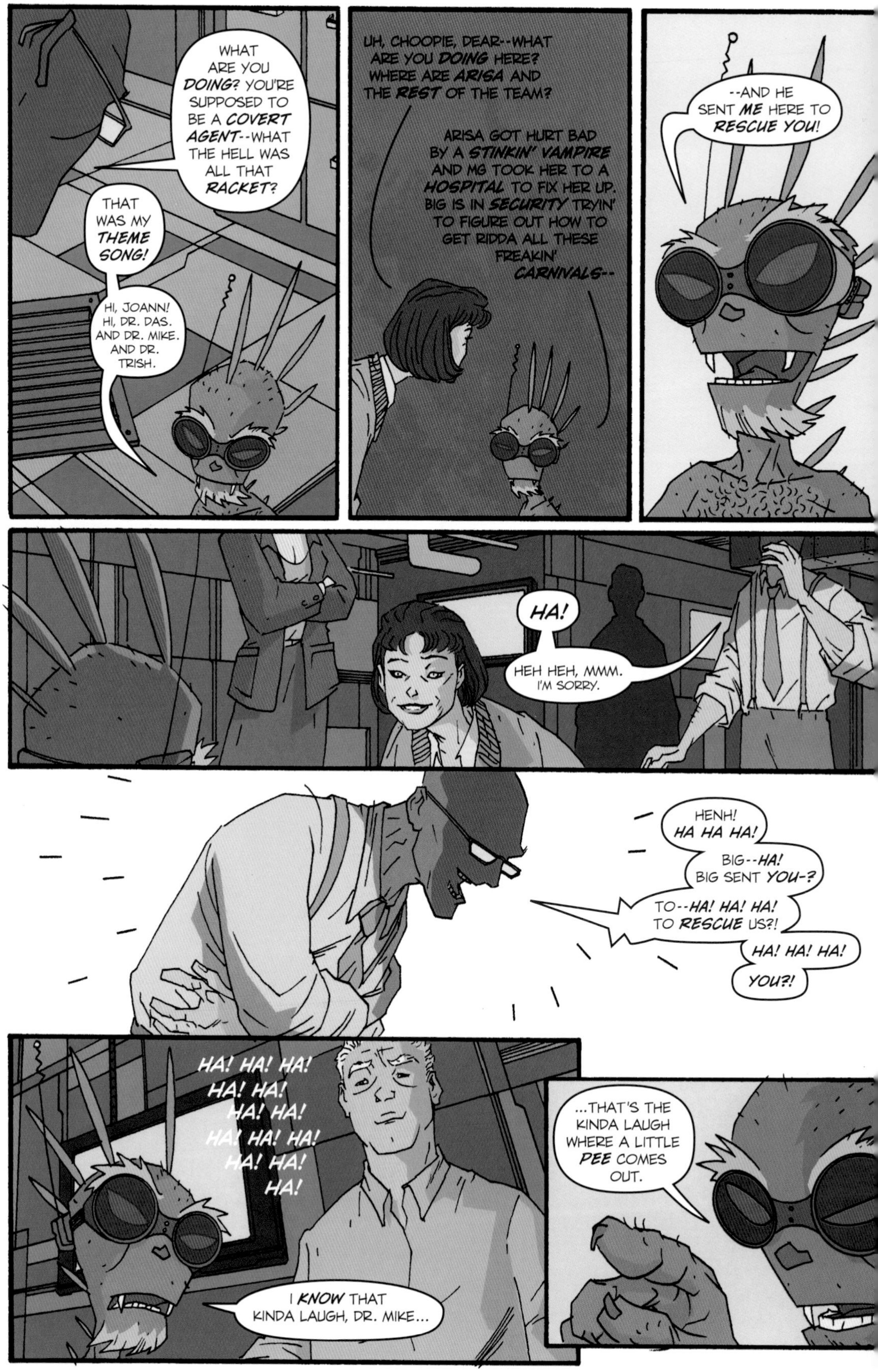

WHAT ARE YOU DOING? YOU'RE SUPPOSED TO BE A COVERT AGENT--WHAT THE HELL WAS ALL THAT RACKET?
THAT WAS MY THEME SONG!
HI, JOANN! HI, DR. DAS. AND DR. MIKE. AND DR. TRISH.
UH, CHOOPIE, DEAR--WHAT ARE YOU DOING HERE? WHERE ARE ARISA AND THE REST OF THE TEAM?
ARISA GOT HURT BAD BY A STINKIN' VAMPIRE AND MG TOOK HER TO A HOSPITAL TO FIX HER UP. BIG IS IN SECURITY TRYIN' TO FIGURE OUT HOW TO GET RIDDA ALL THESE FREAKIN' CARNIVALS--
--AND HE SENT ME HERE TO RESCUE YOU!
HA!
HEH HEH, MMM. I'M SORRY.
HENH! HA HA HA!
BIG--HA! BIG SENT YOU-?
TO--HA! HA! HA! TO RESCUE US?!
HA! HA! HA!
YOU?!
HA! HA! HA! HA! HA! HA! HA! HA! HA! HA! HA! HA! HA!
I KNOW THAT KINDA LAUGH, DR. MIKE...
...THAT'S THE KINDA LAUGH WHERE A LITTLE PEE COMES OUT.

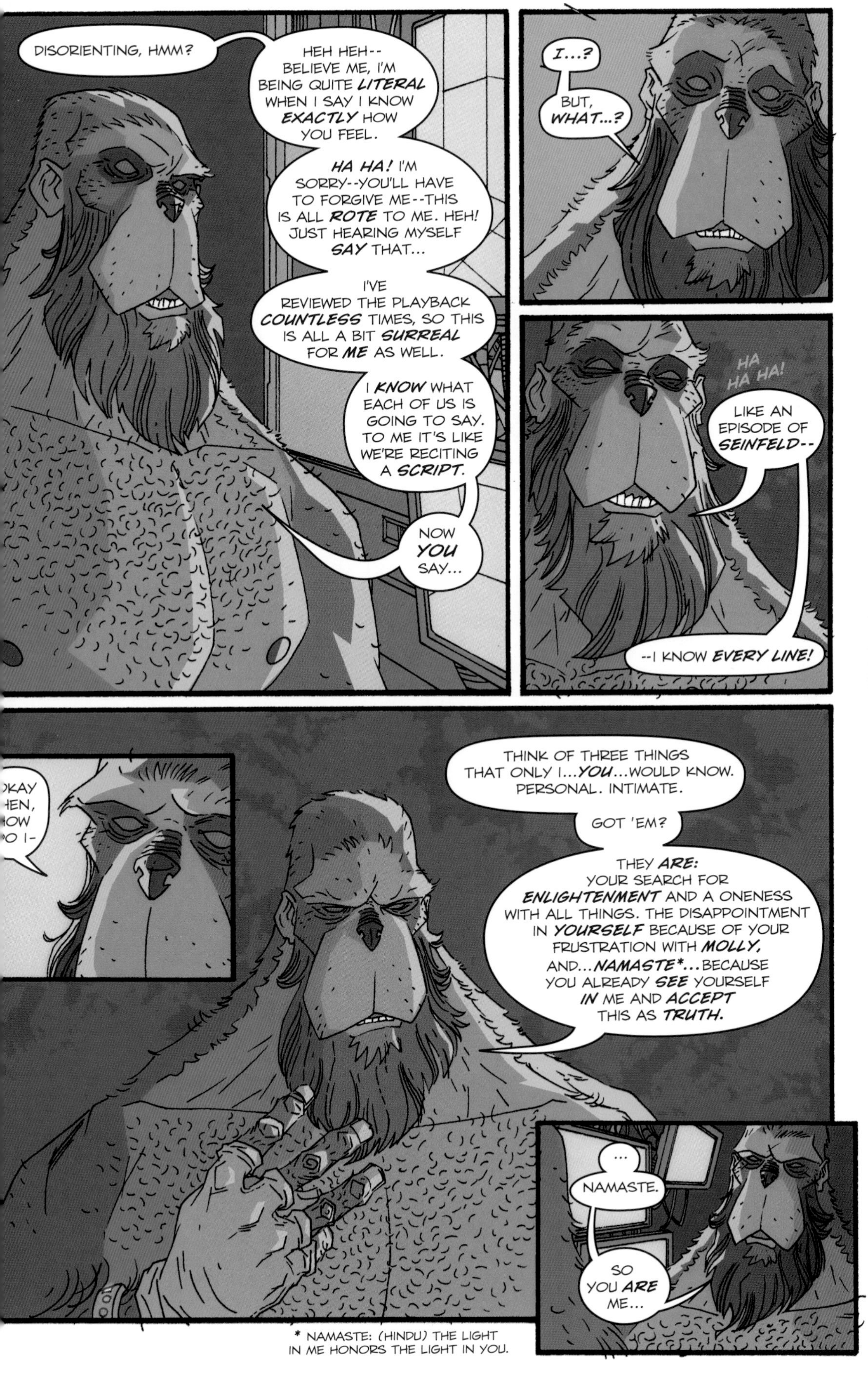
DISORIENTING, HMM?
HEH HEH-- BELIEVE ME, I'M BEING QUITE LITERAL WHEN I SAY I KNOW EXACTLY HOW YOU FEEL.
HA HA! I'M SORRY--YOU'LL HAVE TO FORGIVE ME--THIS IS ALL ROTE TO ME. HEH! JUST HEARING MYSELF SAY THAT...
I'VE REVIEWED THE PLAYBACK COUNTLESS TIMES, SO THIS IS ALL A BIT SURREAL FOR ME AS WELL.
I KNOW WHAT EACH OF US IS GOING TO SAY. TO ME IT'S LIKE WE'RE RECITING A SCRIPT.
NOW YOU SAY...
I...?
BUT, WHAT...?
HA HA HA!
LIKE AN EPISODE OF SEINFELD--
--I KNOW EVERY LINE!
OKAY HEN, HOW DO I-
THINK OF THREE THINGS THAT ONLY I...YOU...WOULD KNOW. PERSONAL. INTIMATE.
GOT 'EM?
THEY ARE: YOUR SEARCH FOR ENLIGHTENMENT AND A ONENESS WITH ALL THINGS. THE DISAPPOINTMENT IN YOURSELF BECAUSE OF YOUR FRUSTRATION WITH MOLLY, AND...NAMASTE*...BECAUSE YOU ALREADY SEE YOURSELF IN ME AND ACCEPT THIS AS TRUTH.
...
NAMASTE.
SO YOU ARE ME...

* NAMASTE: (HINDU) THE LIGHT IN ME HONORS THE LIGHT IN YOU.

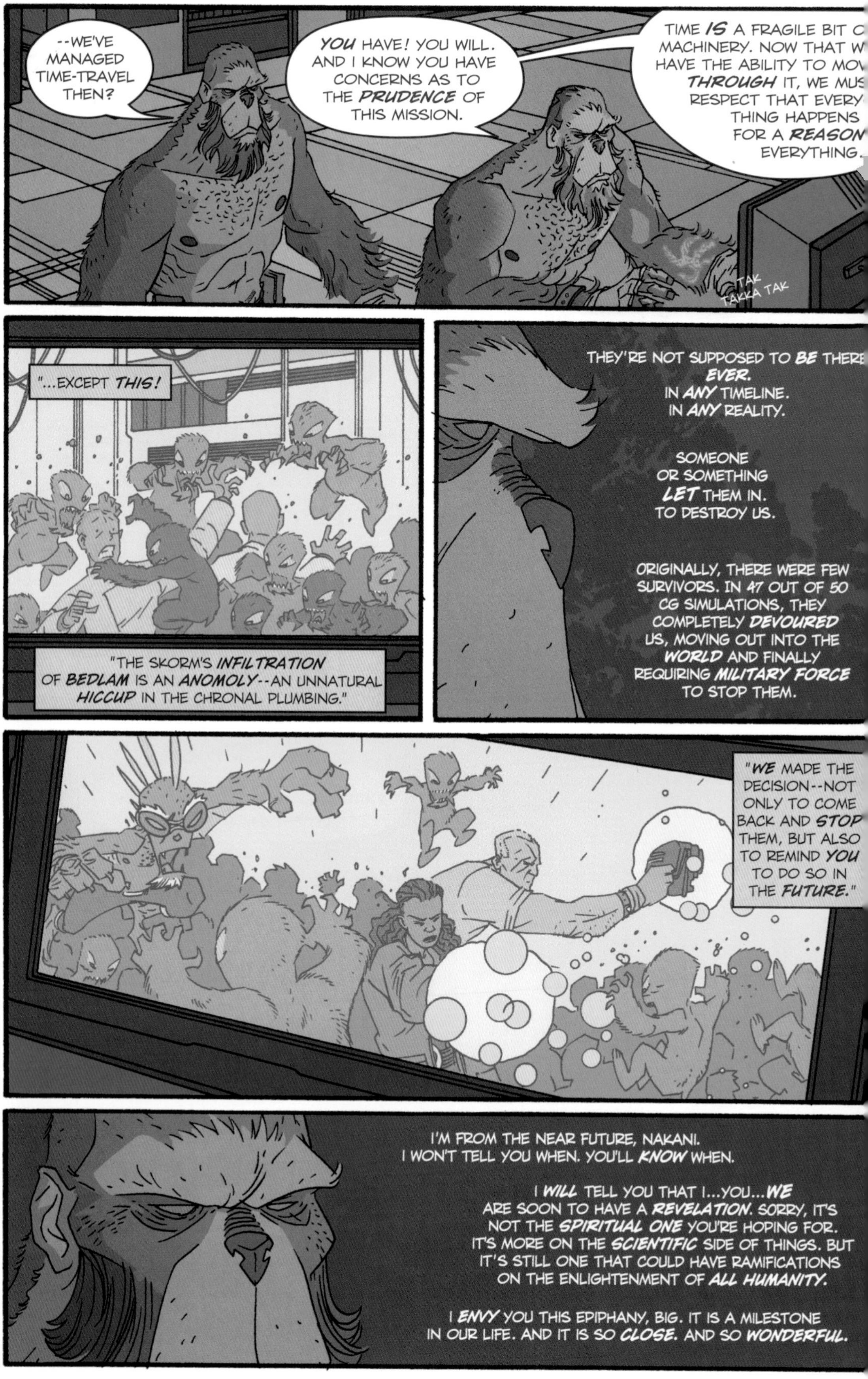
--WE'VE MANAGED TIME-TRAVEL THEN?
YOU HAVE! YOU WILL. AND I KNOW YOU HAVE CONCERNS AS TO THE PRUDENCE OF THIS MISSION.
TIME IS A FRAGILE BIT O MACHINERY. NOW THAT W HAVE THE ABILITY TO MOV THROUGH IT, WE MUS RESPECT THAT EVERY-THING HAPPENS FOR A REASON EVERYTHING.
TAK TAKKA TAK
"...EXCEPT THIS!
"THE SKORM'S INFILTRATION OF BEDLAM IS AN ANOMOLY--AN UNNATURAL HICCUP IN THE CHRONAL PLUMBING."
THEY'RE NOT SUPPOSED TO BE THERE EVER. IN ANY TIMELINE. IN ANY REALITY.
SOMEONE OR SOMETHING LET THEM IN. TO DESTROY US.
ORIGINALLY, THERE WERE FEW SURVIVORS. IN 47 OUT OF 50 CG SIMULATIONS, THEY COMPLETELY DEVOURED US, MOVING OUT INTO THE WORLD AND FINALLY REQUIRING MILITARY FORCE TO STOP THEM.
"WE MADE THE DECISION--NOT ONLY TO COME BACK AND STOP THEM, BUT ALSO TO REMIND YOU TO DO SO IN THE FUTURE."
I'M FROM THE NEAR FUTURE, NAKANI. I WON'T TELL YOU WHEN. YOU'LL KNOW WHEN.
I WILL TELL YOU THAT I...YOU...WE ARE SOON TO HAVE A REVELATION. SORRY, IT'S NOT THE SPIRITUAL ONE YOU'RE HOPING FOR. IT'S MORE ON THE SCIENTIFIC SIDE OF THINGS. BUT IT'S STILL ONE THAT COULD HAVE RAMIFICATIONS ON THE ENLIGHTENMENT OF ALL HUMANITY.
I ENVY YOU THIS EPIPHANY, BIG. IT IS A MILESTONE IN OUR LIFE. AND IT IS SO CLOSE. AND SO WONDERFUL.

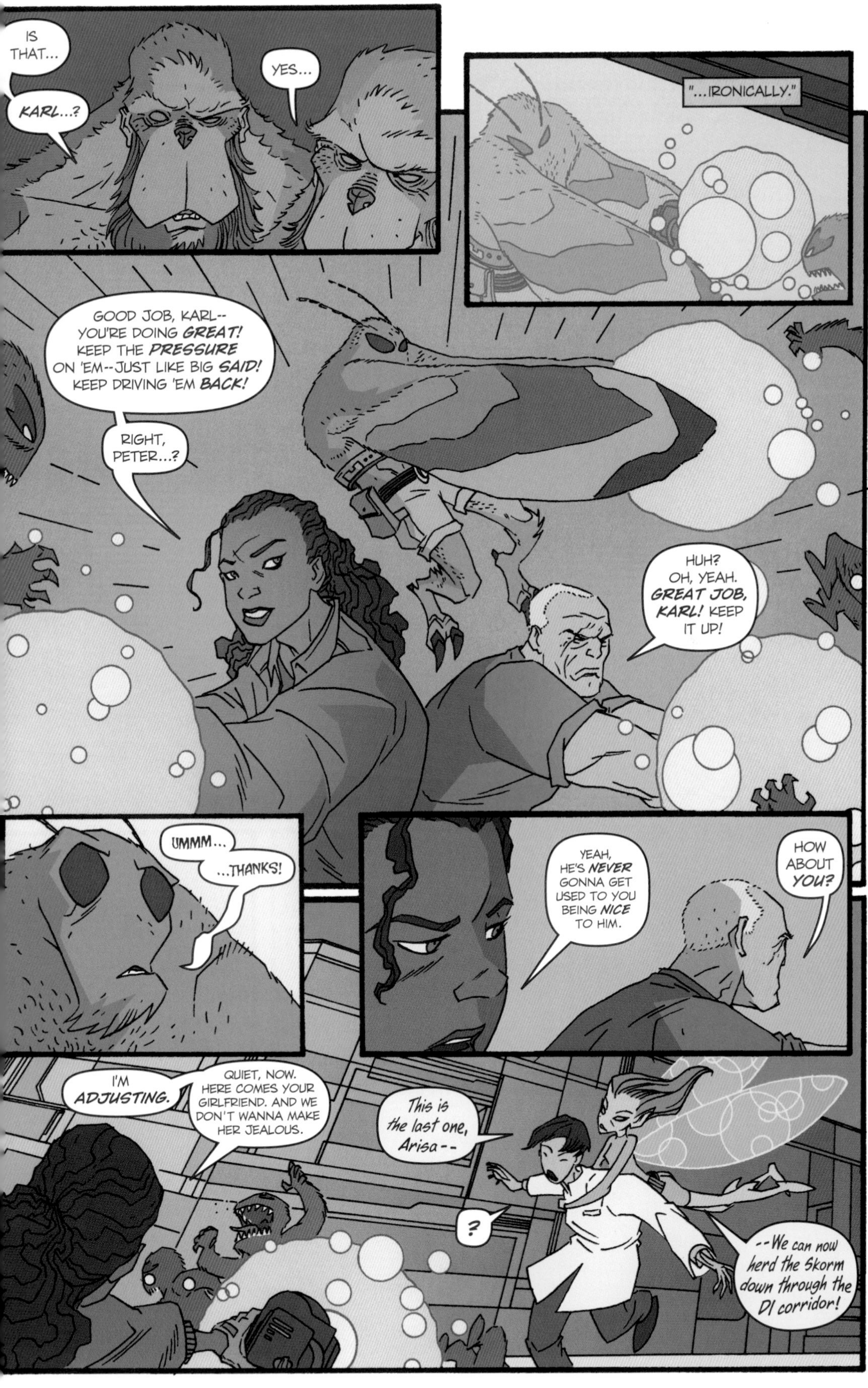

IS THAT...
KARL...?
YES...
"...IRONICALLY."
GOOD JOB, KARL-- YOU'RE DOING GREAT! KEEP THE PRESSURE ON 'EM--JUST LIKE BIG SAID! KEEP DRIVING 'EM BACK!
RIGHT, PETER...?
HUH? OH, YEAH. GREAT JOB, KARL! KEEP IT UP!
UMMM...
...THANKS!
YEAH, HE'S NEVER GONNA GET USED TO YOU BEING NICE TO HIM.
HOW ABOUT YOU?
I'M ADJUSTING.
QUIET, NOW. HERE COMES YOUR GIRLFRIEND. AND WE DON'T WANNA MAKE HER JEALOUS.
This is the last one, Arisa--
?
--We can now herd the Skorm down through the DI corridor!

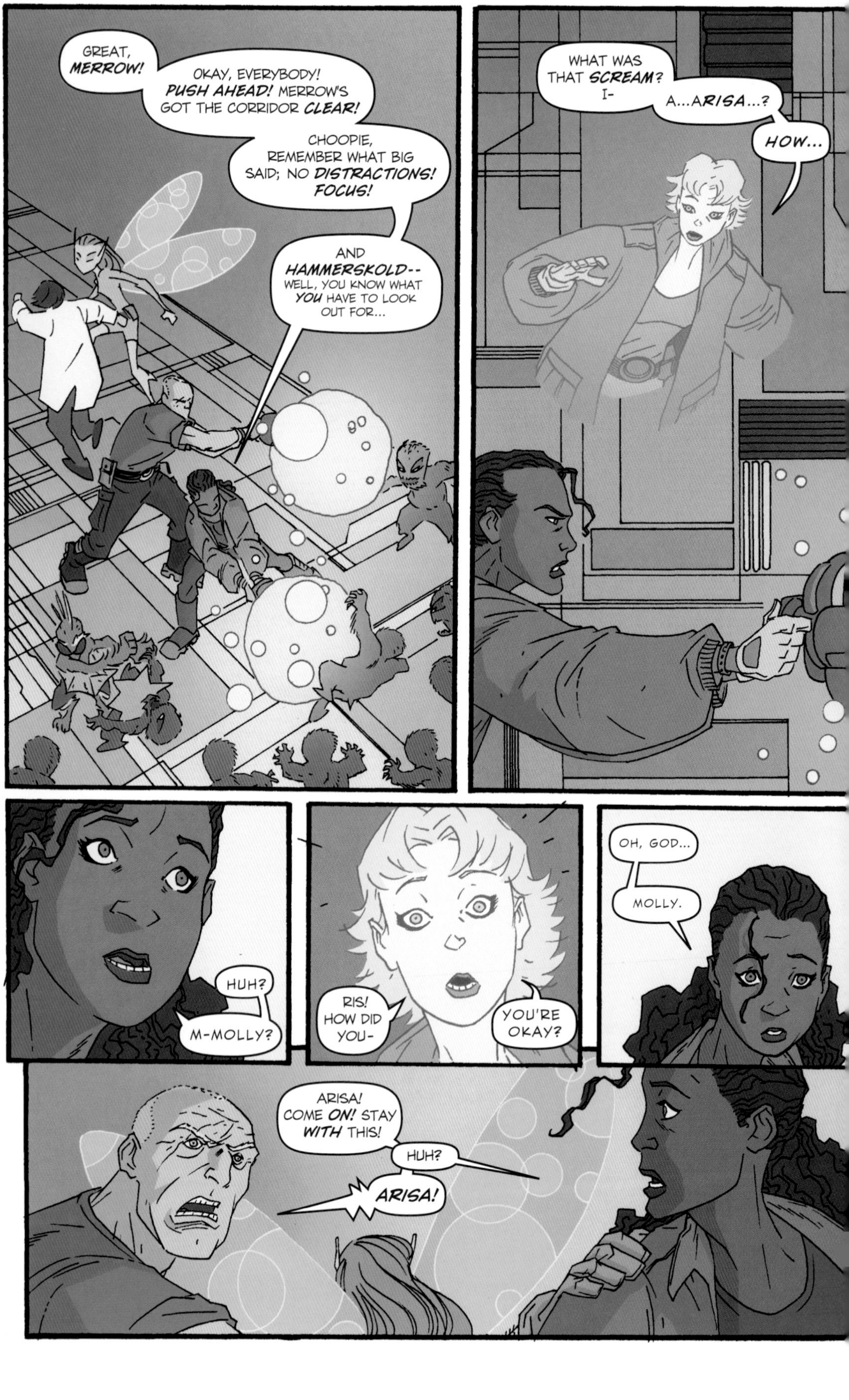
GREAT, MERROW!
OKAY, EVERYBODY! PUSH AHEAD! MERROW'S GOT THE CORRIDOR CLEAR!
CHOOPIE, REMEMBER WHAT BIG SAID; NO DISTRACTIONS! FOCUS!
AND HAMMERSKOLD-- WELL, YOU KNOW WHAT YOU HAVE TO LOOK OUT FOR...
WHAT WAS THAT SCREAM? I-
A...ARISA...?
HOW...
HUH?
M-MOLLY?
RIS! HOW DID YOU-
YOU'RE OKAY?
OH, GOD...
MOLLY.
ARISA! COME ON! STAY WITH THIS!
HUH?
ARISA!

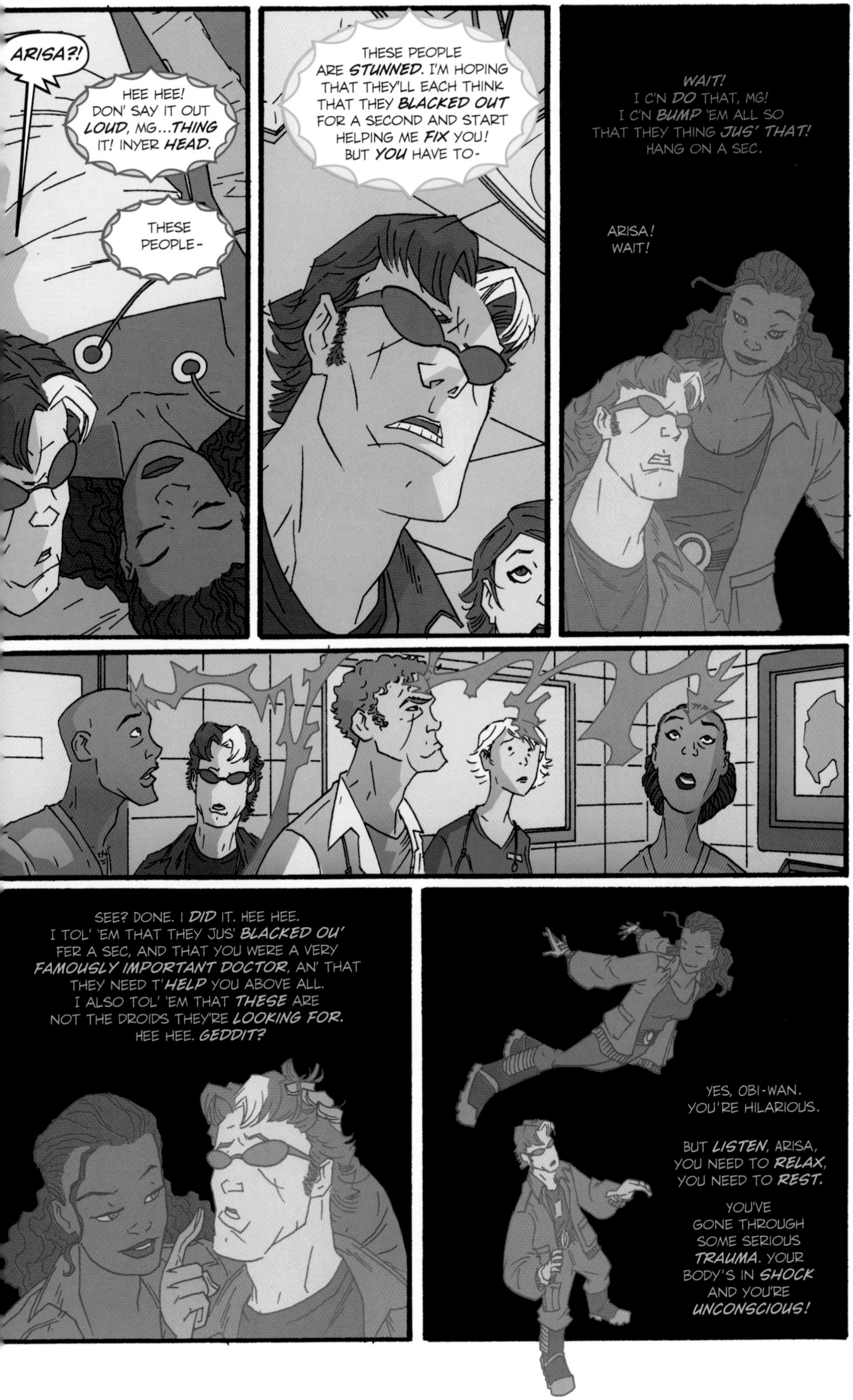
ARISA?!
HEE HEE! DON' SAY IT OUT LOUD, MG...THING IT! INYER HEAD.
THESE PEOPLE-
THESE PEOPLE ARE STUNNED. I'M HOPING THAT THEY'LL EACH THINK THAT THEY BLACKED OUT FOR A SECOND AND START HELPING ME FIX YOU! BUT YOU HAVE TO-
WAIT! I C'N DO THAT, MG! I C'N BUMP 'EM ALL SO THAT THEY THING JUS' THAT! HANG ON A SEC.
ARISA! WAIT!
SEE? DONE. I DID IT. HEE HEE. I TOL' 'EM THAT THEY JUS' BLACKED OU' FER A SEC, AND THAT YOU WERE A VERY FAMOUSLY IMPORTANT DOCTOR, AN' THAT THEY NEED T'HELP YOU ABOVE ALL. I ALSO TOL' 'EM THAT THESE ARE NOT THE DROIDS THEY'RE LOOKING FOR. HEE HEE. GEDDIT?
YES, OBI-WAN. YOU'RE HILARIOUS.
BUT LISTEN, ARISA, YOU NEED TO RELAX, YOU NEED TO REST.
YOU'VE GONE THROUGH SOME SERIOUS TRAUMA. YOUR BODY'S IN SHOCK AND YOU'RE UNCONSCIOUS!

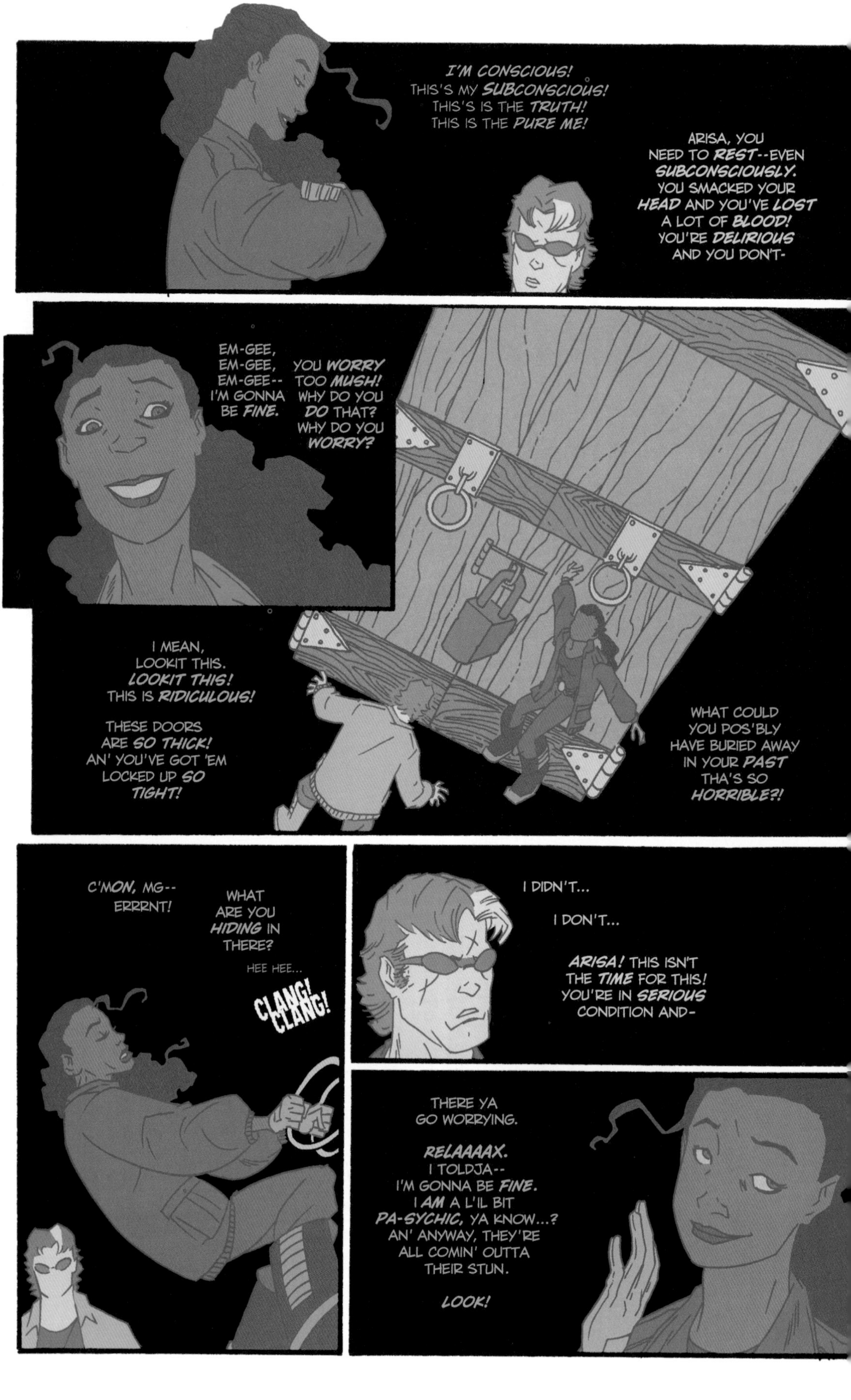
I'M CONSCIOUS! THIS'S MY SUBCONSCIOUS! THIS'S IS THE TRUTH! THIS IS THE PURE ME!
ARISA, YOU NEED TO REST--EVEN SUBCONSCIOUSLY. YOU SMACKED YOUR HEAD AND YOU'VE LOST A LOT OF BLOOD! YOU'RE DELIRIOUS AND YOU DON'T-
EM-GEE, EM-GEE, EM-GEE-- I'M GONNA BE FINE.
YOU WORRY TOO MUSH! WHY DO YOU DO THAT? WHY DO YOU WORRY?
I MEAN, LOOKIT THIS. LOOKIT THIS! THIS IS RIDICULOUS!
THESE DOORS ARE SO THICK! AN' YOU'VE GOT 'EM LOCKED UP SO TIGHT!
WHAT COULD YOU POS'BLY HAVE BURIED AWAY IN YOUR PAST THA'S SO HORRIBLE?!
C'MON, MG-- ERRRNT!
WHAT ARE YOU HIDING IN THERE?
HEE HEE...
CLANG! CLANG!
I DIDN'T...
I DON'T...
ARISA! THIS ISN'T THE TIME FOR THIS! YOU'RE IN SERIOUS CONDITION AND-
THERE YA GO WORRYING.
RELAAAAX. I TOLDJA-- I'M GONNA BE FINE. I AM A L'IL BIT PA-SYCHIC, YA KNOW...? AN' ANYWAY, THEY'RE ALL COMIN' OUTTA THEIR STUN.
LOOK!

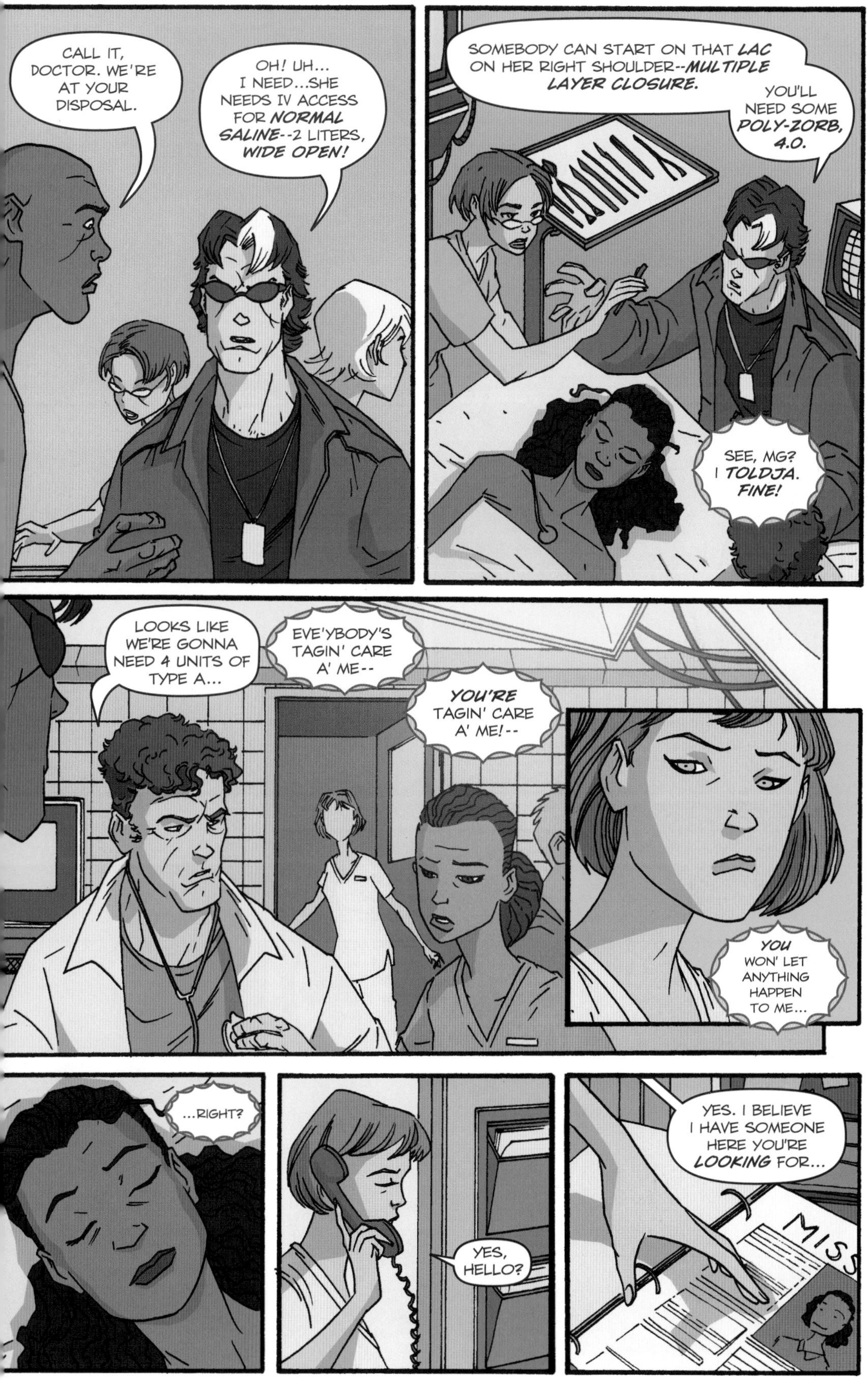
CALL IT, DOCTOR. WE'RE AT YOUR DISPOSAL.
OH! UH... I NEED...SHE NEEDS IV ACCESS FOR NORMAL SALINE--2 LITERS, WIDE OPEN!
SOMEBODY CAN START ON THAT LAC ON HER RIGHT SHOULDER--MULTIPLE LAYER CLOSURE.
YOU'LL NEED SOME POLY-ZORB, 4.0.
SEE, MG? I TOLDJA. FINE!
LOOKS LIKE WE'RE GONNA NEED 4 UNITS OF TYPE A...
EVE'YBODY'S TAGIN' CARE A' ME--
YOU'RE TAGIN' CARE A' ME!--
YOU WON' LET ANYTHING HAPPEN TO ME...
...RIGHT?
YES, HELLO?
YES. I BELIEVE I HAVE SOMEONE HERE YOU'RE LOOKING FOR...
MISS

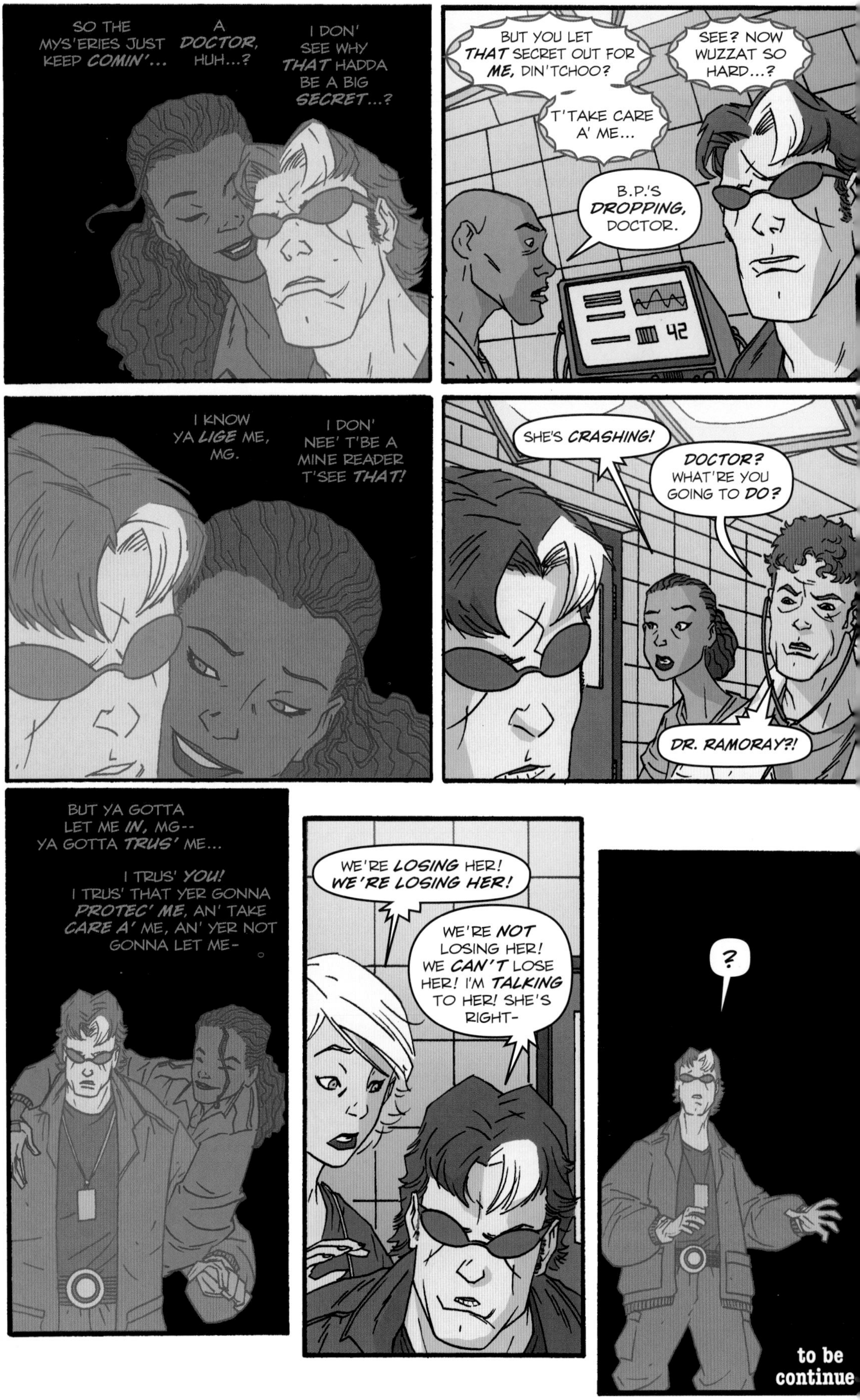
SO THE MYS'ERIES JUST KEEP COMIN'...
A DOCTOR, HUH...?
I DON' SEE WHY THAT HADDA BE A BIG SECRET...?
BUT YOU LET THAT SECRET OUT FOR ME, DIN'TCHOO?
SEE? NOW WUZZAT SO HARD...?
T'TAKE CARE A' ME...
B.P.'S DROPPING, DOCTOR.
42
I KNOW YA LIGE ME, MG.
I DON' NEE' T'BE A MINE READER T'SEE THAT!
SHE'S CRASHING!
DOCTOR? WHAT'RE YOU GOING TO DO?
DR. RAMORAY?!
BUT YA GOTTA LET ME IN, MG-- YA GOTTA TRUS' ME...
I TRUS' YOU! I TRUS' THAT YER GONNA PROTEC' ME, AN' TAKE CARE A' ME, AN' YER NOT GONNA LET ME-
WE'RE LOSING HER! WE'RE LOSING HER!
WE'RE NOT LOSING HER! WE CAN'T LOSE HER! I'M TALKING TO HER! SHE'S RIGHT-
?
to be continue

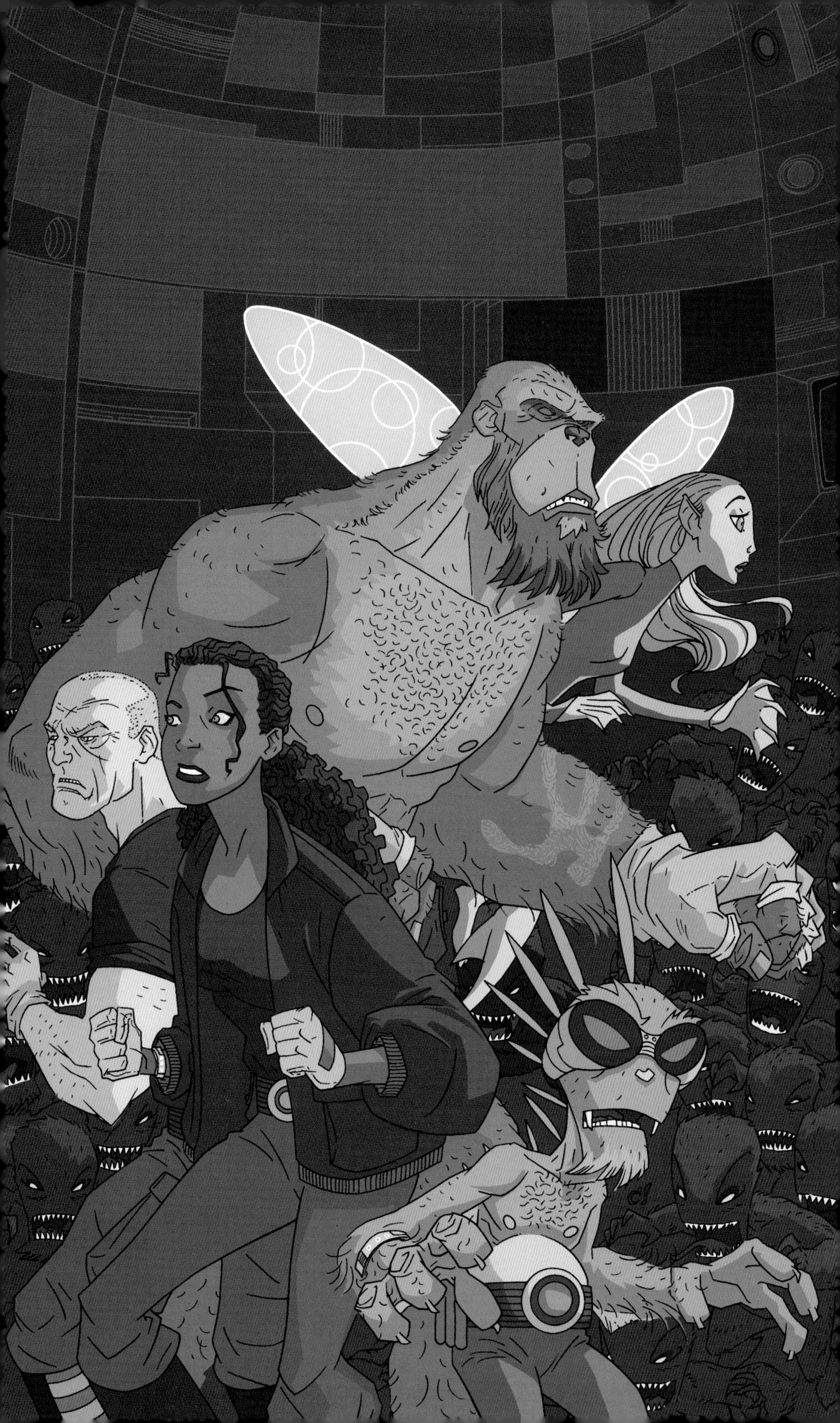

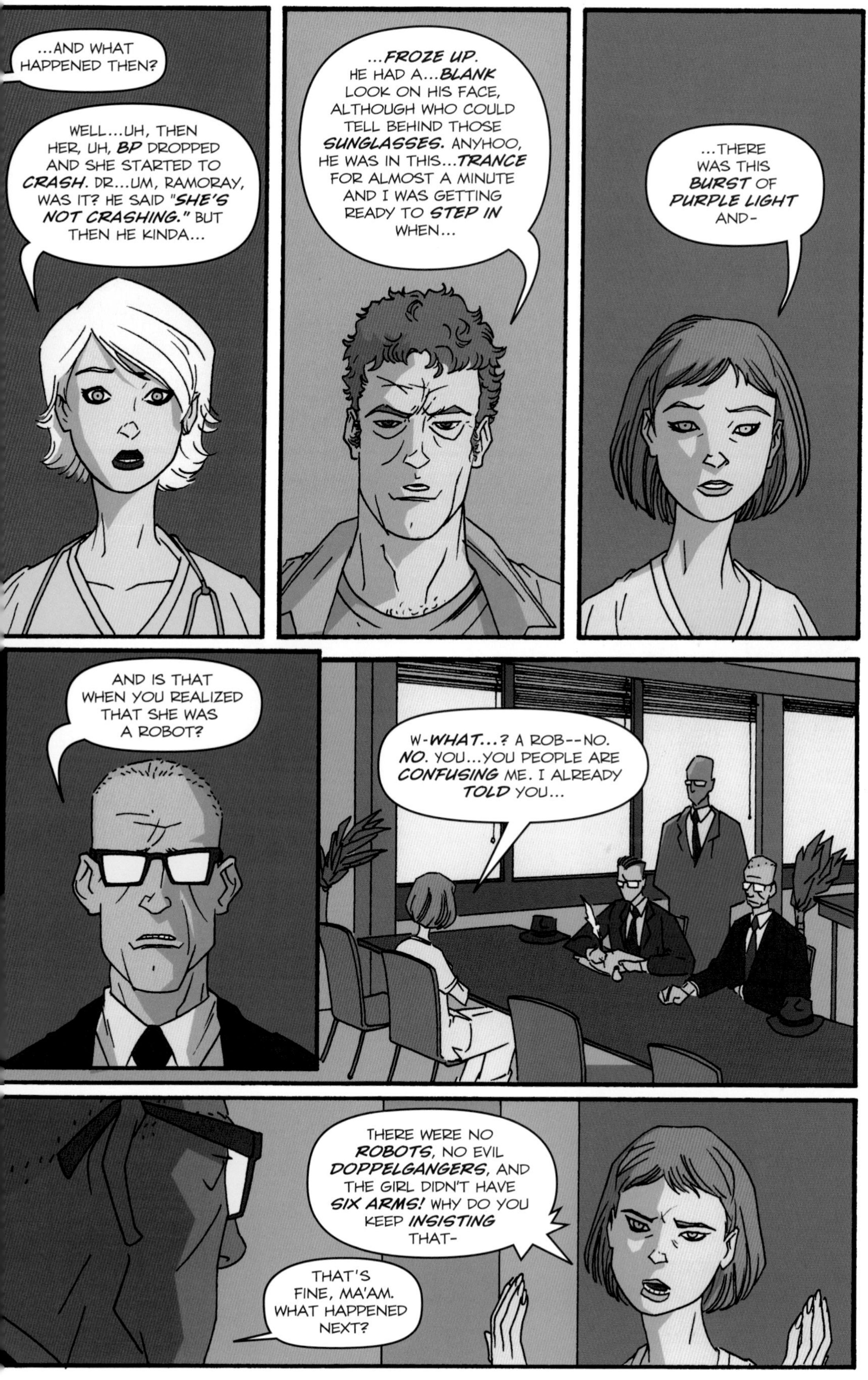
...AND WHAT HAPPENED THEN?
WELL...UH, THEN HER, UH, BP DROPPED AND SHE STARTED TO CRASH. DR...UM, RAMORAY, WAS IT? HE SAID "SHE'S NOT CRASHING." BUT THEN HE KINDA...
...FROZE UP. HE HAD A...BLANK LOOK ON HIS FACE, ALTHOUGH WHO COULD TELL BEHIND THOSE SUNGLASSES. ANYHOO, HE WAS IN THIS...TRANCE FOR ALMOST A MINUTE AND I WAS GETTING READY TO STEP IN WHEN...
...THERE WAS THIS BURST OF PURPLE LIGHT AND-
AND IS THAT WHEN YOU REALIZED THAT SHE WAS A ROBOT?
W-WHAT...? A ROB--NO. NO. YOU...YOU PEOPLE ARE CONFUSING ME. I ALREADY TOLD YOU...
THERE WERE NO ROBOTS, NO EVIL DOPPELGANGERS, AND THE GIRL DIDN'T HAVE SIX ARMS! WHY DO YOU KEEP INSISTING THAT-
THAT'S FINE, MA'AM. WHAT HAPPENED NEXT?

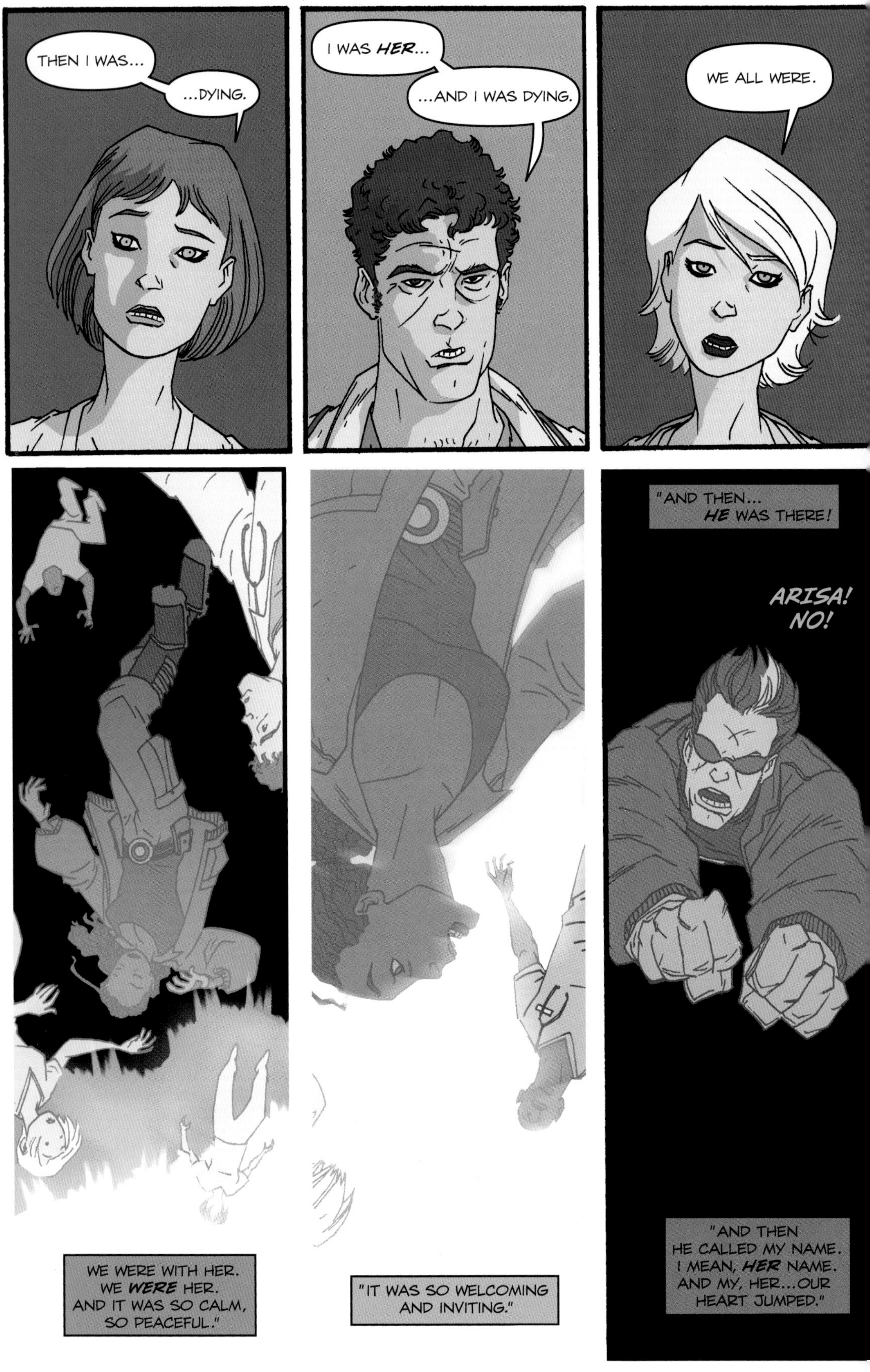

THEN I WAS...
...DYING.
I WAS HER...
...AND I WAS DYING.
WE ALL WERE.
WE WERE WITH HER. WE WERE HER. AND IT WAS SO CALM, SO PEACEFUL."
"IT WAS SO WELCOMING AND INVITING."
"AND THEN... HE WAS THERE!
ARISA! NO!
"AND THEN HE CALLED MY NAME. I MEAN, HER NAME. AND MY, HER...OUR HEART JUMPED."

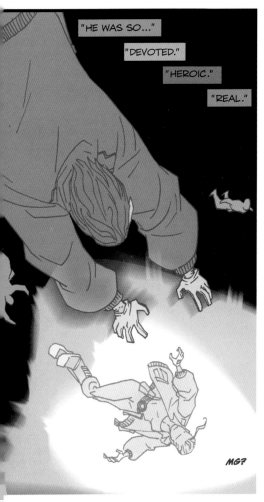

"HE WAS SO..."

"DEVOTED."

"HEROIC."

"REAL."

MG?

YOU CAN'T *GO.* YOU *CAN'T!* THERE'S... THERE'S STILL SO MUCH THAT YOU HAVE TO *DO!*

BUT... I'M SO TIRED. SO *WEAK.*

AND IT'S SO *NICE* HERE.

YOU'RE TIRED. YOU DON'T KNOW WHAT YOU'RE SAYING. YOU HAVE SO MUCH TO LIVE FOR...

LIKE WHAT?

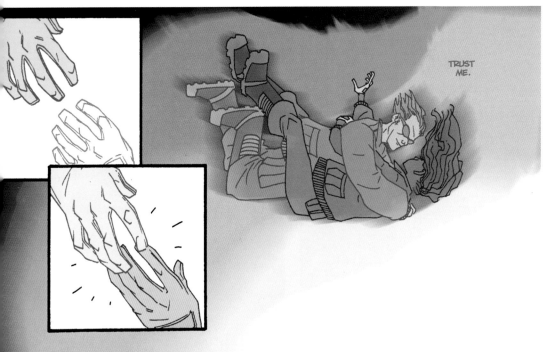

TRUST ME.

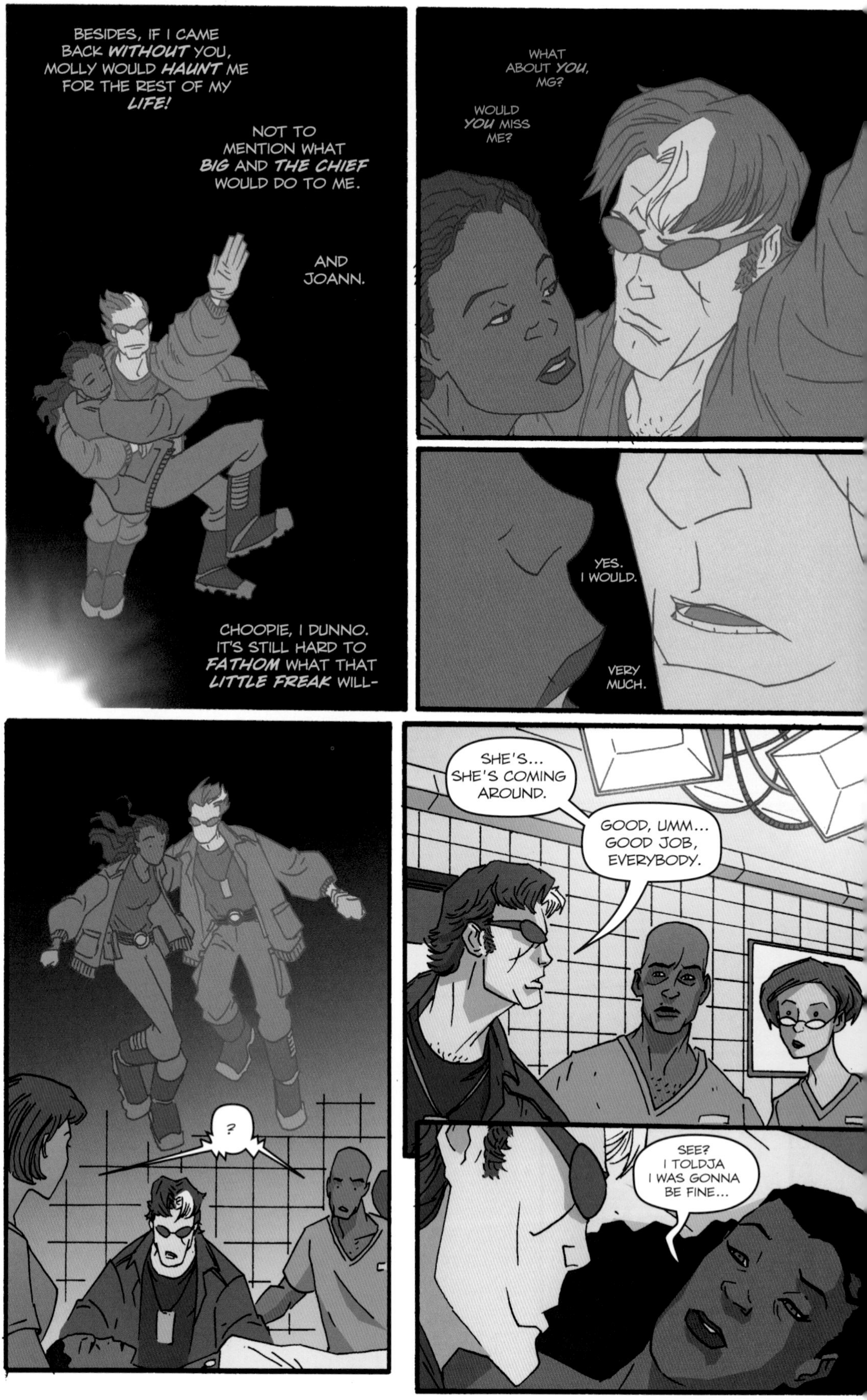
BESIDES, IF I CAME BACK WITHOUT YOU, MOLLY WOULD HAUNT ME FOR THE REST OF MY LIFE!
NOT TO MENTION WHAT BIG AND THE CHIEF WOULD DO TO ME.
AND JOANN.
CHOOPIE, I DUNNO. IT'S STILL HARD TO FATHOM WHAT THAT LITTLE FREAK WILL-
WHAT ABOUT YOU, MG?
WOULD YOU MISS ME?
YES. I WOULD.
VERY MUCH.
?
SHE'S... SHE'S COMING AROUND.
GOOD, UMM... GOOD JOB, EVERYBODY.
SEE? I TOLDJA I WAS GONNA BE FINE...

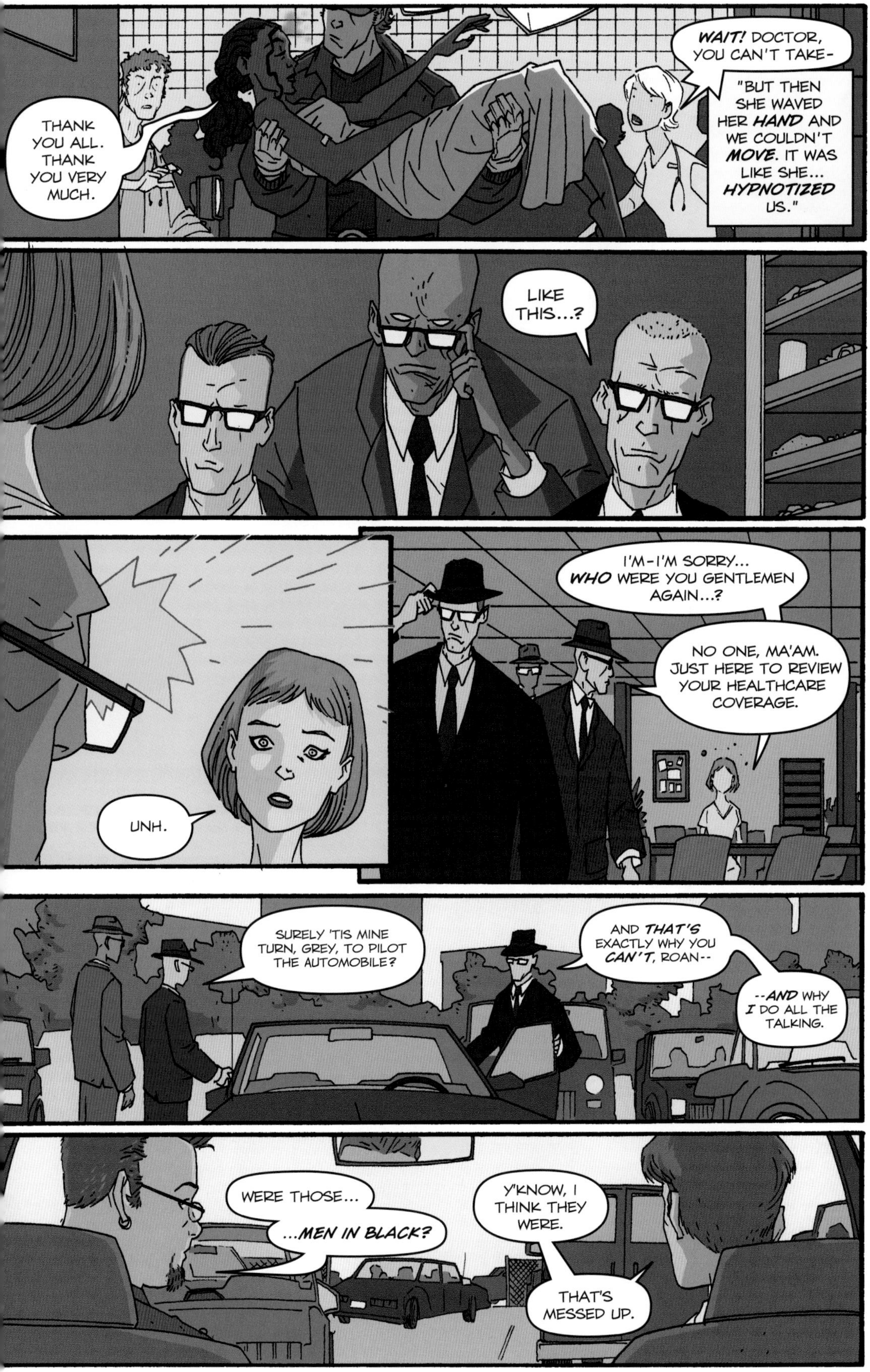
WAIT! DOCTOR, YOU CAN'T TAKE-
"BUT THEN SHE WAVED HER HAND AND WE COULDN'T MOVE. IT WAS LIKE SHE... HYPNOTIZED US."
THANK YOU ALL. THANK YOU VERY MUCH.
LIKE THIS...?
UNH.
I'M-I'M SORRY... WHO WERE YOU GENTLEMEN AGAIN...?
NO ONE, MA'AM. JUST HERE TO REVIEW YOUR HEALTHCARE COVERAGE.
SURELY 'TIS MINE TURN, GREY, TO PILOT THE AUTOMOBILE?
AND THAT'S EXACTLY WHY YOU CAN'T, ROAN--
--AND WHY I DO ALL THE TALKING.
WERE THOSE...
...MEN IN BLACK?
Y'KNOW, I THINK THEY WERE.
THAT'S MESSED UP.

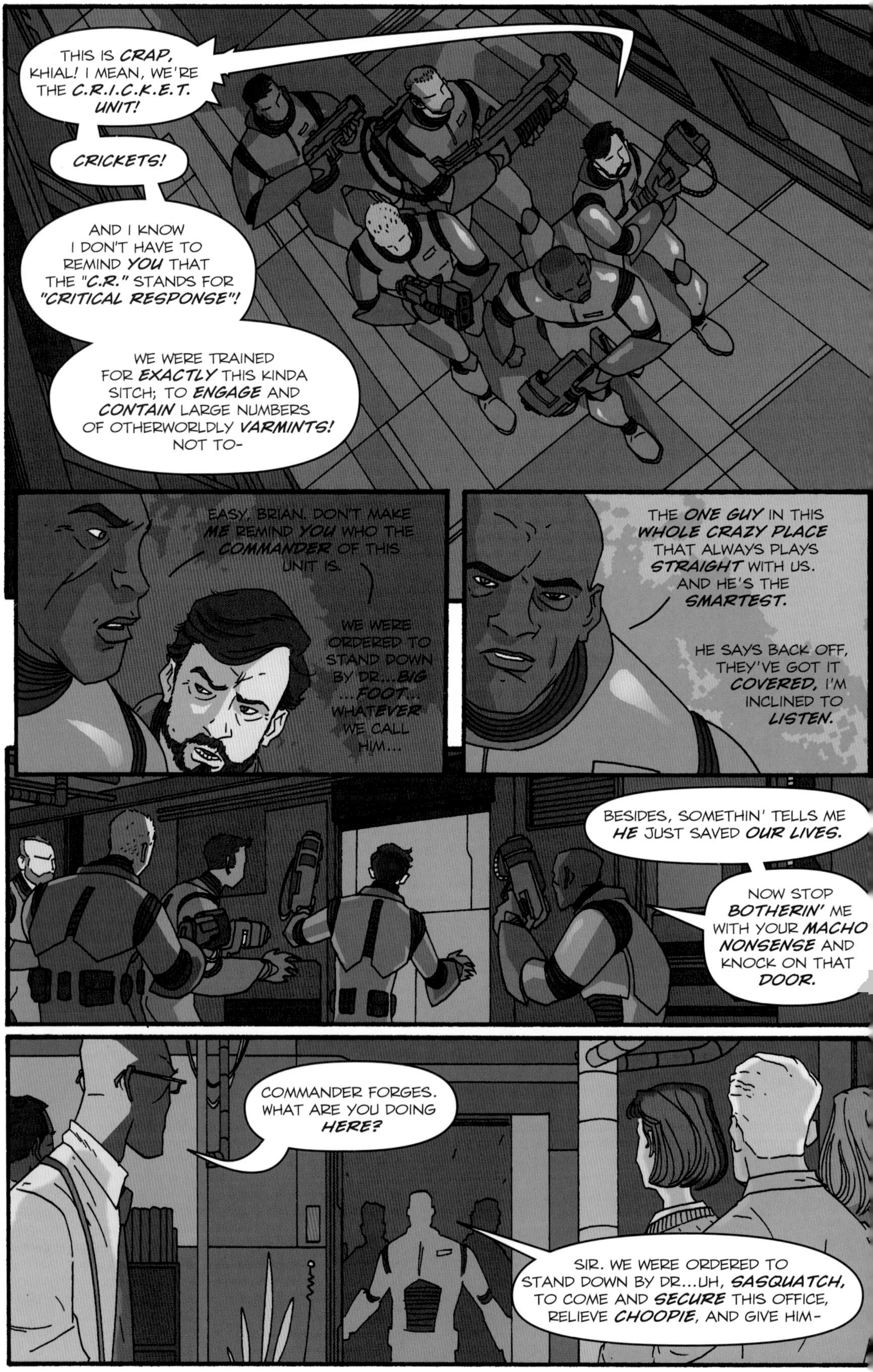
THIS IS CRAP, KHIAL! I MEAN, WE'RE THE C.R.I.C.K.E.T. UNIT!
CRICKETS!
AND I KNOW I DON'T HAVE TO REMIND YOU THAT THE "C.R." STANDS FOR "CRITICAL RESPONSE"!
WE WERE TRAINED FOR EXACTLY THIS KINDA SITCH; TO ENGAGE AND CONTAIN LARGE NUMBERS OF OTHERWORLDLY VARMINTS! NOT TO-
EASY, BRIAN. DON'T MAKE ME REMIND YOU WHO THE COMMANDER OF THIS UNIT IS.
WE WERE ORDERED TO STAND DOWN BY DR...BIG ...FOOT... WHATEVER WE CALL HIM...
THE ONE GUY IN THIS WHOLE CRAZY PLACE THAT ALWAYS PLAYS STRAIGHT WITH US. AND HE'S THE SMARTEST.
HE SAYS BACK OFF, THEY'VE GOT IT COVERED, I'M INCLINED TO LISTEN.
BESIDES, SOMETHIN' TELLS ME HE JUST SAVED OUR LIVES.
NOW STOP BOTHERIN' ME WITH YOUR MACHO NONSENSE AND KNOCK ON THAT DOOR.
COMMANDER FORGES. WHAT ARE YOU DOING HERE?
SIR. WE WERE ORDERED TO STAND DOWN BY DR...UH, SASQUATCH, TO COME AND SECURE THIS OFFICE, RELIEVE CHOOPIE, AND GIVE HIM-

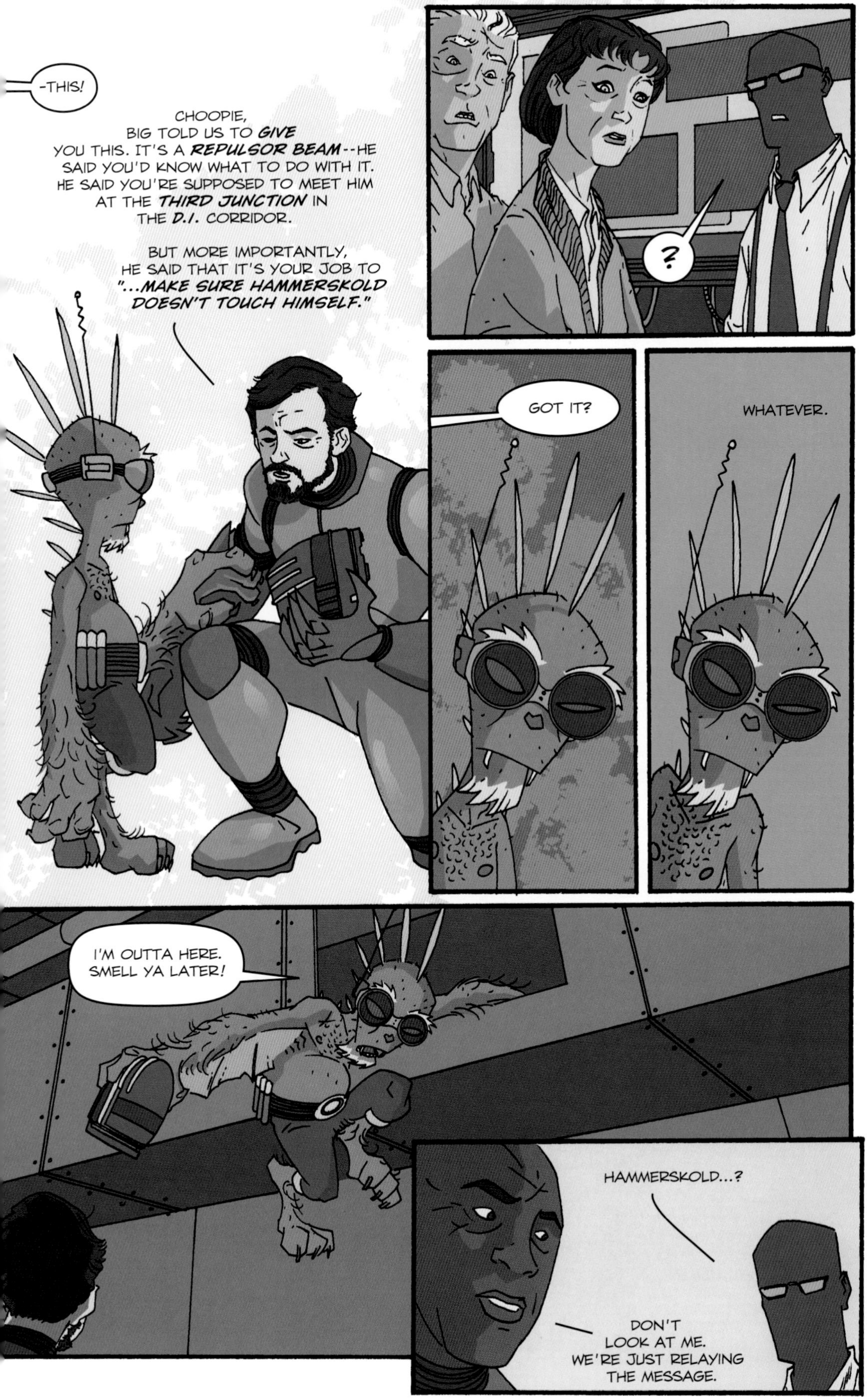
-THIS!
CHOOPIE, BIG TOLD US TO **GIVE** YOU THIS. IT'S A **REPULSOR BEAM**--HE SAID YOU'D KNOW WHAT TO DO WITH IT. HE SAID YOU'RE SUPPOSED TO MEET HIM AT THE **THIRD JUNCTION** IN THE **D.I.** CORRIDOR.
BUT MORE IMPORTANTLY, HE SAID THAT IT'S YOUR JOB TO **"...MAKE SURE HAMMERSKOLD DOESN'T TOUCH HIMSELF."**
?
GOT IT?
WHATEVER.
I'M OUTTA HERE. SMELL YA LATER!
HAMMERSKOLD...?
DON'T LOOK AT ME. WE'RE JUST RELAYING THE MESSAGE.

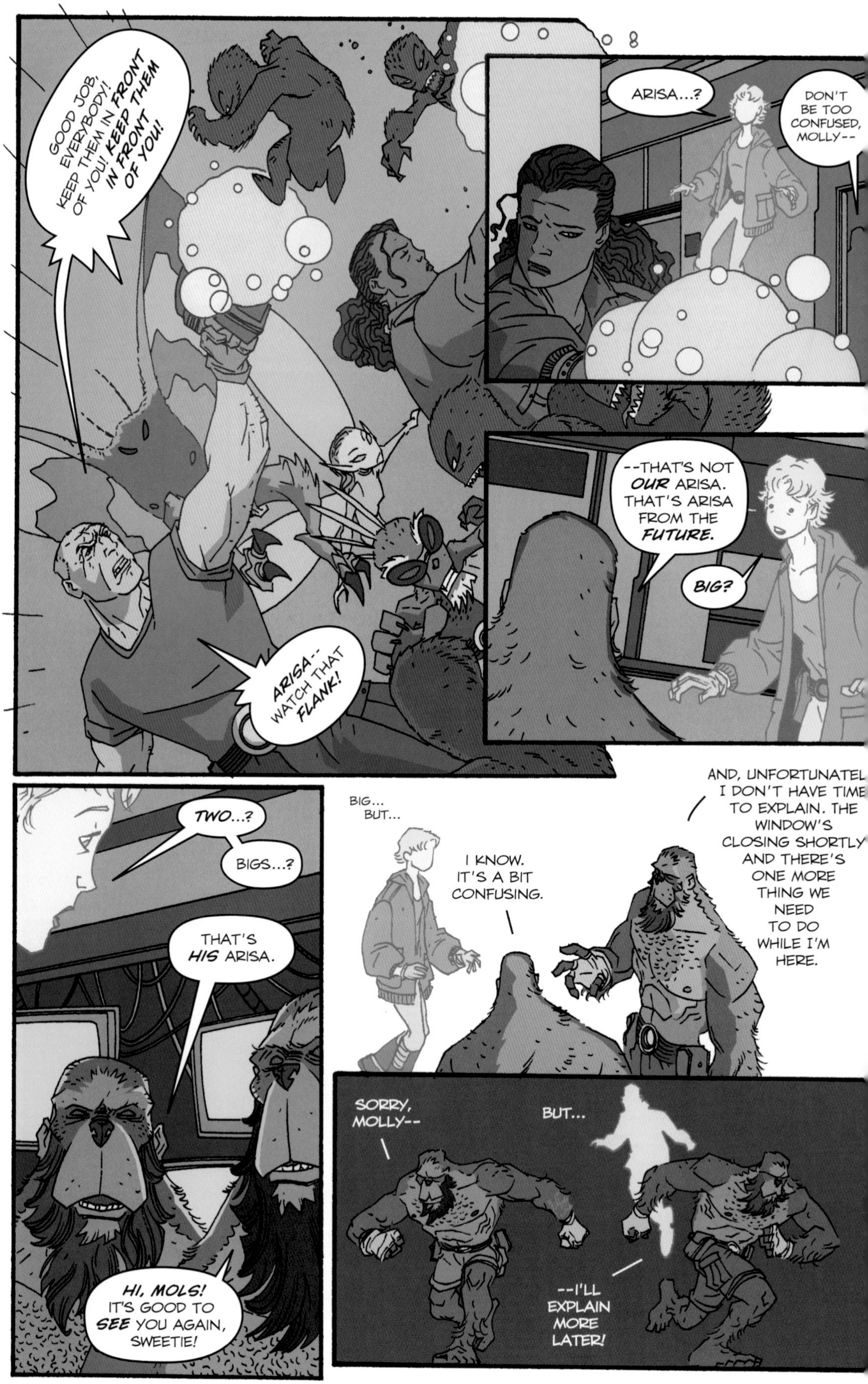
GOOD JOB, EVERYBODY! KEEP THEM IN FRONT OF YOU! KEEP THEM IN FRONT OF YOU!
ARISA--WATCH THAT FLANK!
ARISA...?
DON'T BE TOO CONFUSED, MOLLY--
--THAT'S NOT OUR ARISA. THAT'S ARISA FROM THE FUTURE.
BIG?
TWO...?
BIGS...?
THAT'S HIS ARISA.
HI, MOLS! IT'S GOOD TO SEE YOU AGAIN, SWEETIE!
BIG... BUT...
I KNOW. IT'S A BIT CONFUSING.
AND, UNFORTUNATEL I DON'T HAVE TIME TO EXPLAIN. THE WINDOW'S CLOSING SHORTLY AND THERE'S ONE MORE THING WE NEED TO DO WHILE I'M HERE.
SORRY, MOLLY--
BUT...
--I'LL EXPLAIN MORE LATER!

...TELLIN' YOU RIGHT *NOW,* McCLUSKEY--YOU LET ME *OUTTA* THIS ROOM OR--

AND I'M TELLING *YOU,* COMMANDER HAMMERSKOLD. MY MEN AND I WERE ORDERED TO *DETAIN* YOU AND AGENT THORNTON BY DR....S-SAS...

...QUATCH.

SAS...?

BIG?!!

HE DOESN'T HAVE THE *AUTHORITY* TO-

WHAT THE-?!

BLUE TEAM?! THOSE *GLORY-SEEKING...!* SO *THEY* CAN GET ALL THE *CREDIT?!*

I DON'T *THINK* SO!

THORNTON. JUST A *JOLT.*

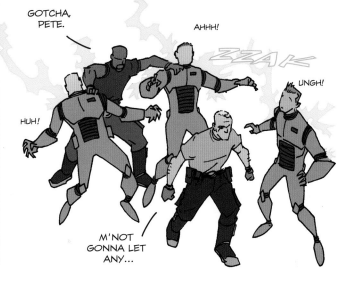

GOTCHA, PETE.

AHHH!

ZZAK

HUH!

UNGH!

M'NOT GONNA LET ANY...

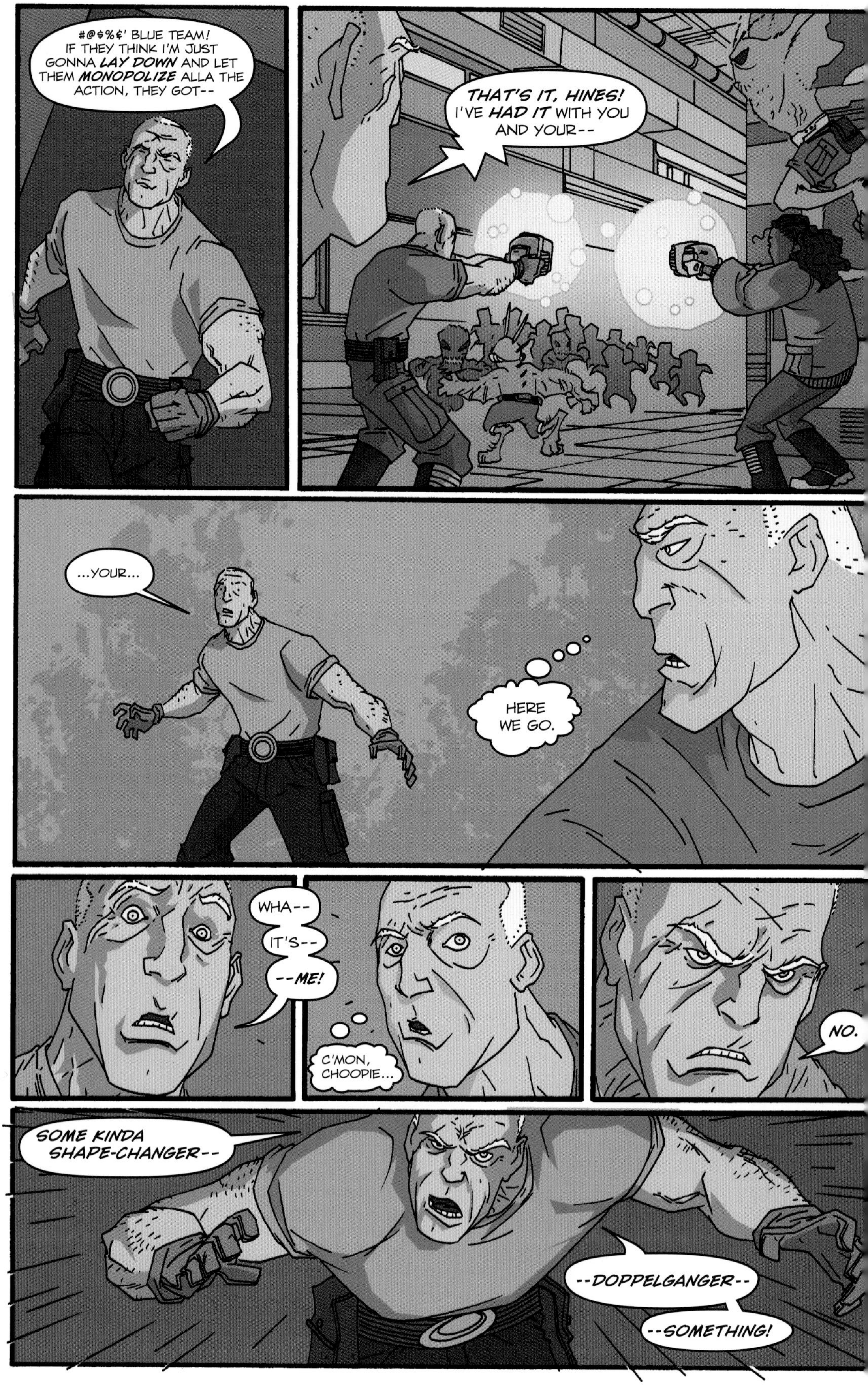
#@$%¢' BLUE TEAM! IF THEY THINK I'M JUST GONNA LAY DOWN AND LET THEM MONOPOLIZE ALLA THE ACTION, THEY GOT--
THAT'S IT, HINES! I'VE HAD IT WITH YOU AND YOUR--
...YOUR...
HERE WE GO.
WHA--
IT'S--
--ME!
C'MON, CHOOPIE...
NO.
SOME KINDA SHAPE-CHANGER--
--DOPPELGANGER--
--SOMETHING!

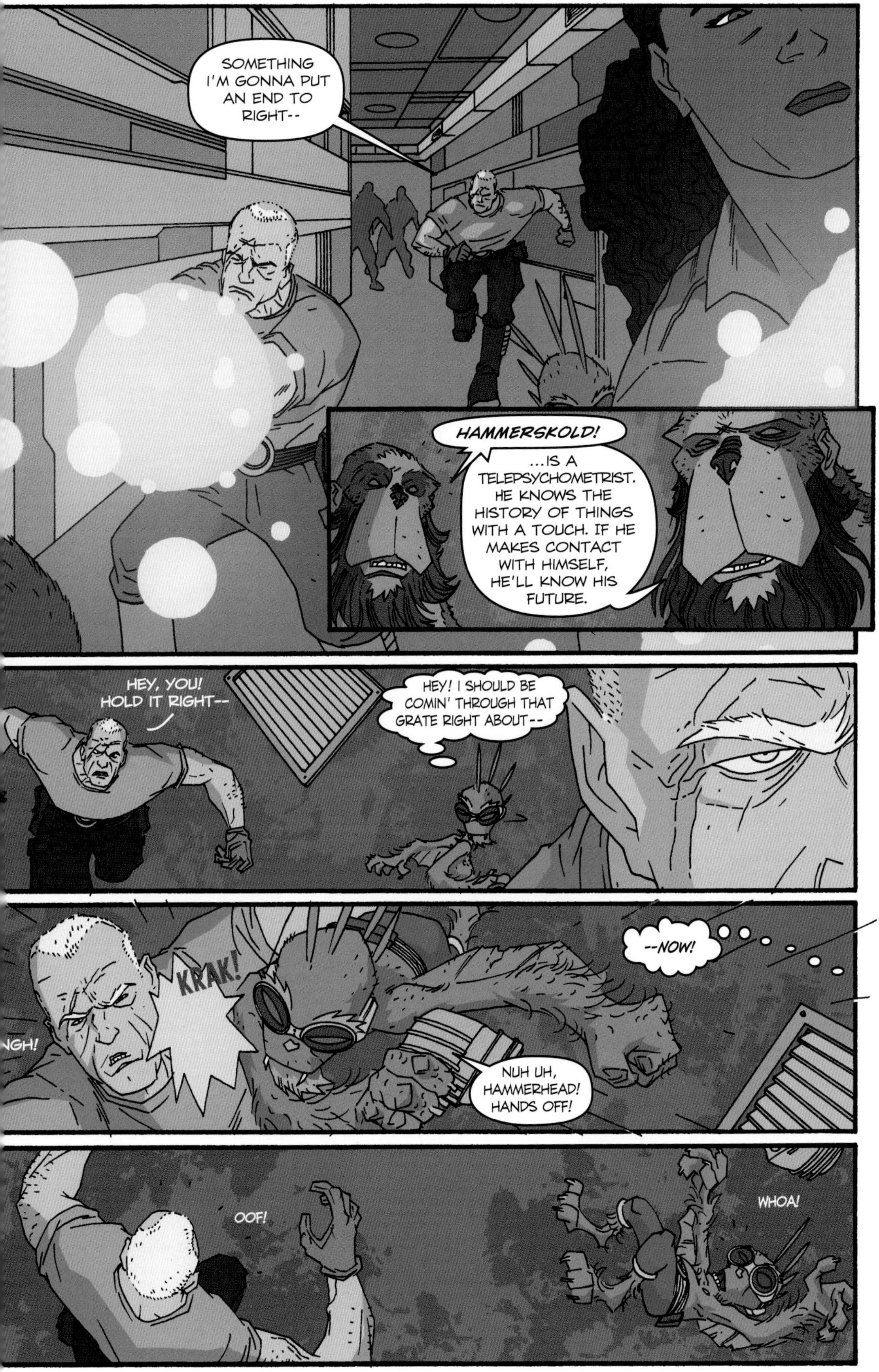

SOMETHING I'M GONNA PUT AN END TO RIGHT--
HAMMERSKOLD!
...IS A TELEPSYCHOMETRIST. HE KNOWS THE HISTORY OF THINGS WITH A TOUCH. IF HE MAKES CONTACT WITH HIMSELF, HE'LL KNOW HIS FUTURE.
HEY, YOU! HOLD IT RIGHT--
HEY! I SHOULD BE COMIN' THROUGH THAT GRATE RIGHT ABOUT--
KRAK!
--NOW!
NGH!
NUH UH, HAMMERHEAD! HANDS OFF!
OOF!
WHOA!

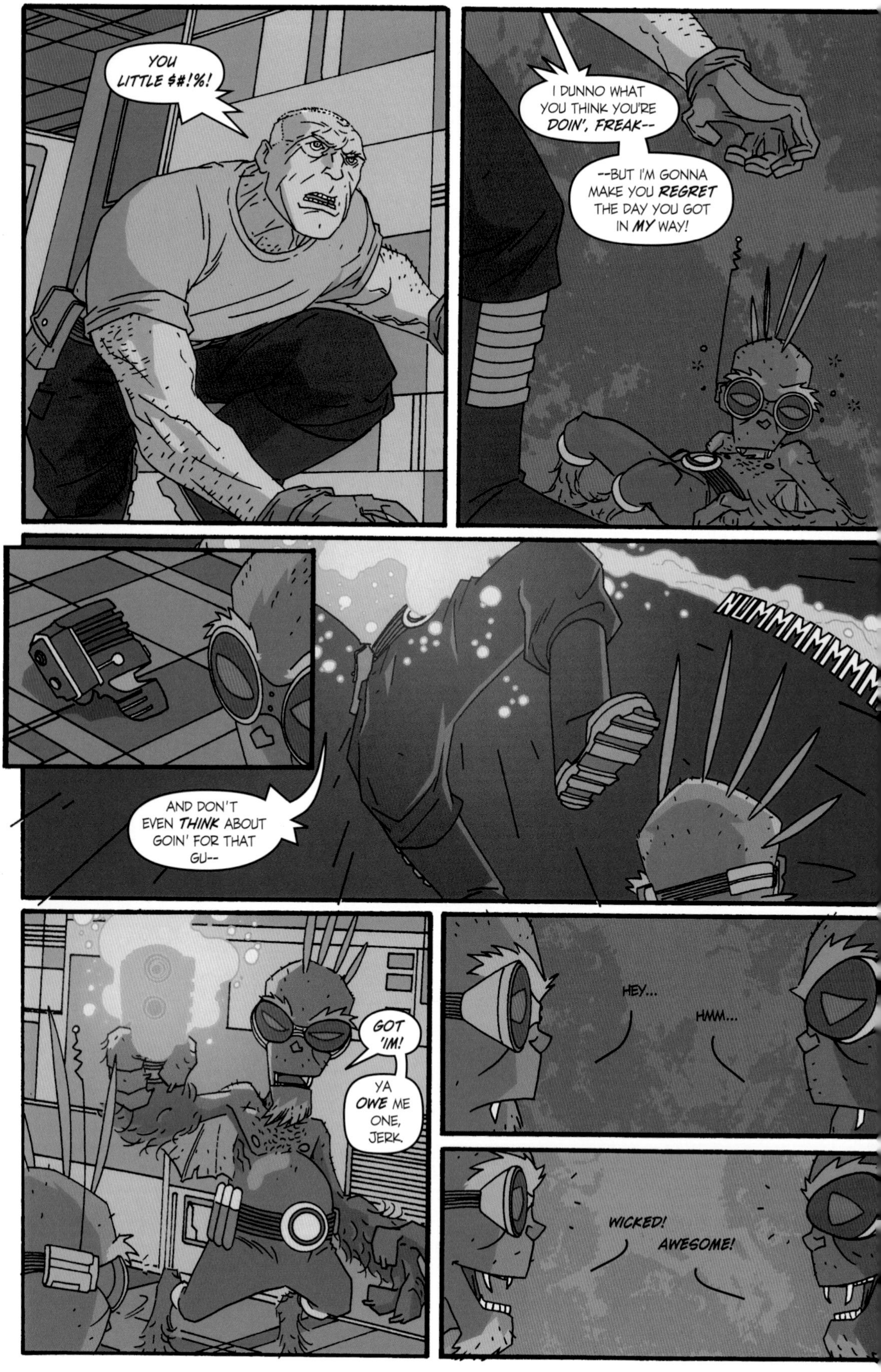
YOU LITTLE $#!%!
I DUNNO WHAT YOU THINK YOU'RE DOIN', FREAK--
--BUT I'M GONNA MAKE YOU REGRET THE DAY YOU GOT IN MY WAY!
NUMMMMMMMM
AND DON'T EVEN THINK ABOUT GOIN' FOR THAT GU--
GOT 'IM!
YA OWE ME ONE, JERK.
HEY...
HMM...
WICKED!
AWESOME!

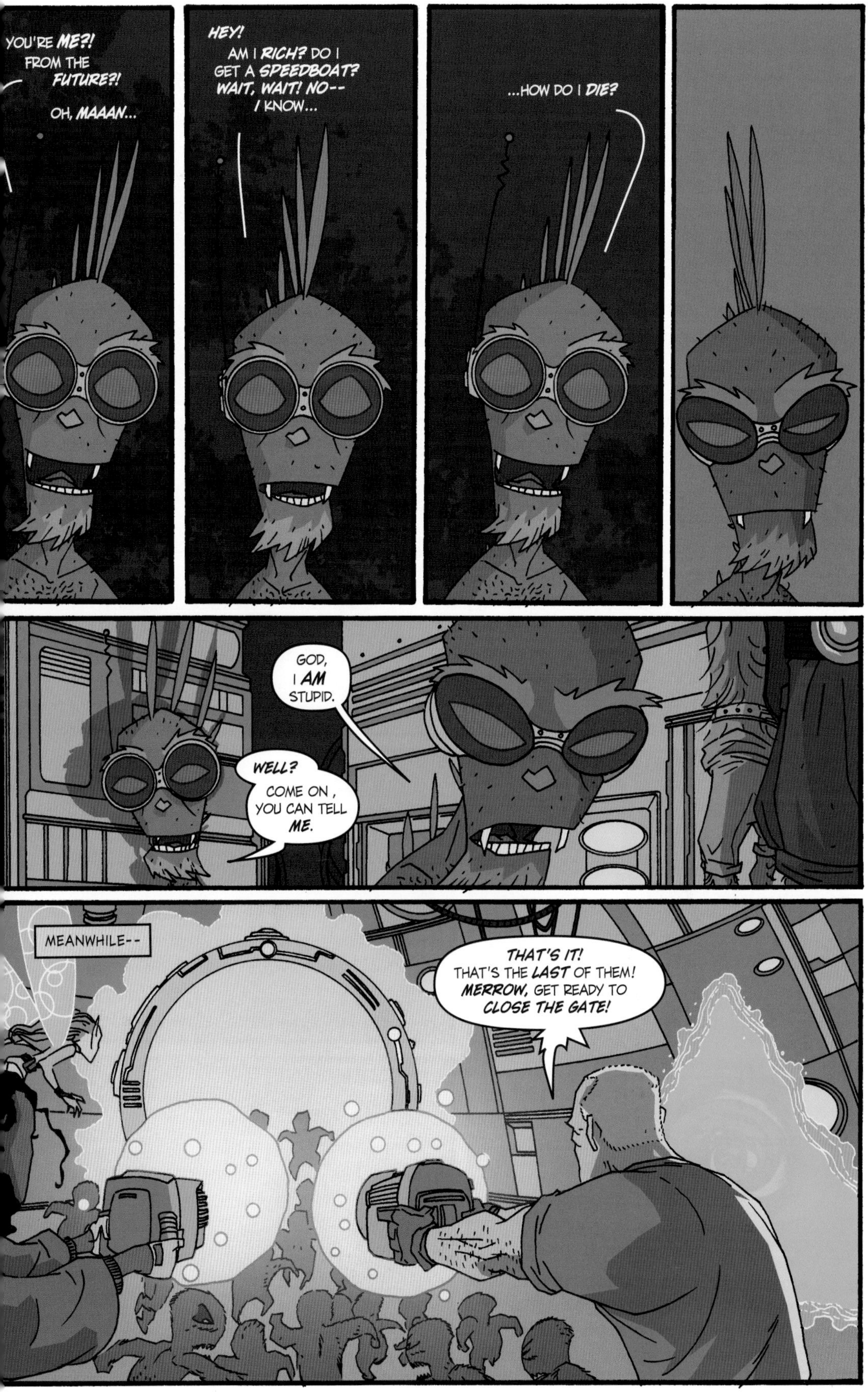
YOU'RE ME?! FROM THE FUTURE?!
OH, MAAAN...
HEY!
AM I RICH? DO I GET A SPEEDBOAT? WAIT, WAIT! NO-- I KNOW...
...HOW DO I DIE?
GOD, I AM STUPID.
WELL? COME ON , YOU CAN TELL ME.
MEANWHILE--
THAT'S IT! THAT'S THE LAST OF THEM! MERROW, GET READY TO CLOSE THE GATE!

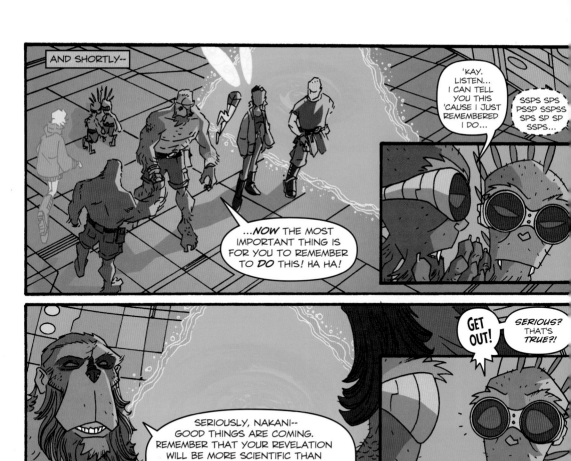

AND SHORTLY--

'KAY. LISTEN... I CAN TELL YOU THIS 'CAUSE I JUST REMEMBERED I DO...

SSPS SPS PSSP SSPSS SPS SP SP SSPS...

...NOW THE MOST IMPORTANT THING IS FOR YOU TO REMEMBER TO DO THIS! HA HA!

GET OUT!

SERIOUS? THAT'S TRUE?!

SERIOUSLY, NAKANI-- GOOD THINGS ARE COMING. REMEMBER THAT YOUR REVELATION WILL BE MORE SCIENTIFIC THAN SPIRITUAL, SO KEEP YOUR MIND-- AND YOUR HEART-- OPEN TO THAT.

ACTUALLY, ALL OF YOU, KEEP YOUR MINDS OPEN TO EVERY POSSIBILITY!

THE CRAZIEST THINGS ARE GOING TO HAPPEN.

PEACE. AHIMSA.

WHAT...?

WAS THAT...?

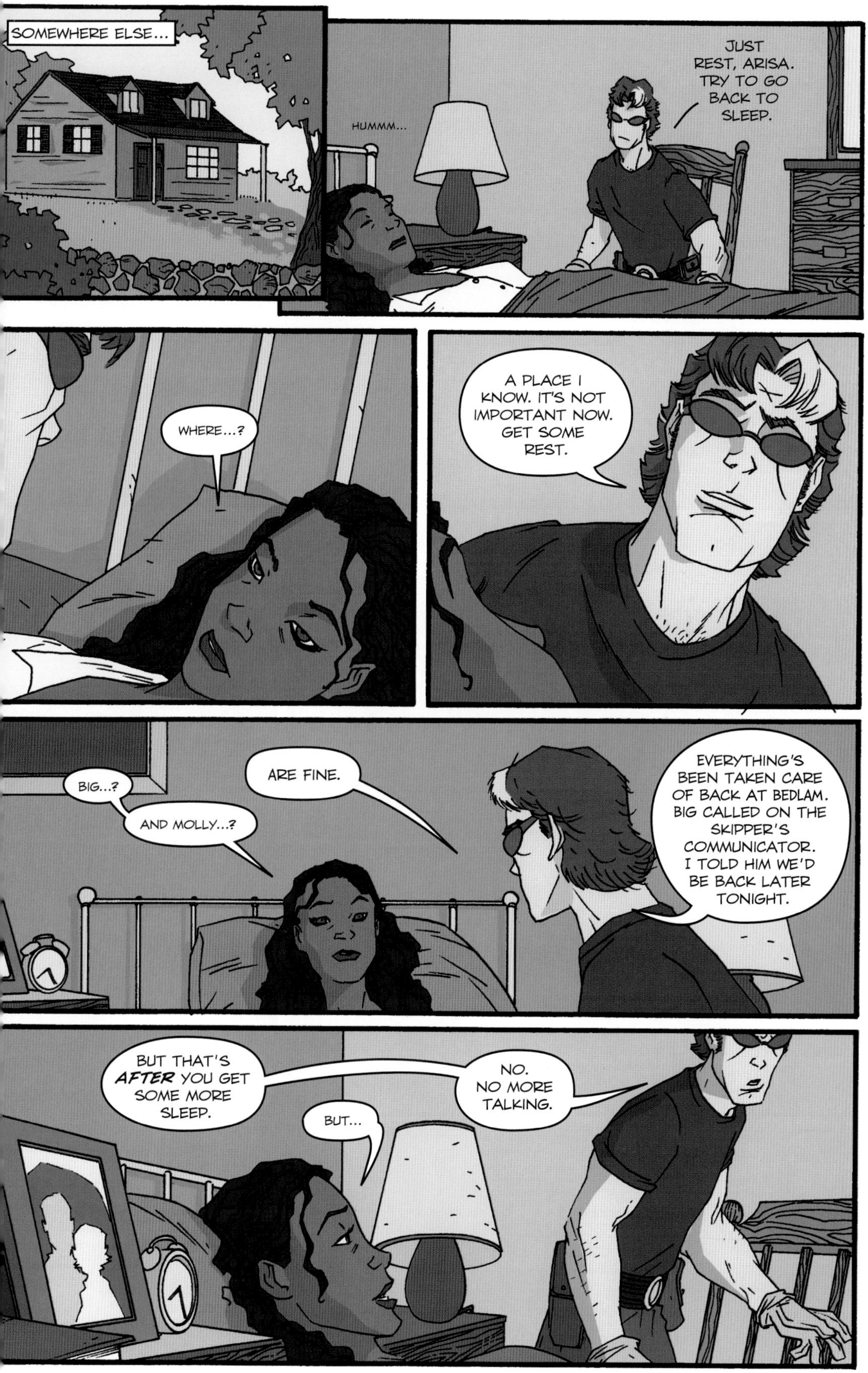
SOMEWHERE ELSE...
HUMMM...
JUST REST, ARISA. TRY TO GO BACK TO SLEEP.
WHERE...?
A PLACE I KNOW. IT'S NOT IMPORTANT NOW. GET SOME REST.
BIG...?
AND MOLLY...?
ARE FINE.
EVERYTHING'S BEEN TAKEN CARE OF BACK AT BEDLAM. BIG CALLED ON THE SKIPPER'S COMMUNICATOR. I TOLD HIM WE'D BE BACK LATER TONIGHT.
BUT...
NO. NO MORE TALKING.
BUT THAT'S *AFTER* YOU GET SOME MORE SLEEP.

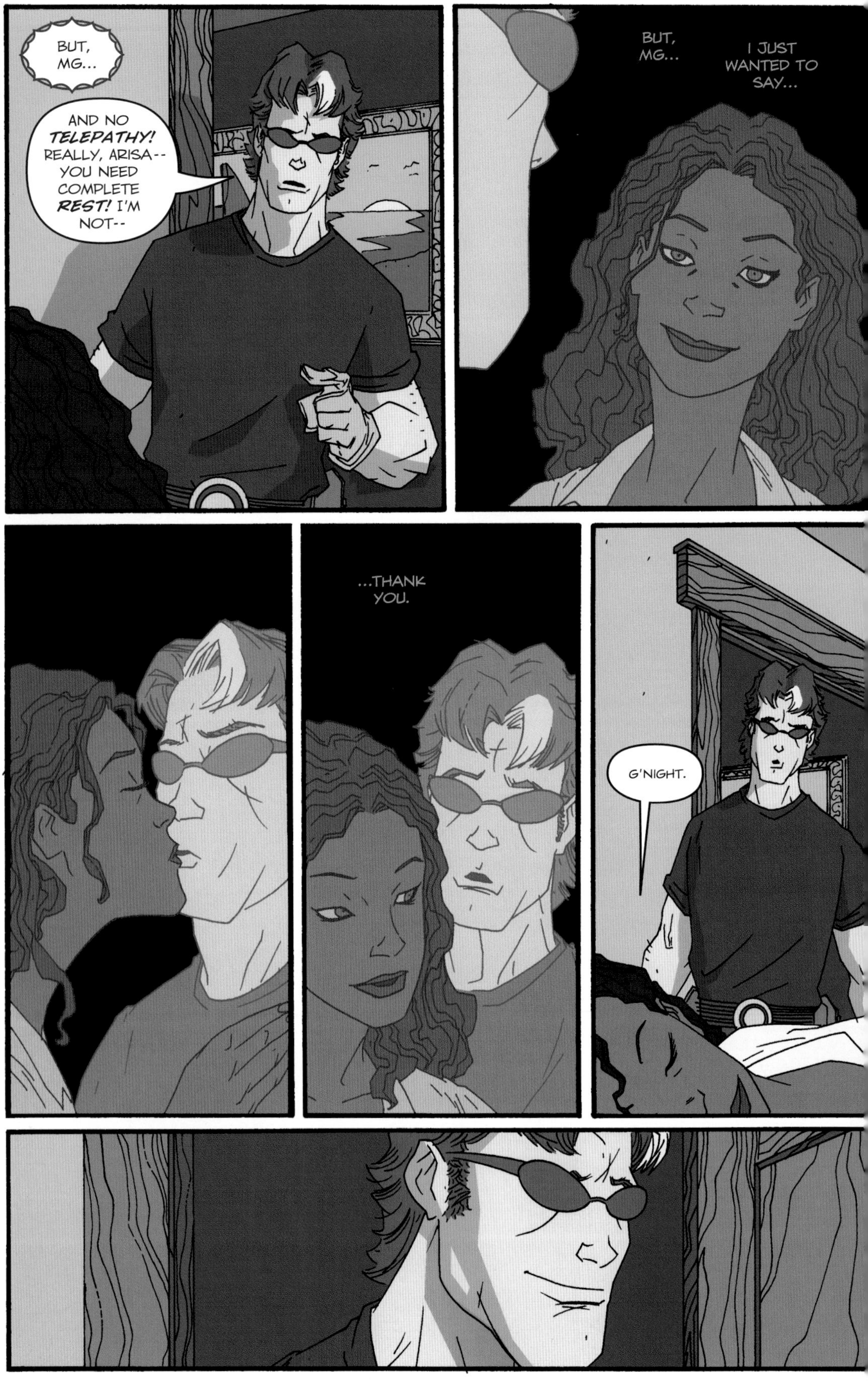
BUT, MG...
AND NO *TELEPATHY!* REALLY, ARISA-- YOU NEED COMPLETE *REST!* I'M NOT--
BUT, MG...
I JUST WANTED TO SAY...
...THANK YOU.
G'NIGHT.

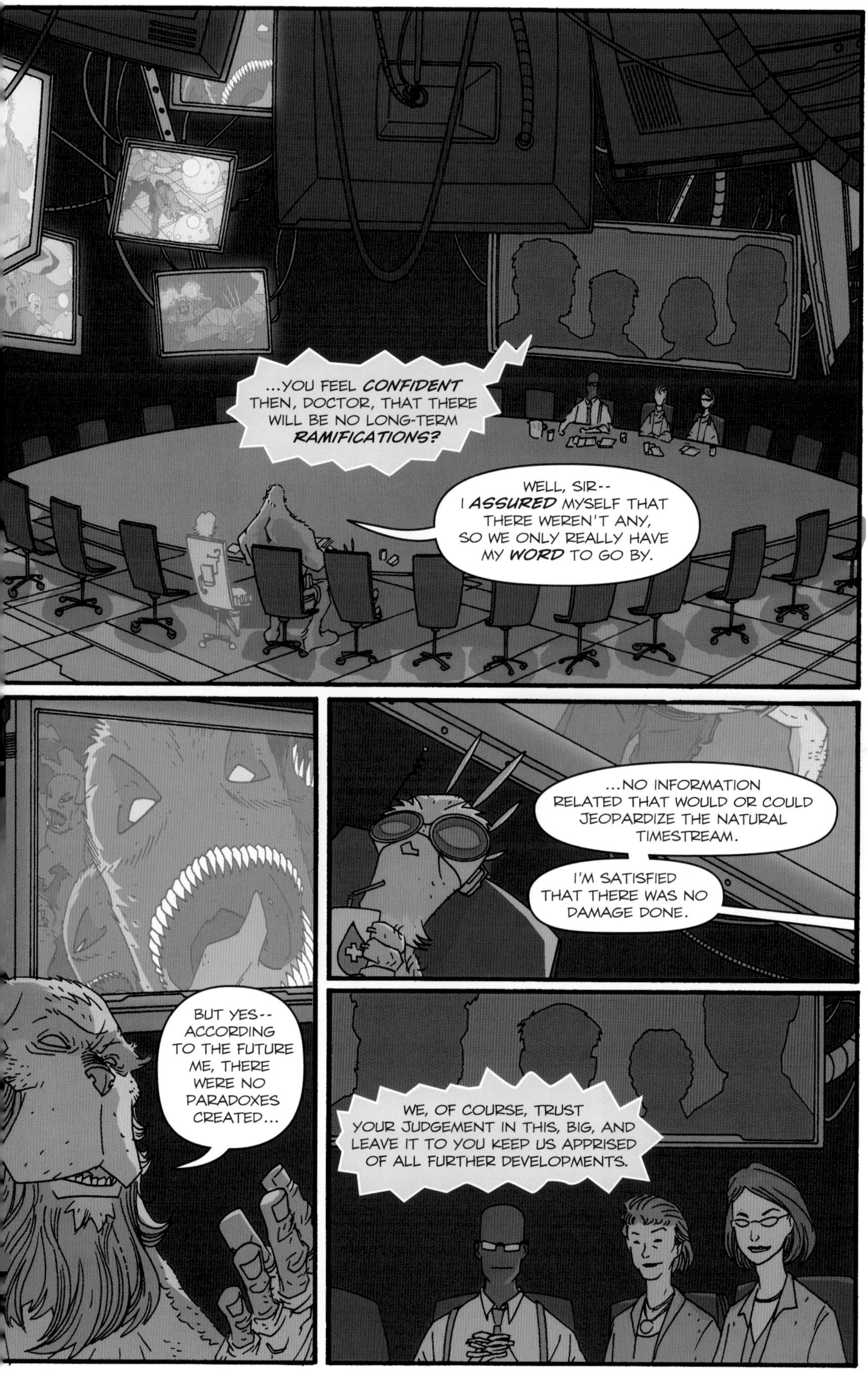
...YOU FEEL CONFIDENT THEN, DOCTOR, THAT THERE WILL BE NO LONG-TERM RAMIFICATIONS?
WELL, SIR-- I ASSURED MYSELF THAT THERE WEREN'T ANY, SO WE ONLY REALLY HAVE MY WORD TO GO BY.
BUT YES-- ACCORDING TO THE FUTURE ME, THERE WERE NO PARADOXES CREATED...
...NO INFORMATION RELATED THAT WOULD OR COULD JEOPARDIZE THE NATURAL TIMESTREAM.
I'M SATISFIED THAT THERE WAS NO DAMAGE DONE.
WE, OF COURSE, TRUST YOUR JUDGEMENT IN THIS, BIG, AND LEAVE IT TO YOU KEEP US APPRISED OF ALL FURTHER DEVELOPMENTS.

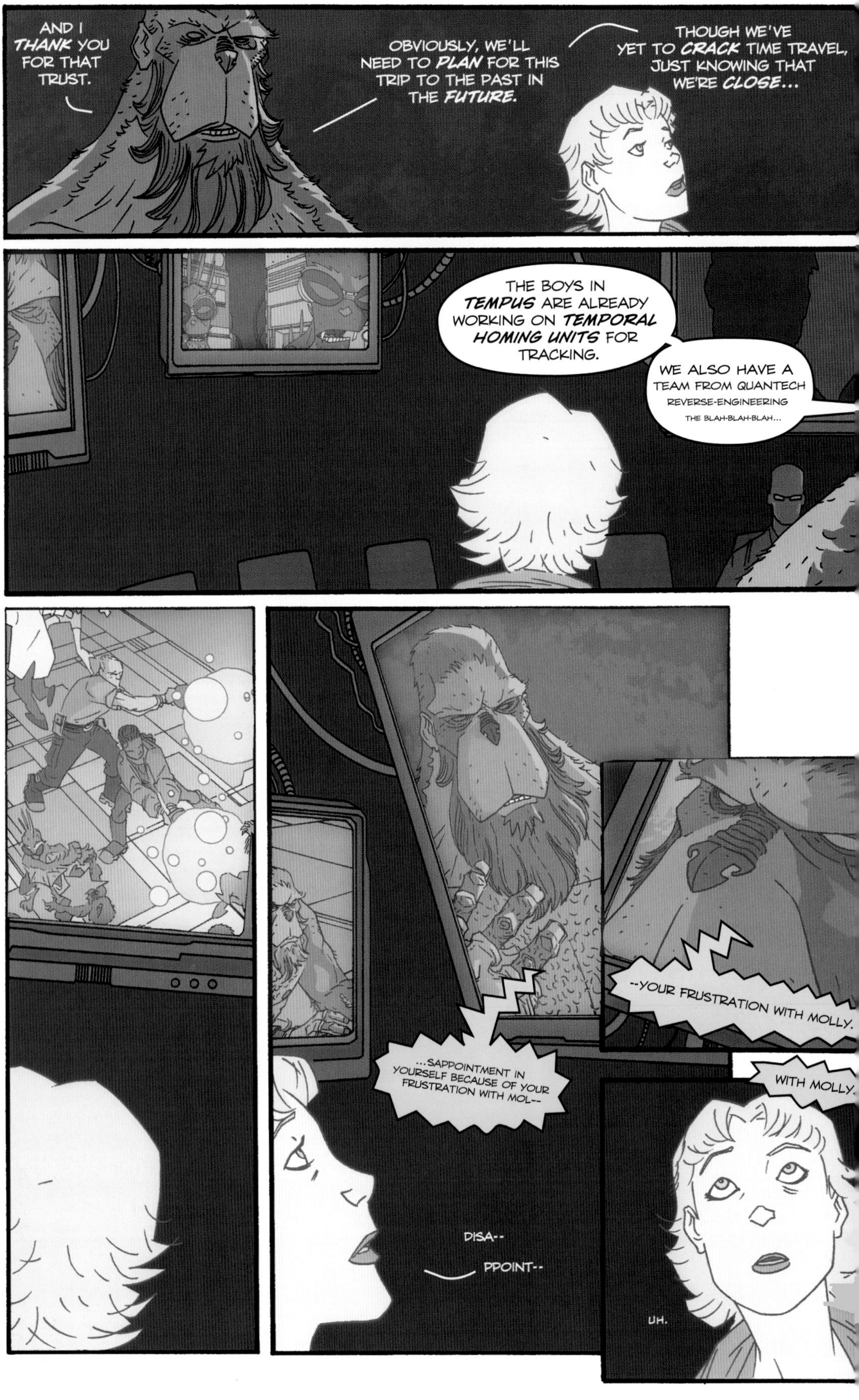
AND I THANK YOU FOR THAT TRUST.
OBVIOUSLY, WE'LL NEED TO PLAN FOR THIS TRIP TO THE PAST IN THE FUTURE.
THOUGH WE'VE YET TO CRACK TIME TRAVEL, JUST KNOWING THAT WE'RE CLOSE...
THE BOYS IN TEMPUS ARE ALREADY WORKING ON TEMPORAL HOMING UNITS FOR TRACKING.
WE ALSO HAVE A TEAM FROM QUANTECH REVERSE-ENGINEERING THE BLAH-BLAH-BLAH...
--YOUR FRUSTRATION WITH MOLLY.
...SAPPOINTMENT IN YOURSELF BECAUSE OF YOUR FRUSTRATION WITH MOL--
WITH MOLLY.
DISA--
PPOINT--
UH.

I...
I HAVE TO *GO!*

MOLLY?

WHAT--

IT'S NOTHING. IT...

WHEN YOU WERE *TALKING* TO YOURSELF YOU SAID... YOU'RE *DISAPPOINTED* IN ME--*FRUSTRATED* WITH ME. I...I KNOW IT WAS IN PRIVATE--I DIDN'T MEAN TO--

MOLLY, THAT'S NOT--

I *TRY*, BIG! I REALLY *DO!* I *WANT* TO HELP, BUT... I *CAN'T!*

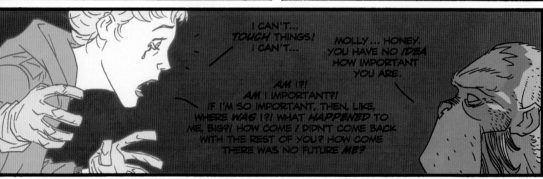

I CAN'T... *TOUCH* THINGS! I CAN'T...

MOLLY... HONEY. YOU HAVE NO *IDEA* HOW IMPORTANT YOU ARE.

AM I?! *AM* I IMPORTANT?! IF I'M SO IMPORTANT, THEN, LIKE, WHERE *WAS* I?! WHAT *HAPPENED* TO ME, BIG?! HOW COME *I* DIDN'T COME BACK WITH THE REST OF YOU? HOW COME THERE WAS NO FUTURE *ME?*

WHAT HAPPENS TO ME, BIG? WHERE WAS I?

> SOB! <

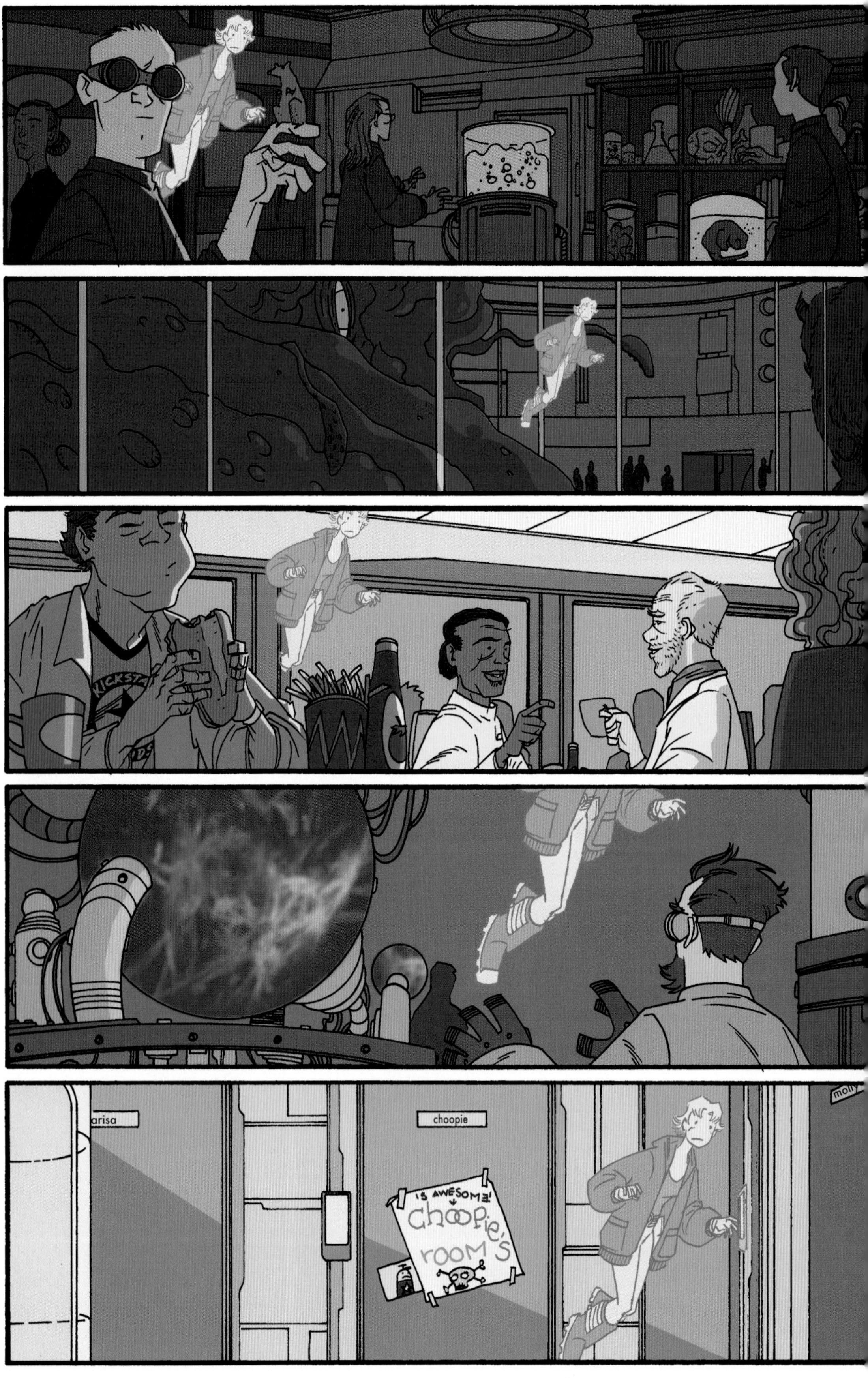
arisa
choopie
molly
IS AWESOME!
choopie's
room

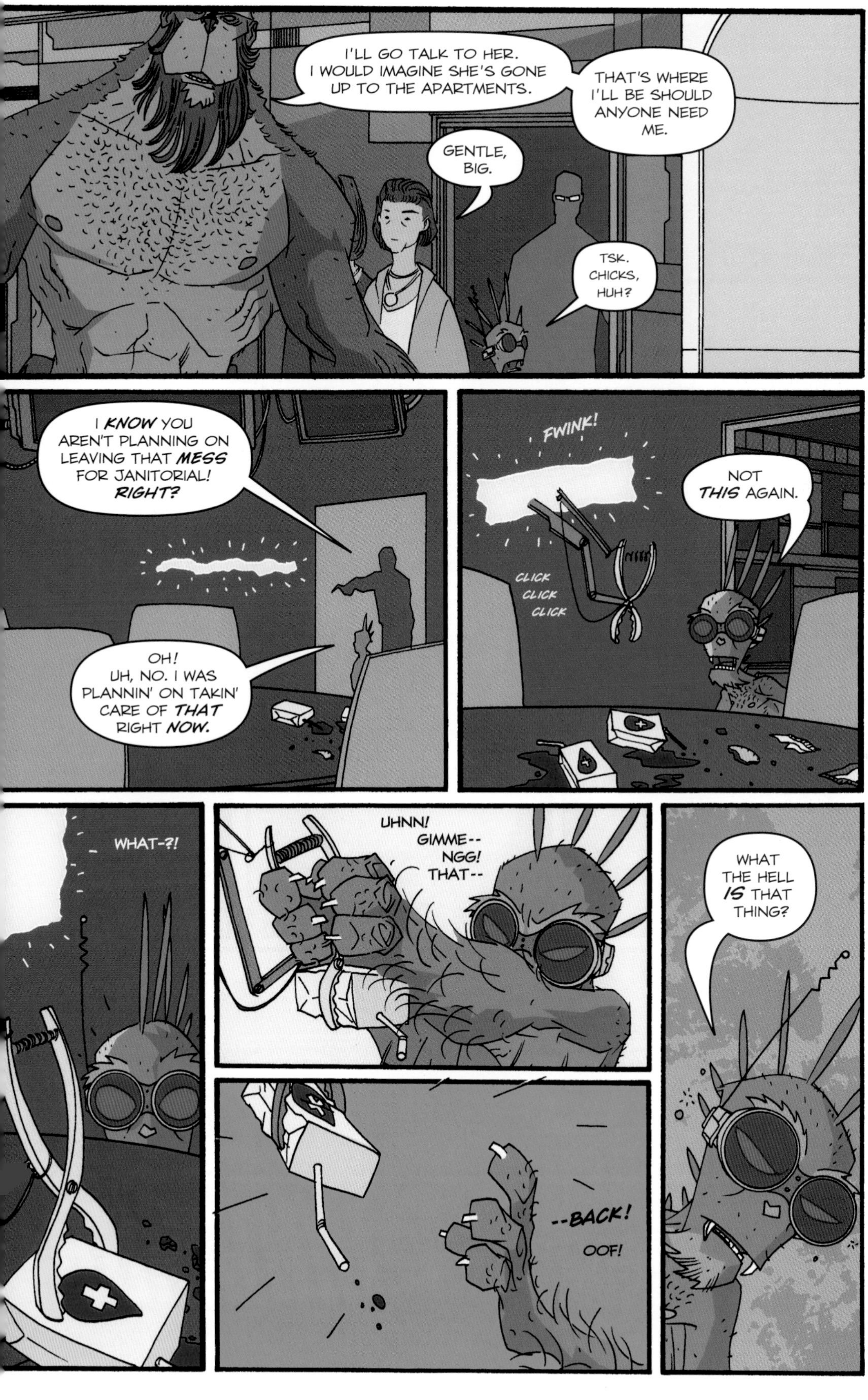
I'LL GO TALK TO HER. I WOULD IMAGINE SHE'S GONE UP TO THE APARTMENTS.
THAT'S WHERE I'LL BE SHOULD ANYONE NEED ME.
GENTLE, BIG.
TSK. CHICKS, HUH?
I KNOW YOU AREN'T PLANNING ON LEAVING THAT MESS FOR JANITORIAL! RIGHT?
OH! UH, NO. I WAS PLANNIN' ON TAKIN' CARE OF THAT RIGHT NOW.
FWINK!
CLICK CLICK CLICK
NOT THIS AGAIN.
WHAT-?!
UHNN! GIMME-- NGG! THAT--
--BACK!
OOF!
WHAT THE HELL IS THAT THING?

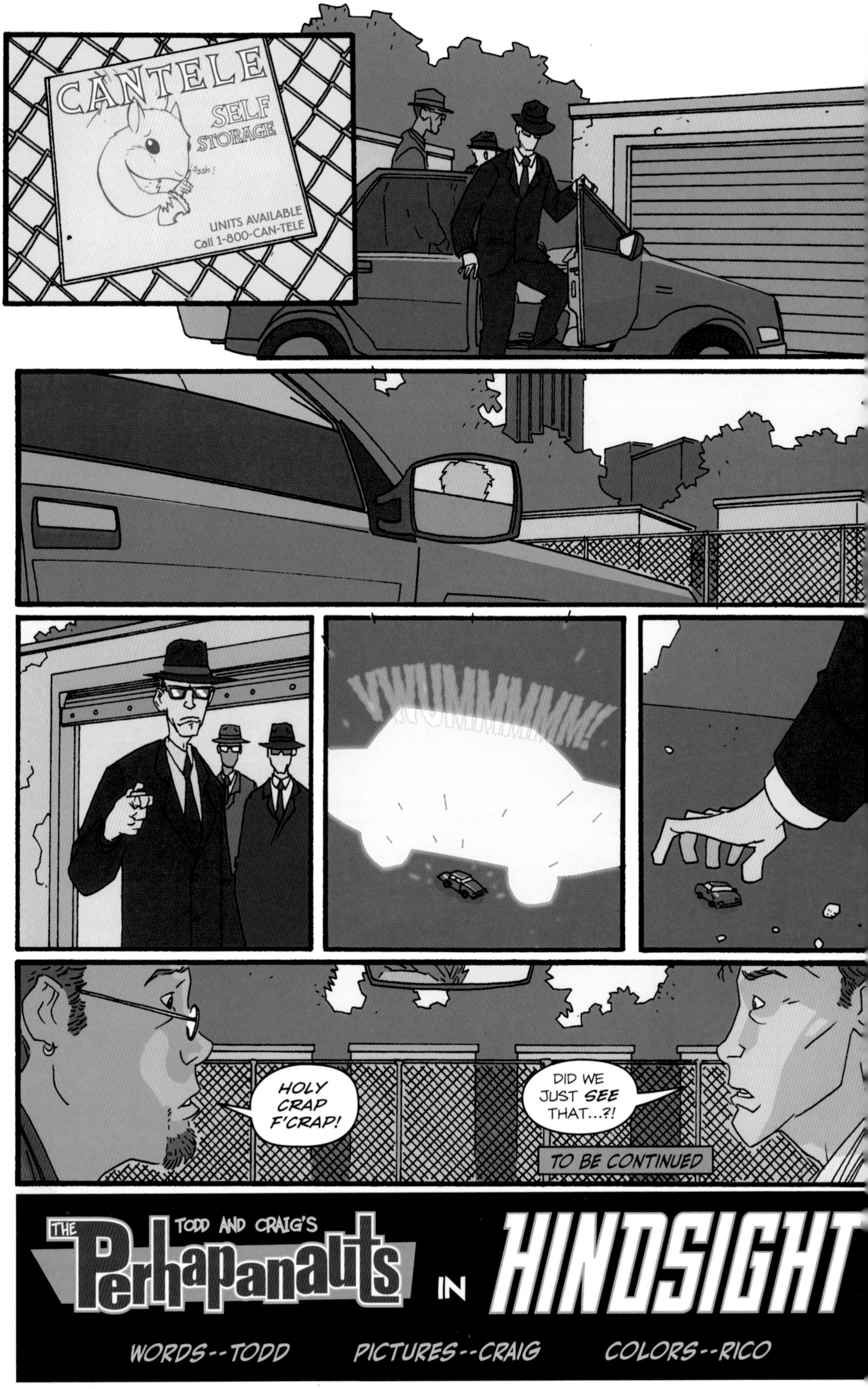
CANTELE
SELF STORAGE
sssh
UNITS AVAILABLE
Call 1-800-CAN-TELE
HOLY CRAP F'CRAP!
DID WE JUST SEE THAT...?!
TO BE CONTINUED

TODD AND CRAIG'S THE Perhapanauts IN HINDSIGHT

WORDS--TODD PICTURES--CRAIG COLORS--RICO

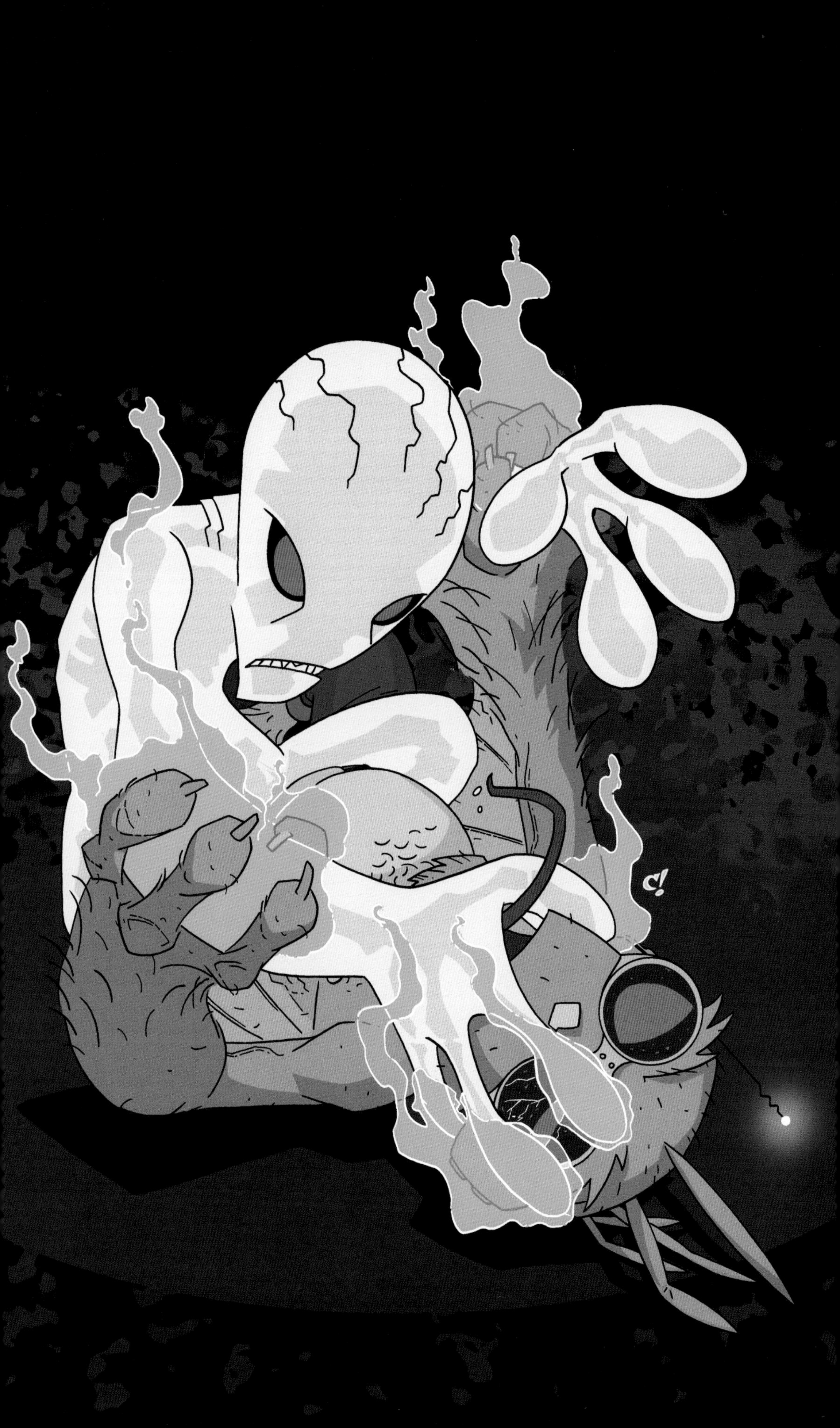
C!

THE PERHAPANAUTS
TODD AND CRAIG'S
IN
The DOVER DEMON

words by todd   pictures by craig   colors by rico

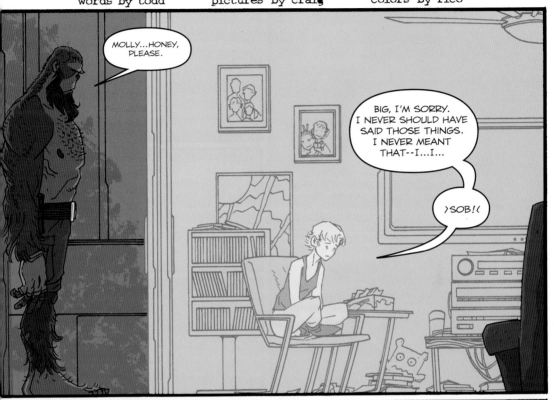

MOLLY...HONEY, PLEASE.

BIG, I'M SORRY. I NEVER SHOULD HAVE SAID THOSE THINGS. I NEVER MEANT THAT--I...I...

>SOB!<

NO. NO, MOLLY. YOU WERE *RIGHT*. YOU HAVE EVERY *RIGHT* TO BE ANGRY, EVERY *RIGHT* TO BE MAD AT ME...AND EVERY RIGHT TO HAVE THE *ANSWERS* TO YOUR QUESTIONS.

MAD AT...

...*YOU?!*

BIG, I--

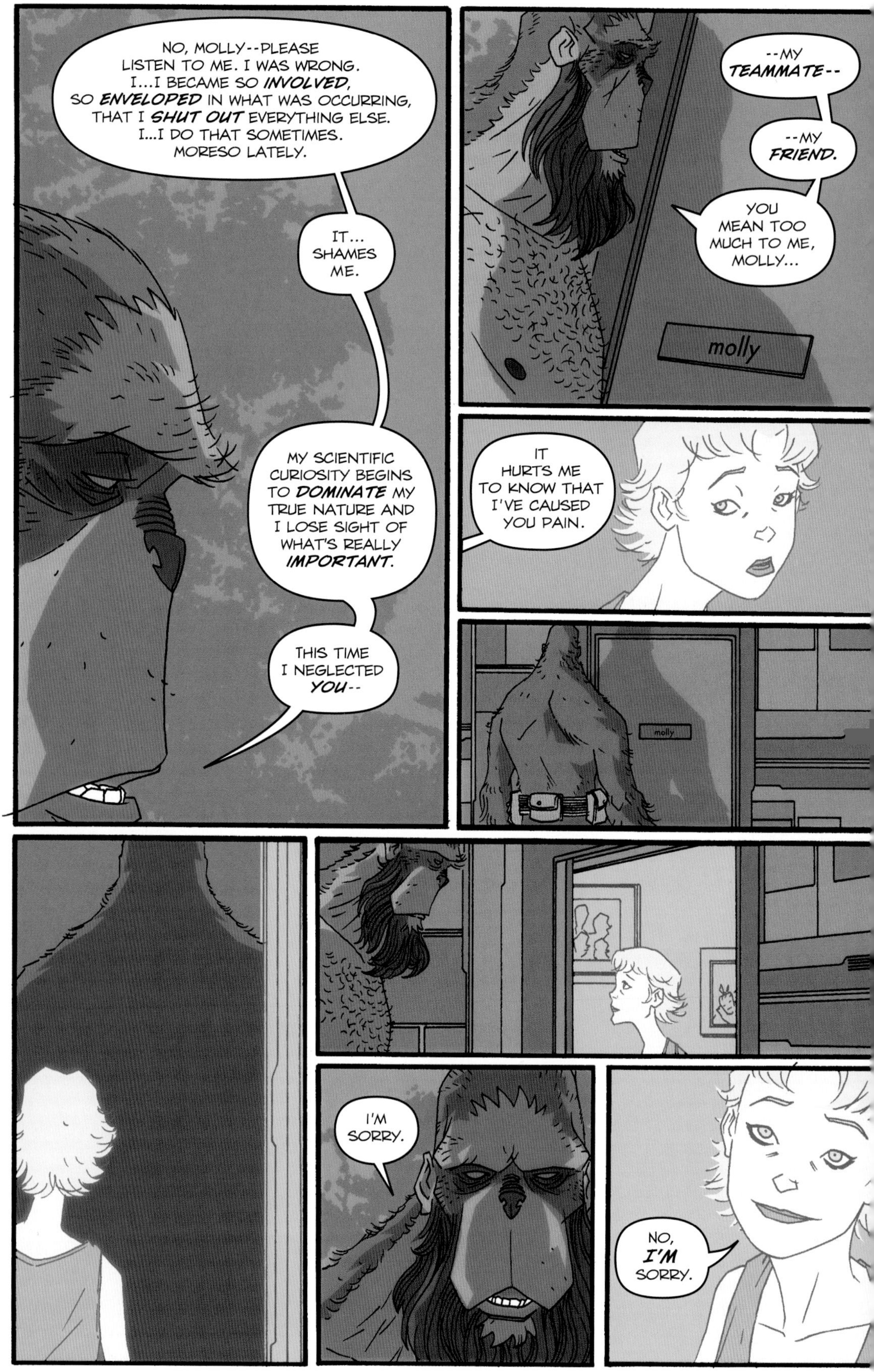
NO, MOLLY--PLEASE LISTEN TO ME. I WAS WRONG. I...I BECAME SO INVOLVED, SO ENVELOPED IN WHAT WAS OCCURRING, THAT I SHUT OUT EVERYTHING ELSE. I...I DO THAT SOMETIMES. MORESO LATELY.
IT... SHAMES ME.
MY SCIENTIFIC CURIOSITY BEGINS TO DOMINATE MY TRUE NATURE AND I LOSE SIGHT OF WHAT'S REALLY IMPORTANT.
THIS TIME I NEGLECTED YOU--
--MY TEAMMATE--
--MY FRIEND.
YOU MEAN TOO MUCH TO ME, MOLLY...
molly
IT HURTS ME TO KNOW THAT I'VE CAUSED YOU PAIN.
molly
I'M SORRY.
NO, I'M SORRY.

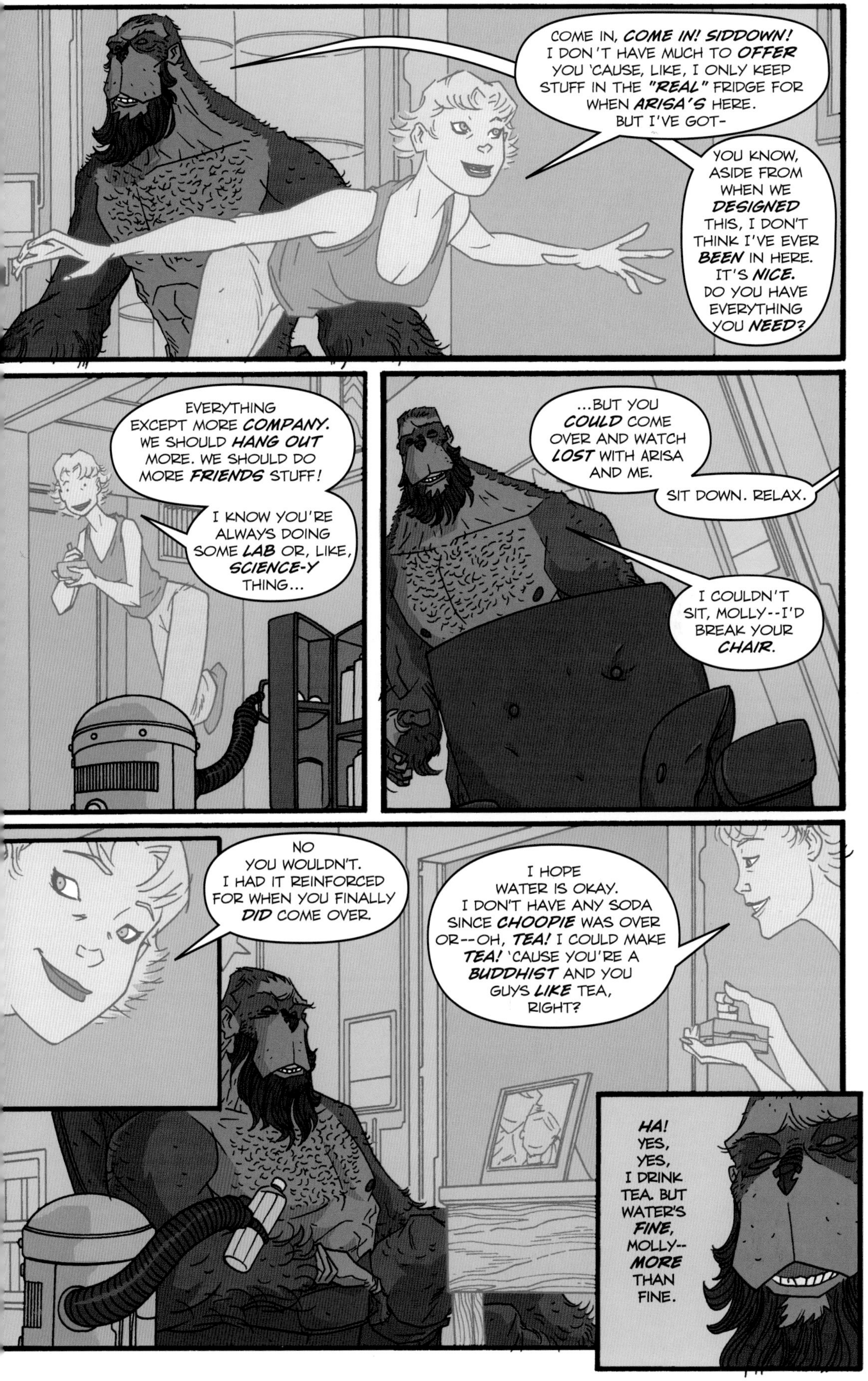
COME IN, COME IN! SIDDOWN! I DON'T HAVE MUCH TO OFFER YOU 'CAUSE, LIKE, I ONLY KEEP STUFF IN THE "REAL" FRIDGE FOR WHEN ARISA'S HERE. BUT I'VE GOT-
YOU KNOW, ASIDE FROM WHEN WE DESIGNED THIS, I DON'T THINK I'VE EVER BEEN IN HERE. IT'S NICE. DO YOU HAVE EVERYTHING YOU NEED?
EVERYTHING EXCEPT MORE COMPANY. WE SHOULD HANG OUT MORE. WE SHOULD DO MORE FRIENDS STUFF!
I KNOW YOU'RE ALWAYS DOING SOME LAB OR, LIKE, SCIENCE-Y THING...
...BUT YOU COULD COME OVER AND WATCH LOST WITH ARISA AND ME.
SIT DOWN. RELAX.
I COULDN'T SIT, MOLLY--I'D BREAK YOUR CHAIR.
NO YOU WOULDN'T. I HAD IT REINFORCED FOR WHEN YOU FINALLY DID COME OVER.
I HOPE WATER IS OKAY. I DON'T HAVE ANY SODA SINCE CHOOPIE WAS OVER OR--OH, TEA! I COULD MAKE TEA! 'CAUSE YOU'RE A BUDDHIST AND YOU GUYS LIKE TEA, RIGHT?
HA! YES, YES, I DRINK TEA. BUT WATER'S FINE, MOLLY--MORE THAN FINE.

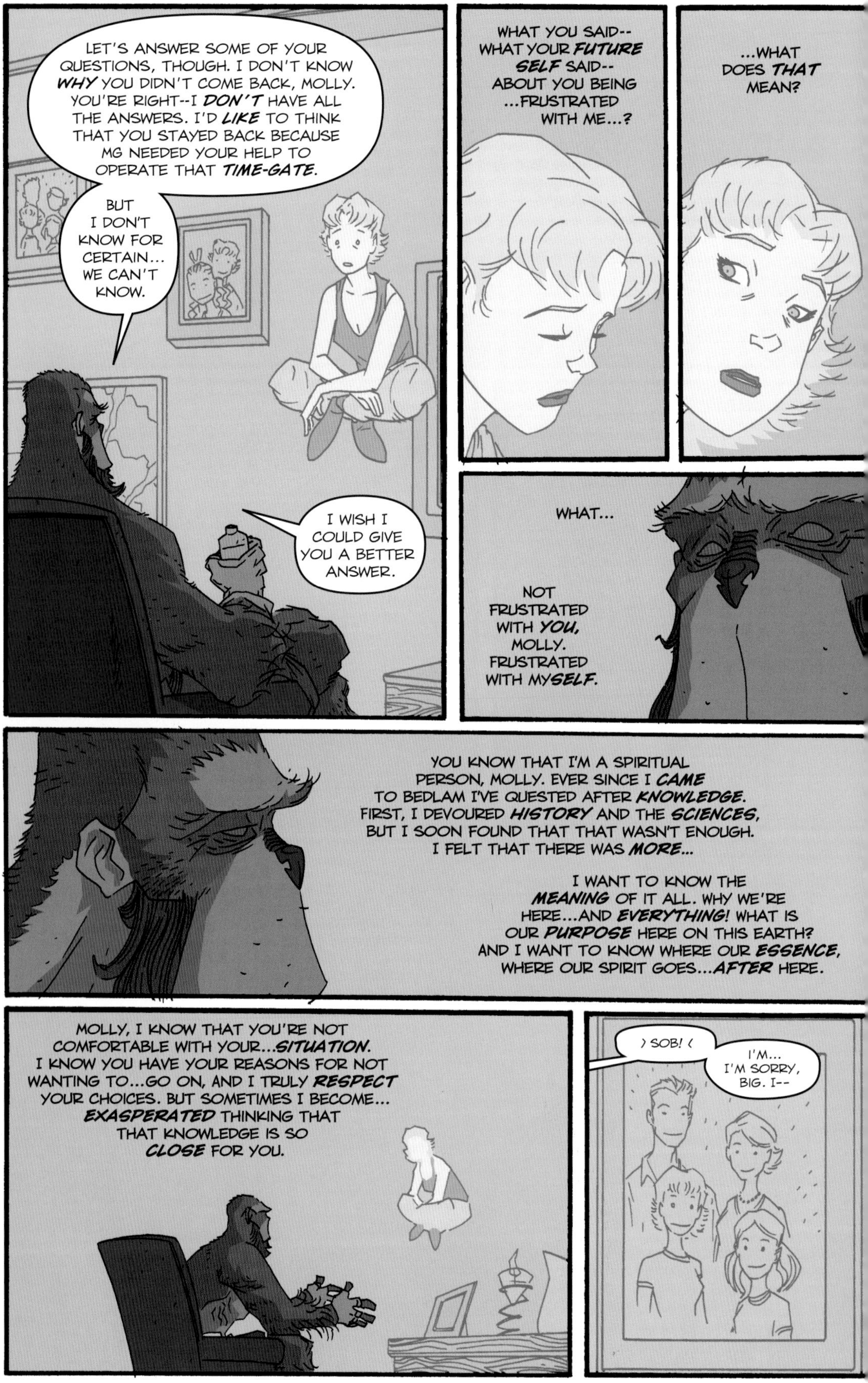
LET'S ANSWER SOME OF YOUR QUESTIONS, THOUGH. I DON'T KNOW WHY YOU DIDN'T COME BACK, MOLLY. YOU'RE RIGHT--I DON'T HAVE ALL THE ANSWERS. I'D LIKE TO THINK THAT YOU STAYED BACK BECAUSE MG NEEDED YOUR HELP TO OPERATE THAT TIME-GATE.
BUT I DON'T KNOW FOR CERTAIN... WE CAN'T KNOW.
I WISH I COULD GIVE YOU A BETTER ANSWER.
WHAT YOU SAID-- WHAT YOUR FUTURE SELF SAID-- ABOUT YOU BEING ...FRUSTRATED WITH ME...?
...WHAT DOES THAT MEAN?
WHAT...
NOT FRUSTRATED WITH YOU, MOLLY. FRUSTRATED WITH MYSELF.
YOU KNOW THAT I'M A SPIRITUAL PERSON, MOLLY. EVER SINCE I CAME TO BEDLAM I'VE QUESTED AFTER KNOWLEDGE. FIRST, I DEVOURED HISTORY AND THE SCIENCES, BUT I SOON FOUND THAT THAT WASN'T ENOUGH. I FELT THAT THERE WAS MORE...
I WANT TO KNOW THE MEANING OF IT ALL. WHY WE'RE HERE...AND EVERYTHING! WHAT IS OUR PURPOSE HERE ON THIS EARTH? AND I WANT TO KNOW WHERE OUR ESSENCE, WHERE OUR SPIRIT GOES...AFTER HERE.
MOLLY, I KNOW THAT YOU'RE NOT COMFORTABLE WITH YOUR...SITUATION. I KNOW YOU HAVE YOUR REASONS FOR NOT WANTING TO...GO ON, AND I TRULY RESPECT YOUR CHOICES. BUT SOMETIMES I BECOME... EXASPERATED THINKING THAT THAT KNOWLEDGE IS SO CLOSE FOR YOU.
› SOB! ‹
I'M... I'M SORRY, BIG. I--

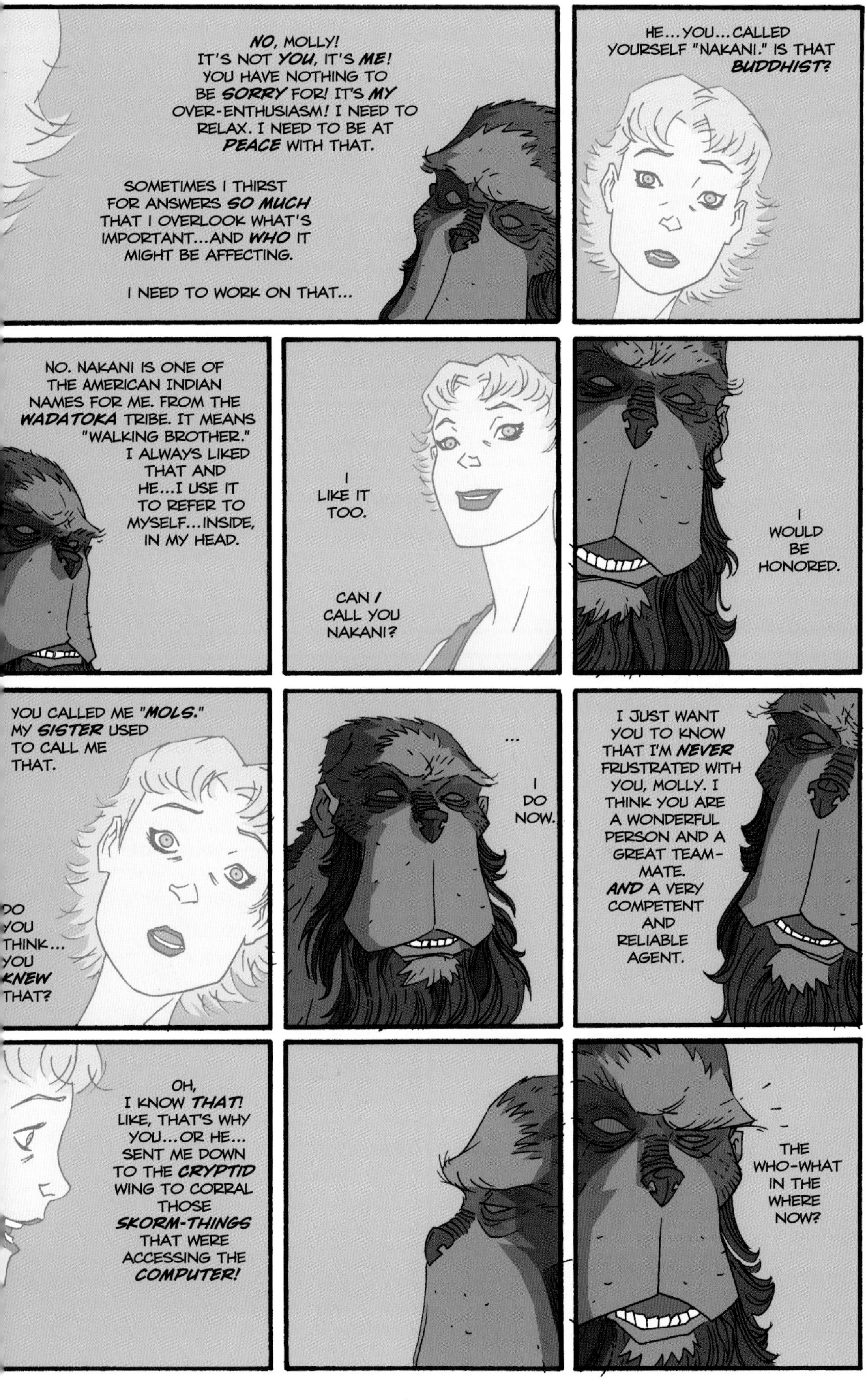
NO, MOLLY! IT'S NOT YOU, IT'S ME! YOU HAVE NOTHING TO BE SORRY FOR! IT'S MY OVER-ENTHUSIASM! I NEED TO RELAX. I NEED TO BE AT PEACE WITH THAT.
SOMETIMES I THIRST FOR ANSWERS SO MUCH THAT I OVERLOOK WHAT'S IMPORTANT...AND WHO IT MIGHT BE AFFECTING.
I NEED TO WORK ON THAT...
HE...YOU...CALLED YOURSELF "NAKANI." IS THAT BUDDHIST?
NO. NAKANI IS ONE OF THE AMERICAN INDIAN NAMES FOR ME. FROM THE WADATOKA TRIBE. IT MEANS "WALKING BROTHER." I ALWAYS LIKED THAT AND HE...I USE IT TO REFER TO MYSELF...INSIDE, IN MY HEAD.
I LIKE IT TOO.
CAN I CALL YOU NAKANI?
I WOULD BE HONORED.
YOU CALLED ME "MOLS." MY SISTER USED TO CALL ME THAT.
DO YOU THINK... YOU KNEW THAT?
...
I DO NOW.
I JUST WANT YOU TO KNOW THAT I'M NEVER FRUSTRATED WITH YOU, MOLLY. I THINK YOU ARE A WONDERFUL PERSON AND A GREAT TEAM-MATE. AND A VERY COMPETENT AND RELIABLE AGENT.
OH, I KNOW THAT! LIKE, THAT'S WHY YOU...OR HE... SENT ME DOWN TO THE CRYPTID WING TO CORRAL THOSE SKORM-THINGS THAT WERE ACCESSING THE COMPUTER!
THE WHO-WHAT IN THE WHERE NOW?

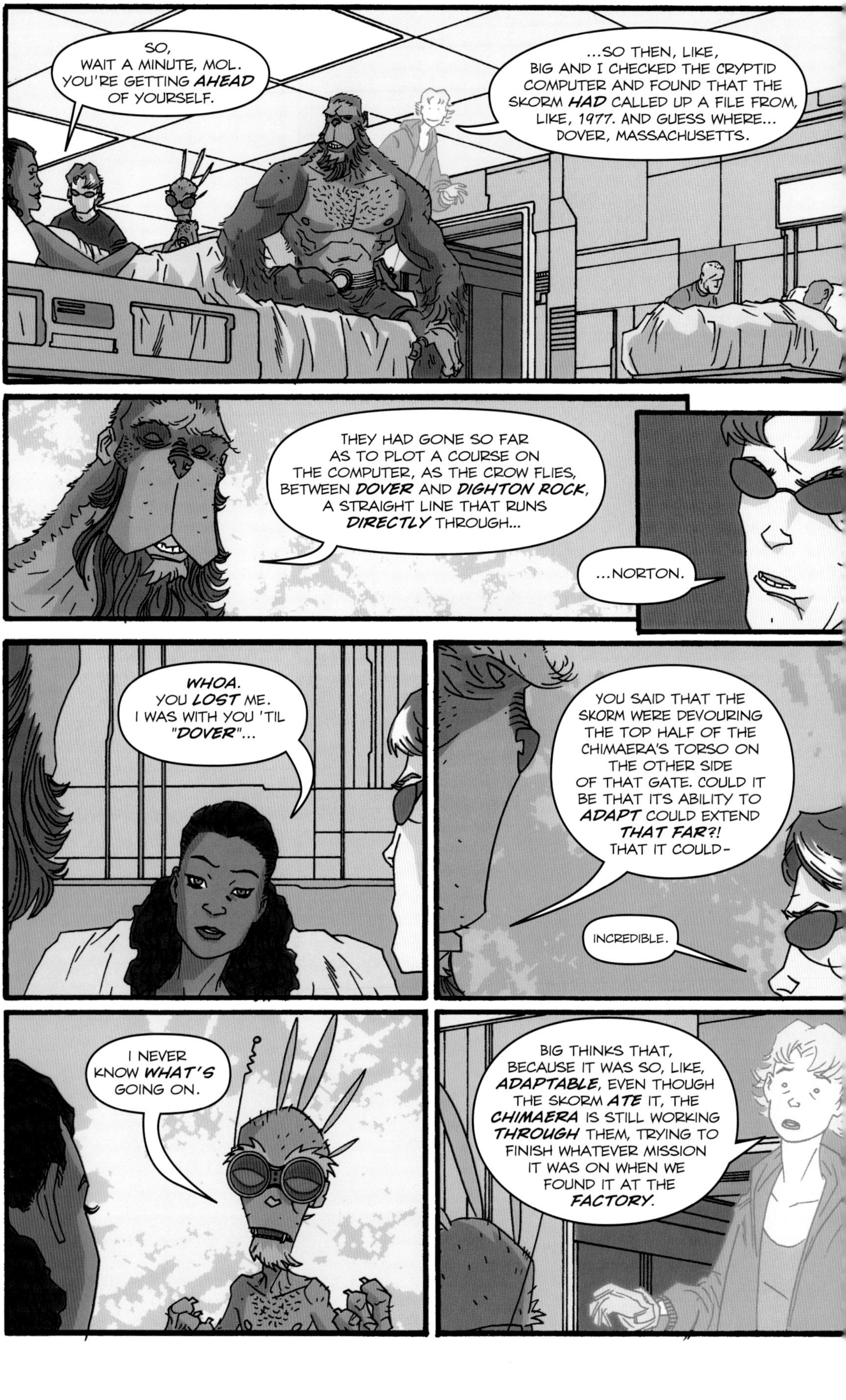
SO, WAIT A MINUTE, MOL. YOU'RE GETTING AHEAD OF YOURSELF.
...SO THEN, LIKE, BIG AND I CHECKED THE CRYPTID COMPUTER AND FOUND THAT THE SKORM HAD CALLED UP A FILE FROM, LIKE, 1977. AND GUESS WHERE... DOVER, MASSACHUSETTS.
THEY HAD GONE SO FAR AS TO PLOT A COURSE ON THE COMPUTER, AS THE CROW FLIES, BETWEEN DOVER AND DIGHTON ROCK, A STRAIGHT LINE THAT RUNS DIRECTLY THROUGH...
...NORTON.
WHOA. YOU LOST ME. I WAS WITH YOU 'TIL "DOVER"...
YOU SAID THAT THE SKORM WERE DEVOURING THE TOP HALF OF THE CHIMAERA'S TORSO ON THE OTHER SIDE OF THAT GATE. COULD IT BE THAT ITS ABILITY TO ADAPT COULD EXTEND THAT FAR?! THAT IT COULD-
INCREDIBLE.
I NEVER KNOW WHAT'S GOING ON.
BIG THINKS THAT, BECAUSE IT WAS SO, LIKE, ADAPTABLE, EVEN THOUGH THE SKORM ATE IT, THE CHIMAERA IS STILL WORKING THROUGH THEM, TRYING TO FINISH WHATEVER MISSION IT WAS ON WHEN WE FOUND IT AT THE FACTORY.

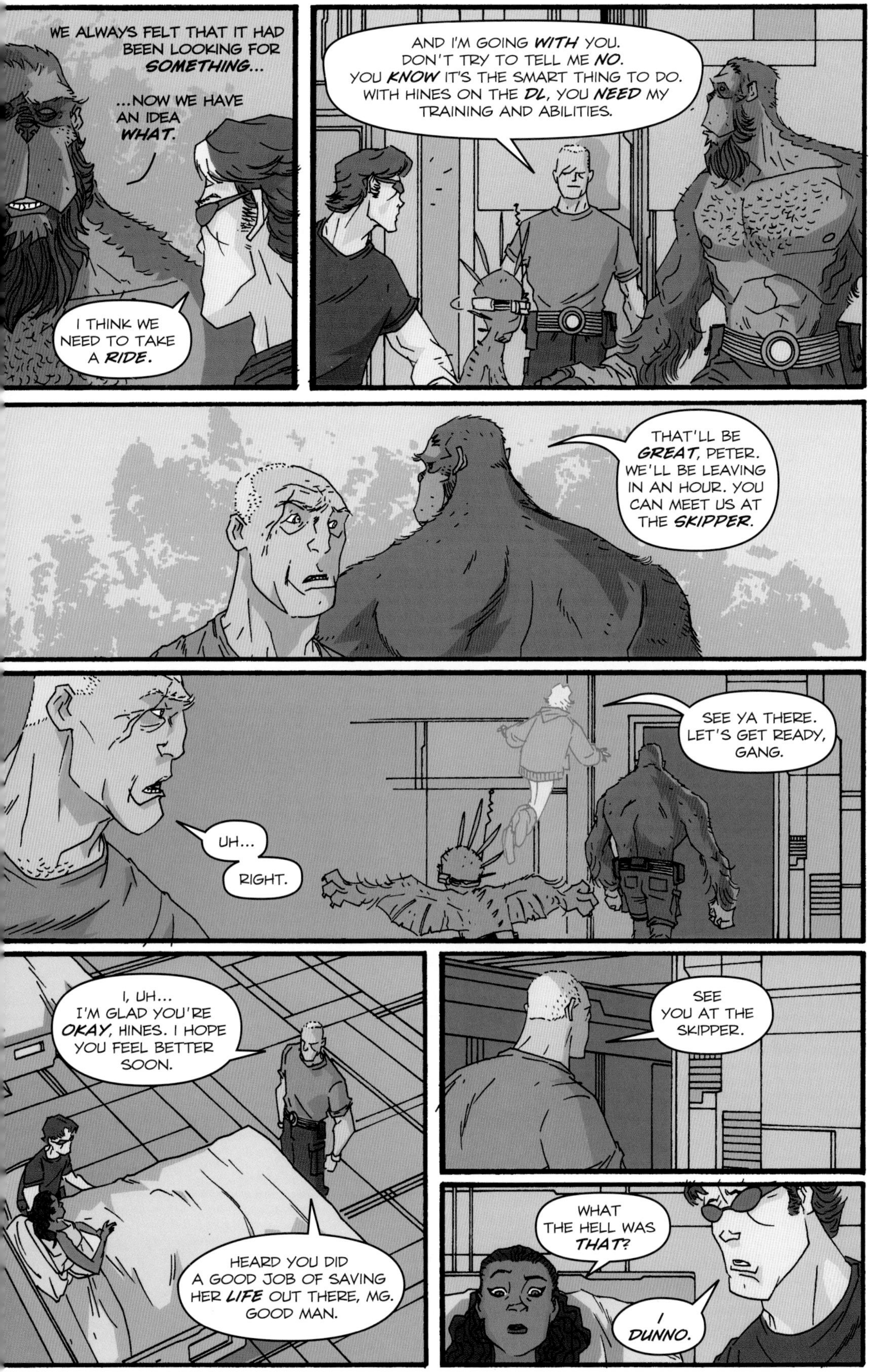

WE ALWAYS FELT THAT IT HAD BEEN LOOKING FOR SOMETHING...
...NOW WE HAVE AN IDEA WHAT.
I THINK WE NEED TO TAKE A RIDE.
AND I'M GOING WITH YOU. DON'T TRY TO TELL ME NO. YOU KNOW IT'S THE SMART THING TO DO. WITH HINES ON THE DL, YOU NEED MY TRAINING AND ABILITIES.
THAT'LL BE GREAT, PETER. WE'LL BE LEAVING IN AN HOUR. YOU CAN MEET US AT THE SKIPPER.
SEE YA THERE. LET'S GET READY, GANG.
UH...
RIGHT.
I, UH... I'M GLAD YOU'RE OKAY, HINES. I HOPE YOU FEEL BETTER SOON.
HEARD YOU DID A GOOD JOB OF SAVING HER LIFE OUT THERE, MG. GOOD MAN.
SEE YOU AT THE SKIPPER.
WHAT THE HELL WAS THAT?
I DUNNO.

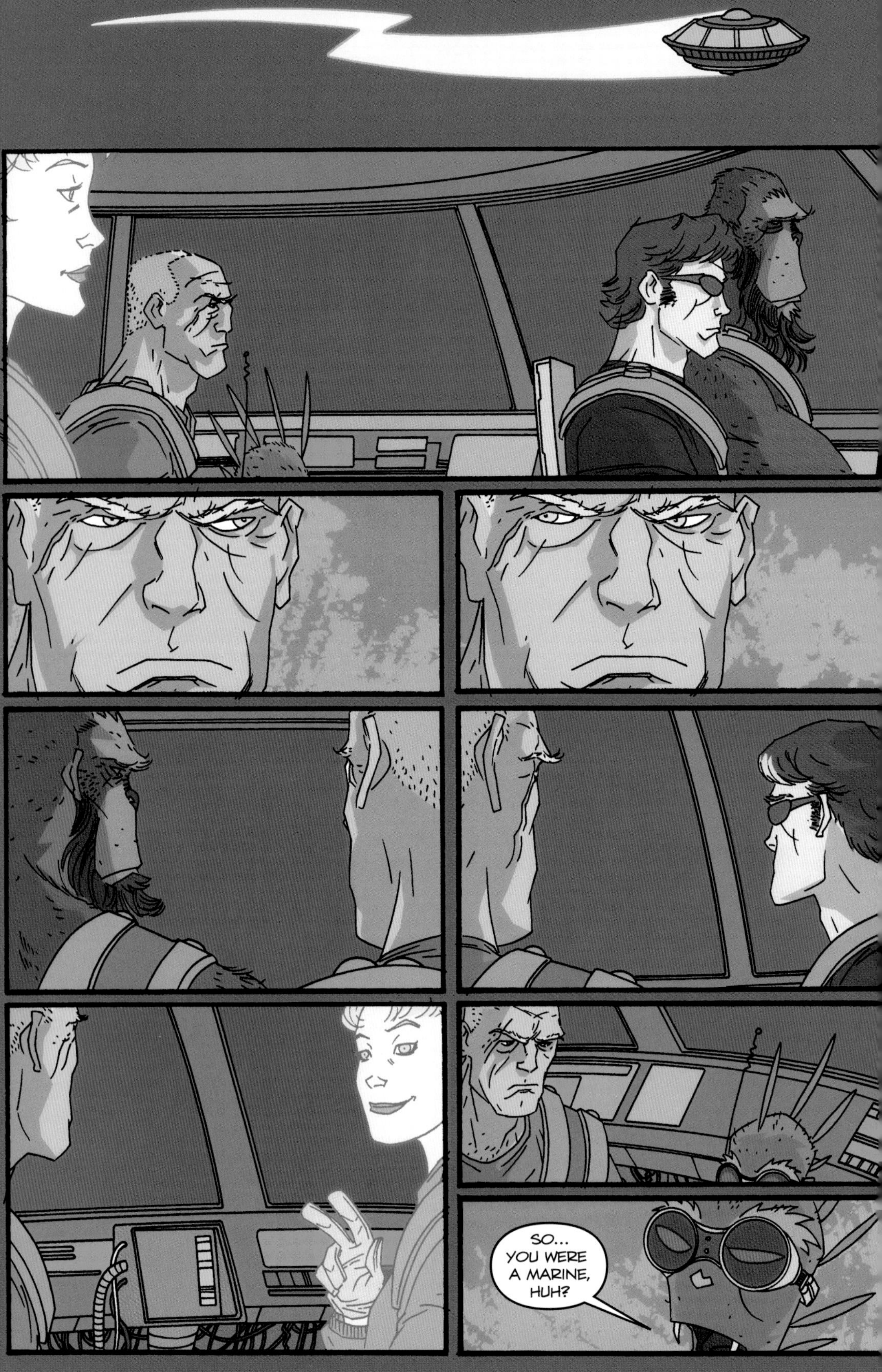
SO...
YOU WERE
A MARINE,
HUH?

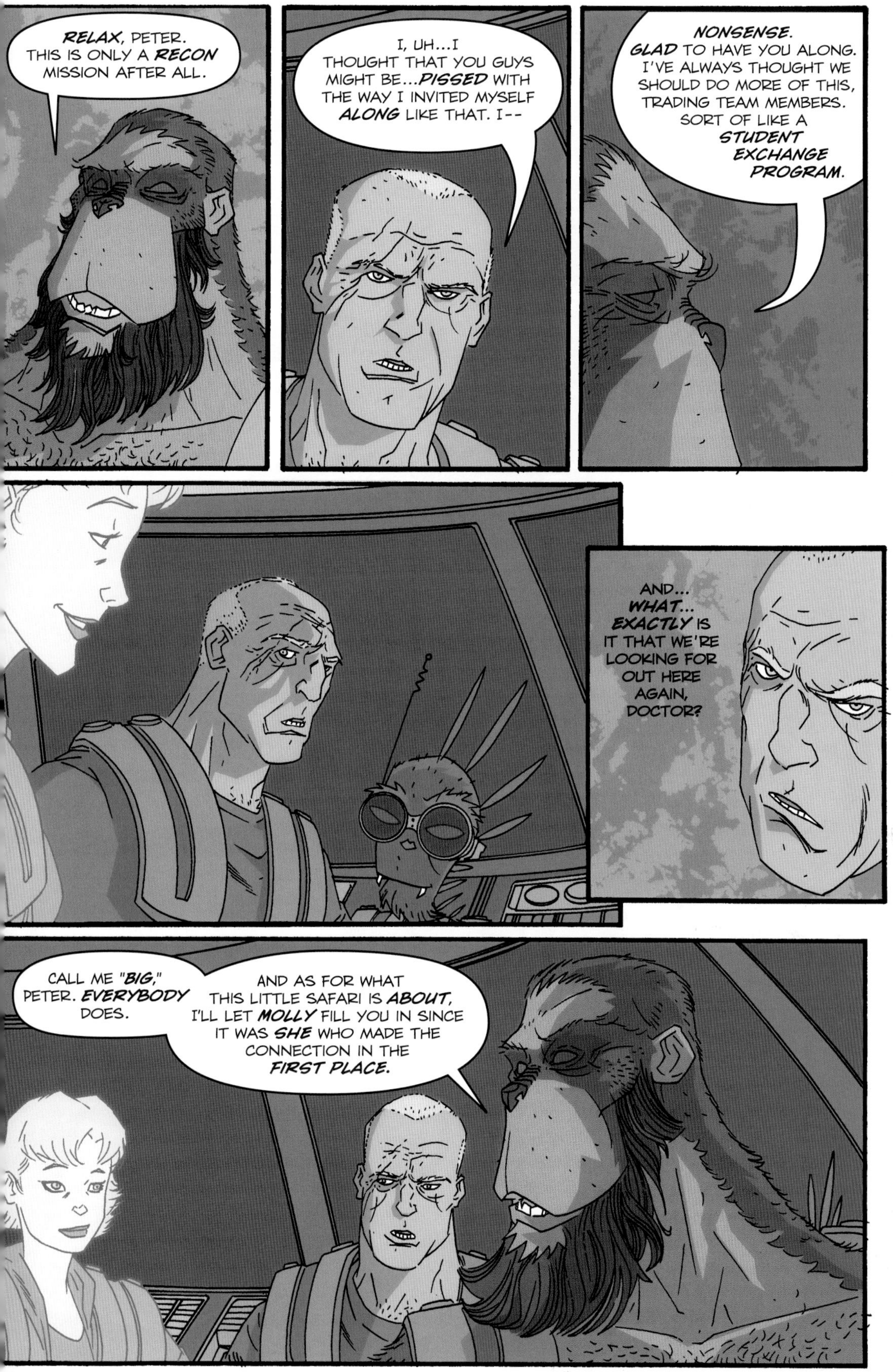
RELAX, PETER. THIS IS ONLY A RECON MISSION AFTER ALL.
I, UH...I THOUGHT THAT YOU GUYS MIGHT BE...PISSED WITH THE WAY I INVITED MYSELF ALONG LIKE THAT. I--
NONSENSE. GLAD TO HAVE YOU ALONG. I'VE ALWAYS THOUGHT WE SHOULD DO MORE OF THIS, TRADING TEAM MEMBERS. SORT OF LIKE A STUDENT EXCHANGE PROGRAM.
AND... WHAT... EXACTLY IS IT THAT WE'RE LOOKING FOR OUT HERE AGAIN, DOCTOR?
CALL ME "BIG," PETER. EVERYBODY DOES.
AND AS FOR WHAT THIS LITTLE SAFARI IS ABOUT, I'LL LET MOLLY FILL YOU IN SINCE IT WAS SHE WHO MADE THE CONNECTION IN THE FIRST PLACE.

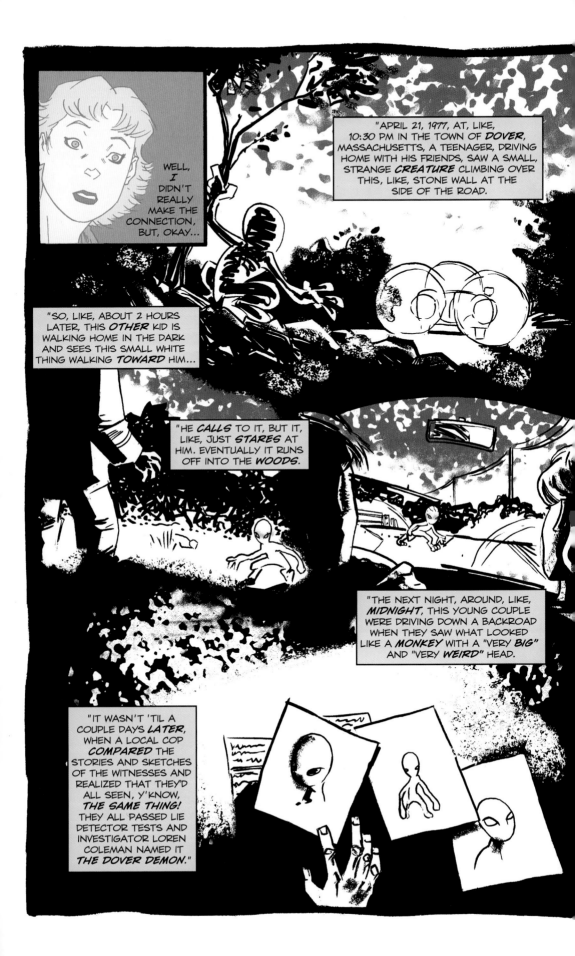

WELL, *I* DIDN'T REALLY MAKE THE CONNECTION, BUT, OKAY...

"APRIL 21, 1977, AT, LIKE, 10:30 PM IN THE TOWN OF *DOVER*, MASSACHUSETTS, A TEENAGER, DRIVING HOME WITH HIS FRIENDS, SAW A SMALL, STRANGE *CREATURE* CLIMBING OVER THIS, LIKE, STONE WALL AT THE SIDE OF THE ROAD.

"SO, LIKE, ABOUT 2 HOURS LATER, THIS *OTHER* KID IS WALKING HOME IN THE DARK AND SEES THIS SMALL WHITE THING WALKING *TOWARD* HIM...

"HE *CALLS* TO IT, BUT IT, LIKE, JUST *STARES* AT HIM. EVENTUALLY IT RUNS OFF INTO THE *WOODS*.

"THE NEXT NIGHT, AROUND, LIKE, *MIDNIGHT*, THIS YOUNG COUPLE WERE DRIVING DOWN A BACKROAD WHEN THEY SAW WHAT LOOKED LIKE A *MONKEY* WITH A "VERY *BIG*" AND "VERY *WEIRD*" HEAD.

"IT WASN'T 'TIL A COUPLE DAYS *LATER*, WHEN A LOCAL COP *COMPARED* THE STORIES AND SKETCHES OF THE WITNESSES AND REALIZED THAT THEY'D ALL SEEN, Y'KNOW, *THE SAME THING!* THEY ALL PASSED LIE DETECTOR TESTS AND INVESTIGATOR LOREN COLEMAN NAMED IT *THE DOVER DEMON*."

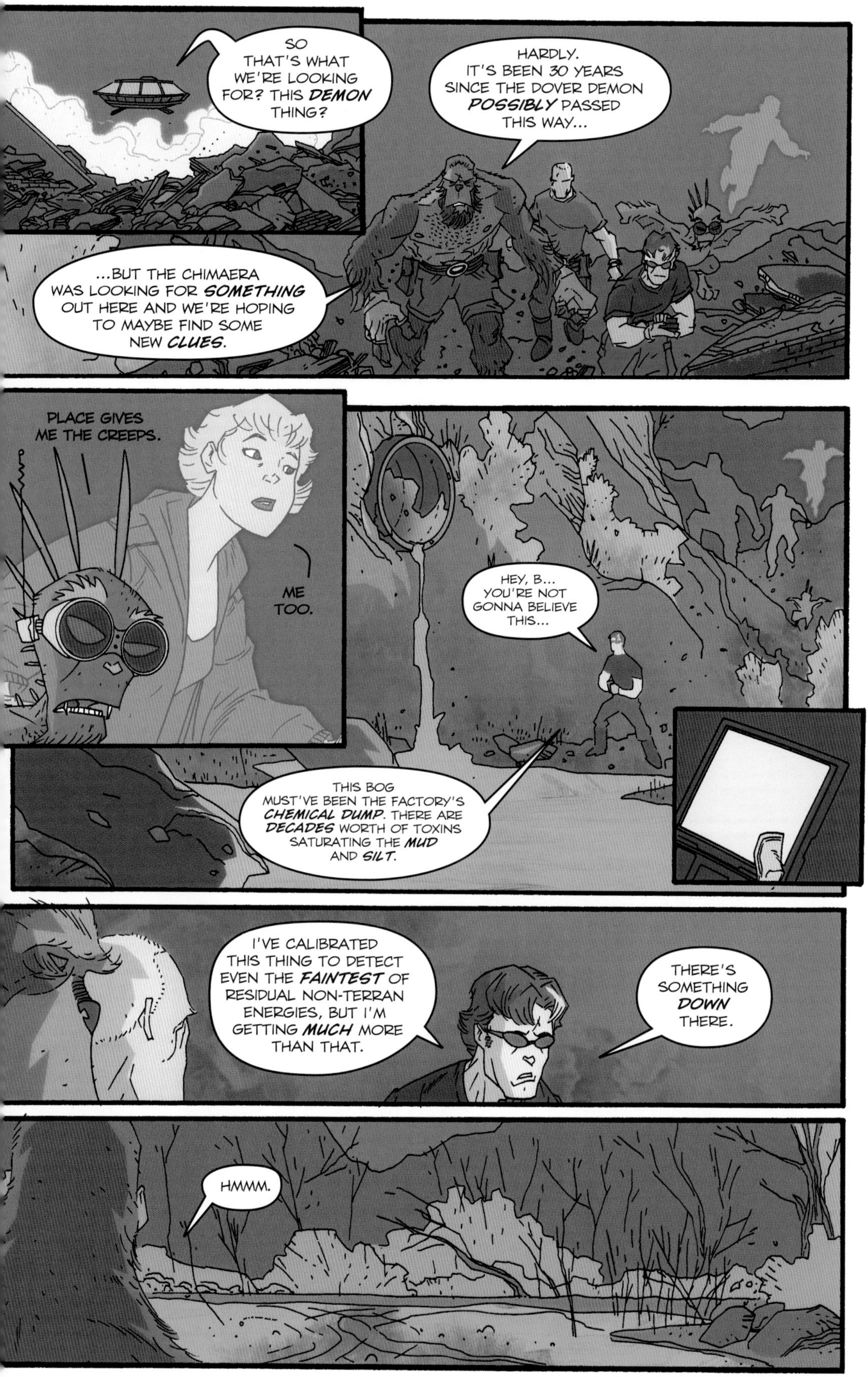
SO THAT'S WHAT WE'RE LOOKING FOR? THIS DEMON THING?
HARDLY. IT'S BEEN 30 YEARS SINCE THE DOVER DEMON POSSIBLY PASSED THIS WAY...
...BUT THE CHIMAERA WAS LOOKING FOR SOMETHING OUT HERE AND WE'RE HOPING TO MAYBE FIND SOME NEW CLUES.
PLACE GIVES ME THE CREEPS.
ME TOO.
HEY, B... YOU'RE NOT GONNA BELIEVE THIS...
THIS BOG MUST'VE BEEN THE FACTORY'S CHEMICAL DUMP. THERE ARE DECADES WORTH OF TOXINS SATURATING THE MUD AND SILT.
I'VE CALIBRATED THIS THING TO DETECT EVEN THE FAINTEST OF RESIDUAL NON-TERRAN ENERGIES, BUT I'M GETTING MUCH MORE THAN THAT.
THERE'S SOMETHING DOWN THERE.
HMMM.

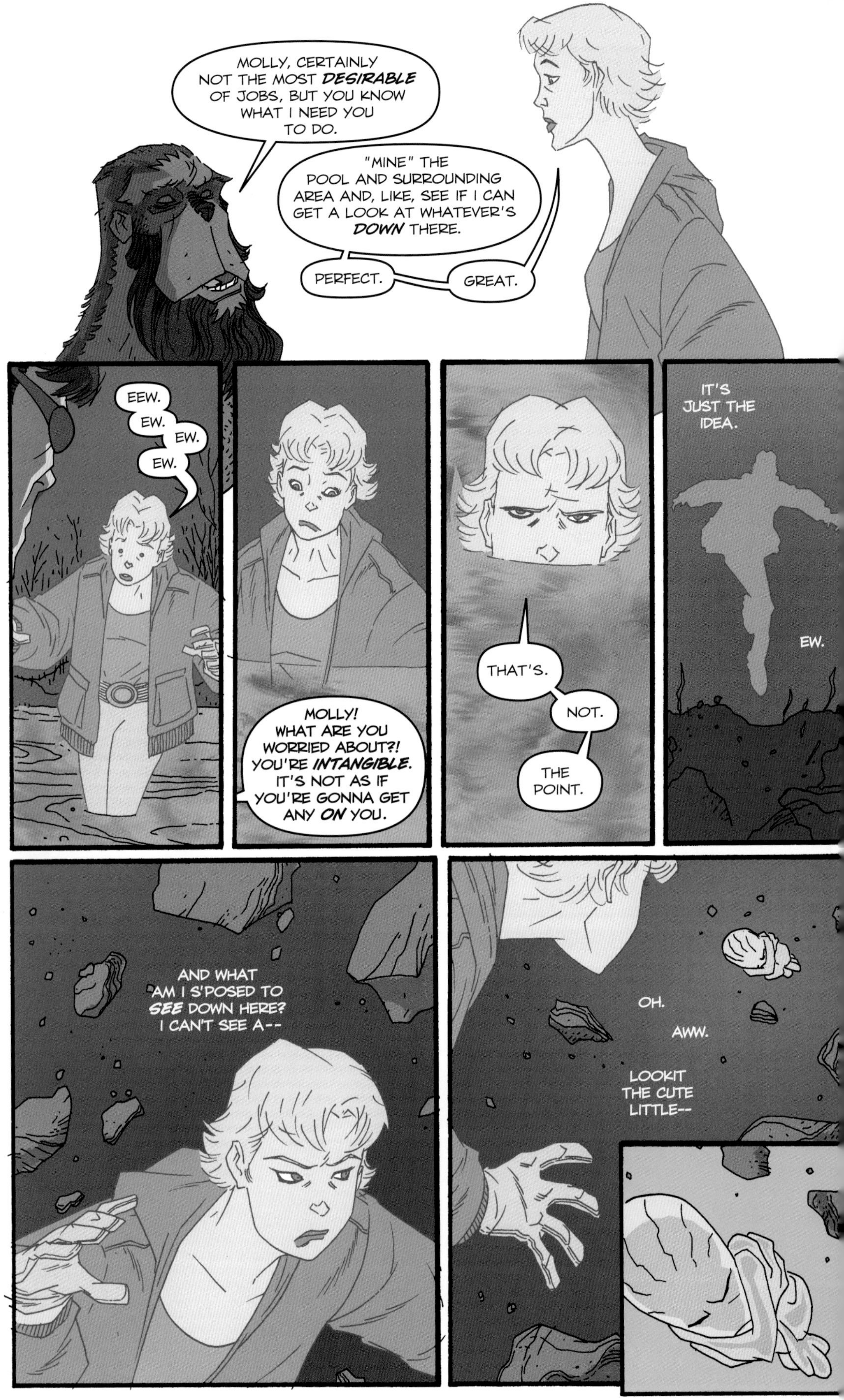
MOLLY, CERTAINLY NOT THE MOST DESIRABLE OF JOBS, BUT YOU KNOW WHAT I NEED YOU TO DO.
"MINE" THE POOL AND SURROUNDING AREA AND, LIKE, SEE IF I CAN GET A LOOK AT WHATEVER'S DOWN THERE.
PERFECT.
GREAT.
EEW.
EW.
EW.
EW.
MOLLY! WHAT ARE YOU WORRIED ABOUT?! YOU'RE INTANGIBLE. IT'S NOT AS IF YOU'RE GONNA GET ANY ON YOU.
THAT'S.
NOT.
THE POINT.
IT'S JUST THE IDEA.
EW.
AND WHAT AM I S'POSED TO SEE DOWN HERE? I CAN'T SEE A--
OH.
AWW.
LOOKIT THE CUTE LITTLE--

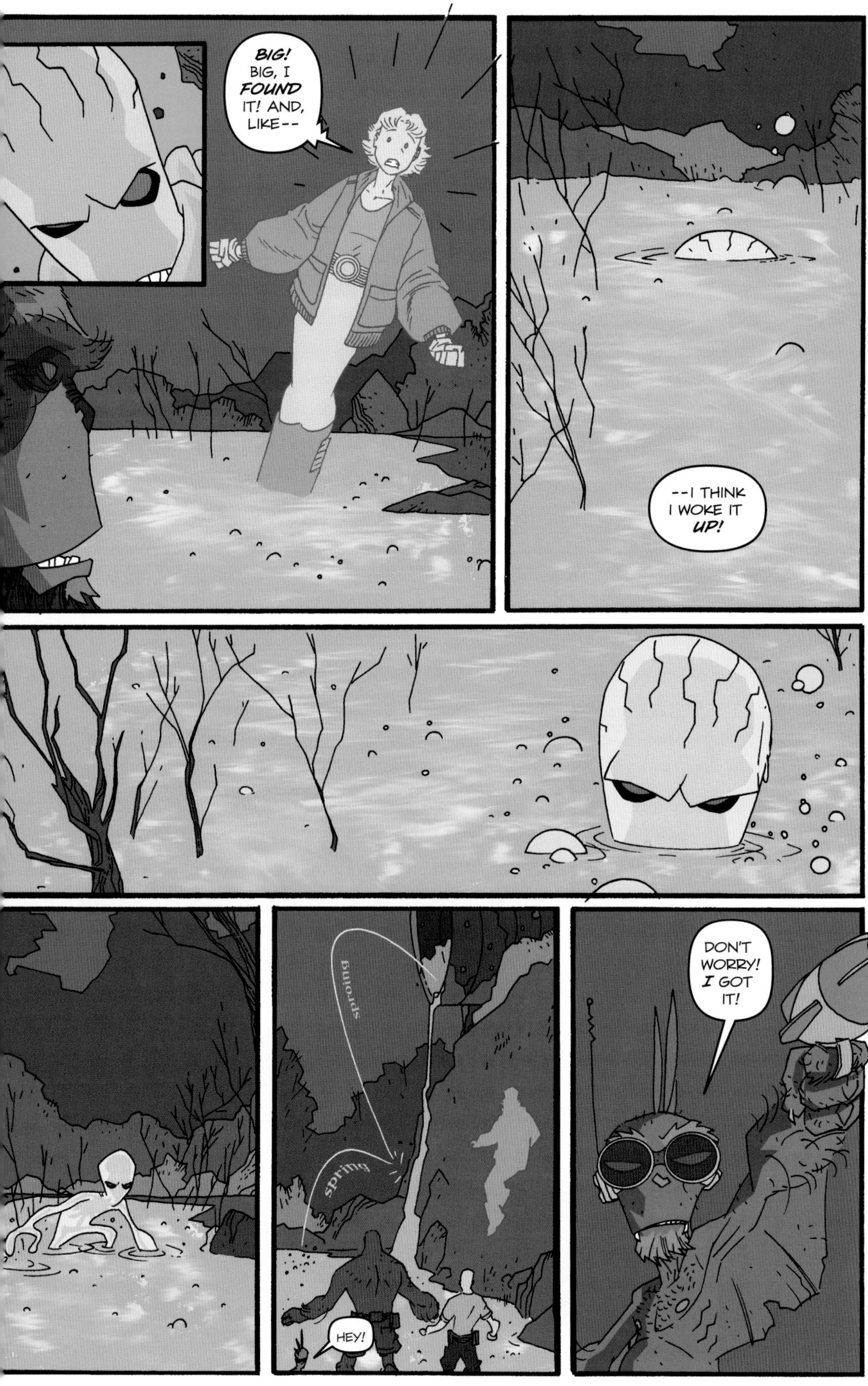
BIG! BIG, I FOUND IT! AND, LIKE--
--I THINK I WOKE IT UP!
spring
sproing
HEY!
DON'T WORRY! I GOT IT!

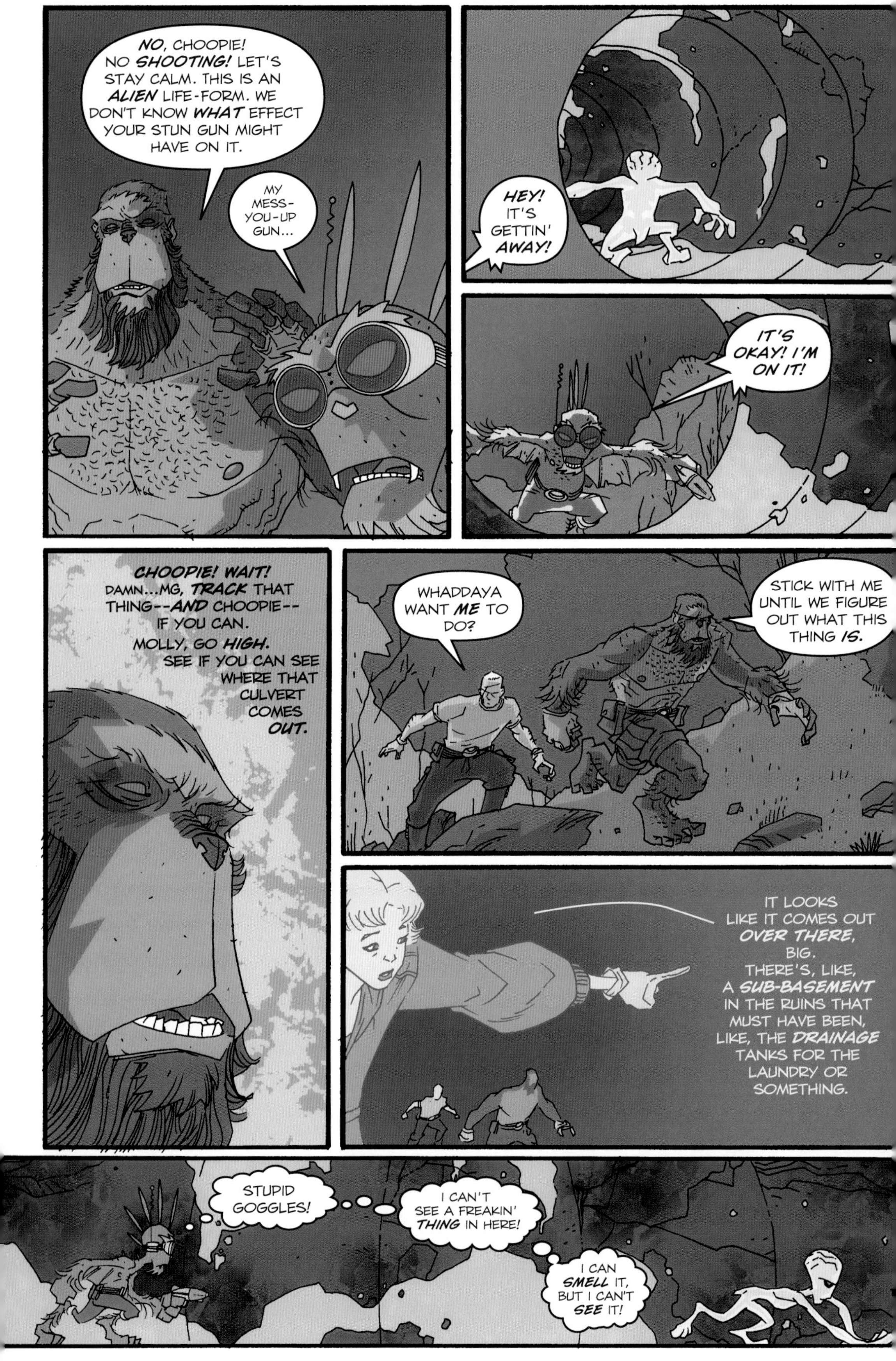
NO, CHOOPIE! NO SHOOTING! LET'S STAY CALM. THIS IS AN ALIEN LIFE-FORM. WE DON'T KNOW WHAT EFFECT YOUR STUN GUN MIGHT HAVE ON IT.
MY MESS-YOU-UP GUN...
HEY! IT'S GETTIN' AWAY!
IT'S OKAY! I'M ON IT!
CHOOPIE! WAIT! DAMN...MG, TRACK THAT THING--AND CHOOPIE--IF YOU CAN.
MOLLY, GO HIGH. SEE IF YOU CAN SEE WHERE THAT CULVERT COMES OUT.
WHADDAYA WANT ME TO DO?
STICK WITH ME UNTIL WE FIGURE OUT WHAT THIS THING IS.
IT LOOKS LIKE IT COMES OUT OVER THERE, BIG. THERE'S, LIKE, A SUB-BASEMENT IN THE RUINS THAT MUST HAVE BEEN, LIKE, THE DRAINAGE TANKS FOR THE LAUNDRY OR SOMETHING.
STUPID GOGGLES!
I CAN'T SEE A FREAKIN' THING IN HERE!
I CAN SMELL IT, BUT I CAN'T SEE IT!

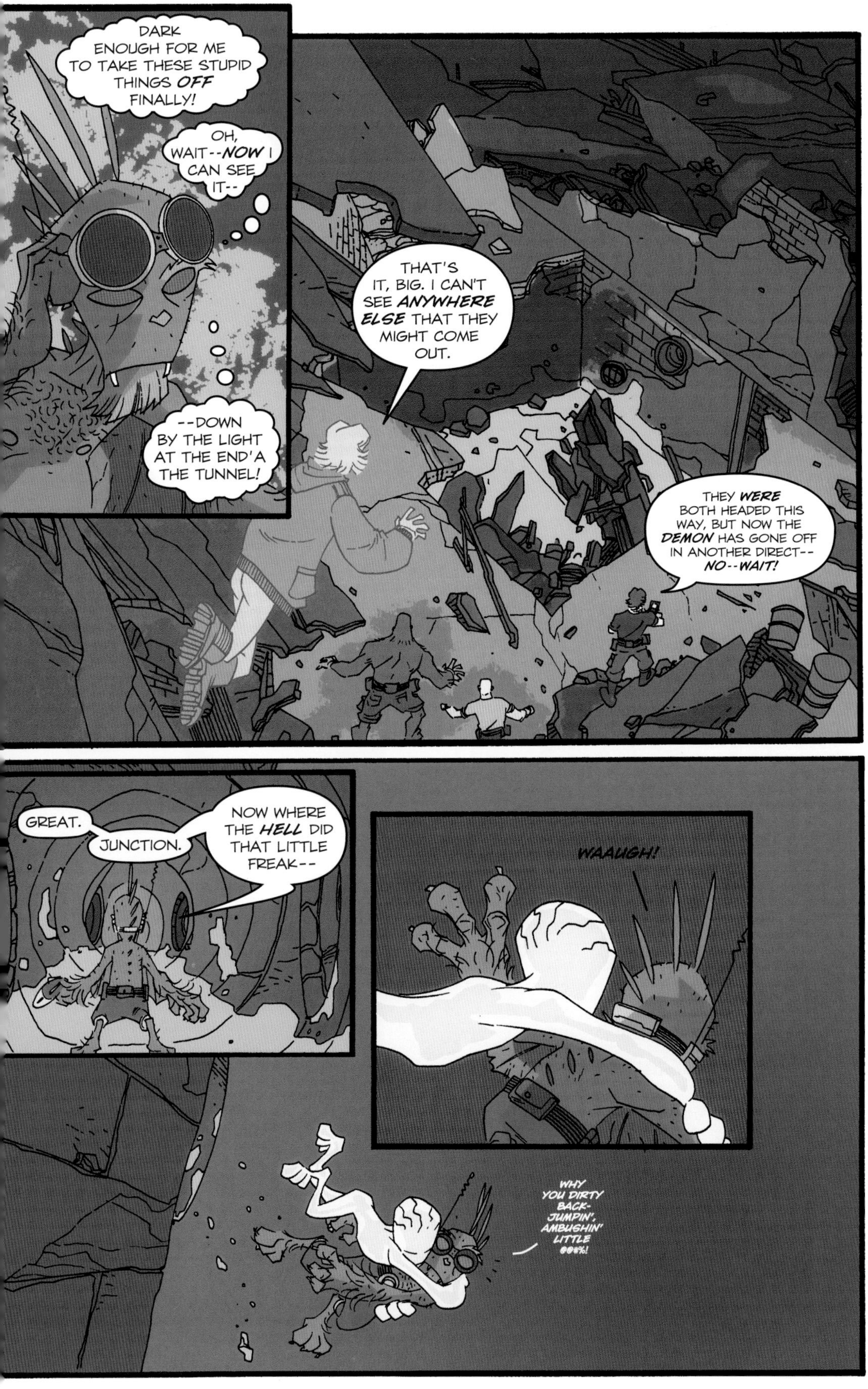
DARK ENOUGH FOR ME TO TAKE THESE STUPID THINGS *OFF* FINALLY!
OH, WAIT--*NOW* I CAN SEE IT--
--DOWN BY THE LIGHT AT THE END'A THE TUNNEL!
THAT'S IT, BIG. I CAN'T SEE *ANYWHERE ELSE* THAT THEY MIGHT COME OUT.
THEY *WERE* BOTH HEADED THIS WAY, BUT NOW THE *DEMON* HAS GONE OFF IN ANOTHER DIRECT-- *NO--WAIT!*
GREAT.
JUNCTION.
NOW WHERE THE *HELL* DID THAT LITTLE FREAK--
WAAUGH!
WHY YOU DIRTY BACK-JUMPIN', AMBUSHIN' LITTLE @@#%!

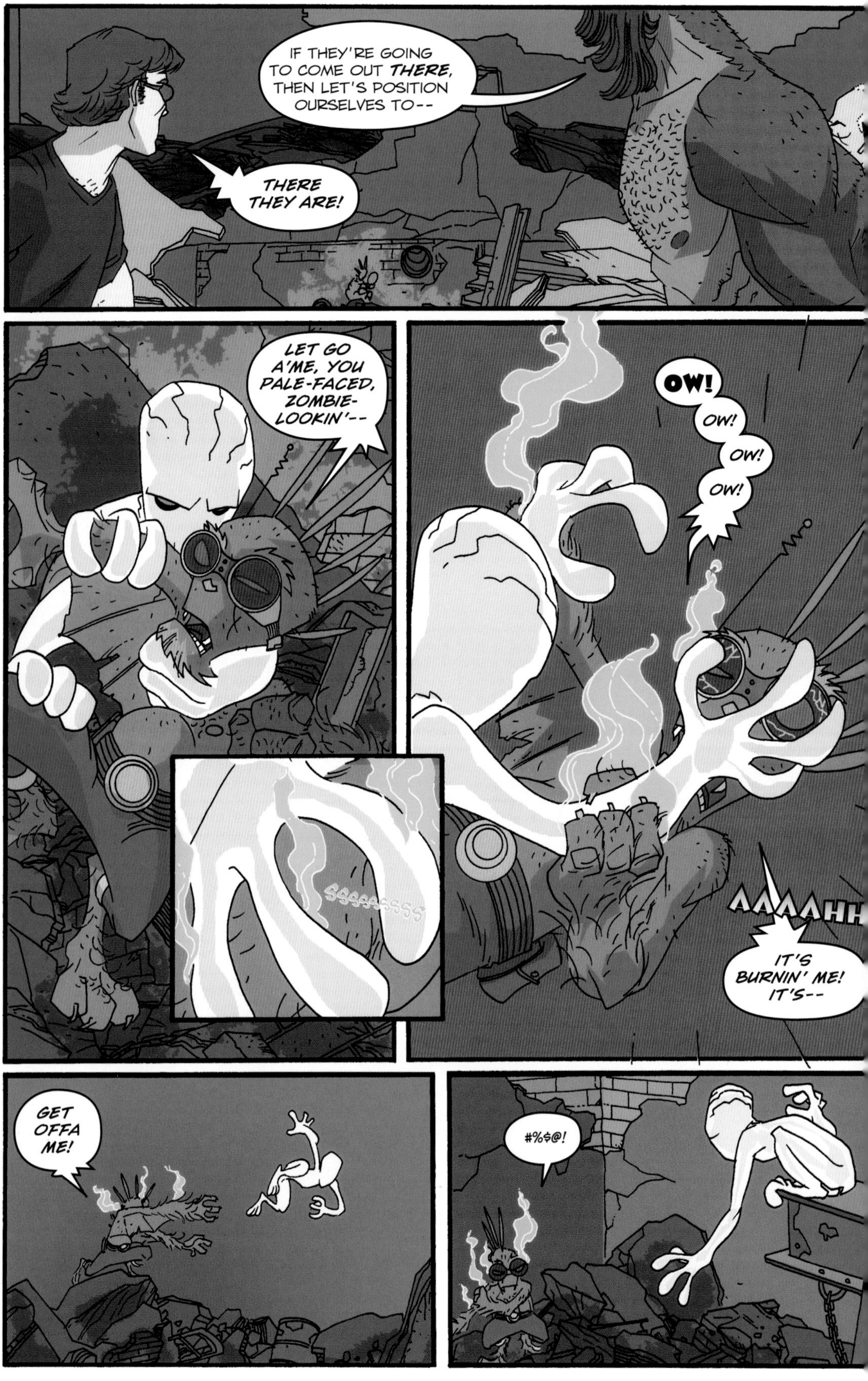
IF THEY'RE GOING TO COME OUT THERE, THEN LET'S POSITION OURSELVES TO--
THERE THEY ARE!
LET GO A'ME, YOU PALE-FACED, ZOMBIE-LOOKIN'--
SSSSSSSSS
OW!
OW!
OW!
OW!
AAAAHH
IT'S BURNIN' ME! IT'S--
GET OFFA ME!
#%$@!

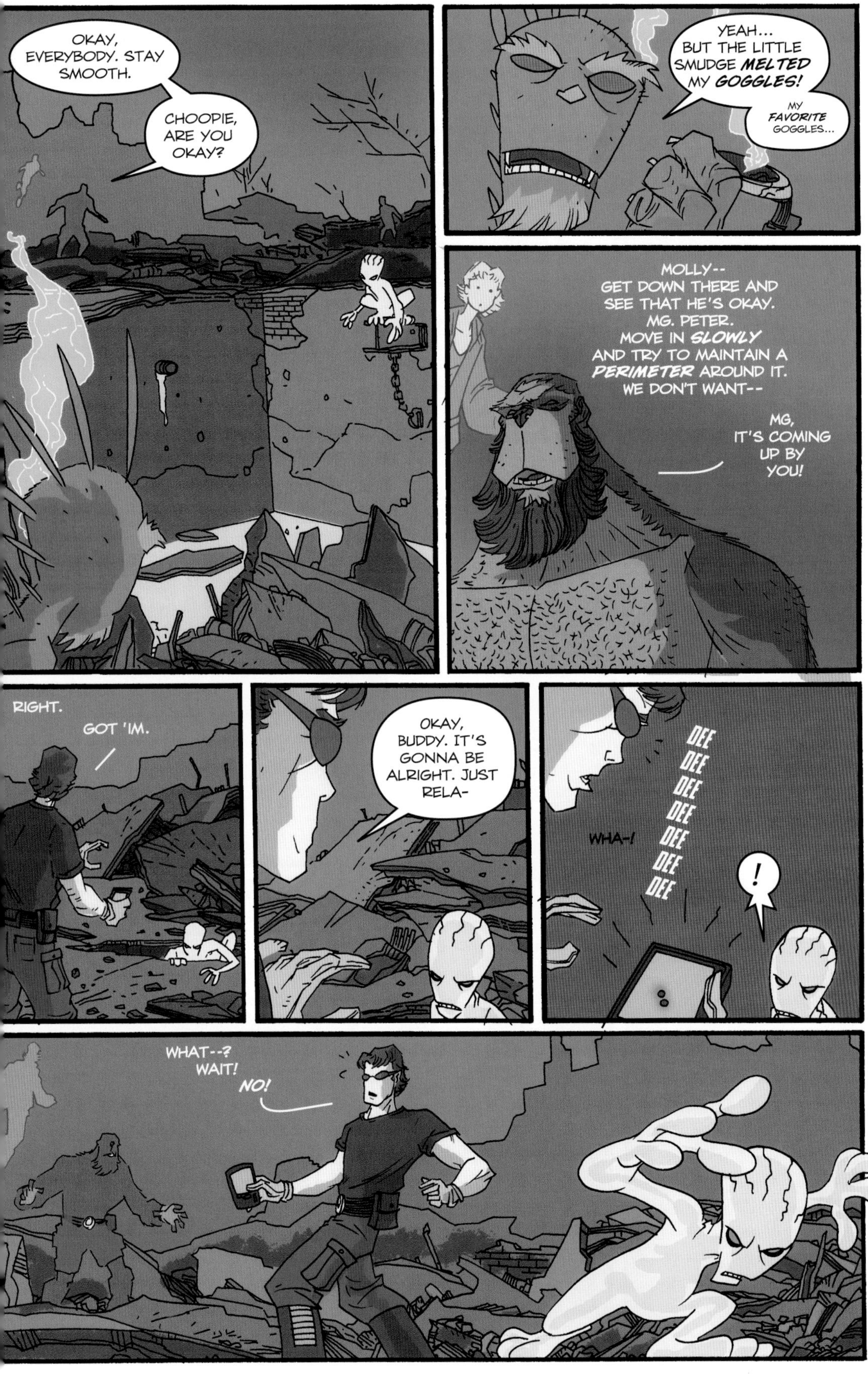
OKAY, EVERYBODY. STAY SMOOTH.
CHOOPIE, ARE YOU OKAY?
YEAH... BUT THE LITTLE SMUDGE MELTED MY GOGGLES!
MY FAVORITE GOGGLES...
MOLLY-- GET DOWN THERE AND SEE THAT HE'S OKAY. MG. PETER. MOVE IN SLOWLY AND TRY TO MAINTAIN A PERIMETER AROUND IT. WE DON'T WANT--
MG, IT'S COMING UP BY YOU!
RIGHT.
GOT 'IM.
OKAY, BUDDY. IT'S GONNA BE ALRIGHT. JUST RELA-
DEE DEE DEE DEE DEE DEE DEE
WHA-!
!
WHAT--? WAIT!
NO!

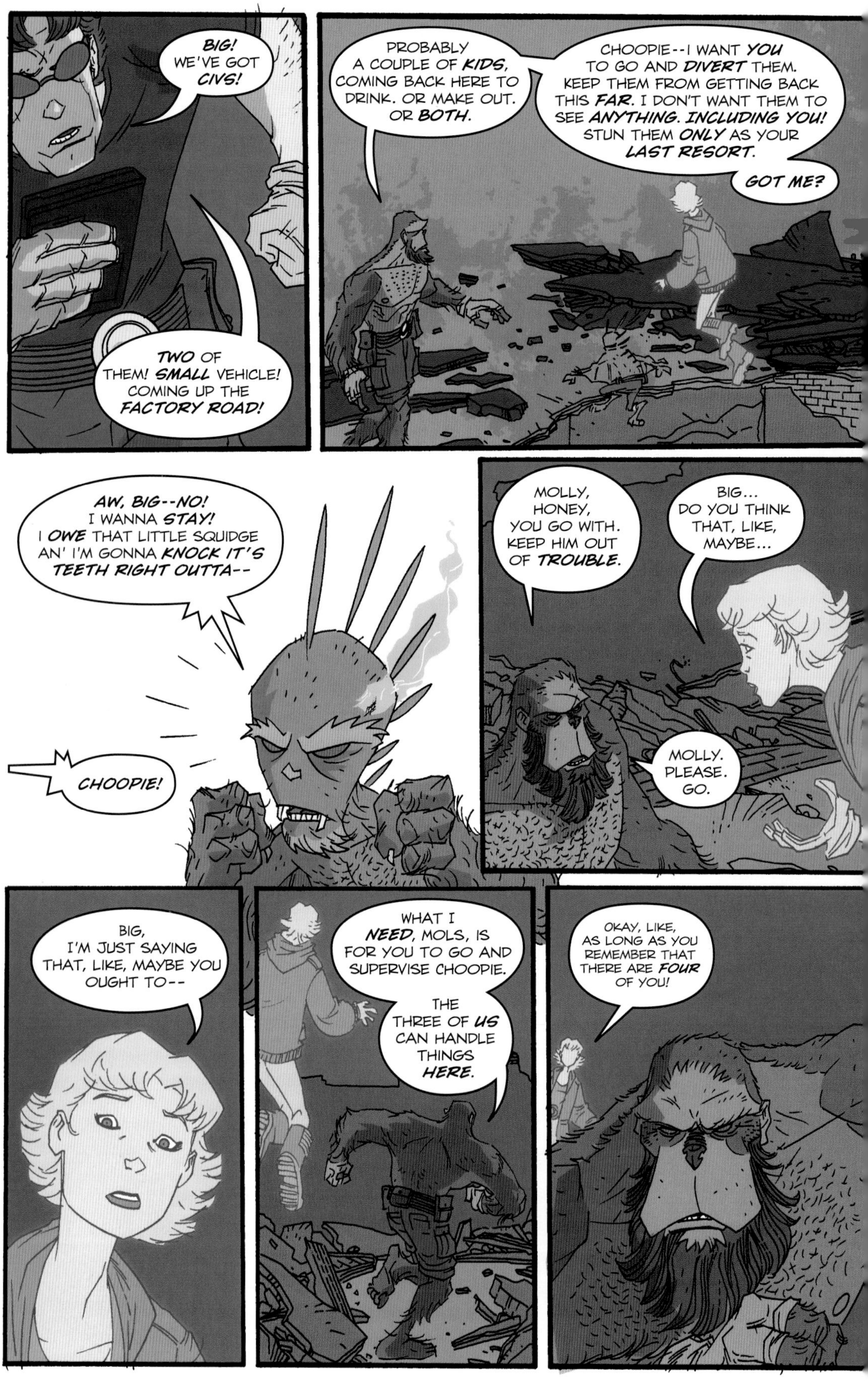
BIG! WE'VE GOT CIVS!
TWO OF THEM! SMALL VEHICLE! COMING UP THE FACTORY ROAD!
PROBABLY A COUPLE OF KIDS, COMING BACK HERE TO DRINK. OR MAKE OUT. OR BOTH.
CHOOPIE--I WANT YOU TO GO AND DIVERT THEM. KEEP THEM FROM GETTING BACK THIS FAR. I DON'T WANT THEM TO SEE ANYTHING. INCLUDING YOU! STUN THEM ONLY AS YOUR LAST RESORT.
GOT ME?
AW, BIG--NO! I WANNA STAY! I OWE THAT LITTLE SQUIDGE AN' I'M GONNA KNOCK IT'S TEETH RIGHT OUTTA--
CHOOPIE!
MOLLY, HONEY, YOU GO WITH. KEEP HIM OUT OF TROUBLE.
BIG... DO YOU THINK THAT, LIKE, MAYBE...
MOLLY. PLEASE. GO.
BIG, I'M JUST SAYING THAT, LIKE, MAYBE YOU OUGHT TO--
WHAT I NEED, MOLS, IS FOR YOU TO GO AND SUPERVISE CHOOPIE.
THE THREE OF US CAN HANDLE THINGS HERE.
OKAY, LIKE, AS LONG AS YOU REMEMBER THAT THERE ARE FOUR OF YOU!

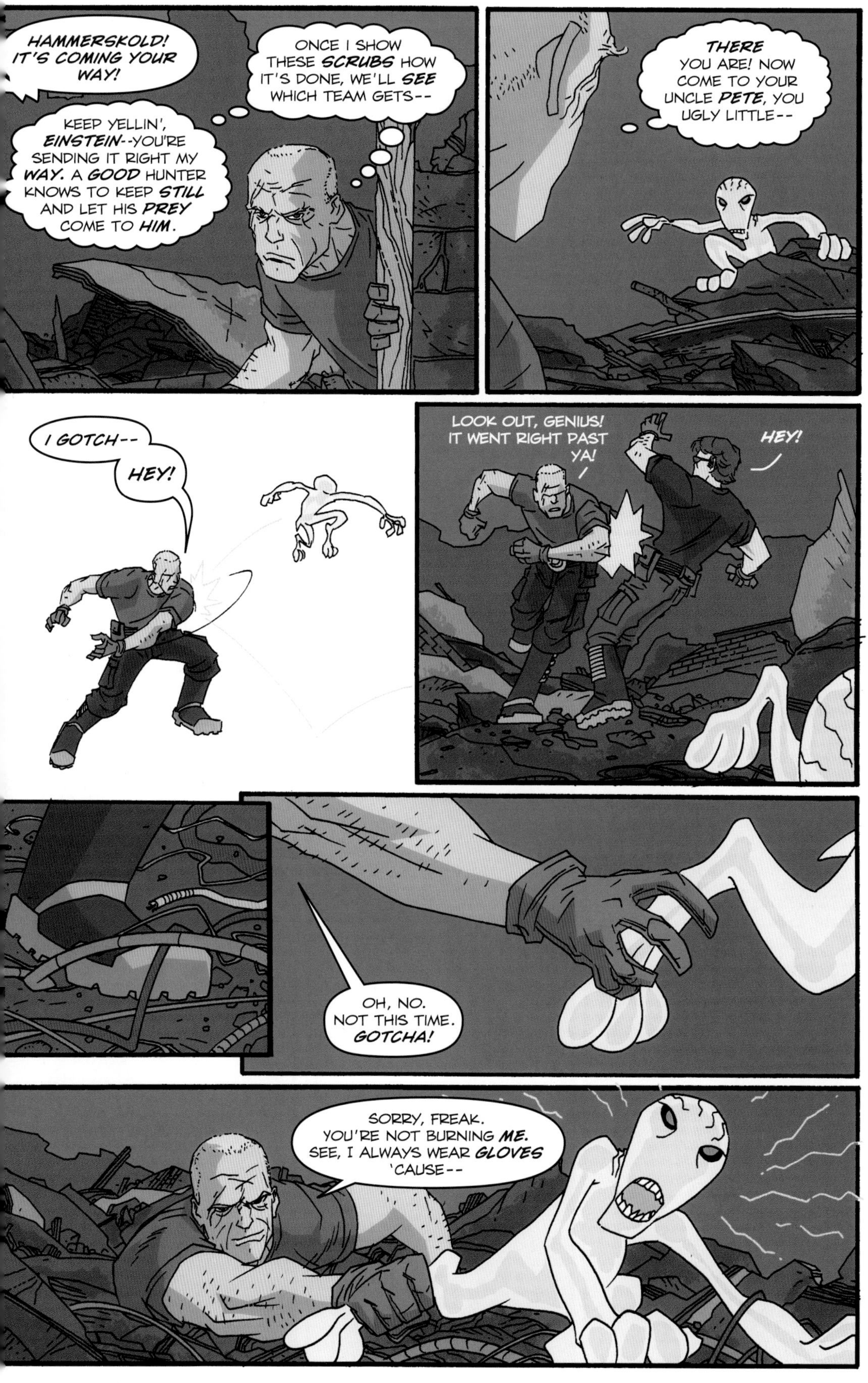
HAMMERSKOLD! IT'S COMING YOUR WAY!
ONCE I SHOW THESE SCRUBS HOW IT'S DONE, WE'LL SEE WHICH TEAM GETS--
KEEP YELLIN', EINSTEIN--YOU'RE SENDING IT RIGHT MY WAY. A GOOD HUNTER KNOWS TO KEEP STILL AND LET HIS PREY COME TO HIM.
THERE YOU ARE! NOW COME TO YOUR UNCLE PETE, YOU UGLY LITTLE--
I GOTCH--
HEY!
LOOK OUT, GENIUS! IT WENT RIGHT PAST YA!
HEY!
OH, NO. NOT THIS TIME. GOTCHA!
SORRY, FREAK. YOU'RE NOT BURNING ME. SEE, I ALWAYS WEAR GLOVES 'CAUSE--

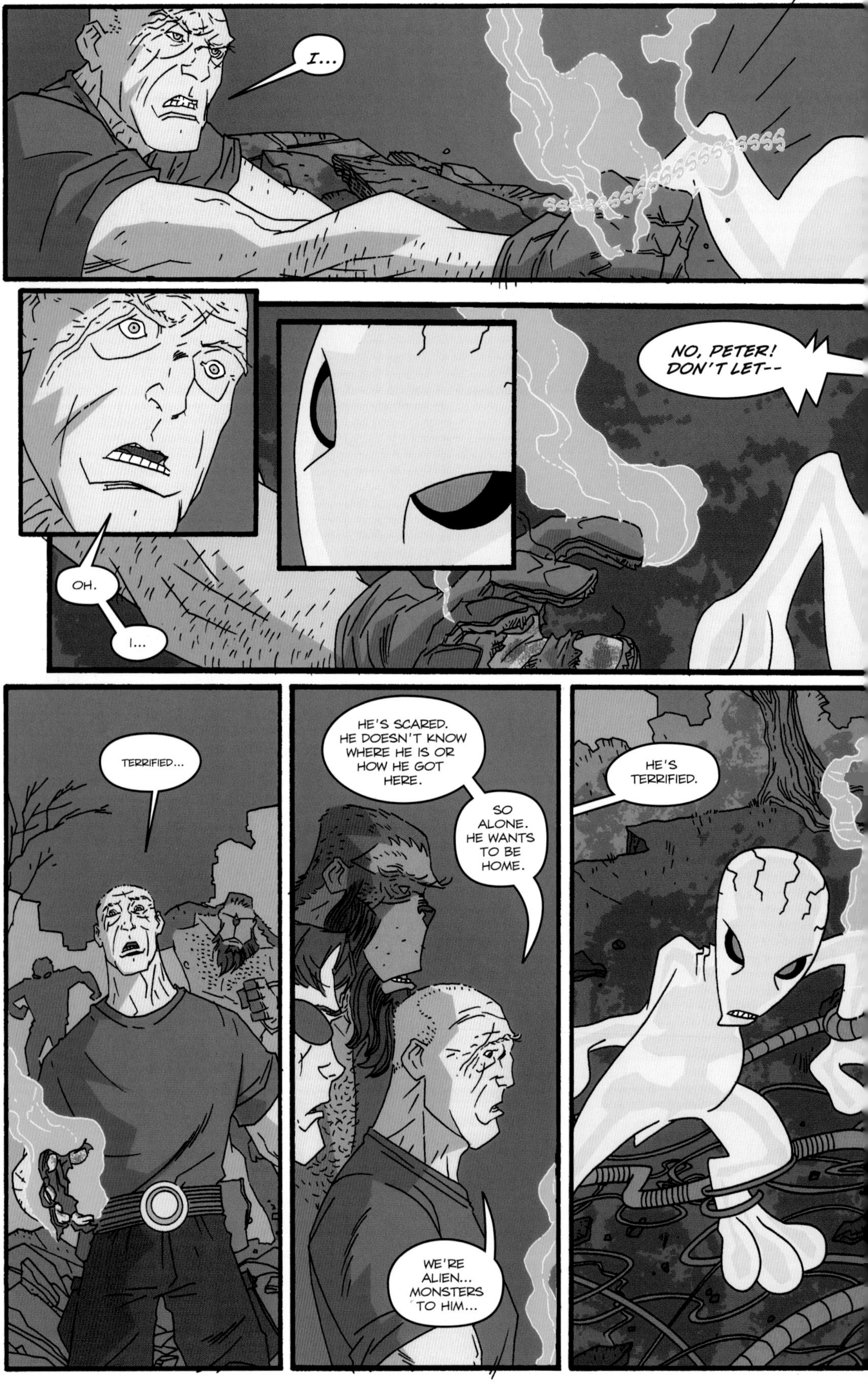
I...
SSSSSSSSSSSSSSSSSSSSSSSS
OH.
I...
NO, PETER! DON'T LET--
TERRIFIED...
HE'S SCARED. HE DOESN'T KNOW WHERE HE IS OR HOW HE GOT HERE.
SO ALONE. HE WANTS TO BE HOME.
WE'RE ALIEN... MONSTERS TO HIM...
HE'S TERRIFIED.

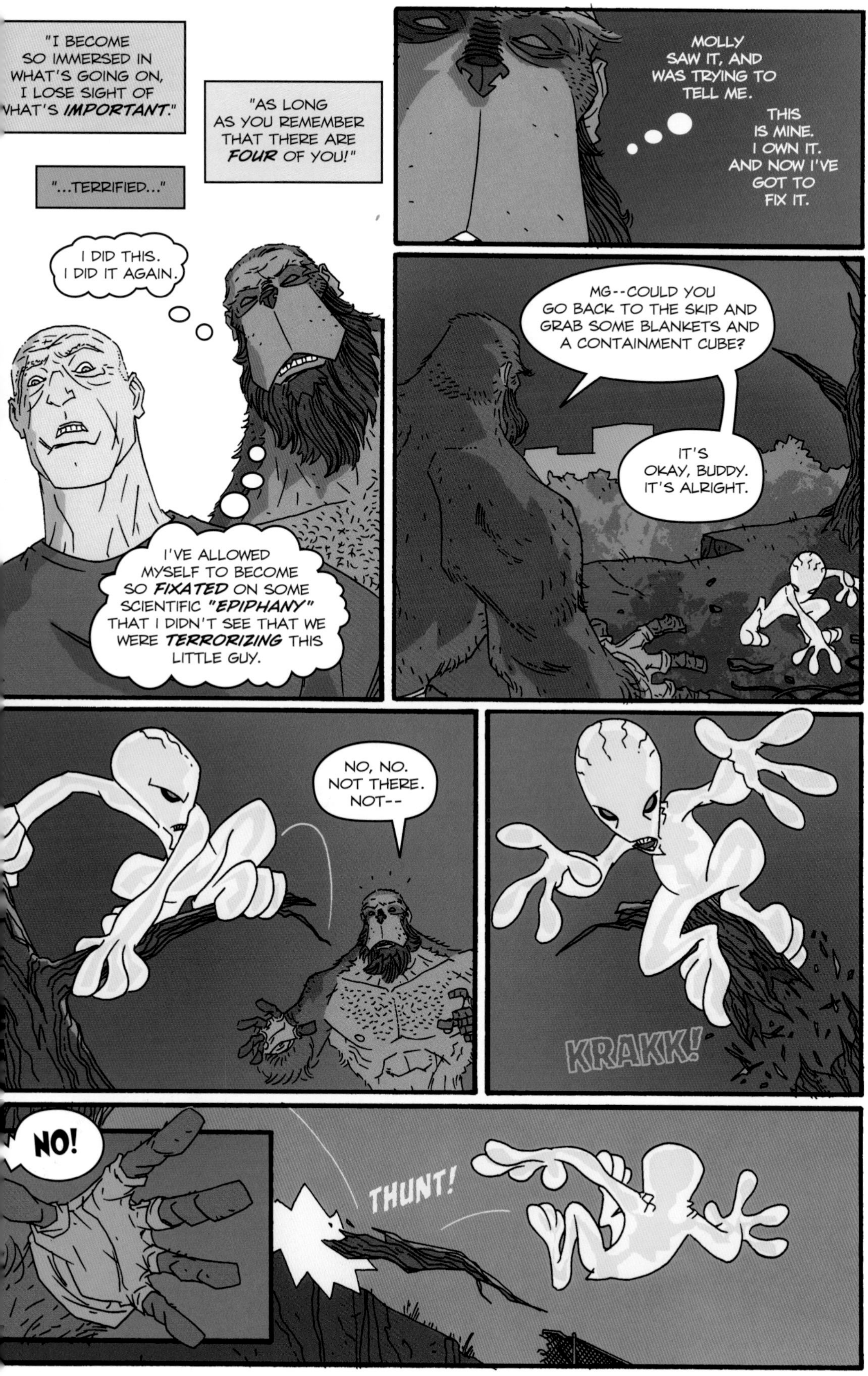
"I BECOME SO IMMERSED IN WHAT'S GOING ON, I LOSE SIGHT OF WHAT'S IMPORTANT."
"AS LONG AS YOU REMEMBER THAT THERE ARE FOUR OF YOU!"
"...TERRIFIED..."
MOLLY SAW IT, AND WAS TRYING TO TELL ME.
THIS IS MINE. I OWN IT. AND NOW I'VE GOT TO FIX IT.
I DID THIS. I DID IT AGAIN.
I'VE ALLOWED MYSELF TO BECOME SO FIXATED ON SOME SCIENTIFIC "EPIPHANY" THAT I DIDN'T SEE THAT WE WERE TERRORIZING THIS LITTLE GUY.
MG--COULD YOU GO BACK TO THE SKIP AND GRAB SOME BLANKETS AND A CONTAINMENT CUBE?
IT'S OKAY, BUDDY. IT'S ALRIGHT.
NO, NO. NOT THERE. NOT--
KRAKK!
NO!
THUNT!

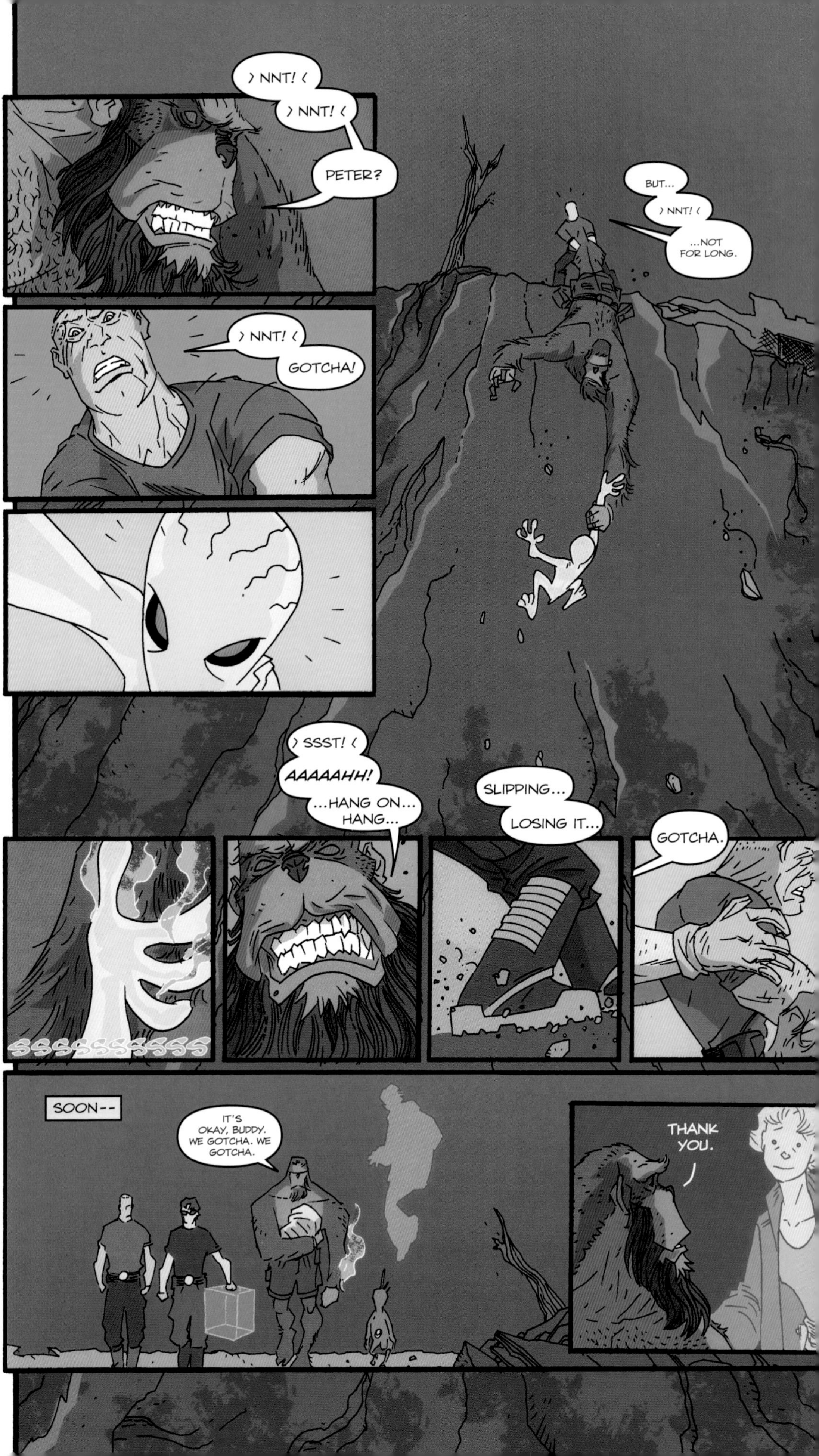

› NNT! ‹
› NNT! ‹
PETER?
BUT...
› NNT! ‹
...NOT FOR LONG.
› NNT! ‹
GOTCHA!
› SSST! ‹
AAAAAHH!
...HANG ON... HANG...
SLIPPING...
LOSING IT...
GOTCHA.
SSSSSSSSSSS
SOON--
IT'S OKAY, BUDDY. WE GOTCHA. WE GOTCHA.
THANK YOU.

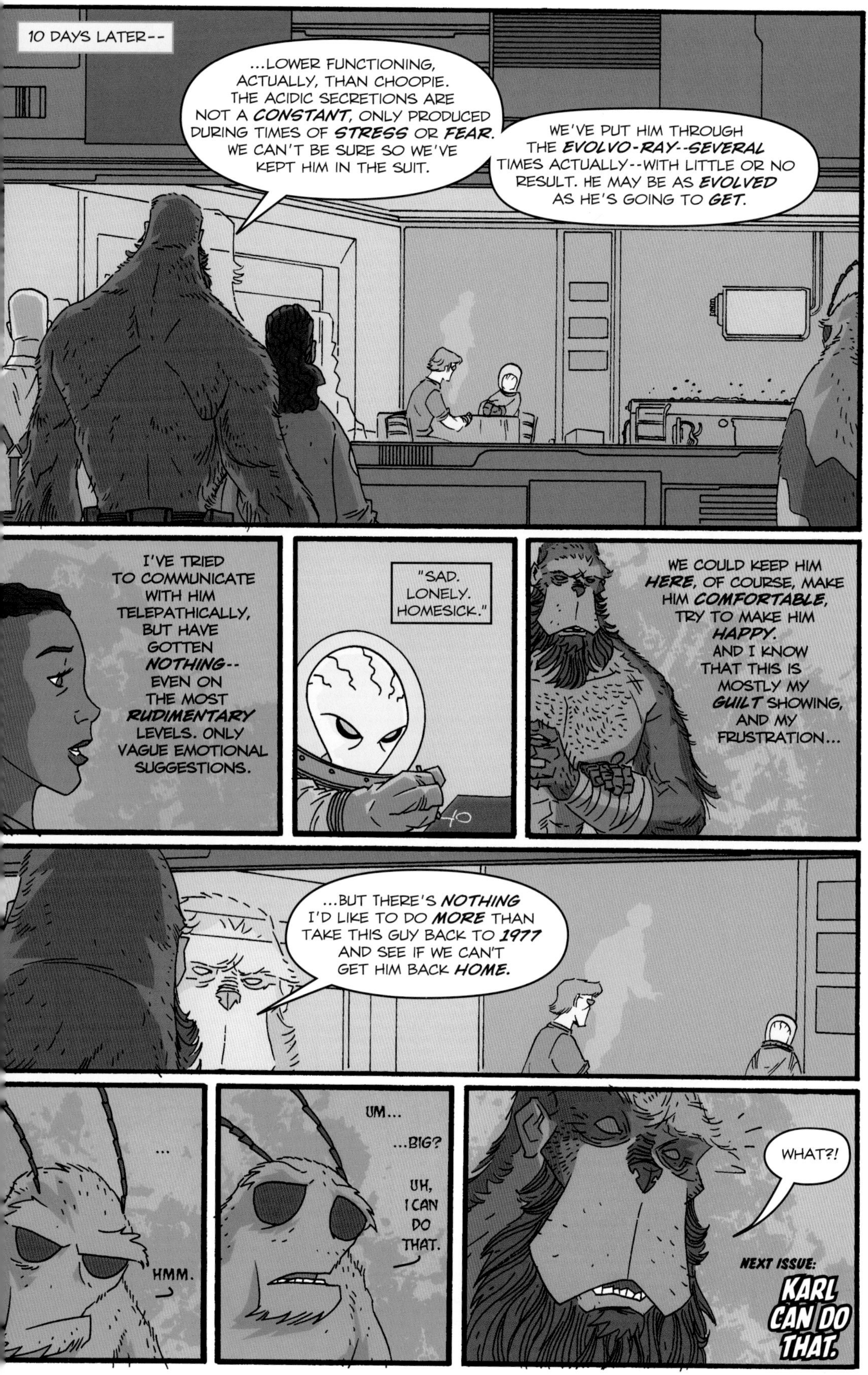
10 DAYS LATER--
...LOWER FUNCTIONING, ACTUALLY, THAN CHOOPIE. THE ACIDIC SECRETIONS ARE NOT A CONSTANT, ONLY PRODUCED DURING TIMES OF STRESS OR FEAR. WE CAN'T BE SURE SO WE'VE KEPT HIM IN THE SUIT.
WE'VE PUT HIM THROUGH THE EVOLVO-RAY--SEVERAL TIMES ACTUALLY--WITH LITTLE OR NO RESULT. HE MAY BE AS EVOLVED AS HE'S GOING TO GET.
I'VE TRIED TO COMMUNICATE WITH HIM TELEPATHICALLY, BUT HAVE GOTTEN NOTHING-- EVEN ON THE MOST RUDIMENTARY LEVELS. ONLY VAGUE EMOTIONAL SUGGESTIONS.
"SAD. LONELY. HOMESICK."
WE COULD KEEP HIM HERE, OF COURSE, MAKE HIM COMFORTABLE, TRY TO MAKE HIM HAPPY. AND I KNOW THAT THIS IS MOSTLY MY GUILT SHOWING, AND MY FRUSTRATION...
...BUT THERE'S NOTHING I'D LIKE TO DO MORE THAN TAKE THIS GUY BACK TO 1977 AND SEE IF WE CAN'T GET HIM BACK HOME.
...
HMM.
UM...
...BIG?
UH, I CAN DO THAT.
WHAT?!
NEXT ISSUE:
KARL CAN DO THAT.

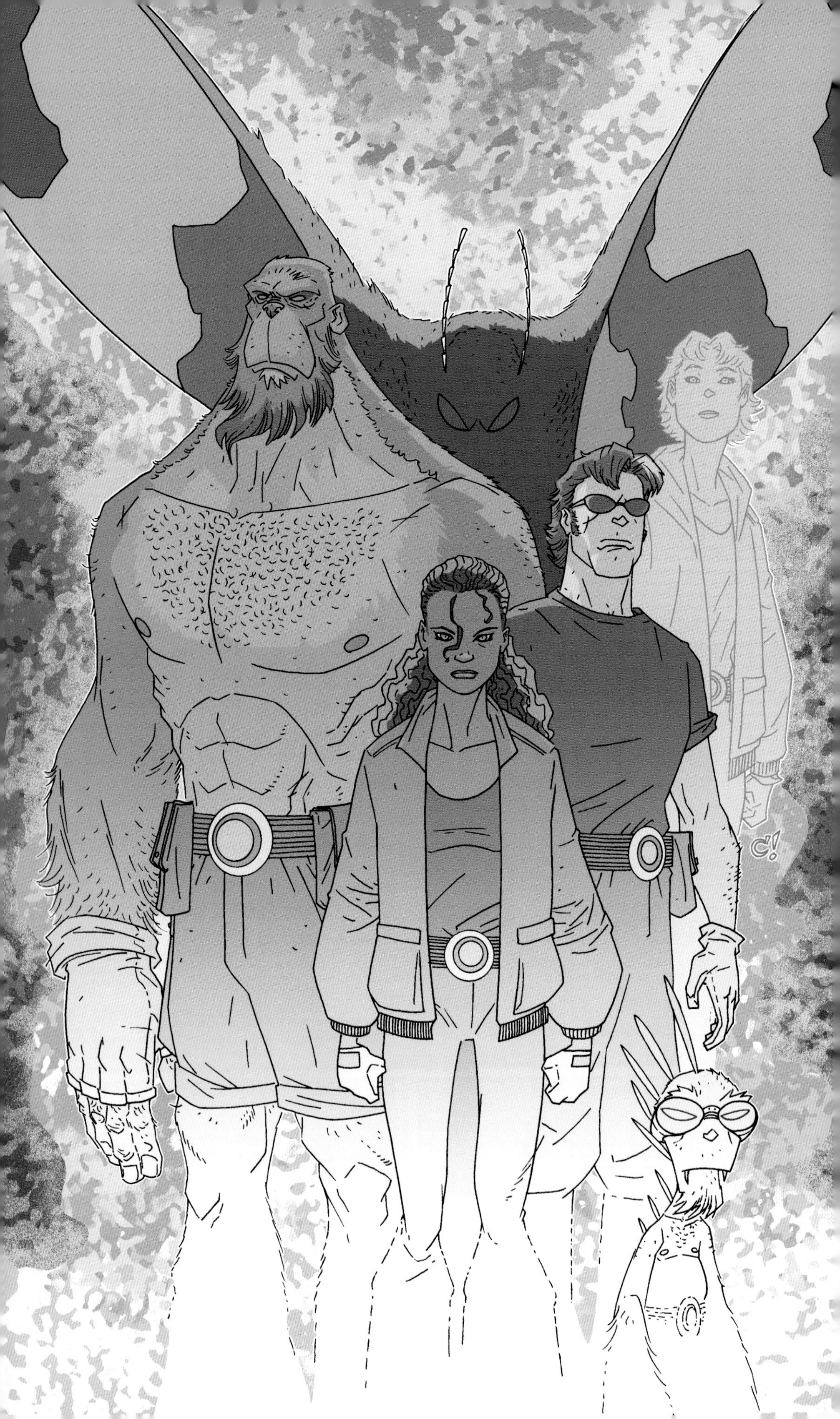

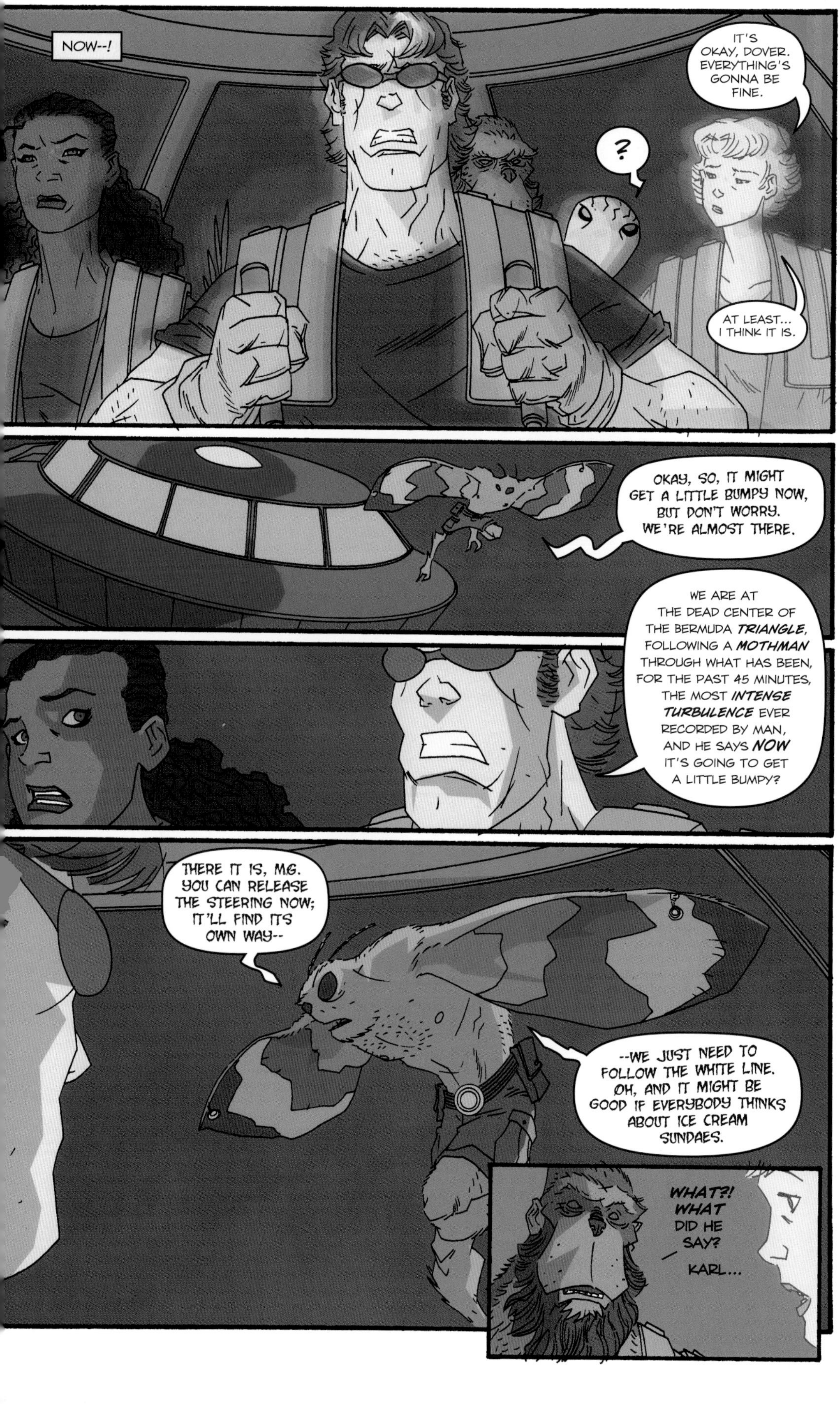
NOW--!
IT'S OKAY, DOVER. EVERYTHING'S GONNA BE FINE.
?
AT LEAST... I THINK IT IS.
OKAY, SO, IT MIGHT GET A LITTLE BUMPY NOW, BUT DON'T WORRY. WE'RE ALMOST THERE.
WE ARE AT THE DEAD CENTER OF THE BERMUDA TRIANGLE, FOLLOWING A MOTHMAN THROUGH WHAT HAS BEEN, FOR THE PAST 45 MINUTES, THE MOST INTENSE TURBULENCE EVER RECORDED BY MAN, AND HE SAYS NOW IT'S GOING TO GET A LITTLE BUMPY?
THERE IT IS, M.G. YOU CAN RELEASE THE STEERING NOW; IT'LL FIND ITS OWN WAY--
--WE JUST NEED TO FOLLOW THE WHITE LINE. OH, AND IT MIGHT BE GOOD IF EVERYBODY THINKS ABOUT ICE CREAM SUNDAES.
WHAT?! WHAT DID HE SAY?
KARL...

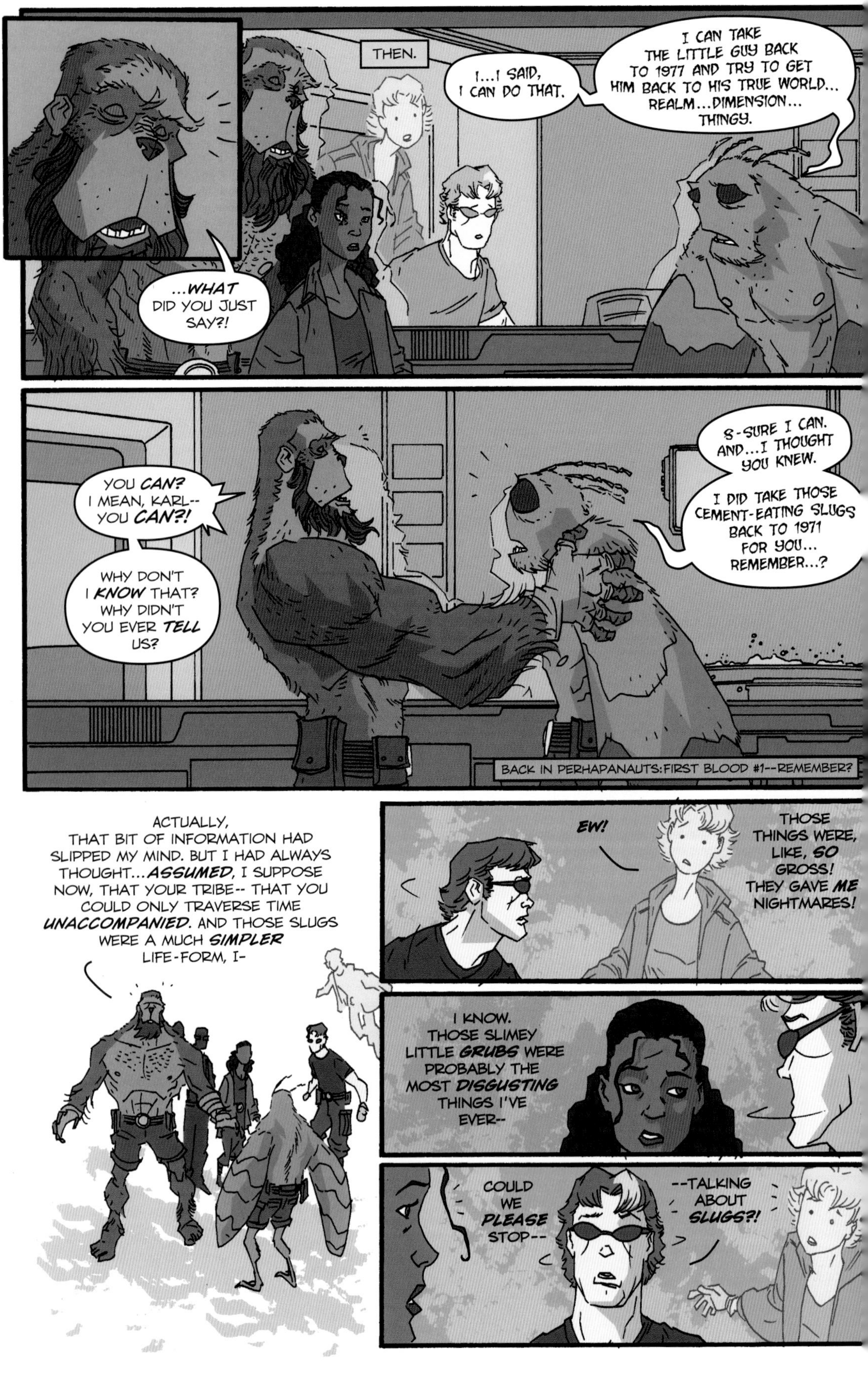

THEN.
...WHAT DID YOU JUST SAY?!
I...I SAID, I CAN DO THAT.
I CAN TAKE THE LITTLE GUY BACK TO 1977 AND TRY TO GET HIM BACK TO HIS TRUE WORLD... REALM...DIMENSION... THINGY.
YOU CAN? I MEAN, KARL-- YOU CAN?!
WHY DON'T I KNOW THAT? WHY DIDN'T YOU EVER TELL US?
S-SURE I CAN. AND...I THOUGHT YOU KNEW.
I DID TAKE THOSE CEMENT-EATING SLUGS BACK TO 1971 FOR YOU... REMEMBER...?
BACK IN PERHAPANAUTS:FIRST BLOOD #1--REMEMBER?
ACTUALLY, THAT BIT OF INFORMATION HAD SLIPPED MY MIND. BUT I HAD ALWAYS THOUGHT...ASSUMED, I SUPPOSE NOW, THAT YOUR TRIBE-- THAT YOU COULD ONLY TRAVERSE TIME UNACCOMPANIED. AND THOSE SLUGS WERE A MUCH SIMPLER LIFE-FORM, I-
EW!
THOSE THINGS WERE, LIKE, SO GROSS! THEY GAVE ME NIGHTMARES!
I KNOW. THOSE SLIMEY LITTLE GRUBS WERE PROBABLY THE MOST DISGUSTING THINGS I'VE EVER--
COULD WE PLEASE STOP--
--TALKING ABOUT SLUGS?!

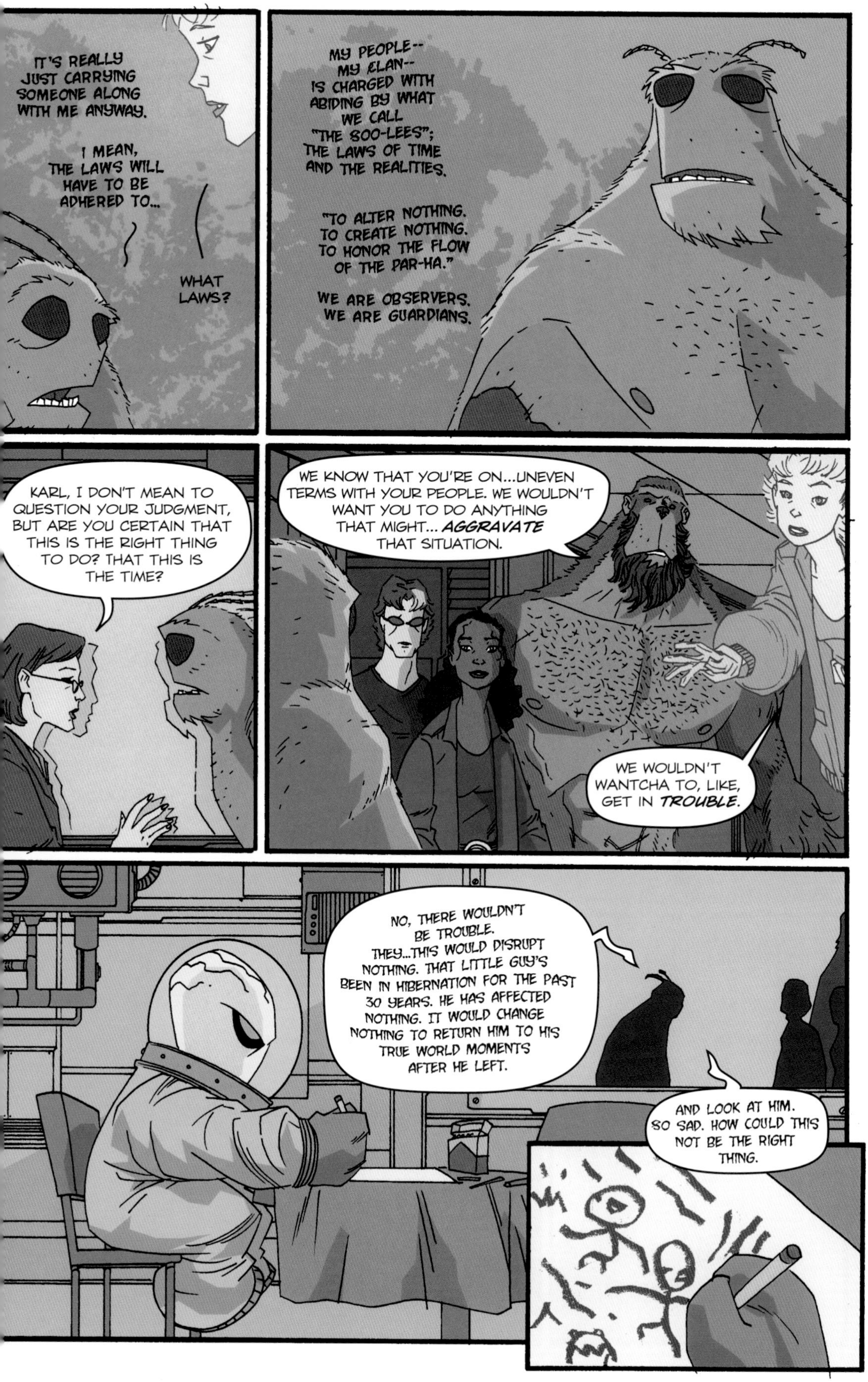
IT'S REALLY JUST CARRYING SOMEONE ALONG WITH ME ANYWAY.
I MEAN, THE LAWS WILL HAVE TO BE ADHERED TO...
WHAT LAWS?
MY PEOPLE-- MY CLAN-- IS CHARGED WITH ABIDING BY WHAT WE CALL "THE SOO-LEES"; THE LAWS OF TIME AND THE REALITIES.
"TO ALTER NOTHING. TO CREATE NOTHING. TO HONOR THE FLOW OF THE PAR-HA."
WE ARE OBSERVERS. WE ARE GUARDIANS.
KARL, I DON'T MEAN TO QUESTION YOUR JUDGMENT, BUT ARE YOU CERTAIN THAT THIS IS THE RIGHT THING TO DO? THAT THIS IS THE TIME?
WE KNOW THAT YOU'RE ON...UNEVEN TERMS WITH YOUR PEOPLE. WE WOULDN'T WANT YOU TO DO ANYTHING THAT MIGHT... AGGRAVATE THAT SITUATION.
WE WOULDN'T WANTCHA TO, LIKE, GET IN TROUBLE.
NO, THERE WOULDN'T BE TROUBLE. THEY...THIS WOULD DISRUPT NOTHING. THAT LITTLE GUY'S BEEN IN HIBERNATION FOR THE PAST 30 YEARS. HE HAS AFFECTED NOTHING. IT WOULD CHANGE NOTHING TO RETURN HIM TO HIS TRUE WORLD MOMENTS AFTER HE LEFT.
AND LOOK AT HIM. SO SAD. HOW COULD THIS NOT BE THE RIGHT THING.

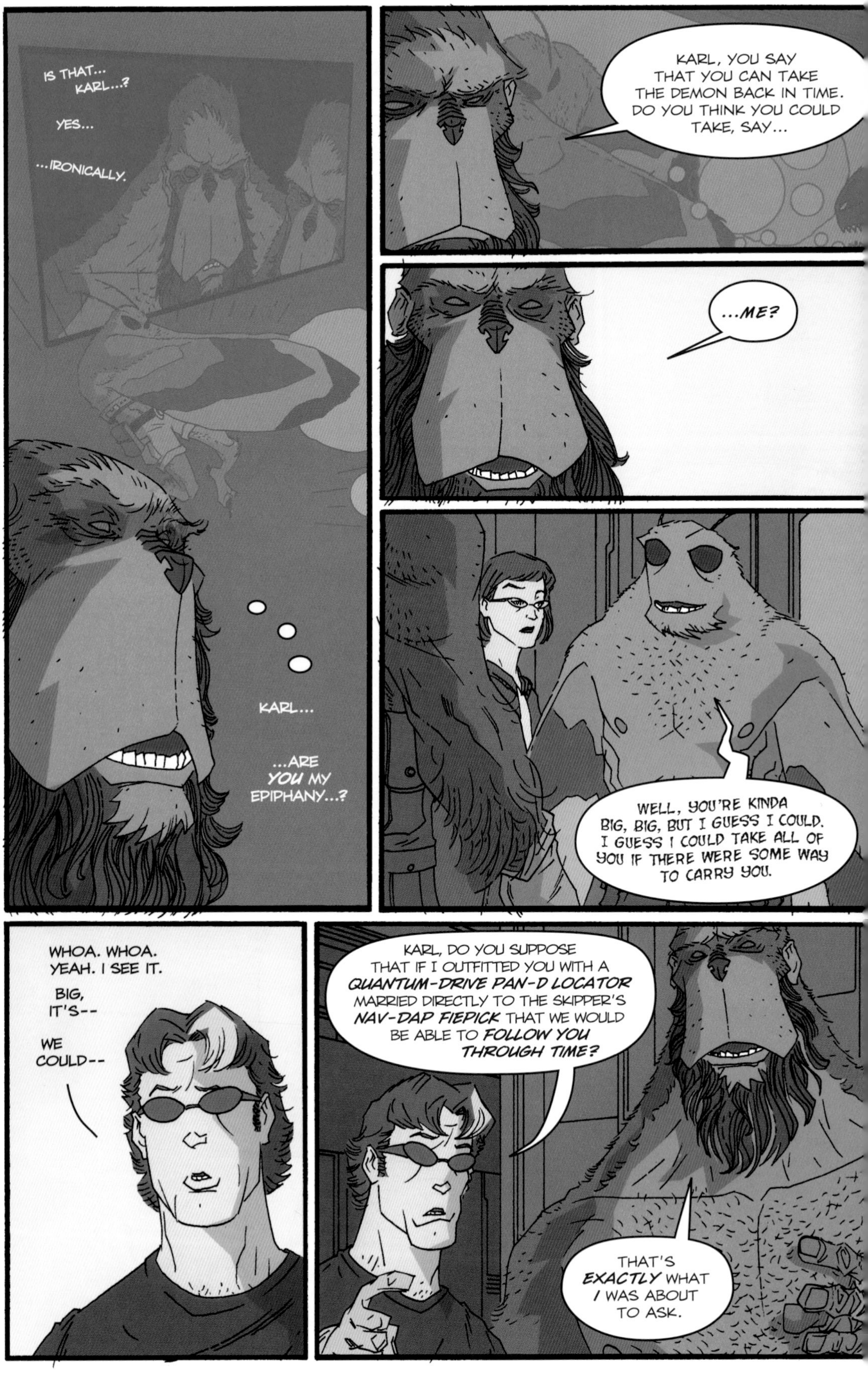
IS THAT... KARL...?
YES...
...IRONICALLY.
KARL...
...ARE YOU MY EPIPHANY...?
KARL, YOU SAY THAT YOU CAN TAKE THE DEMON BACK IN TIME. DO YOU THINK YOU COULD TAKE, SAY...
...ME?
WELL, YOU'RE KINDA BIG, BIG, BUT I GUESS I COULD. I GUESS I COULD TAKE ALL OF YOU IF THERE WERE SOME WAY TO CARRY YOU.
WHOA. WHOA. YEAH. I SEE IT.
BIG, IT'S--
WE COULD--
KARL, DO YOU SUPPOSE THAT IF I OUTFITTED YOU WITH A QUANTUM-DRIVE PAN-D LOCATOR MARRIED DIRECTLY TO THE SKIPPER'S NAV-DAP FIEPICK THAT WE WOULD BE ABLE TO FOLLOW YOU THROUGH TIME?
THAT'S EXACTLY WHAT I WAS ABOUT TO ASK.

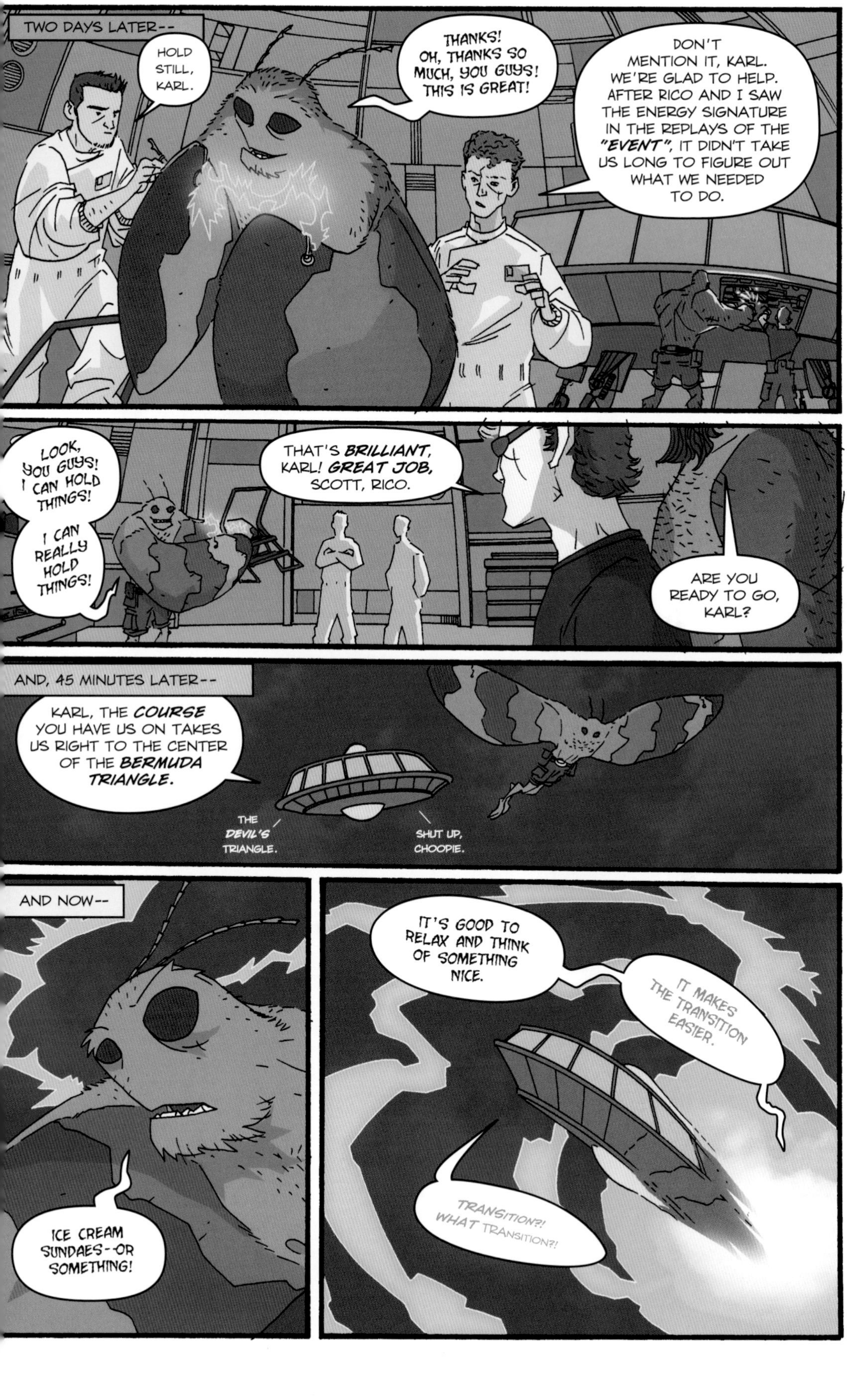
TWO DAYS LATER--
HOLD STILL, KARL.
THANKS! OH, THANKS SO MUCH, YOU GUYS! THIS IS GREAT!
DON'T MENTION IT, KARL. WE'RE GLAD TO HELP. AFTER RICO AND I SAW THE ENERGY SIGNATURE IN THE REPLAYS OF THE "EVENT", IT DIDN'T TAKE US LONG TO FIGURE OUT WHAT WE NEEDED TO DO.
LOOK, YOU GUYS! I CAN HOLD THINGS!
I CAN REALLY HOLD THINGS!
THAT'S BRILLIANT, KARL! GREAT JOB, SCOTT, RICO.
ARE YOU READY TO GO, KARL?
AND, 45 MINUTES LATER--
KARL, THE COURSE YOU HAVE US ON TAKES US RIGHT TO THE CENTER OF THE BERMUDA TRIANGLE.
THE DEVIL'S TRIANGLE.
SHUT UP, CHOOPIE.
AND NOW--
ICE CREAM SUNDAES--OR SOMETHING!
IT'S GOOD TO RELAX AND THINK OF SOMETHING NICE.
IT MAKES THE TRANSITION EASIER.
TRANSITION?! WHAT TRANSITION?!

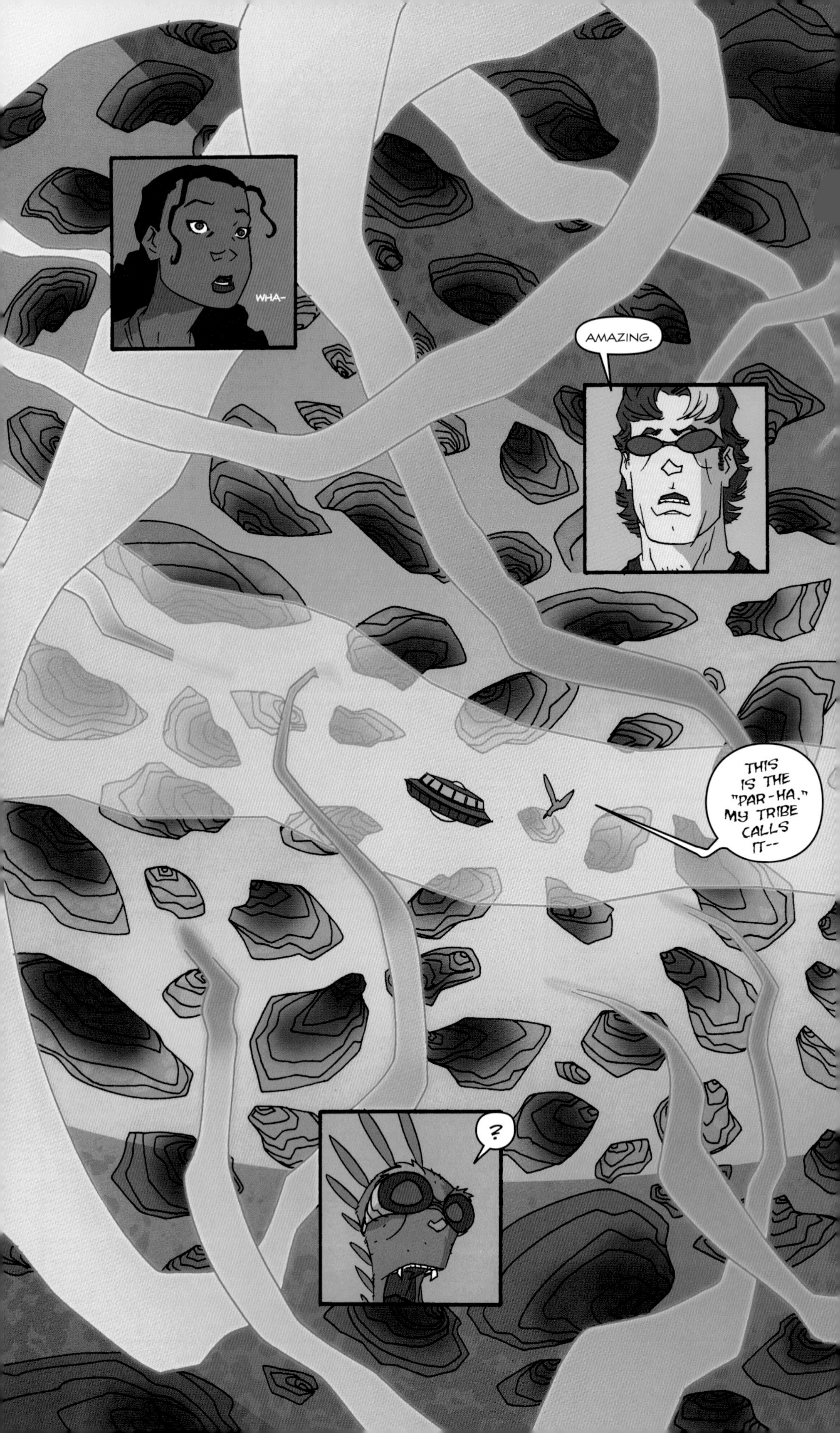
WHA-
AMAZING.
THIS IS THE "PAR-HA." MY TRIBE CALLS IT--
?

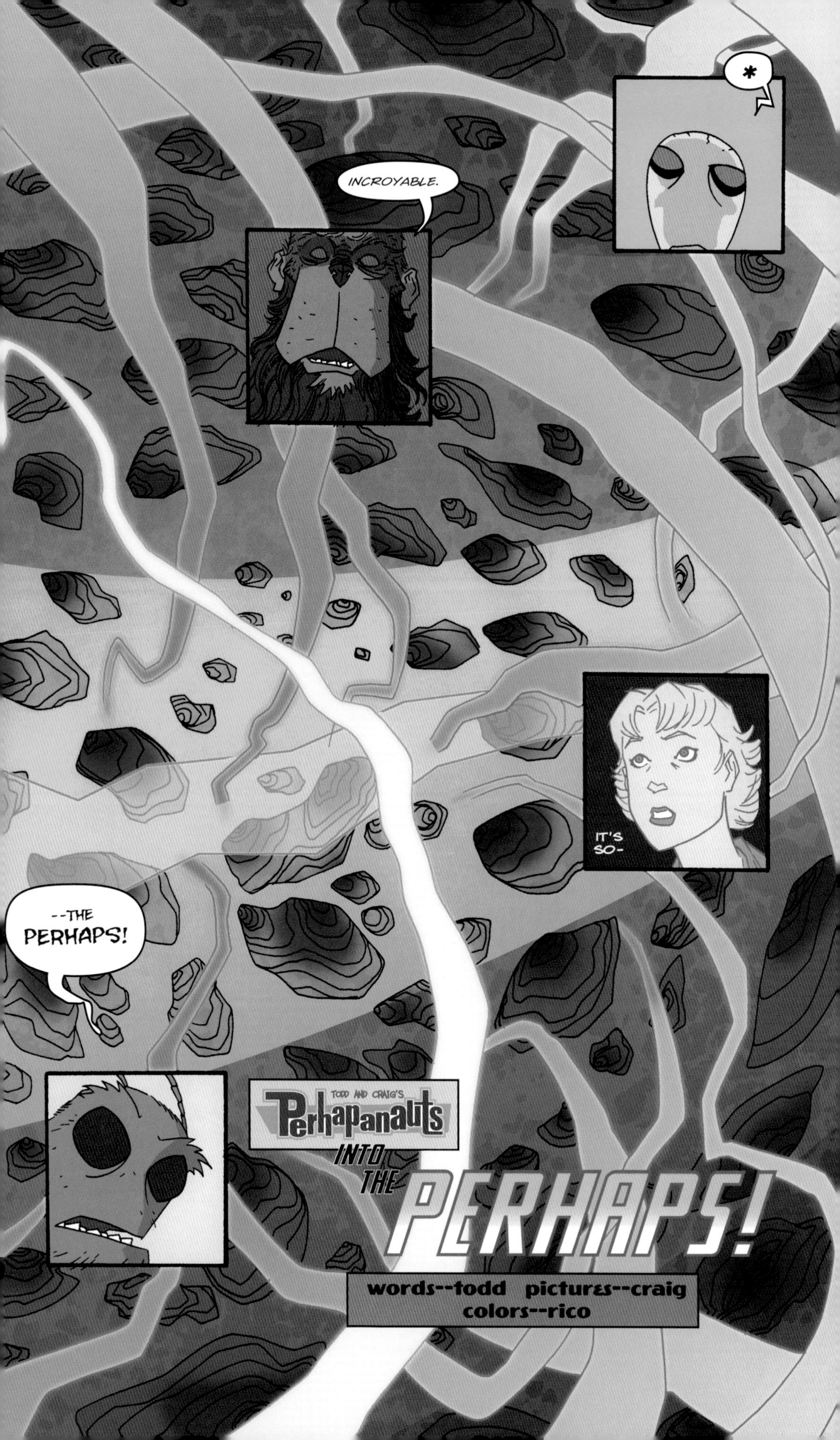
*
INCROYABLE.
IT'S SO-
--THE PERHAPS!
TODD AND CRAIG'S
Perhapanauts
INTO THE PERHAPS!
words--todd pictures--craig
colors--rico

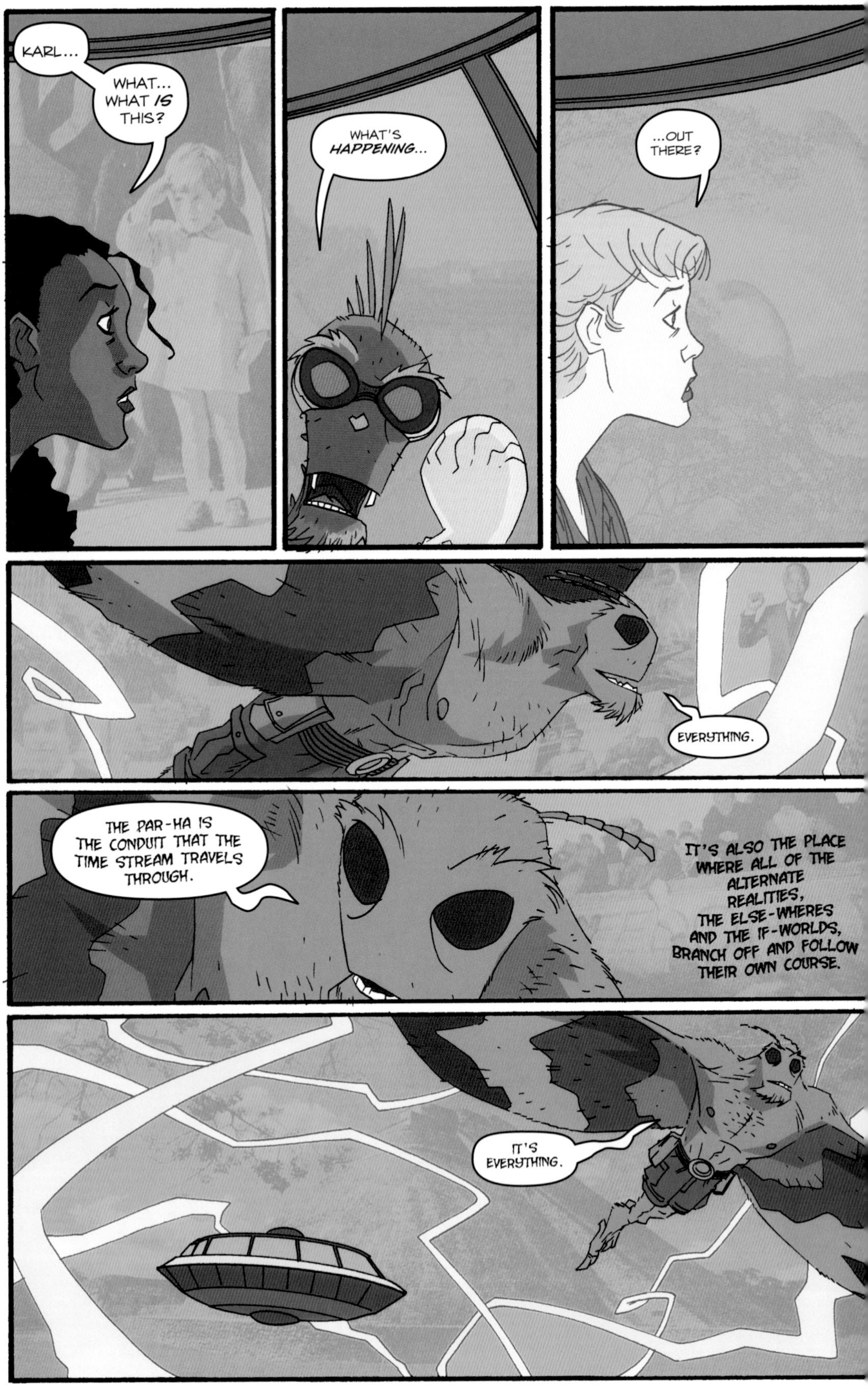
KARL...
WHAT... WHAT *IS* THIS?
WHAT'S *HAPPENING*...
...OUT THERE?
EVERYTHING.
THE PAR-HA IS THE CONDUIT THAT THE TIME STREAM TRAVELS THROUGH.
IT'S ALSO THE PLACE WHERE ALL OF THE ALTERNATE REALITIES, THE ELSE-WHERES AND THE IF-WORLDS, BRANCH OFF AND FOLLOW THEIR OWN COURSE.
IT'S EVERYTHING.

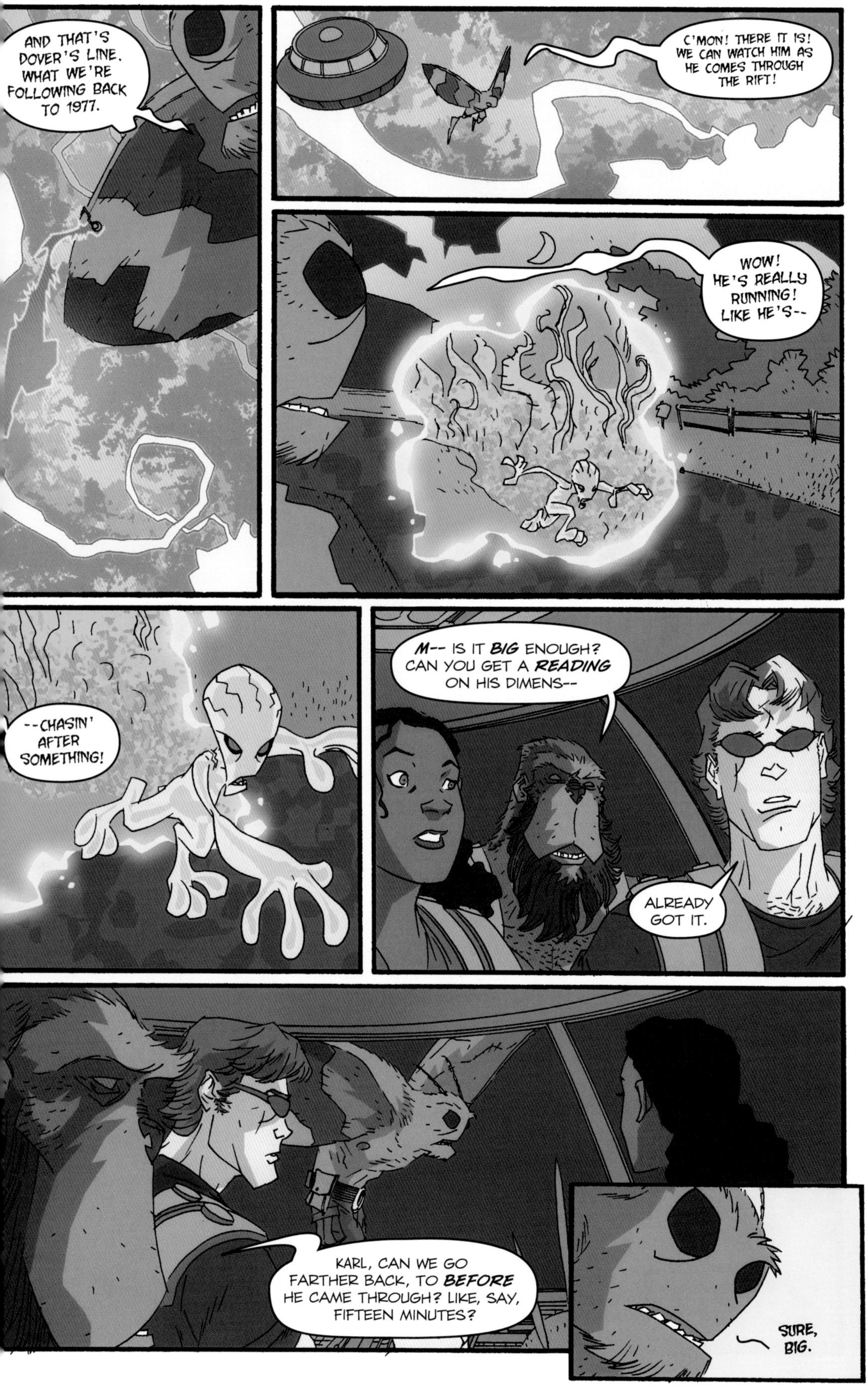
AND THAT'S DOVER'S LINE. WHAT WE'RE FOLLOWING BACK TO 1977.
C'MON! THERE IT IS! WE CAN WATCH HIM AS HE COMES THROUGH THE RIFT!
WOW! HE'S REALLY RUNNING! LIKE HE'S--
--CHASIN' AFTER SOMETHING!
M-- IS IT BIG ENOUGH? CAN YOU GET A READING ON HIS DIMENS--
ALREADY GOT IT.
KARL, CAN WE GO FARTHER BACK, TO BEFORE HE CAME THROUGH? LIKE, SAY, FIFTEEN MINUTES?
SURE, BIG.

AND, MOMENTS LATER--

OKAY, KARL... NOW!

AND HE SHOULD HAVE THE D-GATE OPEN RIGHT ABOUT...

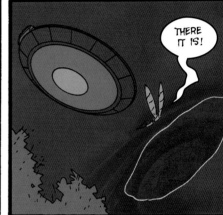

THERE IT IS!

SO...DOVER... THIS IS YOUR WORLD, HUH? IT'S VERY... UH...

COLORFUL.

IT'S BEAUTIFUL.

IT'S SQUISHY.

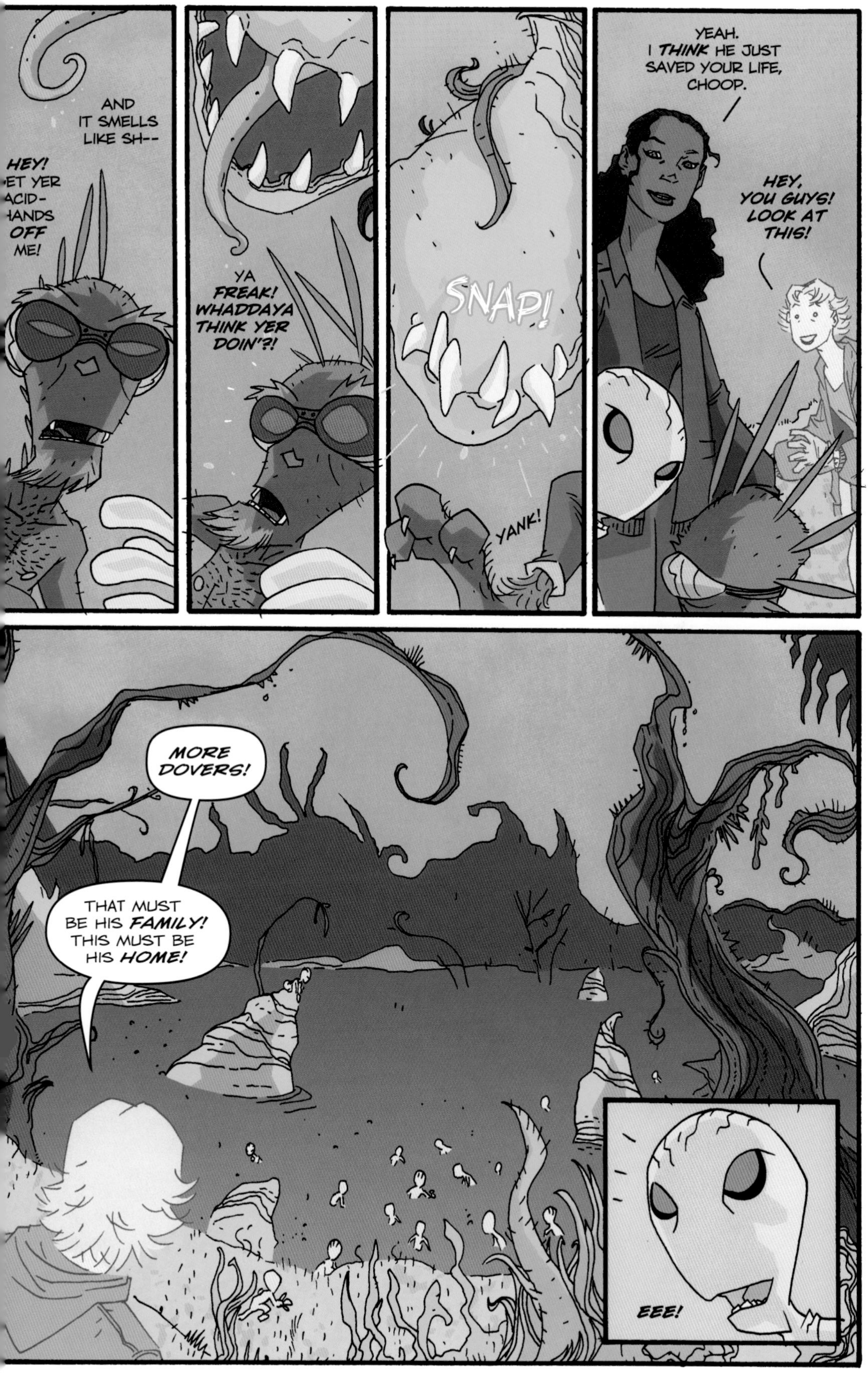
AND IT SMELLS LIKE SH--
HEY! ET YER ACID-HANDS OFF ME!
YA FREAK! WHADDAYA THINK YER DOIN'?!
SNAP!
YANK!
YEAH. I THINK HE JUST SAVED YOUR LIFE, CHOOP.
HEY, YOU GUYS! LOOK AT THIS!
MORE DOVERS!
THAT MUST BE HIS FAMILY! THIS MUST BE HIS HOME!
EEE!

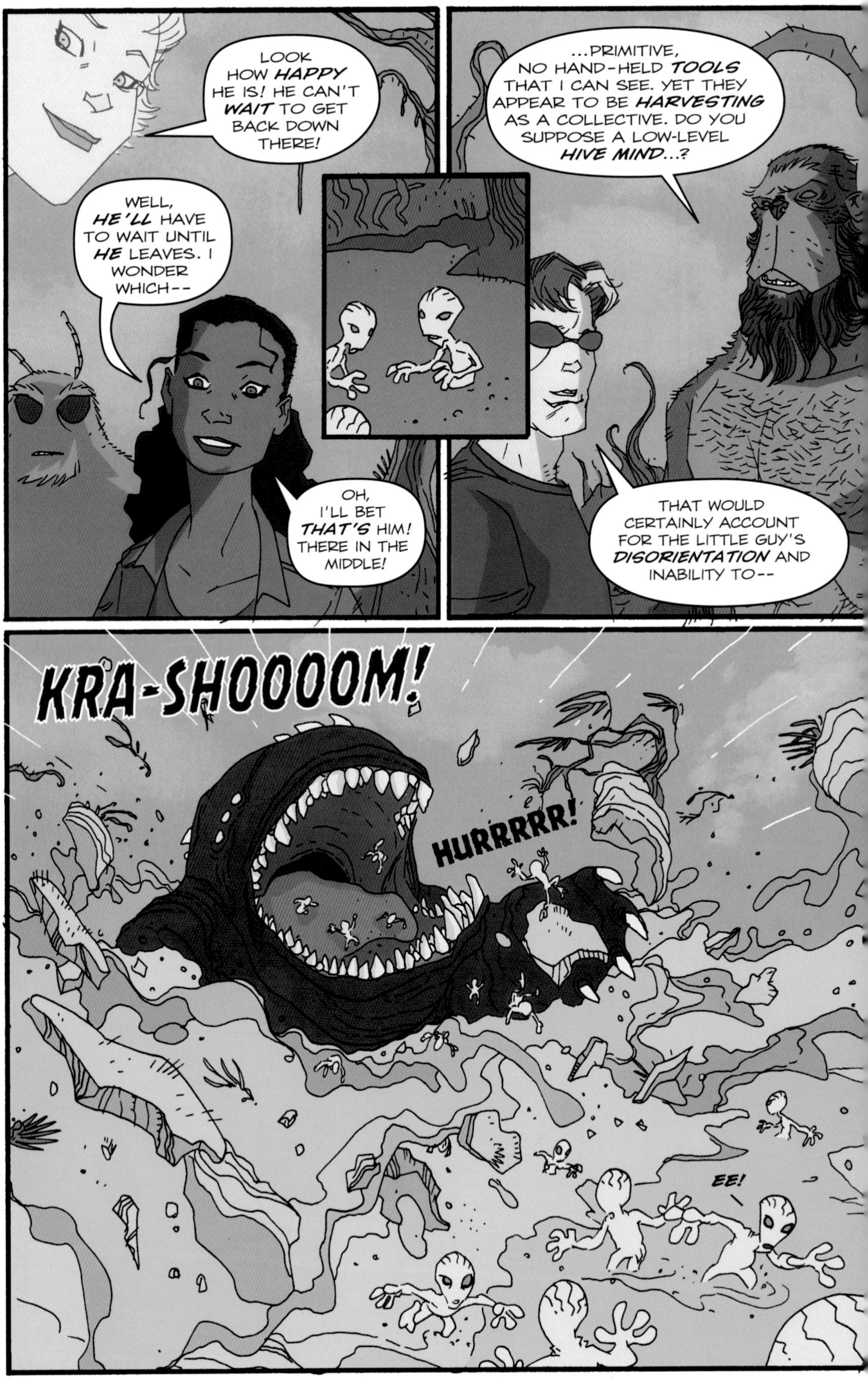
LOOK HOW HAPPY HE IS! HE CAN'T WAIT TO GET BACK DOWN THERE!
WELL, HE'LL HAVE TO WAIT UNTIL HE LEAVES. I WONDER WHICH--
OH, I'LL BET THAT'S HIM! THERE IN THE MIDDLE!
...PRIMITIVE, NO HAND-HELD TOOLS THAT I CAN SEE. YET THEY APPEAR TO BE HARVESTING AS A COLLECTIVE. DO YOU SUPPOSE A LOW-LEVEL HIVE MIND...?
THAT WOULD CERTAINLY ACCOUNT FOR THE LITTLE GUY'S DISORIENTATION AND INABILITY TO--
KRA-SHOOOOM!
HURRRRR!
EE!

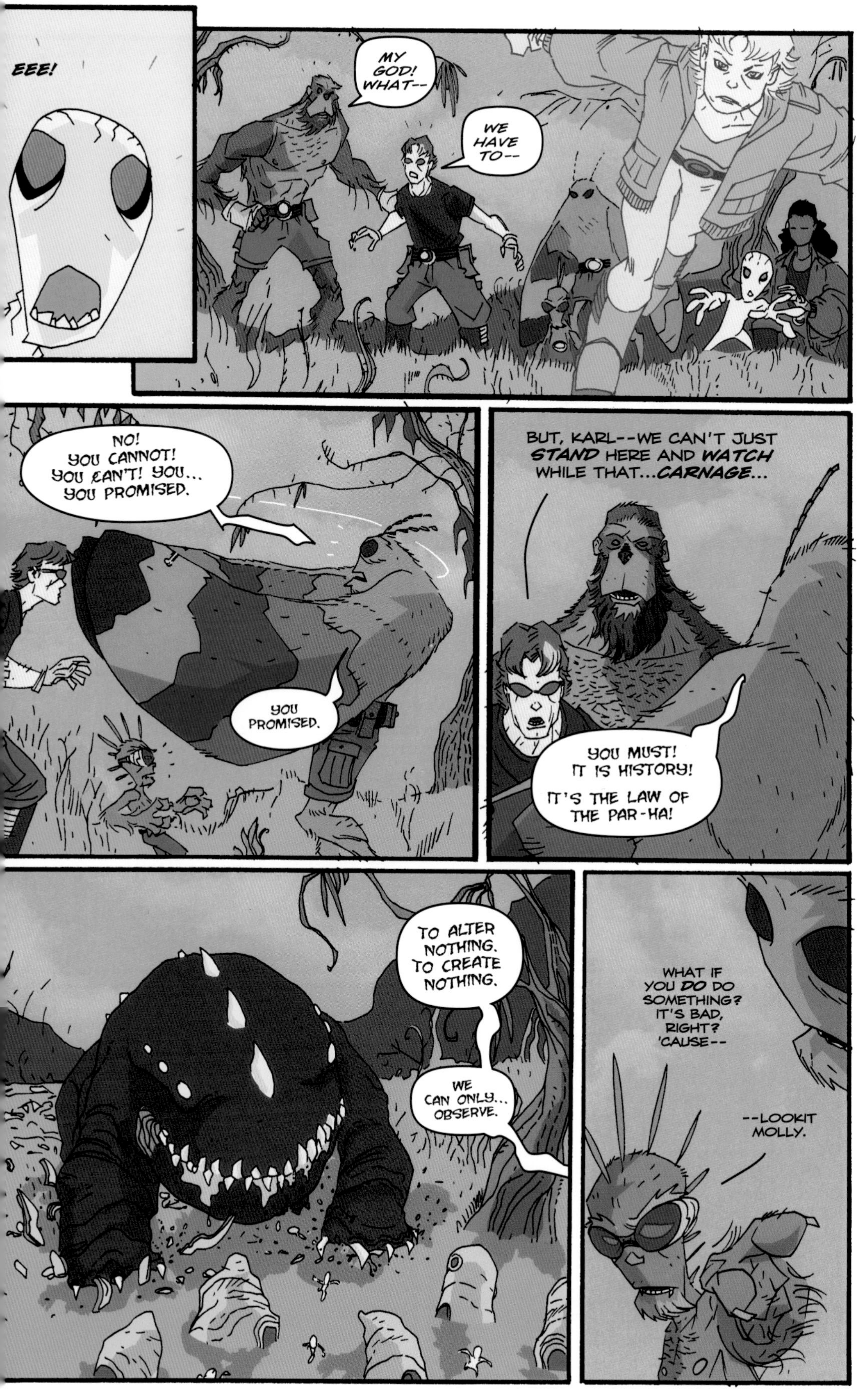
EEE!
MY GOD! WHAT--
WE HAVE TO--
NO! YOU CANNOT! YOU CAN'T! YOU... YOU PROMISED.
YOU PROMISED.
BUT, KARL--WE CAN'T JUST STAND HERE AND WATCH WHILE THAT...CARNAGE...
YOU MUST! IT IS HISTORY!
IT'S THE LAW OF THE PAR-HA!
TO ALTER NOTHING. TO CREATE NOTHING.
WE CAN ONLY... OBSERVE.
WHAT IF YOU DO DO SOMETHING? IT'S BAD, RIGHT? 'CAUSE--
--LOOKIT MOLLY.

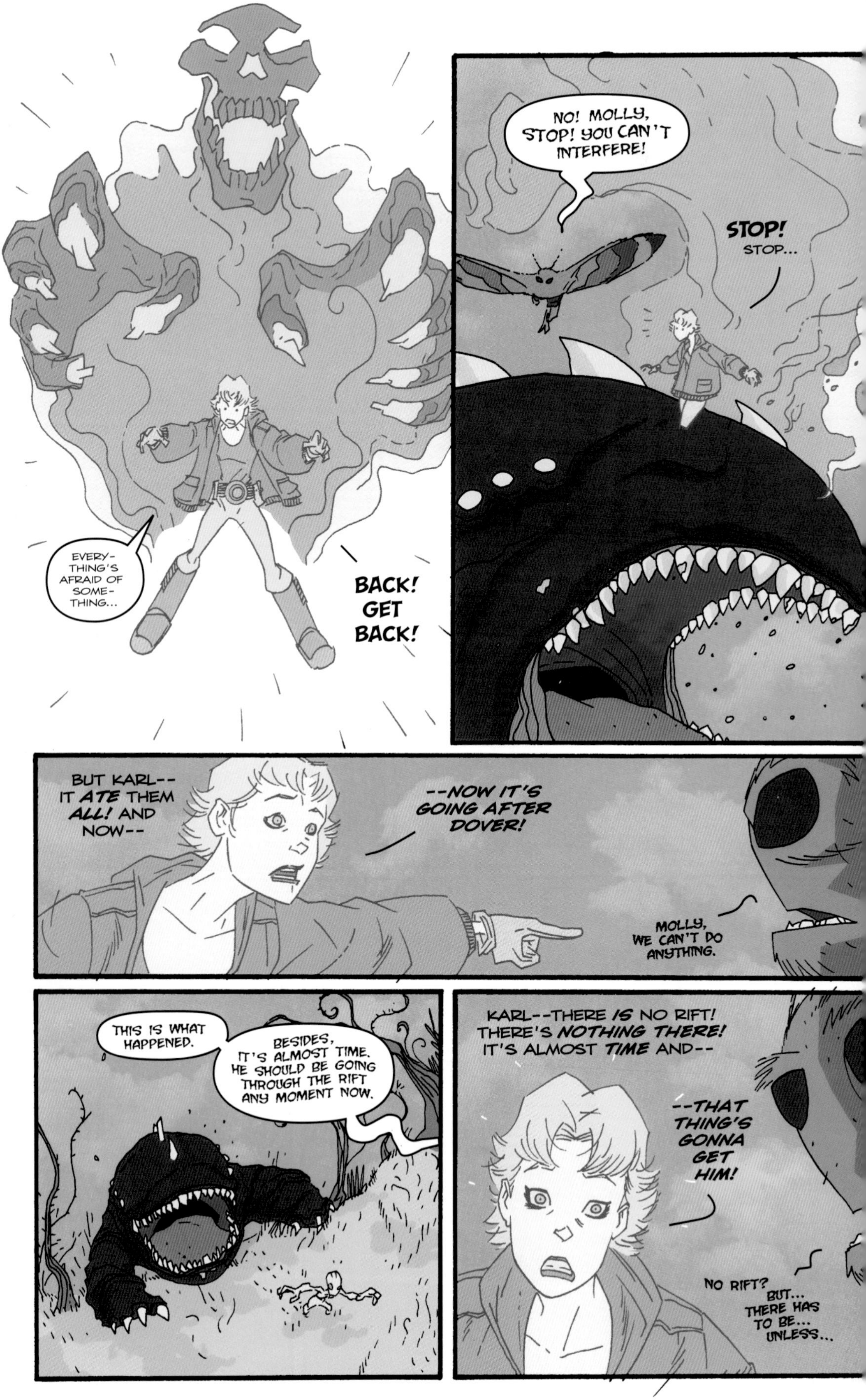
EVERY-THING'S AFRAID OF SOME-THING...
BACK! GET BACK!
NO! MOLLY, STOP! YOU CAN'T INTERFERE!
STOP! STOP...
BUT KARL-- IT ATE THEM ALL! AND NOW--
--NOW IT'S GOING AFTER DOVER!
MOLLY, WE CAN'T DO ANYTHING.
THIS IS WHAT HAPPENED.
BESIDES, IT'S ALMOST TIME. HE SHOULD BE GOING THROUGH THE RIFT ANY MOMENT NOW.
KARL--THERE IS NO RIFT! THERE'S NOTHING THERE! IT'S ALMOST TIME AND--
--THAT THING'S GONNA GET HIM!
NO RIFT? BUT... THERE HAS TO BE... UNLESS...

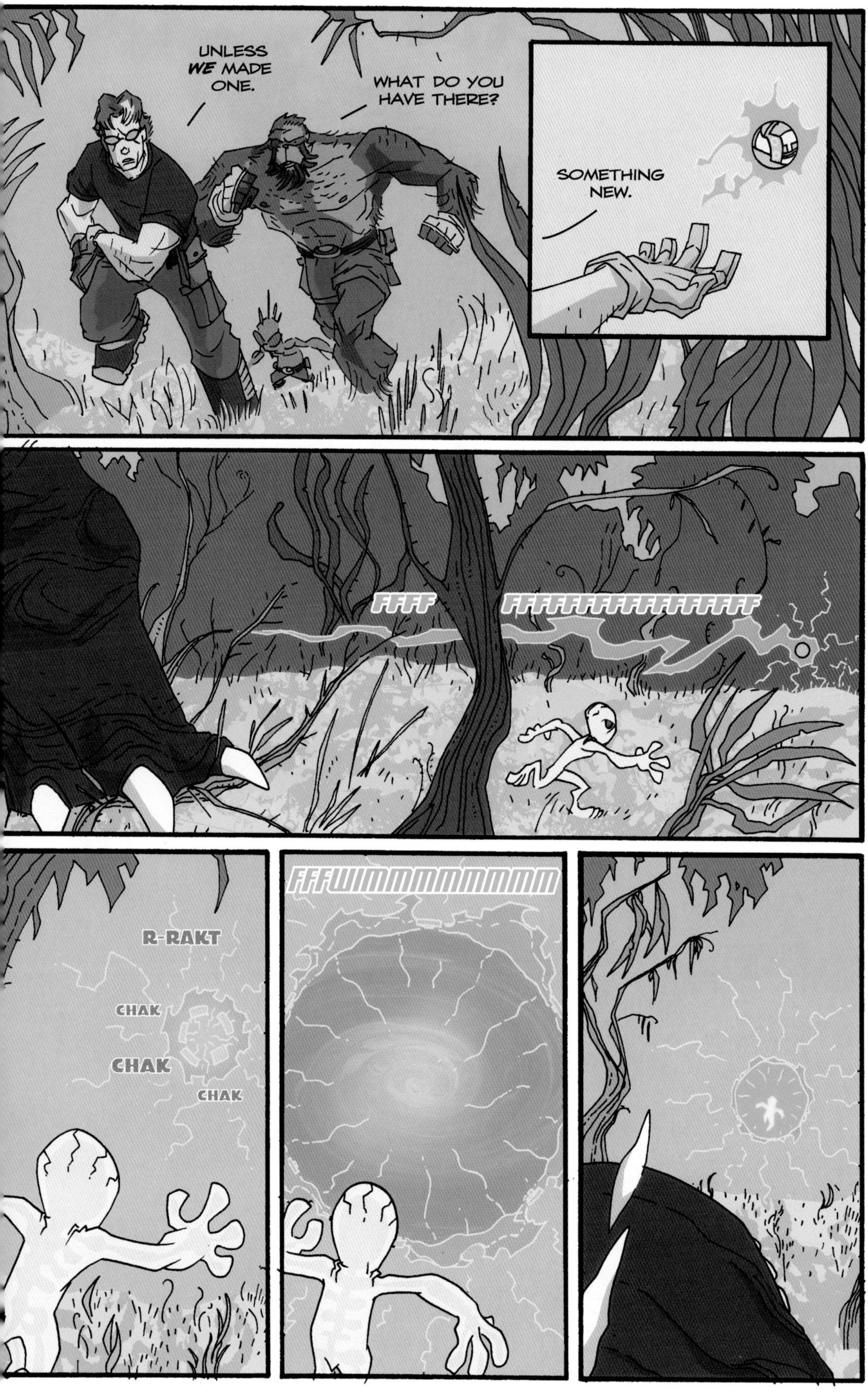
UNLESS *WE* MADE ONE.
WHAT DO YOU HAVE THERE?
SOMETHING NEW.
FFFF FFFFFFFFFFFFFFFFF
R-RAKT
CHAK
CHAK
CHAK
FFFWIMMMMMMMM

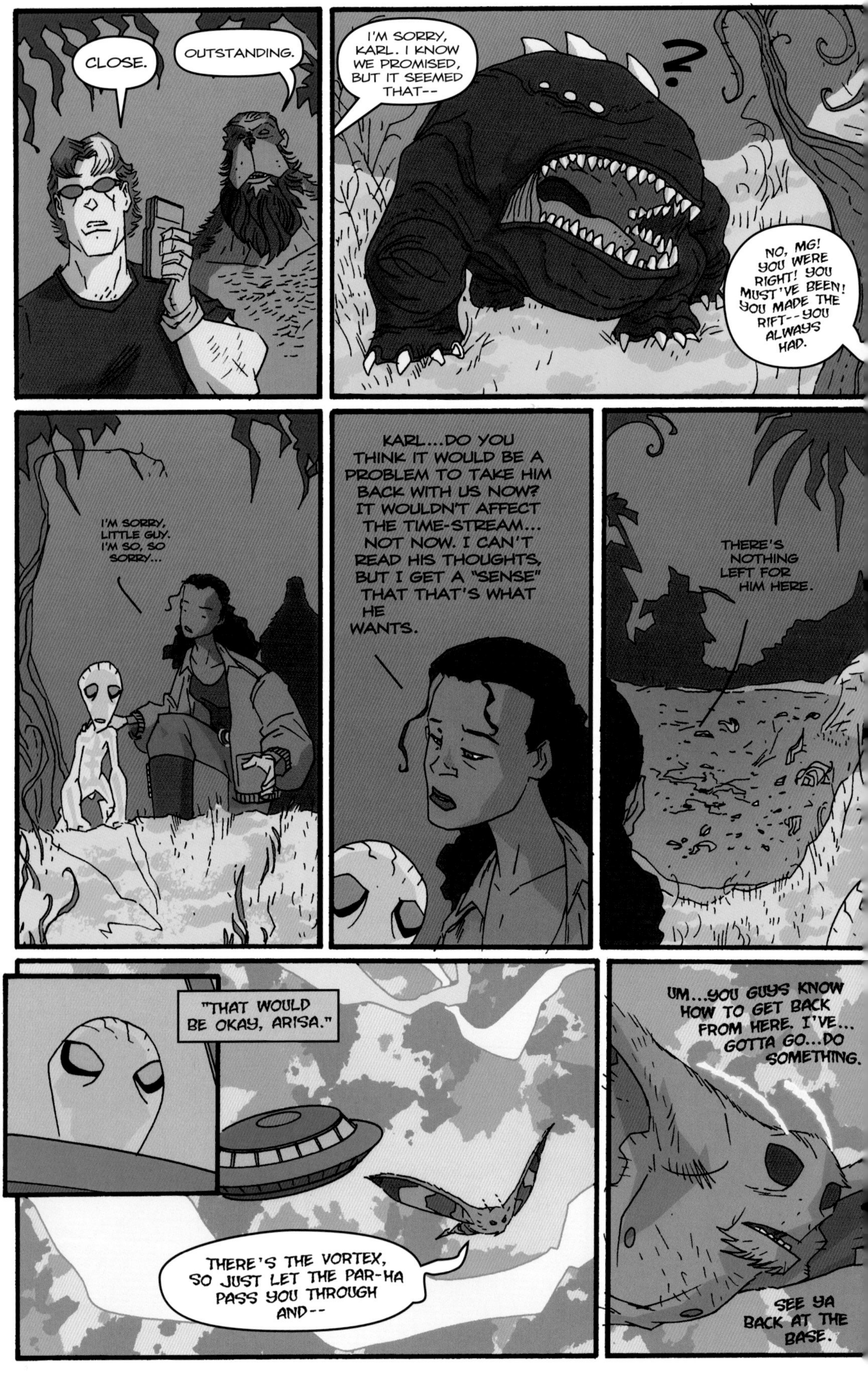

CLOSE.
OUTSTANDING.
I'M SORRY, KARL. I KNOW WE PROMISED, BUT IT SEEMED THAT--
?
NO, MG! YOU WERE RIGHT! YOU MUST'VE BEEN! YOU MADE THE RIFT--YOU ALWAYS HAD.
I'M SORRY, LITTLE GUY. I'M SO, SO SORRY...
KARL...DO YOU THINK IT WOULD BE A PROBLEM TO TAKE HIM BACK WITH US NOW? IT WOULDN'T AFFECT THE TIME-STREAM... NOT NOW. I CAN'T READ HIS THOUGHTS, BUT I GET A "SENSE" THAT THAT'S WHAT HE WANTS.
THERE'S NOTHING LEFT FOR HIM HERE.
"THAT WOULD BE OKAY, ARISA."
THERE'S THE VORTEX, SO JUST LET THE PAR-HA PASS YOU THROUGH AND--
UM...YOU GUYS KNOW HOW TO GET BACK FROM HERE. I'VE... GOTTA GO...DO SOMETHING.
SEE YA BACK AT THE BASE.

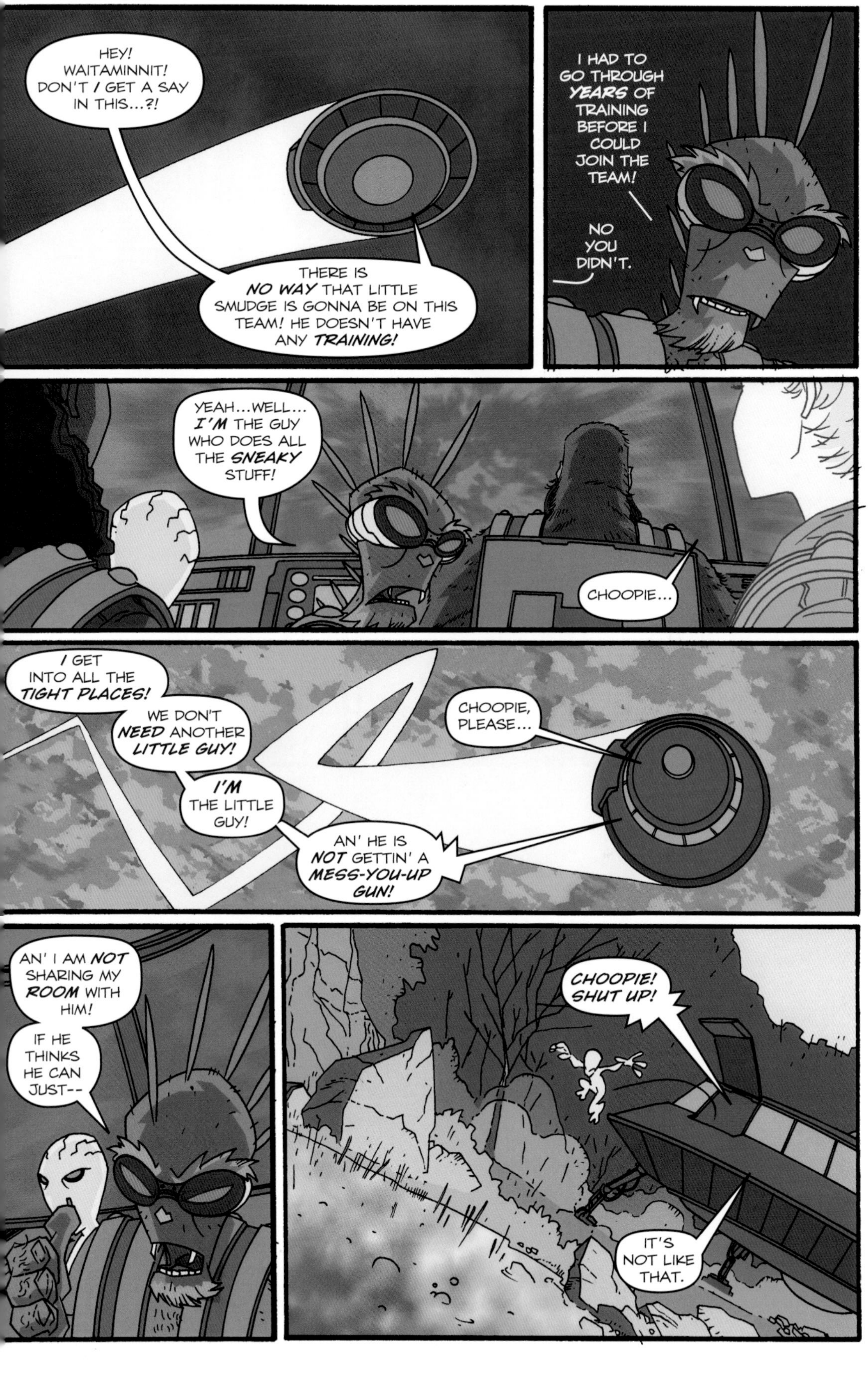
HEY! WAITAMINNIT! DON'T I GET A SAY IN THIS...?!
THERE IS NO WAY THAT LITTLE SMUDGE IS GONNA BE ON THIS TEAM! HE DOESN'T HAVE ANY TRAINING!
I HAD TO GO THROUGH YEARS OF TRAINING BEFORE I COULD JOIN THE TEAM!
NO YOU DIDN'T.
YEAH...WELL... I'M THE GUY WHO DOES ALL THE SNEAKY STUFF!
CHOOPIE...
I GET INTO ALL THE TIGHT PLACES!
WE DON'T NEED ANOTHER LITTLE GUY!
I'M THE LITTLE GUY!
CHOOPIE, PLEASE...
AN' HE IS NOT GETTIN' A MESS-YOU-UP GUN!
AN' I AM NOT SHARING MY ROOM WITH HIM!
IF HE THINKS HE CAN JUST--
CHOOPIE! SHUT UP!
IT'S NOT LIKE THAT.

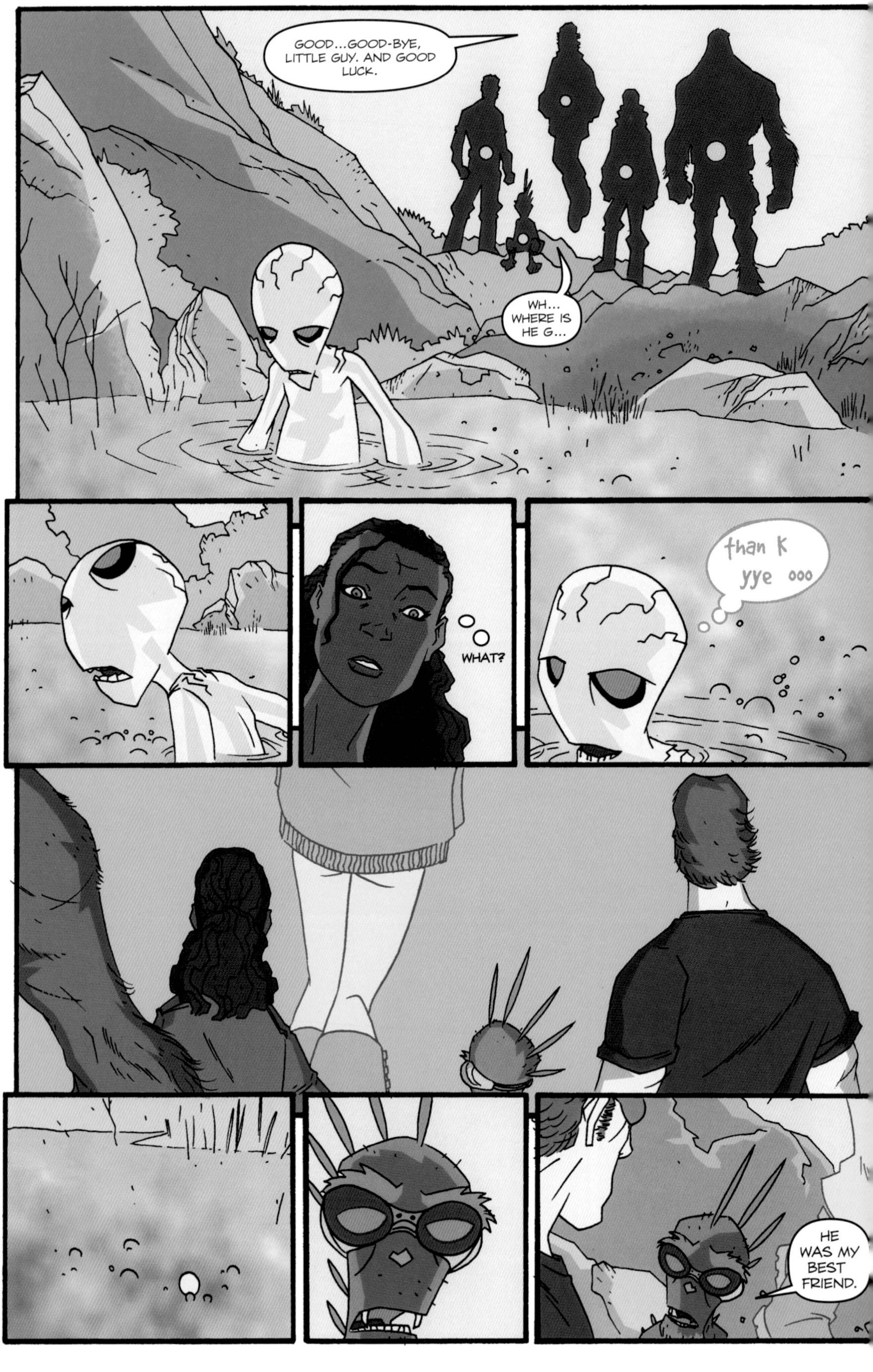
GOOD...GOOD-BYE, LITTLE GUY. AND GOOD LUCK.
WH... WHERE IS HE G...
WHAT?
than k yye ooo
HE WAS MY BEST FRIEND.

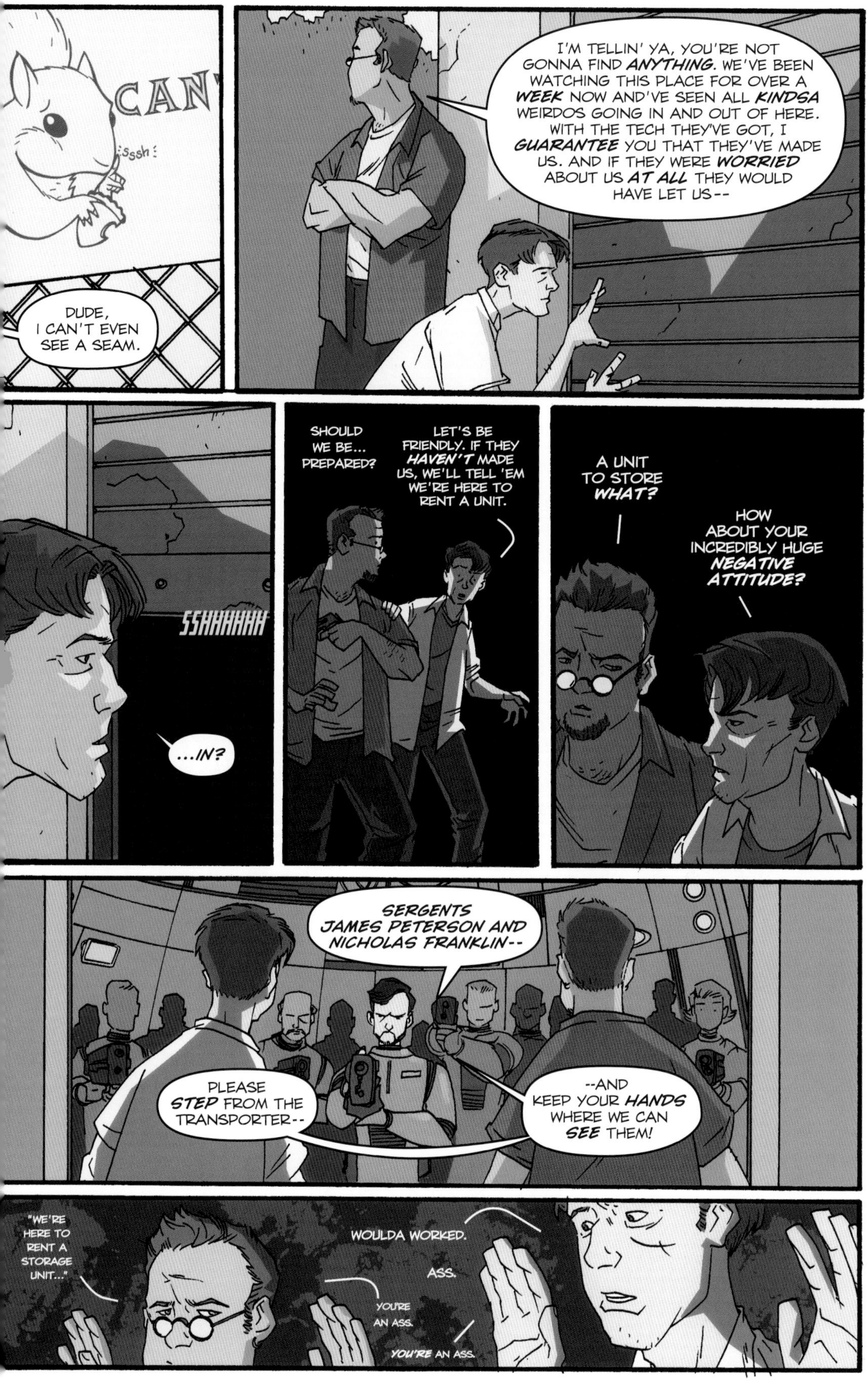
CAN'
:ssh:
I'M TELLIN' YA, YOU'RE NOT GONNA FIND ANYTHING. WE'VE BEEN WATCHING THIS PLACE FOR OVER A WEEK NOW AND'VE SEEN ALL KINDSA WEIRDOS GOING IN AND OUT OF HERE. WITH THE TECH THEY'VE GOT, I GUARANTEE YOU THAT THEY'VE MADE US. AND IF THEY WERE WORRIED ABOUT US AT ALL THEY WOULD HAVE LET US--
DUDE, I CAN'T EVEN SEE A SEAM.
SSHHHHHH
...IN?
SHOULD WE BE... PREPARED?
LET'S BE FRIENDLY. IF THEY HAVEN'T MADE US, WE'LL TELL 'EM WE'RE HERE TO RENT A UNIT.
A UNIT TO STORE WHAT?
HOW ABOUT YOUR INCREDIBLY HUGE NEGATIVE ATTITUDE?
SERGENTS JAMES PETERSON AND NICHOLAS FRANKLIN--
PLEASE STEP FROM THE TRANSPORTER--
--AND KEEP YOUR HANDS WHERE WE CAN SEE THEM!
"WE'RE HERE TO RENT A STORAGE UNIT..."
WOULDA WORKED.
ASS.
YOU'RE AN ASS.
YOU'RE AN ASS.

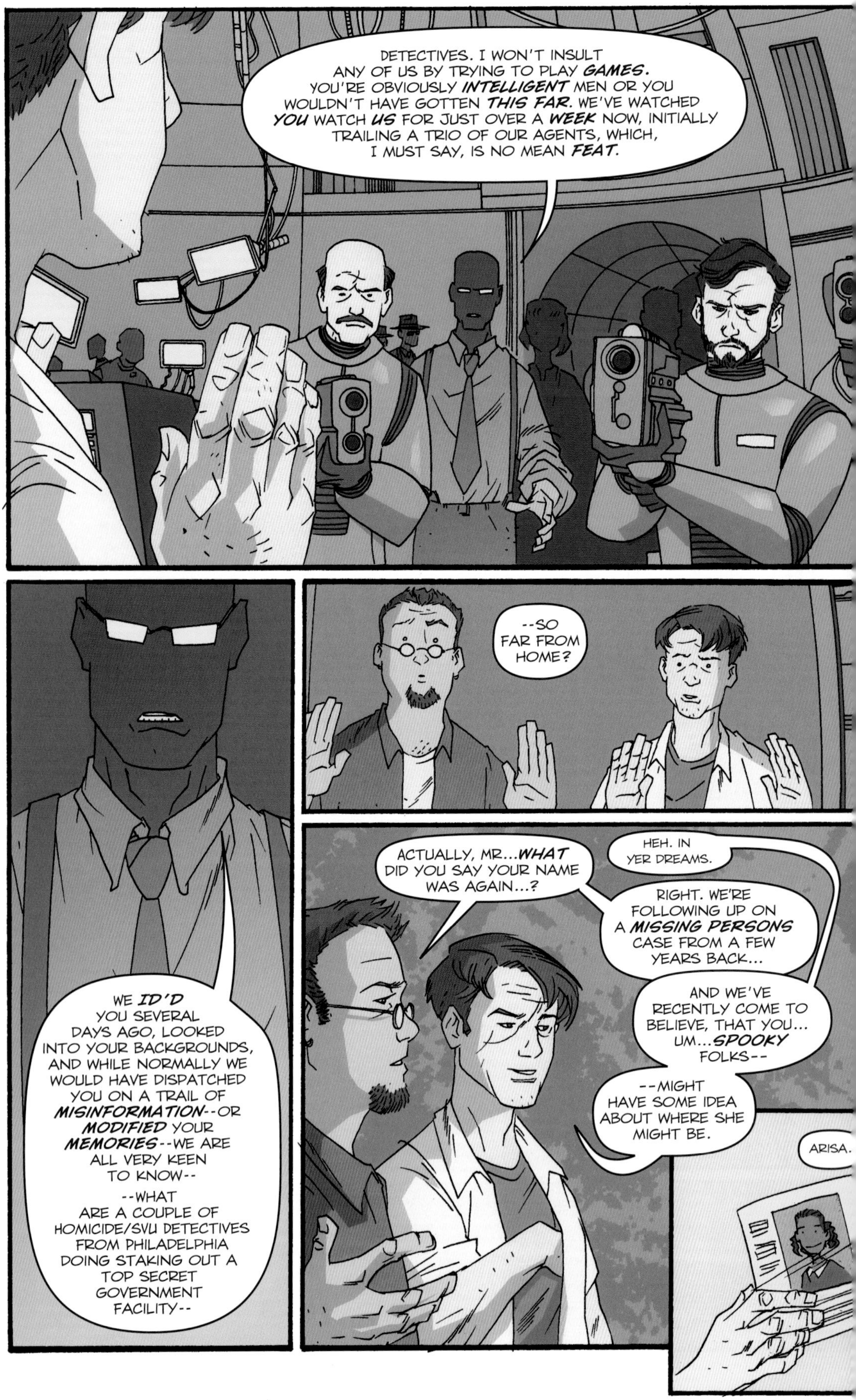
DETECTIVES. I WON'T INSULT ANY OF US BY TRYING TO PLAY *GAMES.* YOU'RE OBVIOUSLY *INTELLIGENT* MEN OR YOU WOULDN'T HAVE GOTTEN *THIS FAR.* WE'VE WATCHED *YOU* WATCH *US* FOR JUST OVER A *WEEK* NOW, INITIALLY TRAILING A TRIO OF OUR AGENTS, WHICH, I MUST SAY, IS NO MEAN *FEAT.*
WE *ID'D* YOU SEVERAL DAYS AGO, LOOKED INTO YOUR BACKGROUNDS, AND WHILE NORMALLY WE WOULD HAVE DISPATCHED YOU ON A TRAIL OF *MISINFORMATION*--OR *MODIFIED* YOUR *MEMORIES*--WE ARE ALL VERY KEEN TO KNOW--
--WHAT ARE A COUPLE OF HOMICIDE/SVU DETECTIVES FROM PHILADELPHIA DOING STAKING OUT A TOP SECRET GOVERNMENT FACILITY--
--SO FAR FROM HOME?
ACTUALLY, MR...*WHAT* DID YOU SAY YOUR NAME WAS AGAIN...?
HEH. IN YER DREAMS.
RIGHT. WE'RE FOLLOWING UP ON A *MISSING PERSONS* CASE FROM A FEW YEARS BACK...
AND WE'VE RECENTLY COME TO BELIEVE, THAT YOU... UM...*SPOOKY* FOLKS--
--MIGHT HAVE SOME IDEA ABOUT WHERE SHE MIGHT BE.
ARISA.

SORRY.

IIIII'M GONNA TAKE THAT AS A *"YES."*

OH, ABSOLUTELY.

sweeet sweeet sweeet sweeet sweeer sweee swe

**INTEGRITY BREACH!
INTEGRITY BREACH!**

SIR, SHOULD I—

AWAIT MY ORDER, MULCAHY.

FWINK!

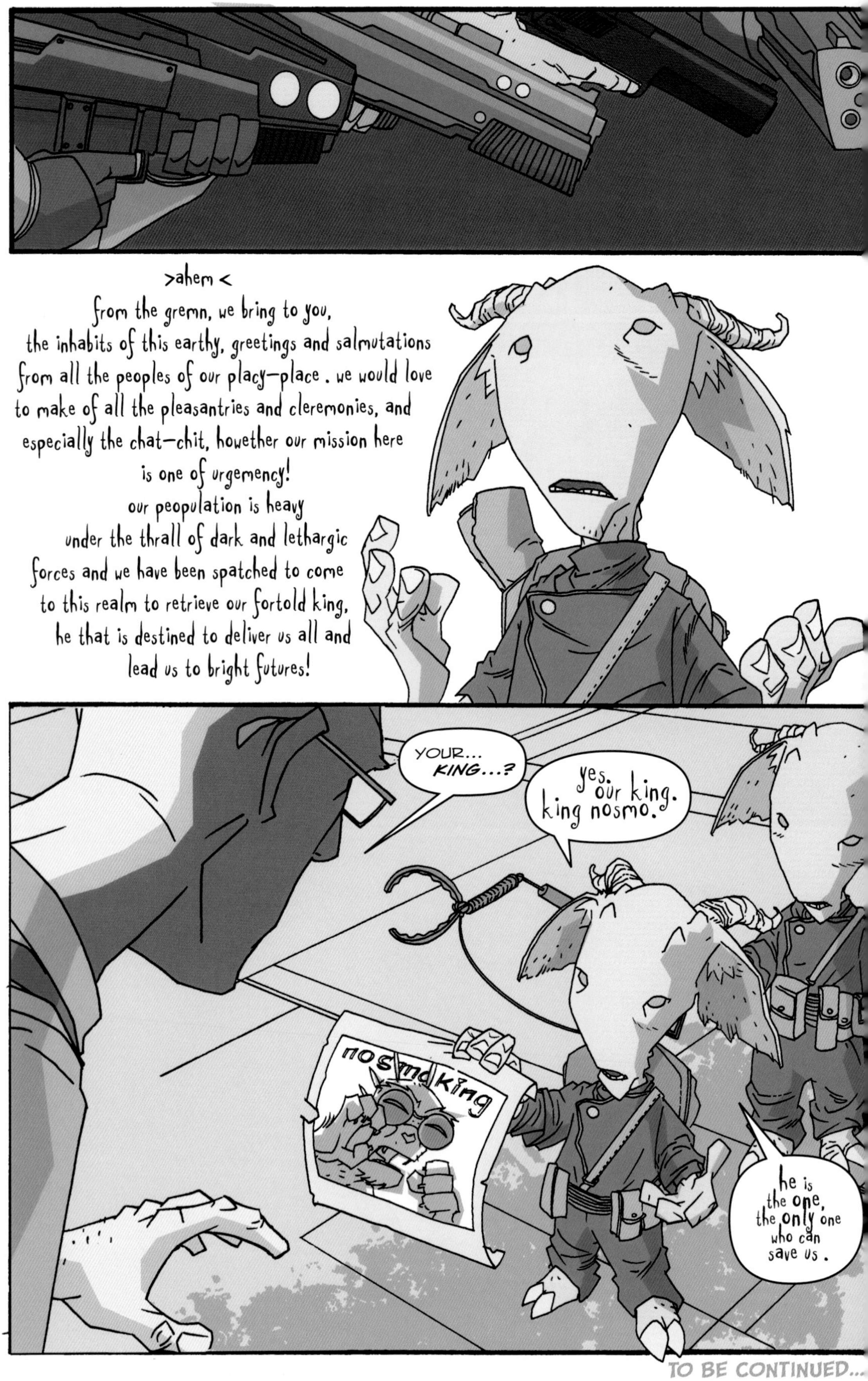
>ahem <
from the gremn, we bring to you, the inhabits of this earthy, greetings and salmutations from all the peoples of our placy-place . we would love to make of all the pleasantries and cleremonies, and especially the chat-chit, howether our mission here is one of urgemency! our peopulation is heavy under the thrall of dark and lethargic forces and we have been spatched to come to this realm to retrieve our fortold king, he that is destined to deliver us all and lead us to bright futures!
YOUR... KING...?
yes. our king. king nosmo.
he is the one, the only one who can save us .
TO BE CONTINUED...

GALLERY

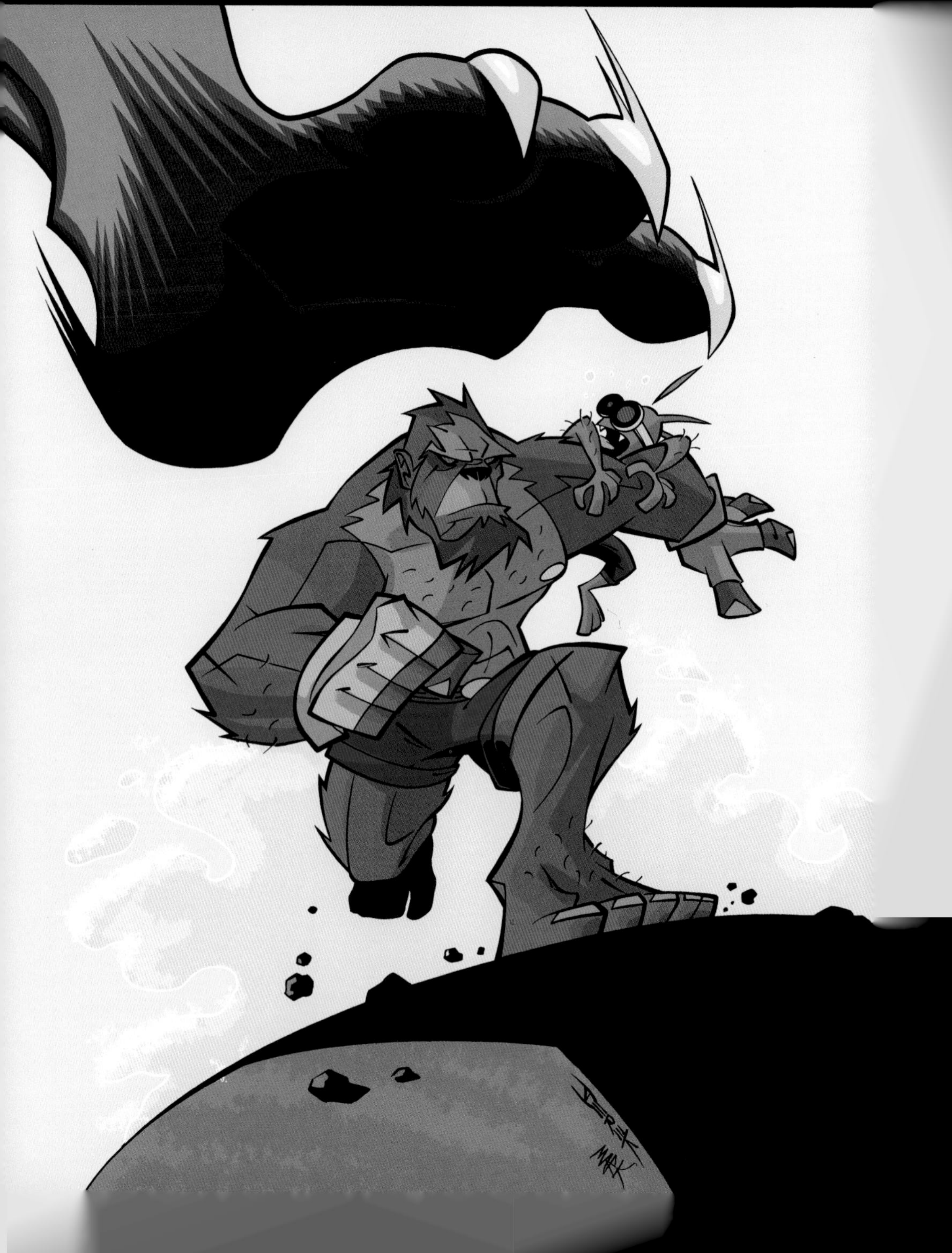

KELLY YATES

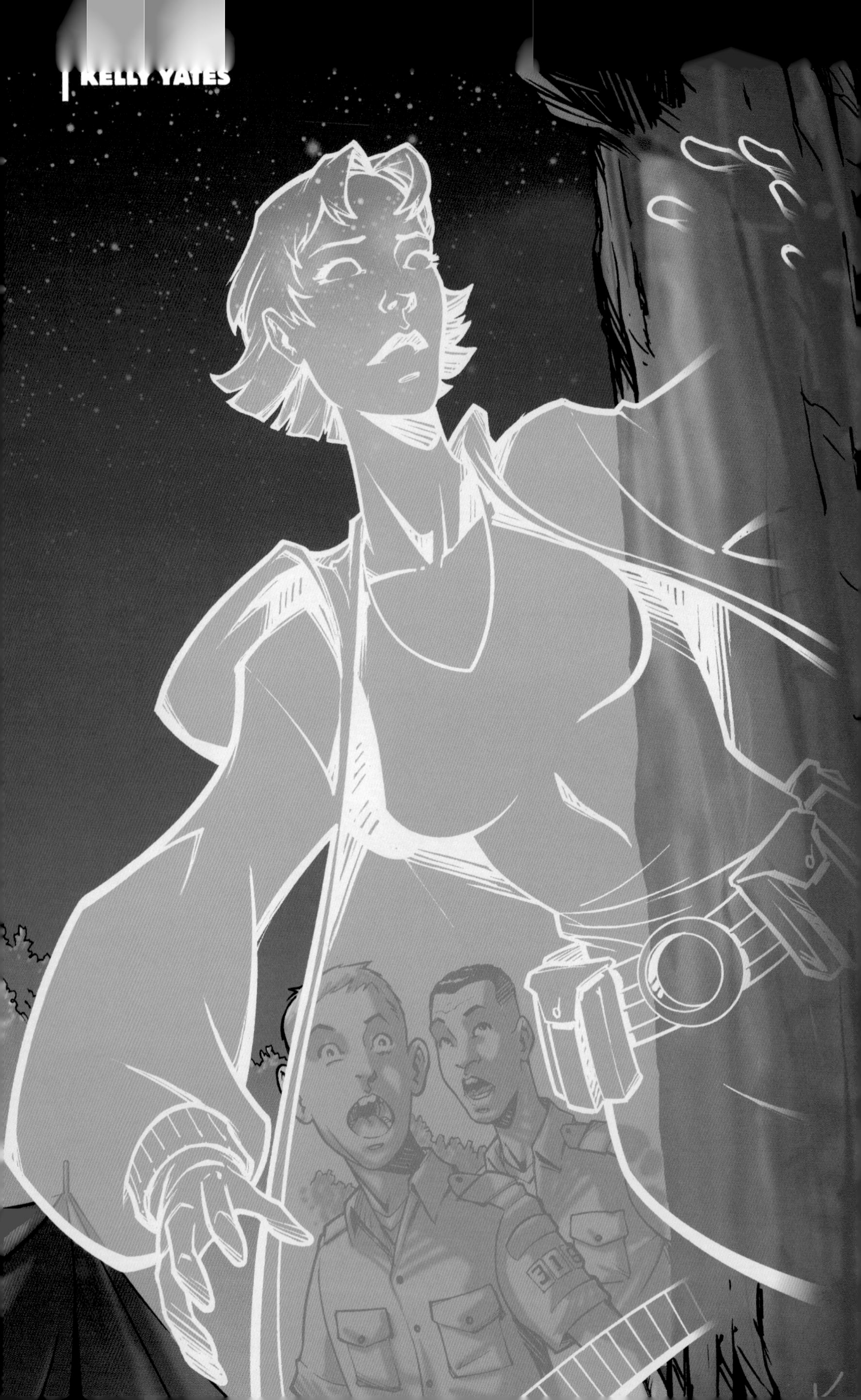

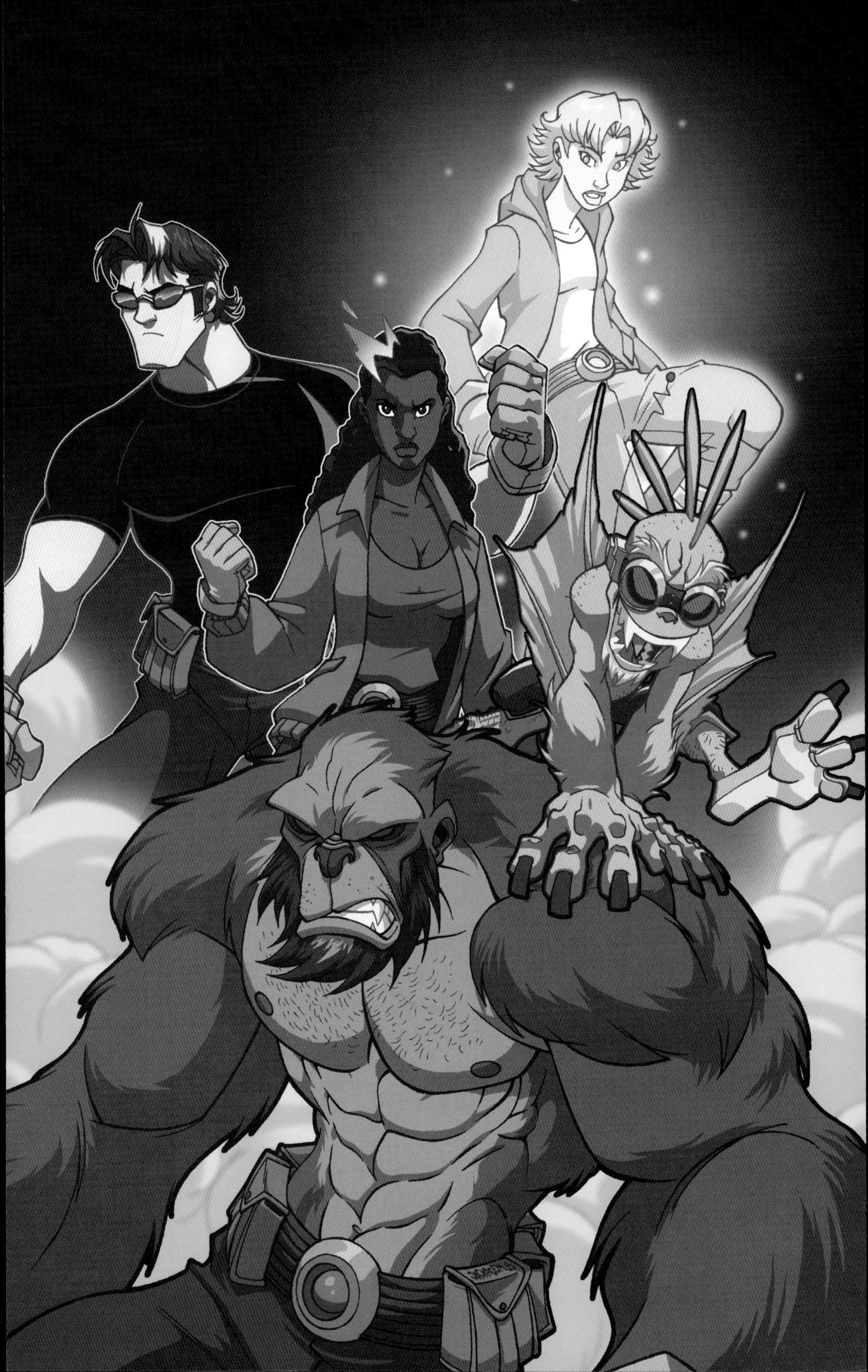

JONBOY MEYERS
COLORS BY SCOTT KESTER

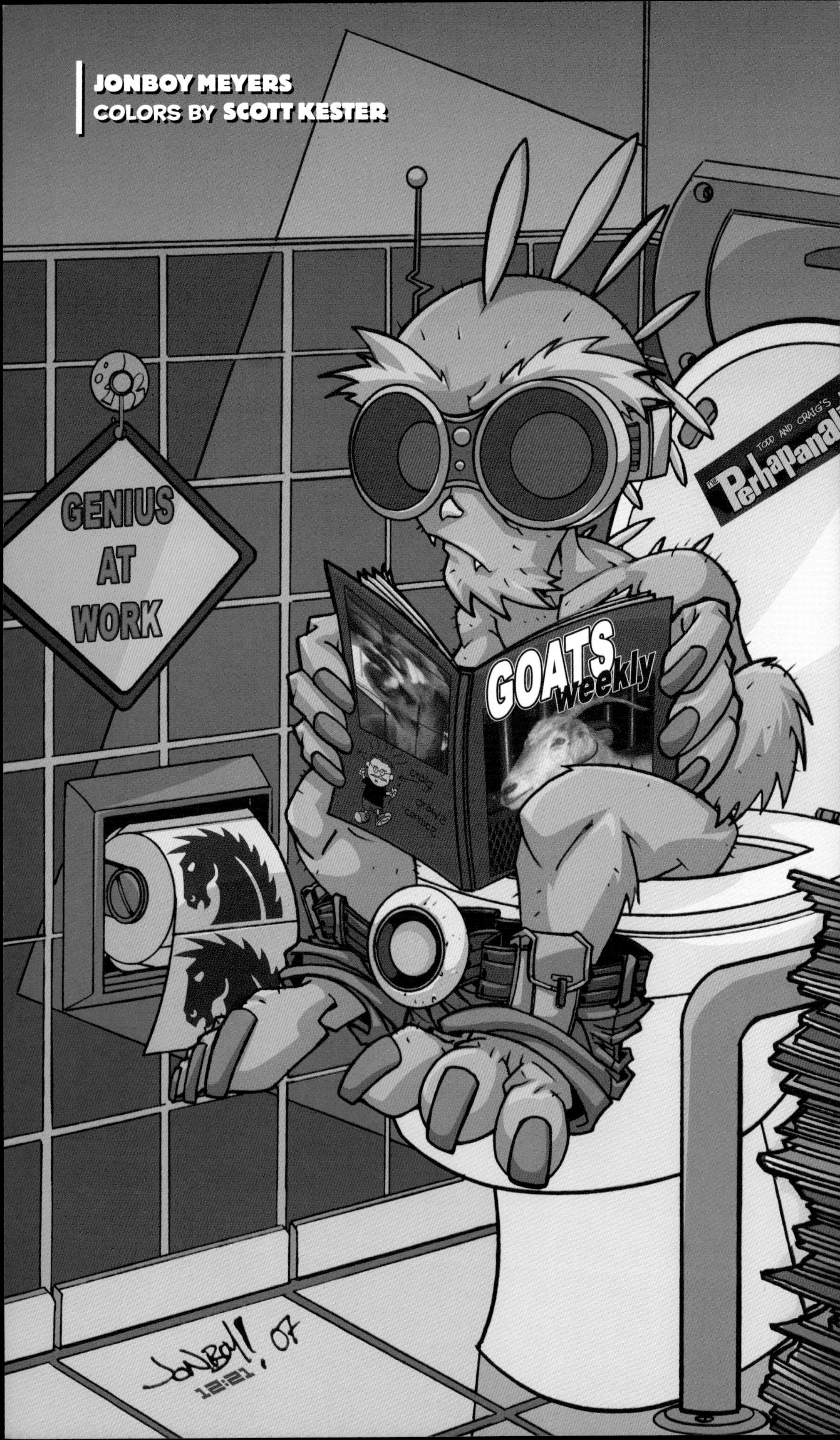
GENIUS AT WORK
GOATS weekly
craig
craig's comics
TODD AND CRAIG'S
THE
JONBOY! '07
12:21

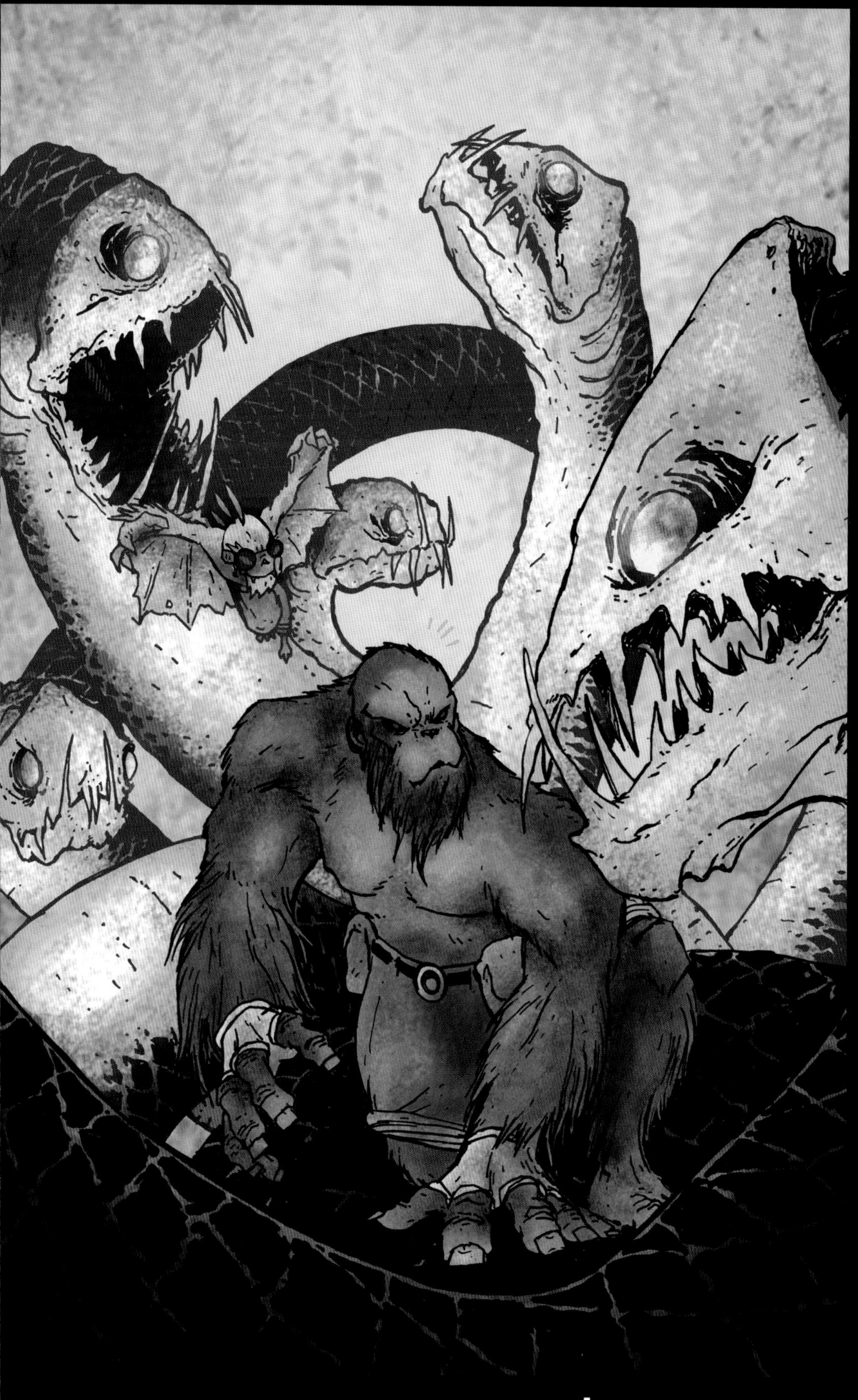

DAVID PETERSEN

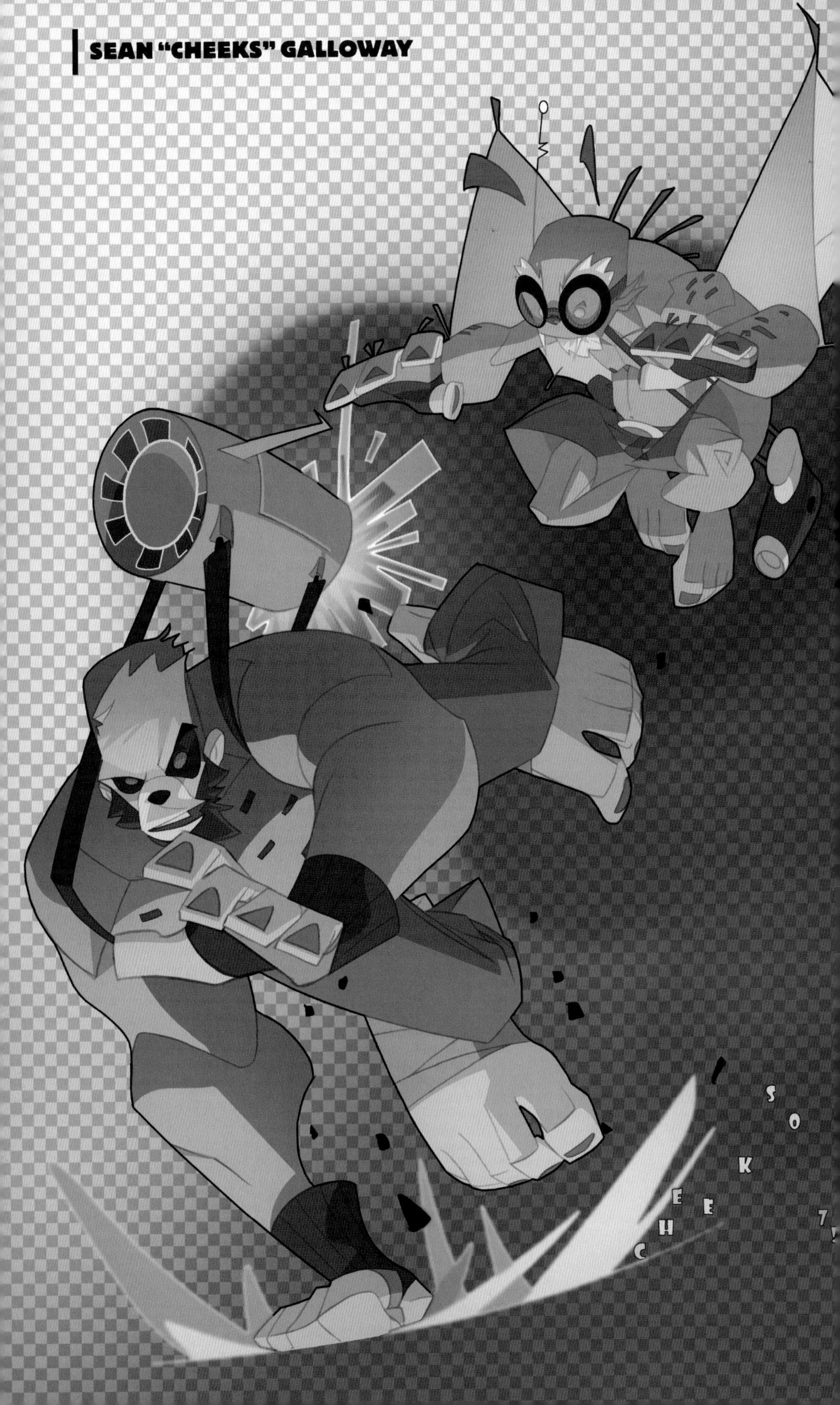
CHEEKS O7!

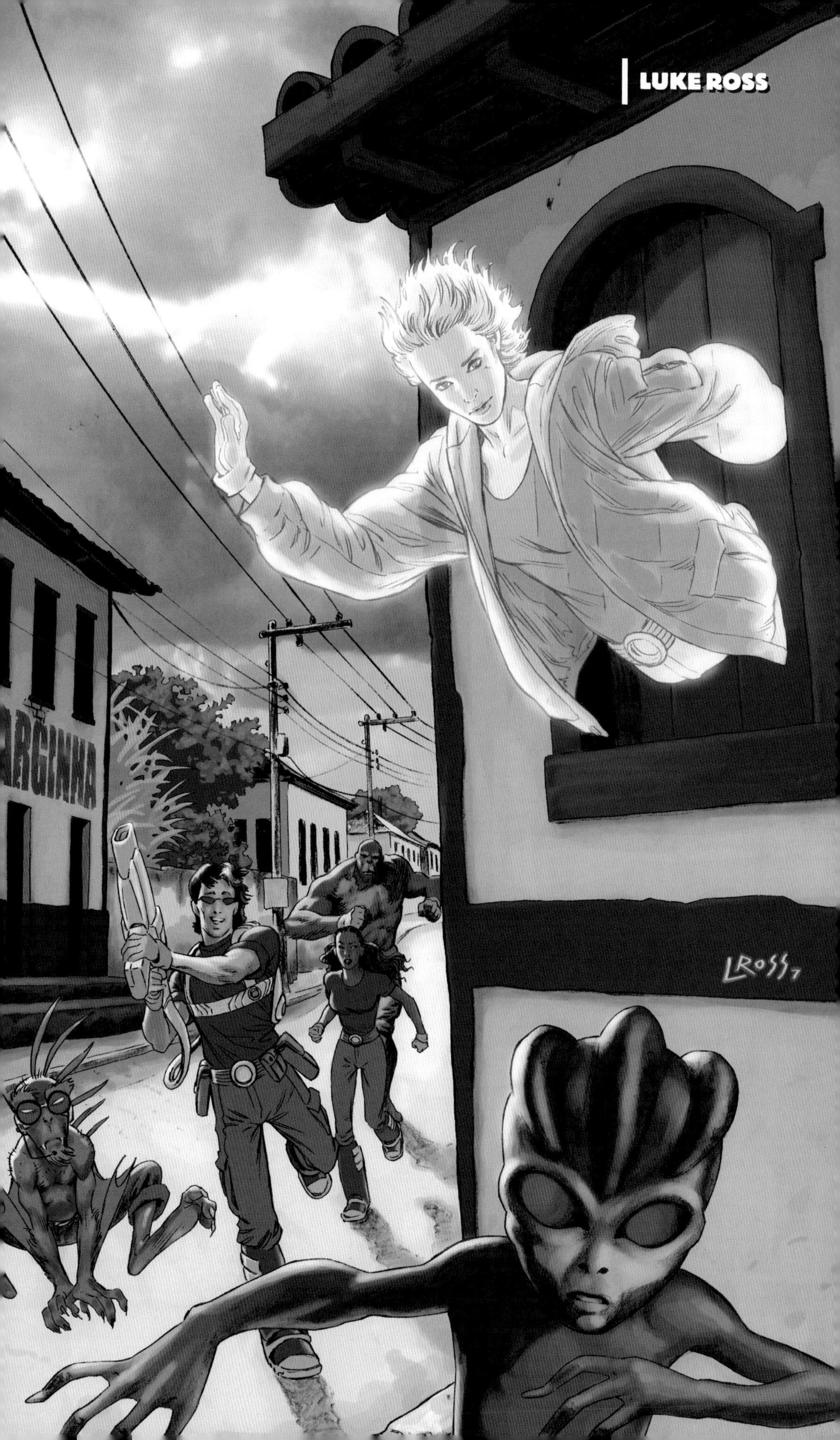
ARGINHA
LROSS 7

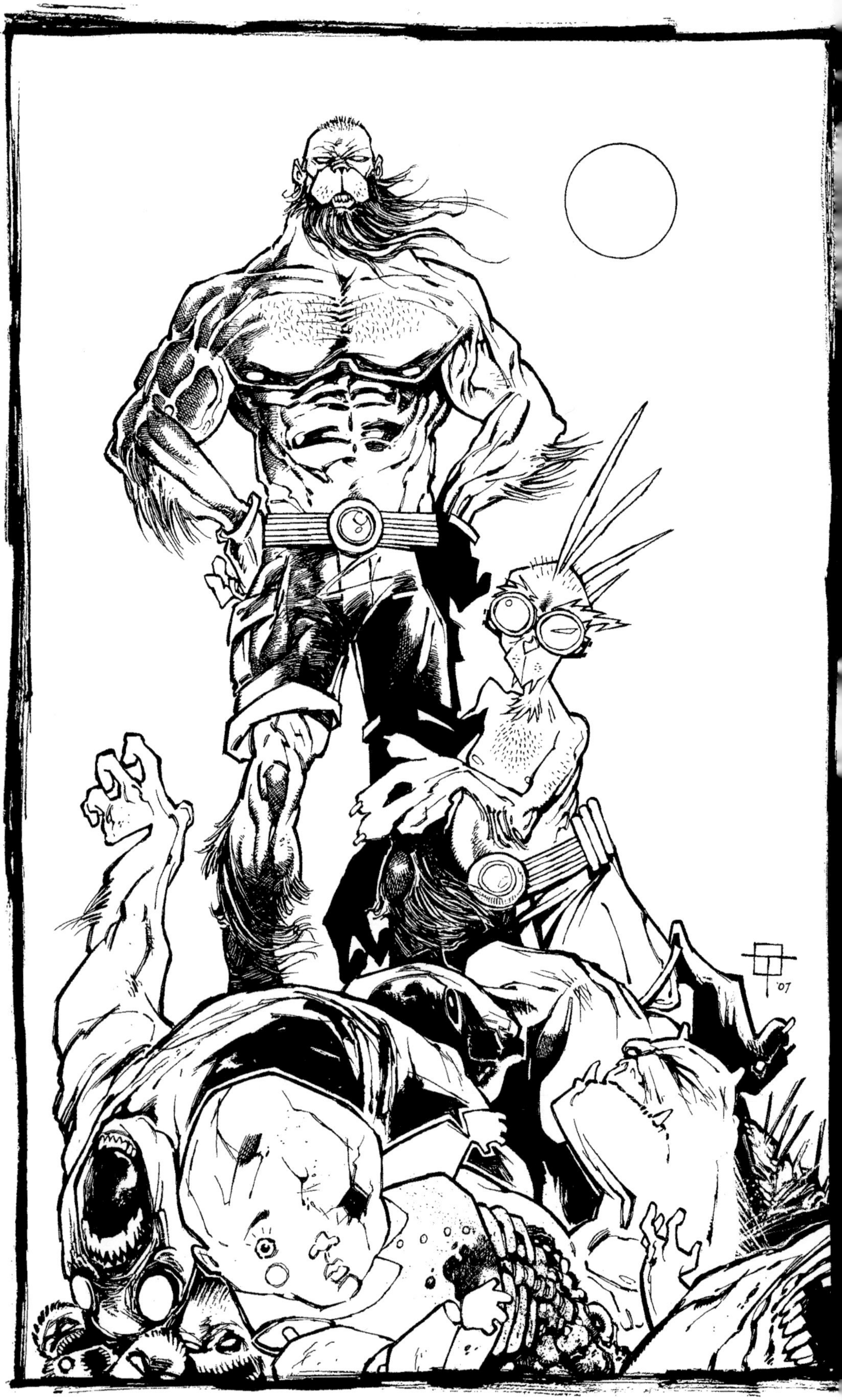
'07

TED MCKEEVER

ANDY KUHN
COLORS BY SEAN "CHEEKS" GALLOWAY

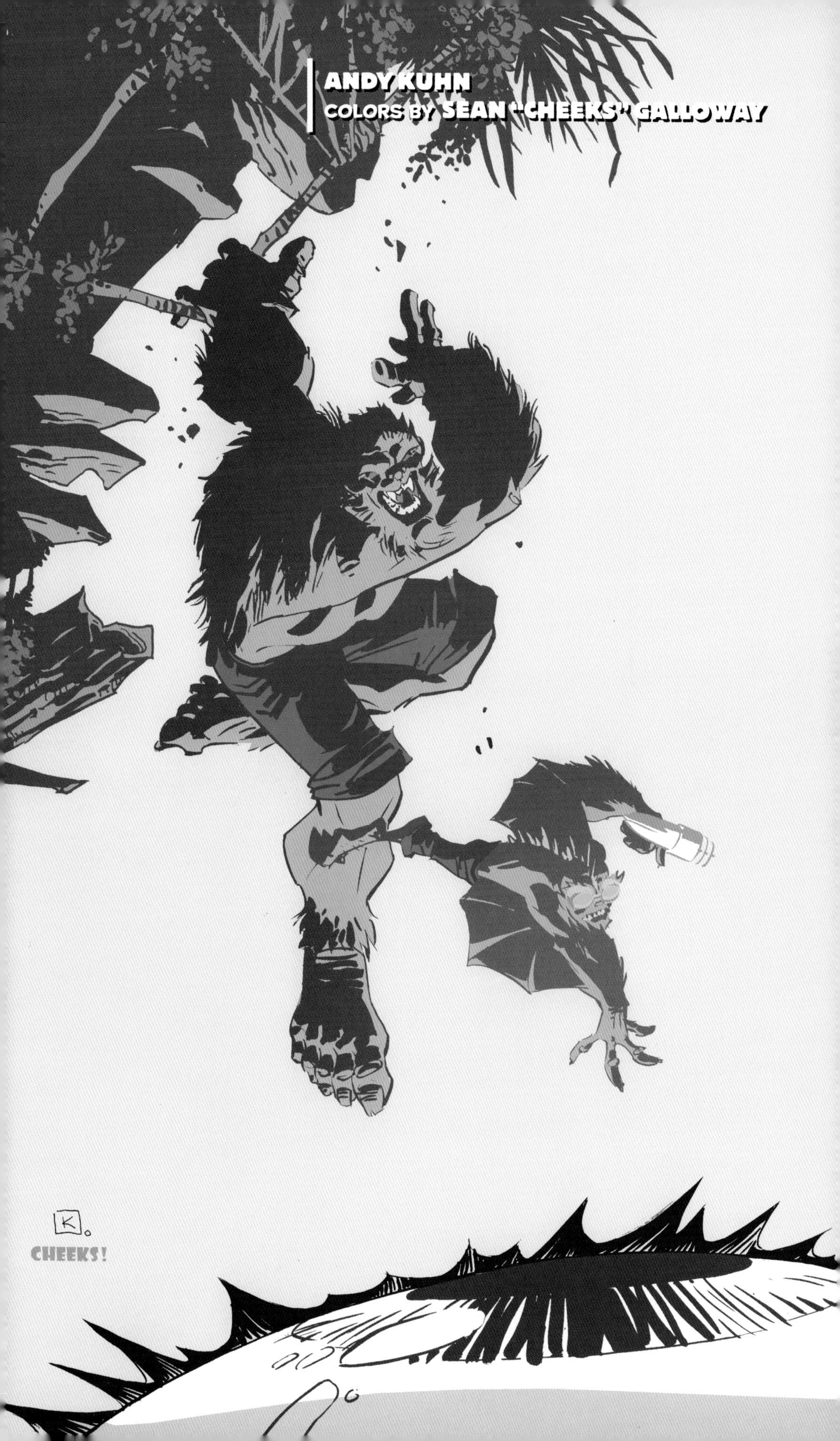
K
CHEEKS!

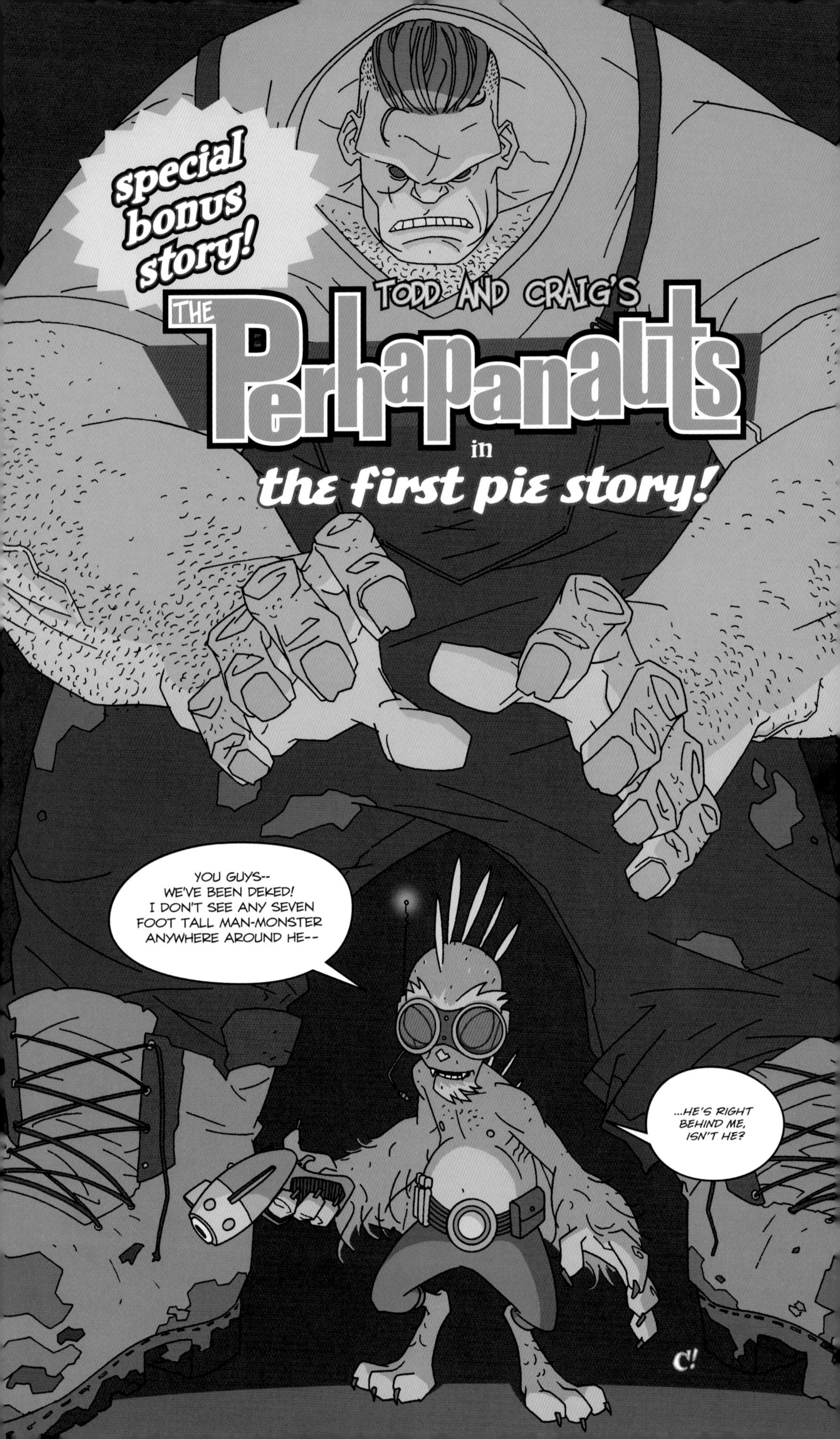
special bonus story!
TODD AND CRAIG'S
THE Perhapanauts
in
the first pie story!
YOU GUYS-- WE'VE BEEN DEKED! I DON'T SEE ANY SEVEN FOOT TALL MAN-MONSTER ANYWHERE AROUND HE--
...HE'S RIGHT BEHIND ME, ISN'T HE?
C!

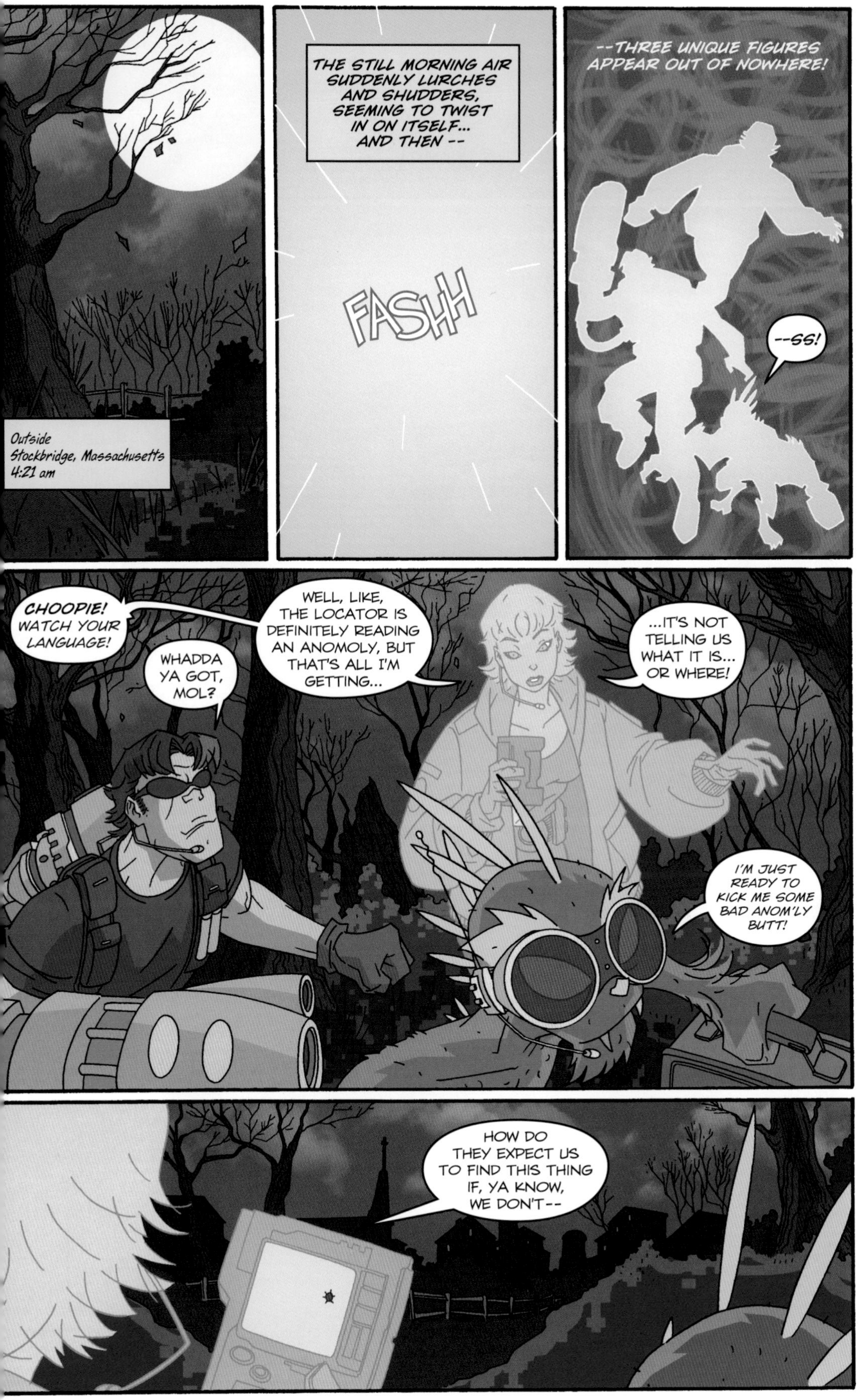
Outside
Stockbridge, Massachusetts
4:21 am
THE STILL MORNING AIR SUDDENLY LURCHES AND SHUDDERS, SEEMING TO TWIST IN ON ITSELF... AND THEN --
FASHH
--THREE UNIQUE FIGURES APPEAR OUT OF NOWHERE!
--SS!
CHOOPIE! WATCH YOUR LANGUAGE!
WHADDA YA GOT, MOL?
WELL, LIKE, THE LOCATOR IS DEFINITELY READING AN ANOMOLY, BUT THAT'S ALL I'M GETTING...
...IT'S NOT TELLING US WHAT IT IS... OR WHERE!
I'M JUST READY TO KICK ME SOME BAD ANOM'LY BUTT!
HOW DO THEY EXPECT US TO FIND THIS THING IF, YA KNOW, WE DON'T--

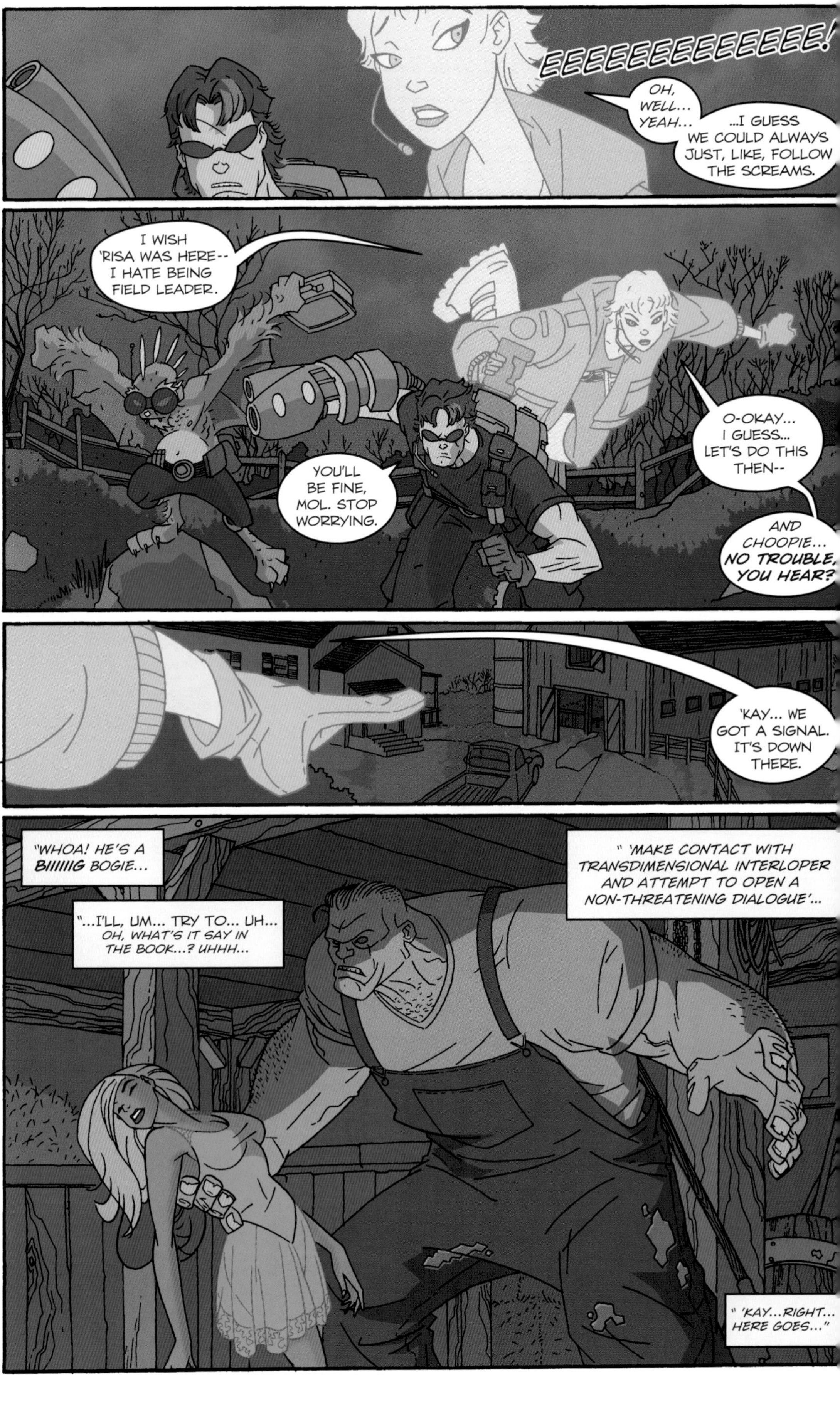
EEEEEEEEEEEEEE!
OH, WELL... YEAH...
...I GUESS WE COULD ALWAYS JUST, LIKE, FOLLOW THE SCREAMS.
I WISH 'RISA WAS HERE-- I HATE BEING FIELD LEADER.
YOU'LL BE FINE, MOL. STOP WORRYING.
O-OKAY... I GUESS... LET'S DO THIS THEN--
AND CHOOPIE... NO TROUBLE, YOU HEAR?
'KAY... WE GOT A SIGNAL. IT'S DOWN THERE.
"WHOA! HE'S A BIIIIIG BOGIE...
"...I'LL, UM... TRY TO... UH... OH, WHAT'S IT SAY IN THE BOOK...? UHHH...
" 'MAKE CONTACT WITH TRANSDIMENSIONAL INTERLOPER AND ATTEMPT TO OPEN A NON-THREATENING DIALOGUE'...
" 'KAY...RIGHT... HERE GOES..."

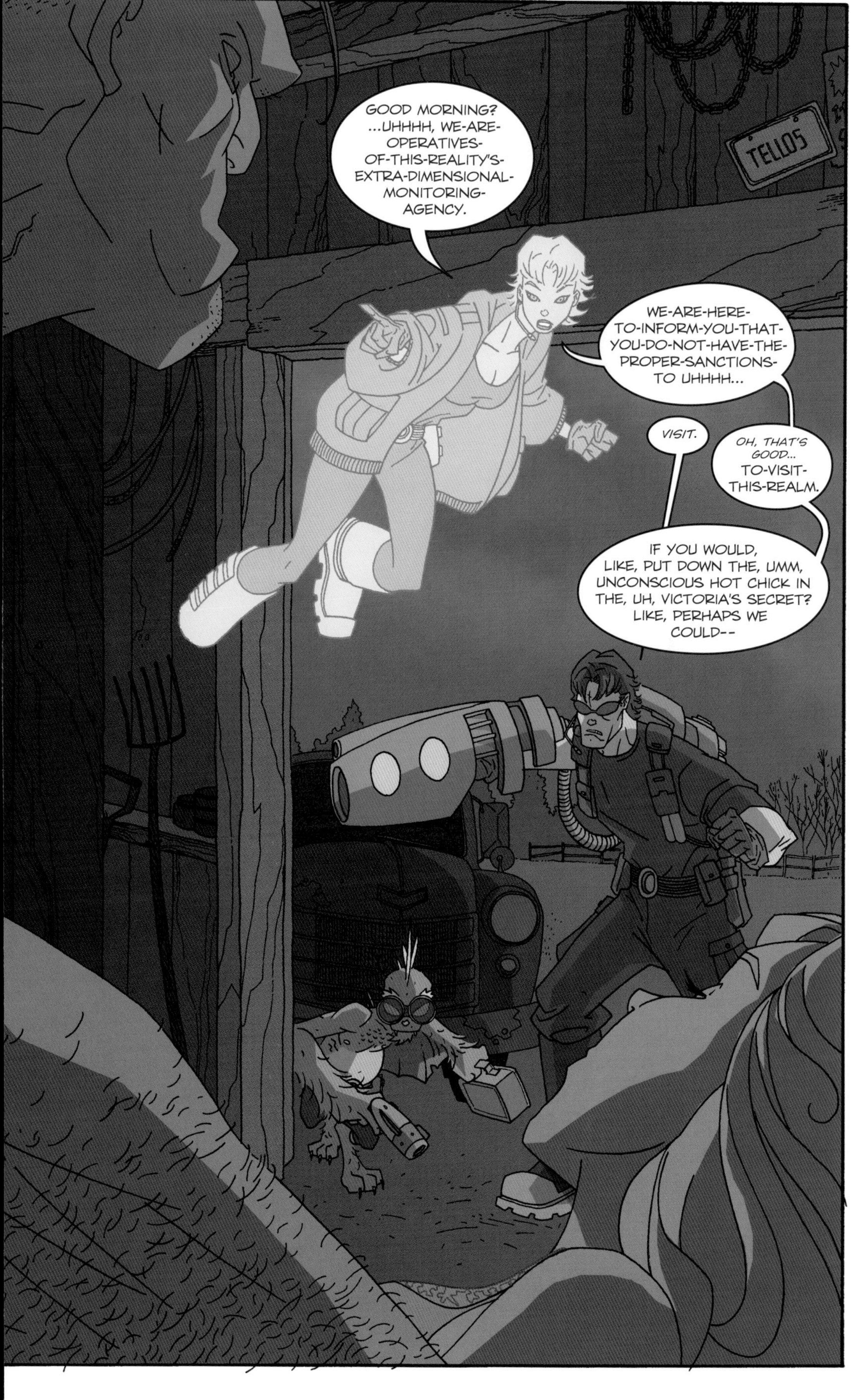
TELLOS
GOOD MORNING? ...UHHHH, WE-ARE-OPERATIVES-OF-THIS-REALITY'S-EXTRA-DIMENSIONAL-MONITORING-AGENCY.
WE-ARE-HERE-TO-INFORM-YOU-THAT-YOU-DO-NOT-HAVE-THE-PROPER-SANCTIONS-TO UHHHH...
VISIT.
OH, THAT'S GOOD... TO-VISIT-THIS-REALM.
IF YOU WOULD, LIKE, PUT DOWN THE, UMM, UNCONSCIOUS HOT CHICK IN THE, UH, VICTORIA'S SECRET? LIKE, PERHAPS WE COULD--

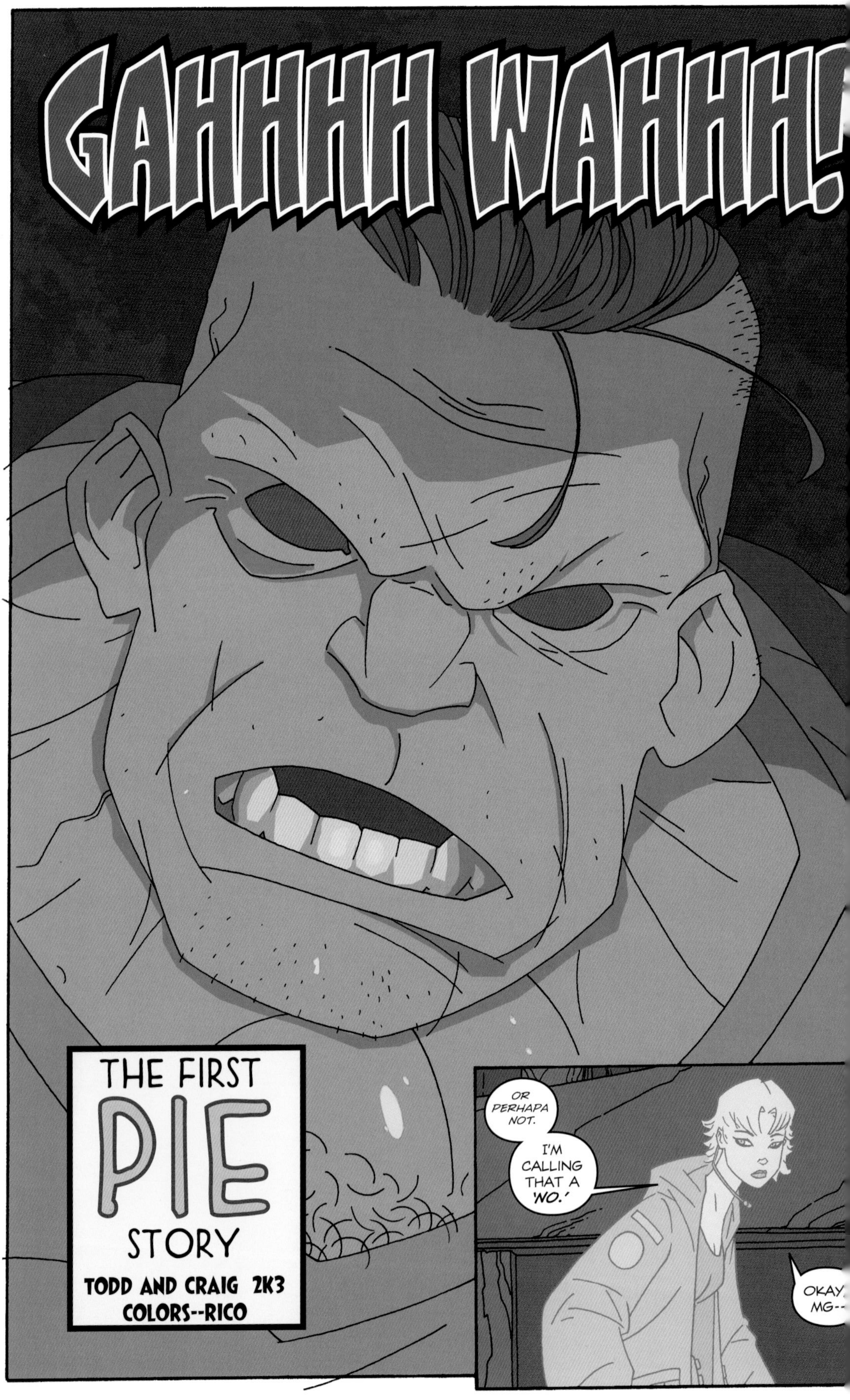
GAHHHH WAHHH!
THE FIRST PIE STORY
TODD AND CRAIG 2K3
COLORS--RICO
OR PERHAPA NOT.
I'M CALLING THAT A 'NO.'
OKAY
MG--

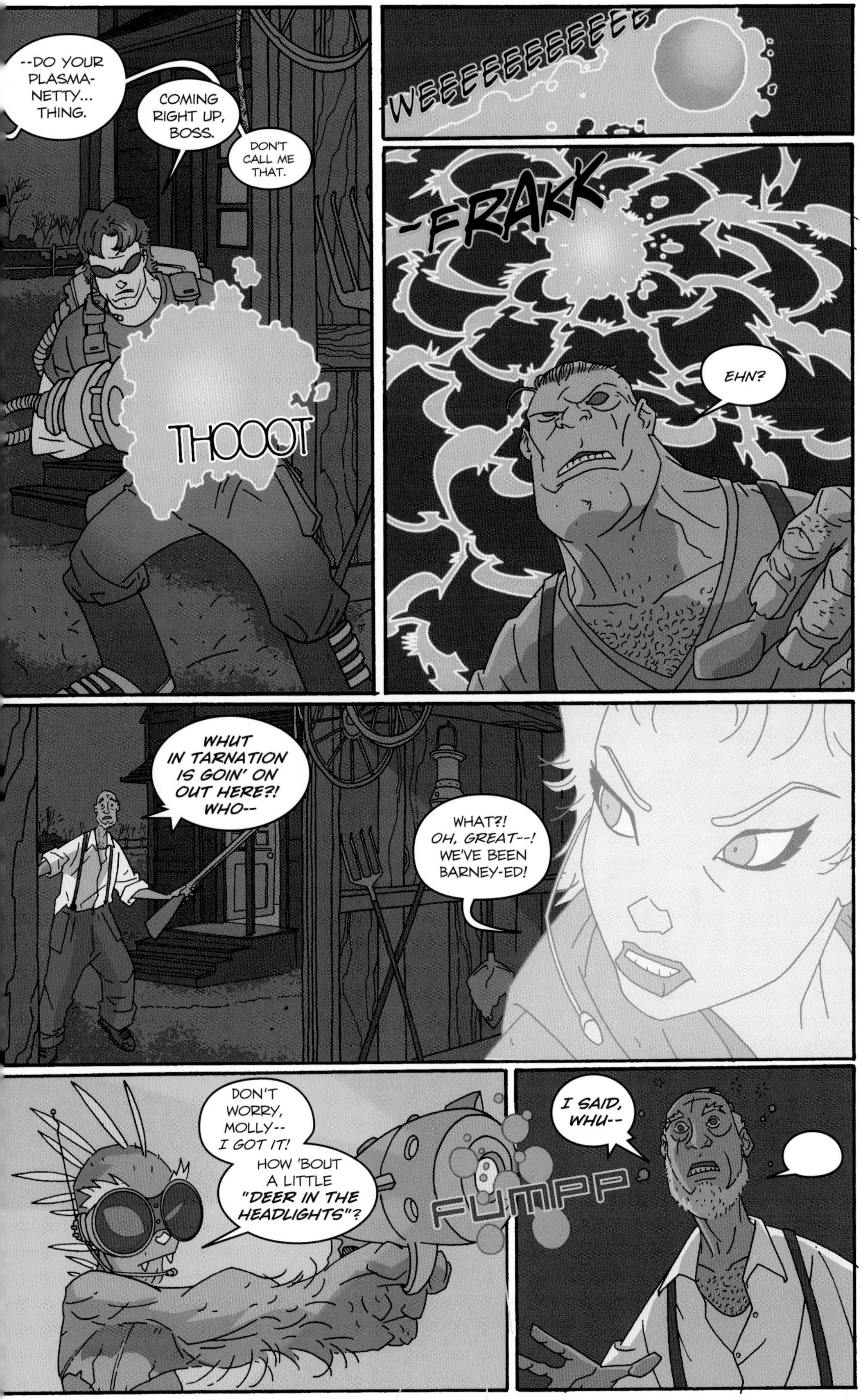

--DO YOUR PLASMA-NETTY... THING.
COMING RIGHT UP, BOSS.
DON'T CALL ME THAT.
THOOOT
WEEEEEEEEEEEEE
-FRAKK
EHN?
WHUT IN TARNATION IS GOIN' ON OUT HERE?! WHO--
WHAT?! OH, GREAT--! WE'VE BEEN BARNEY-ED!
DON'T WORRY, MOLLY-- I GOT IT!
HOW 'BOUT A LITTLE "DEER IN THE HEADLIGHTS"?
FUMPP
I SAID, WHU--

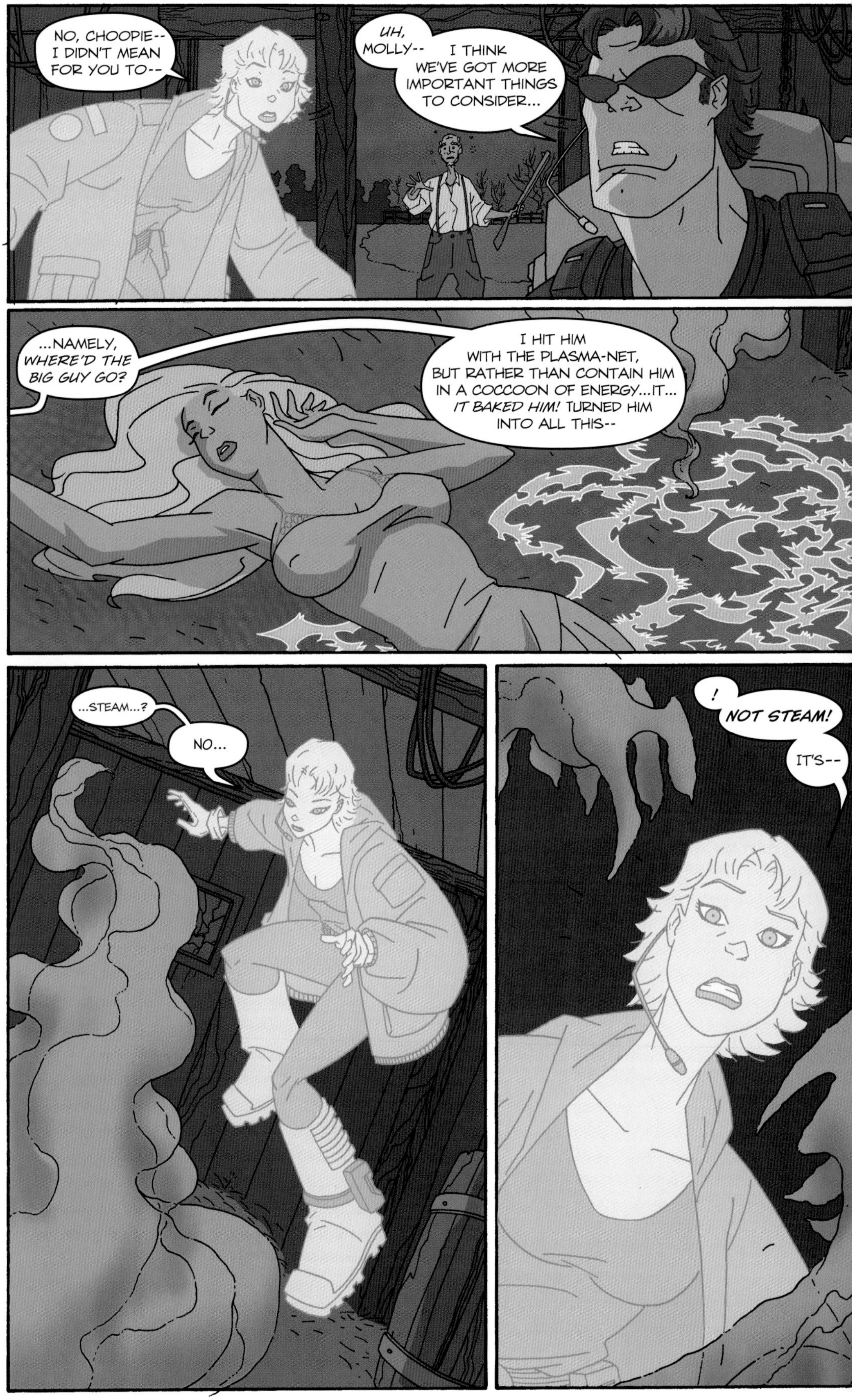
NO, CHOOPIE-- I DIDN'T MEAN FOR YOU TO--
UH, MOLLY--
I THINK WE'VE GOT MORE IMPORTANT THINGS TO CONSIDER...
...NAMELY, WHERE'D THE BIG GUY GO?
I HIT HIM WITH THE PLASMA-NET, BUT RATHER THAN CONTAIN HIM IN A COCCOON OF ENERGY...IT... IT BAKED HIM! TURNED HIM INTO ALL THIS--
...STEAM...?
NO...
!
NOT STEAM!
IT'S--

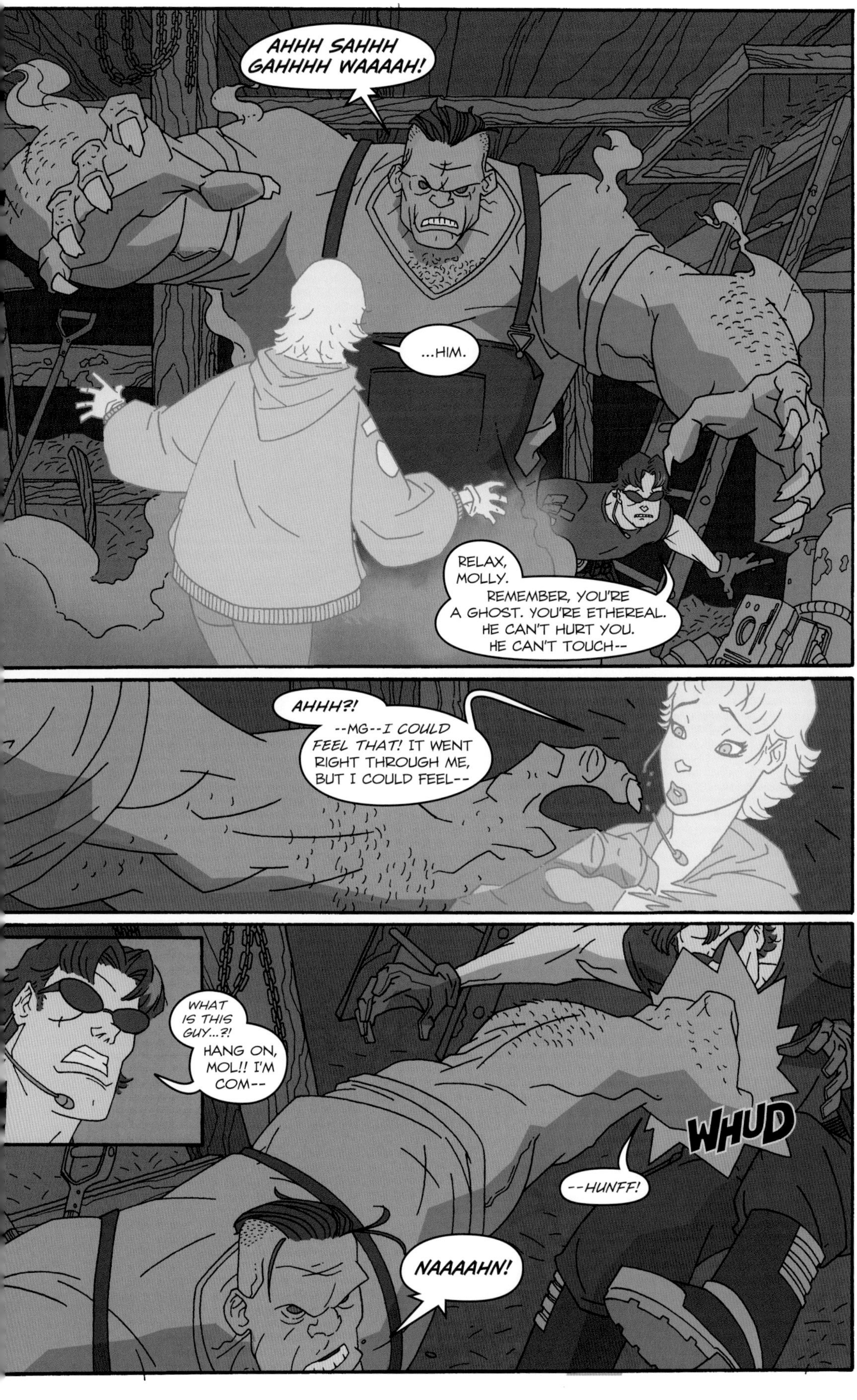
AHHH SAHHH GAHHHH WAAAAH!
...HIM.
RELAX, MOLLY. REMEMBER, YOU'RE A GHOST. YOU'RE ETHEREAL. HE CAN'T HURT YOU. HE CAN'T TOUCH--
AHHH?!
--MG--I COULD FEEL THAT! IT WENT RIGHT THROUGH ME, BUT I COULD FEEL--
WHAT IS THIS GUY...?!
HANG ON, MOL!! I'M COM--
WHUD
--HUNFF!
NAAAAHN!

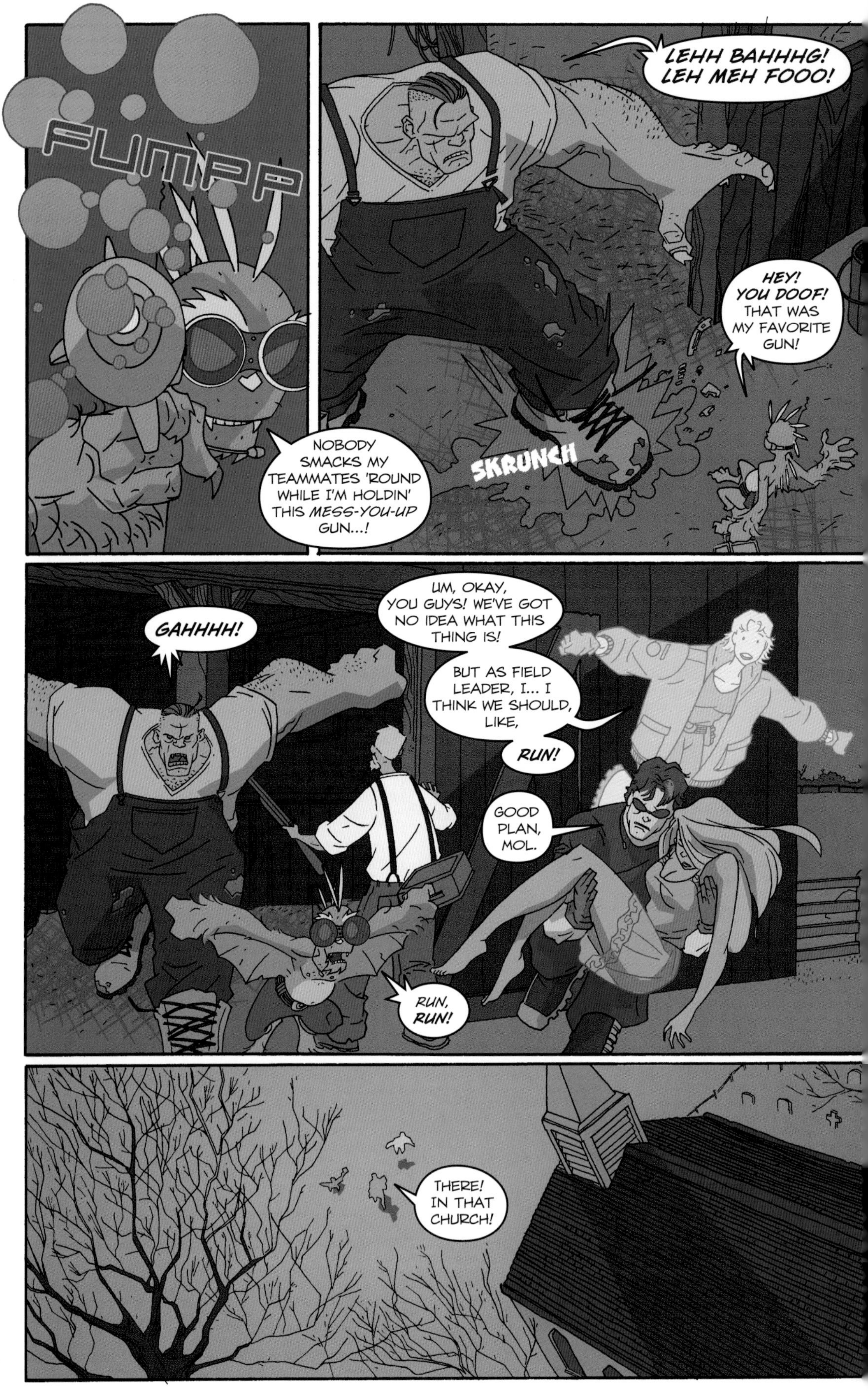
FUMPP
LEHH BAHHHG! LEH MEH FOOO!
NOBODY SMACKS MY TEAMMATES 'ROUND WHILE I'M HOLDIN' THIS *MESS-YOU-UP* GUN...!
SKRUNCH
HEY! YOU DOOF! THAT WAS MY FAVORITE GUN!
GAHHHH!
UM, OKAY, YOU GUYS! WE'VE GOT NO IDEA WHAT THIS THING IS!
BUT AS FIELD LEADER, I... I THINK WE SHOULD, LIKE,
RUN!
GOOD PLAN, MOL.
RUN, RUN!
THERE! IN THAT CHURCH!

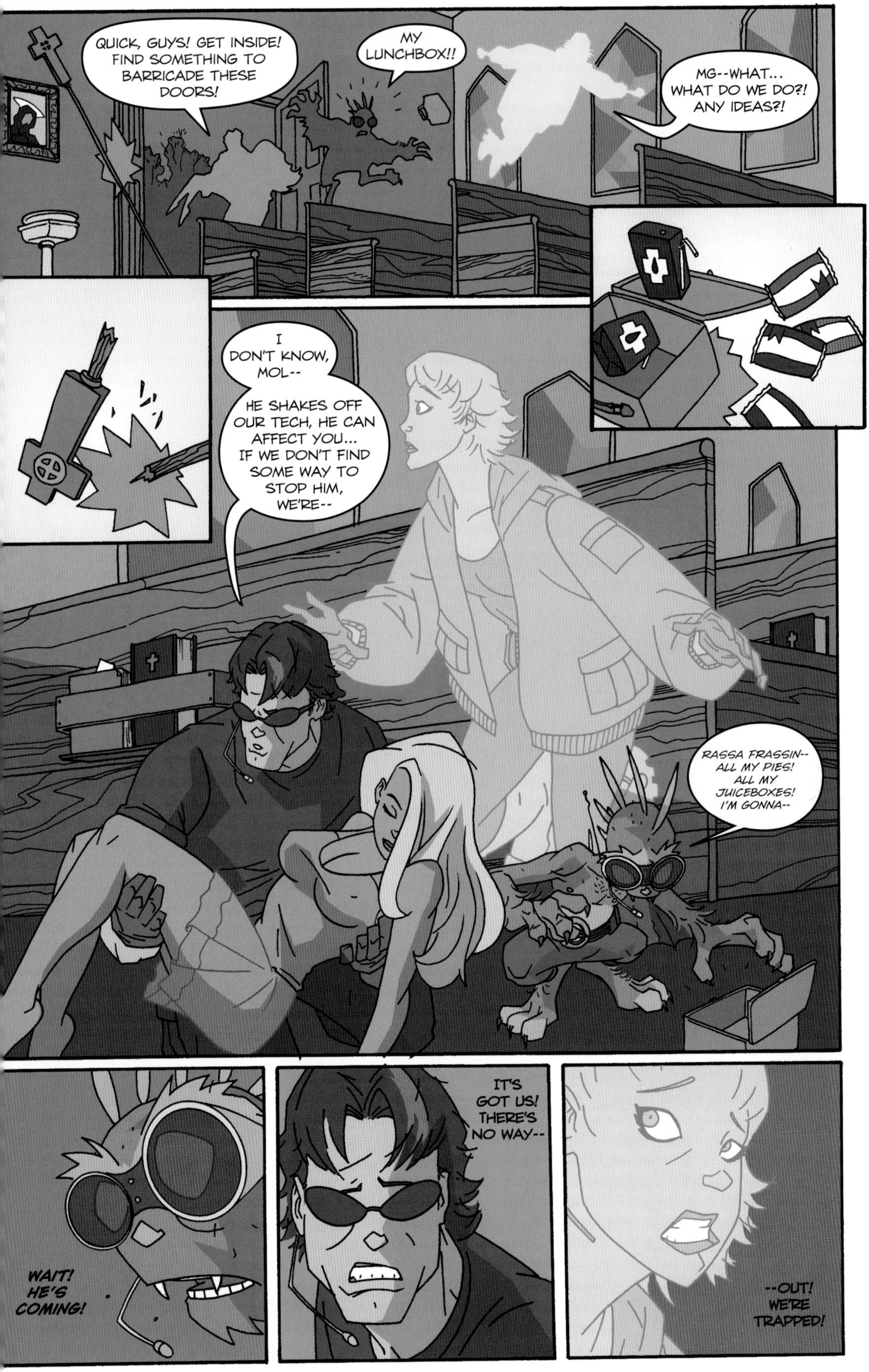
QUICK, GUYS! GET INSIDE! FIND SOMETHING TO BARRICADE THESE DOORS!
MY LUNCHBOX!!
MG--WHAT... WHAT DO WE DO?! ANY IDEAS?!
I DON'T KNOW, MOL--
HE SHAKES OFF OUR TECH, HE CAN AFFECT YOU... IF WE DON'T FIND SOME WAY TO STOP HIM, WE'RE--
RASSA FRASSIN-- ALL MY PIES! ALL MY JUICEBOXES! I'M GONNA--
WAIT! HE'S COMING!
IT'S GOT US! THERE'S NO WAY--
--OUT! WE'RE TRAPPED!

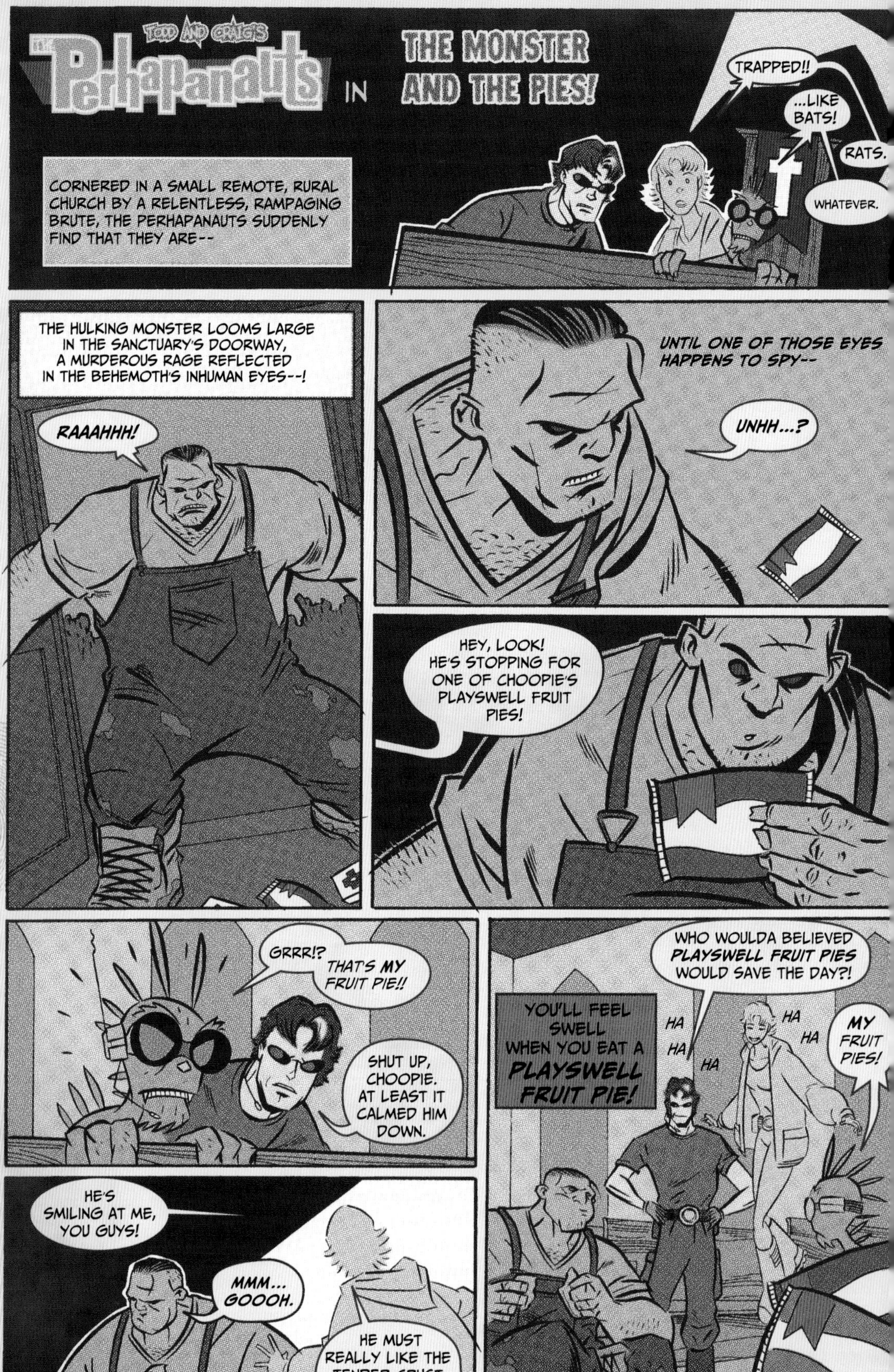
TODD AND CRAIG'S
THE Perhapanauts IN THE MONSTER AND THE PIES!
CORNERED IN A SMALL REMOTE, RURAL CHURCH BY A RELENTLESS, RAMPAGING BRUTE, THE PERHAPANAUTS SUDDENLY FIND THAT THEY ARE--
TRAPPED!!
...LIKE BATS!
RATS.
WHATEVER.
THE HULKING MONSTER LOOMS LARGE IN THE SANCTUARY'S DOORWAY, A MURDEROUS RAGE REFLECTED IN THE BEHEMOTH'S INHUMAN EYES--!
RAAAHHH!
UNTIL ONE OF THOSE EYES HAPPENS TO SPY--
UNHH...?
HEY, LOOK! HE'S STOPPING FOR ONE OF CHOOPIE'S PLAYSWELL FRUIT PIES!
GRRR!? THAT'S MY FRUIT PIE!!
SHUT UP, CHOOPIE. AT LEAST IT CALMED HIM DOWN.
HE'S SMILING AT ME, YOU GUYS!
MMM... GOOOH.
HE MUST REALLY LIKE THE TENDER CRUST AND REAL FRUIT FILLING!
WHO WOULDA BELIEVED PLAYSWELL FRUIT PIES WOULD SAVE THE DAY?!
YOU'LL FEEL SWELL WHEN YOU EAT A PLAYSWELL FRUIT PIE!
HA HA HA HA HA
MY FRUIT PIES!

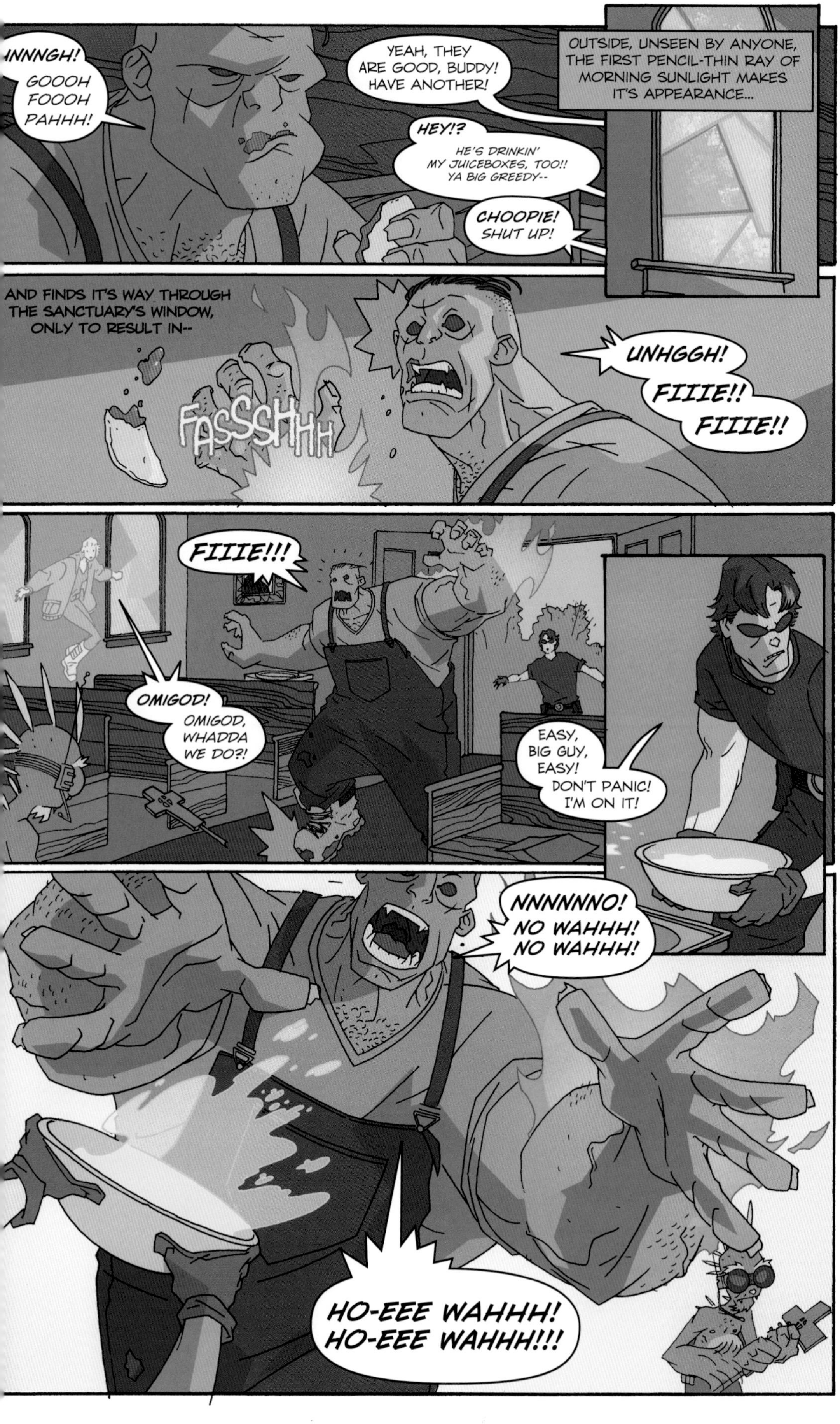
NNNGH! GOOOH FOOOH PAHHH!
YEAH, THEY ARE GOOD, BUDDY! HAVE ANOTHER!
OUTSIDE, UNSEEN BY ANYONE, THE FIRST PENCIL-THIN RAY OF MORNING SUNLIGHT MAKES IT'S APPEARANCE...
HEY!? HE'S DRINKIN' MY JUICEBOXES, TOO!! YA BIG GREEDY--
CHOOPIE! SHUT UP!
AND FINDS IT'S WAY THROUGH THE SANCTUARY'S WINDOW, ONLY TO RESULT IN--
FASSSHHH
UNHGGH! FIIIE!! FIIIE!!
FIIIE!!!
OMIGOD! OMIGOD, WHADDA WE DO?!
EASY, BIG GUY, EASY! DON'T PANIC! I'M ON IT!
NNNNNNO! NO WAHHH! NO WAHHH!
HO-EEE WAHHH! HO-EEE WAHHH!!!

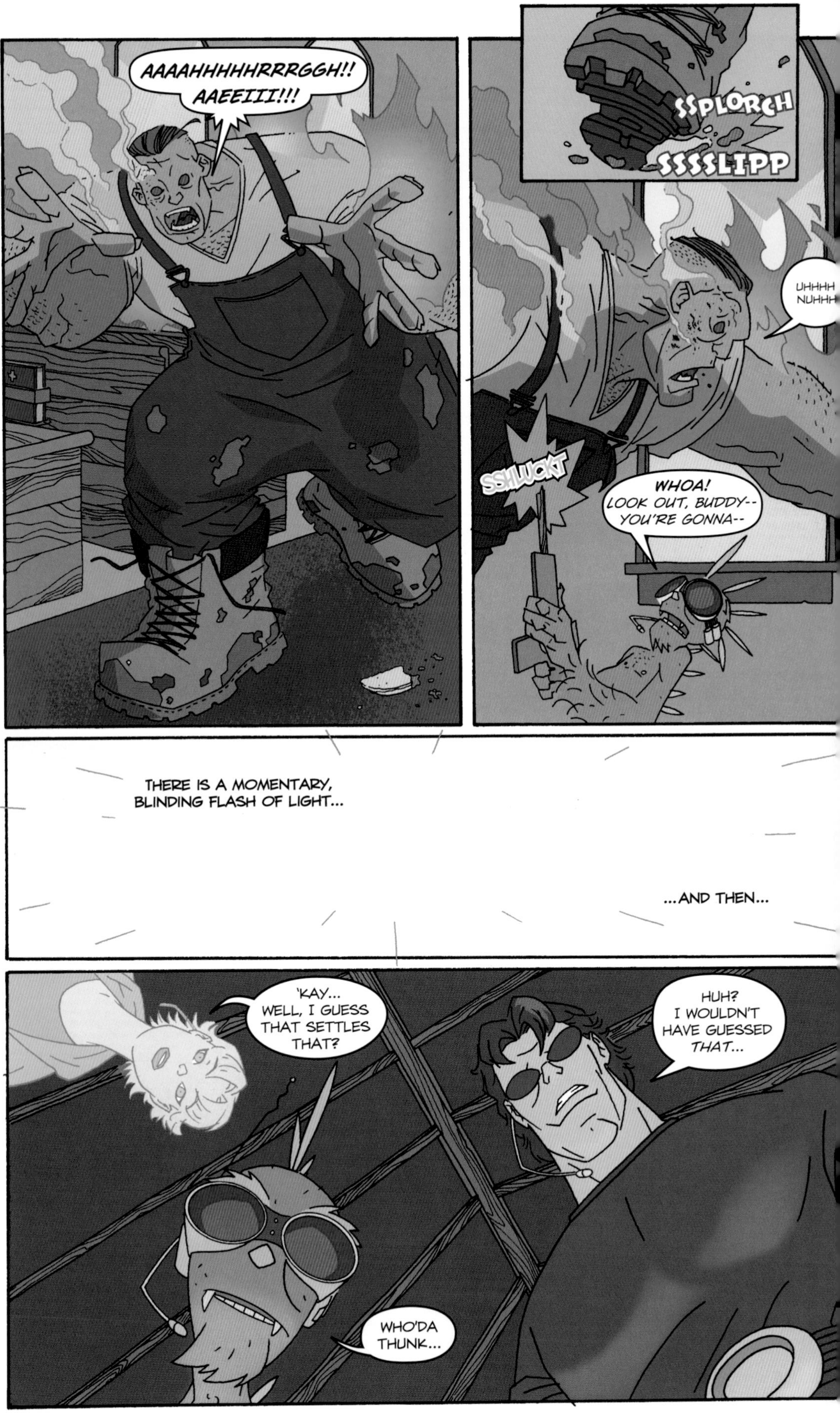
AAAAHHHHHRRRGGH!! AAEEIII!!!
SSPLORCH
SSSSLIPP
UHHHH NUHHH
SSHLUCKT
WHOA! LOOK OUT, BUDDY-- YOU'RE GONNA--
THERE IS A MOMENTARY, BLINDING FLASH OF LIGHT...
...AND THEN...
'KAY... WELL, I GUESS THAT SETTLES THAT?
HUH? I WOULDN'T HAVE GUESSED THAT...
WHO'DA THUNK...

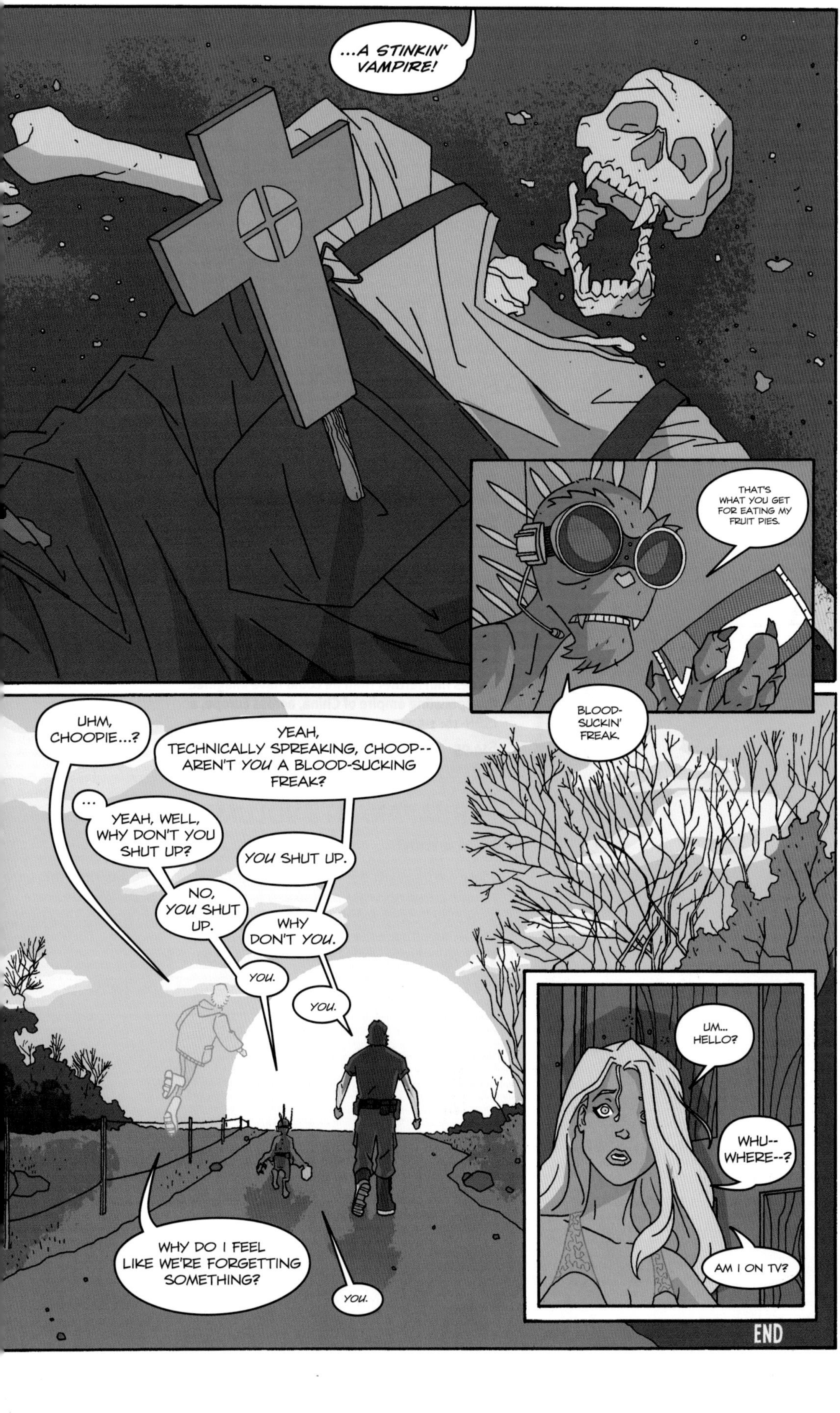
...A STINKIN' VAMPIRE!
THAT'S WHAT YOU GET FOR EATING MY FRUIT PIES.
BLOOD-SUCKIN' FREAK.
UHM, CHOOPIE...?
YEAH, TECHNICALLY SPREAKING, CHOOP-- AREN'T YOU A BLOOD-SUCKING FREAK?
... YEAH, WELL, WHY DON'T YOU SHUT UP?
YOU SHUT UP.
NO, YOU SHUT UP.
WHY DON'T YOU.
YOU.
YOU.
WHY DO I FEEL LIKE WE'RE FORGETTING SOMETHING?
YOU.
UM... HELLO?
WHU-- WHERE--?
AM I ON TV?
END

ACTION! ADVENTURE! EXCITEMENT!

ISN'T IT TIME YOU PICKED UP ANOTHER GREAT TITLE FROM DARK HORSE BOOKS?

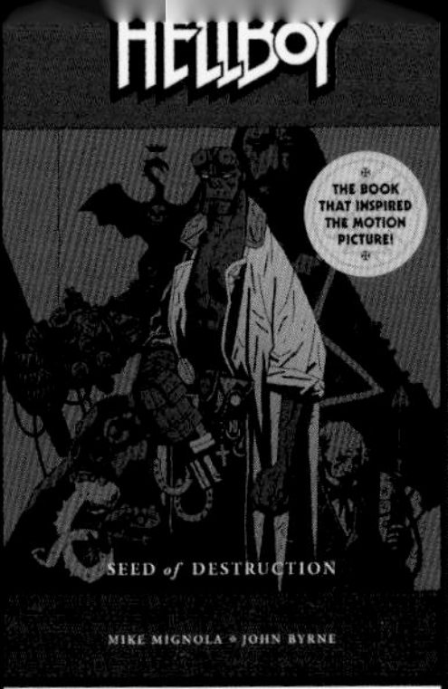
HELLBOY
THE BOOK THAT INSPIRED THE MOTION PICTURE!
SEED of DESTRUCTION
MIKE MIGNOLA • JOHN BYRNE

HELLBOY VOLUME 1:
Seed of Destruction

When strangeness threatens to engulf the world, a strange man will come to save it. Sent to investigate a mystery with supernatural overtones, Hellboy discovers the secrets of his own origins, and his link to the Nazi occultists who promised Hitler a final solution in the form of a demonic avatar.
ISBN-10: 1-59307-094-2 / ISBN-13: 978-1-59307-094-6
$17.95

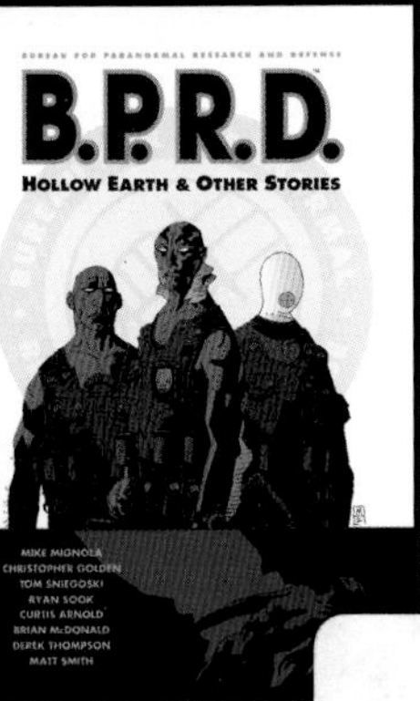
B.P.R.D.
HOLLOW EARTH & OTHER STORIES
MIKE MIGNOLA
CHRISTOPHER GOLDEN
TOM SNIEGOSKI
RYAN SOOK
CURTIS ARNOLD
BRIAN McDONALD
DEREK THOMPSON
MATT SMITH

BPRD VOLUME 1:
Hollow Earth and Other Stories

Hellboy's departure from the Bureau for Paranormal Research and Defense has left the other supernatural members questioning their futures. But when a vision appears to Abe Sapien warning of danger for the missing Liz Sherman, he takes a very irregular group of agents on a mission that could lead them right through the center of the earth. This story is collected here with rare Hellboy, Abe Sapien, and Lobster Johnston related stories!
...1-862-9

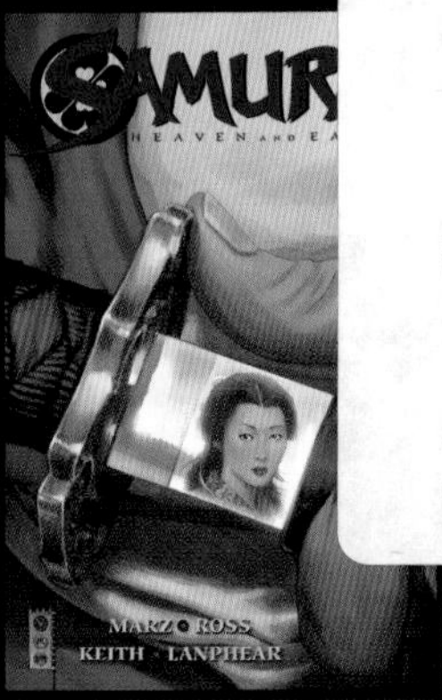
MARZ • ROSS
KEITH • LANPHEAR

...reunited with the love of ...ies, as his pursuit of Yoshiko ...—from his native Japan to ...nd finally to Paris itself!
...-388-6

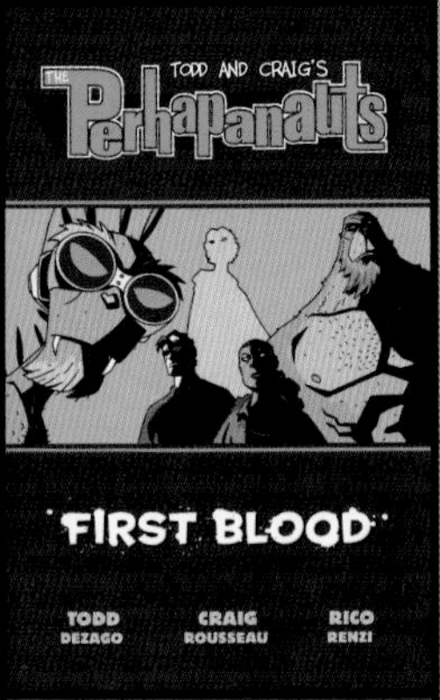
TODD AND CRAIG'S
THE Perhapanauts
FIRST BLOOD
TODD DEZAGO
CRAIG ROUSSEAU
RICO RENZI

PERHAPANAUTS VOLUME 1:
First Blood

There are places in this world where the fabric of reality has worn thin and terrible creatures cross over to lurk in the night. But BEDLAM is dedicated to finding these creatures and sending them back from whence they came, and its agents are the Perhapanauts!
ISBN-10: 1-59307-607-X / ISBN-13: 978-1-59307-607-8
$15.95

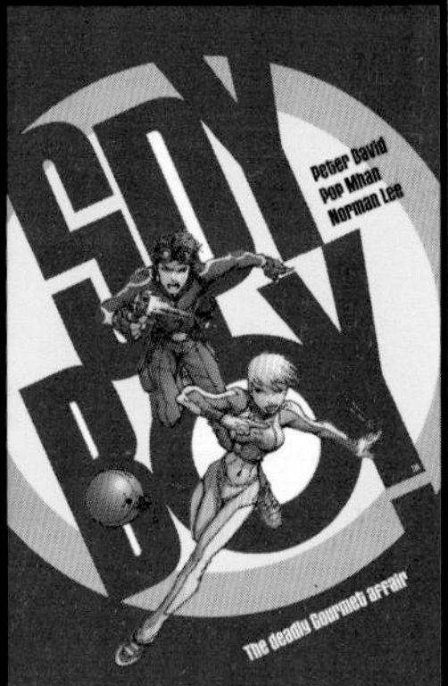
Peter David
Pop Mhan
Norman Lee
The Deadly Gourmet Affair

SPYBOY VOLUME 1:
The Deadly Gourmet Affair

What if you were an international super spy? What if you had the latest technology at your fingertips? What if you had martial-arts training to hone your mind and body into the perfect living weapon? What if you didn't know it? But what if others did?
ISBN-10: 1-56971-463-0 / ISBN-13: 978-1-56971-463-8
$8.95

DARK HORSE BOOKS

AVAILABLE AT YOUR LOCAL COMICS SHOP OR BOOKSTORE
TO FIND A COMICS SHOP IN YOUR AREA, CALL 1-888-266-4226.
For more information or to order direct: • On the web: darkhorse.com • E-mail: mailorder@darkhorse.com
• Phone: 1-800-862-0052 Mon.-Fri. 9 A.M. to 5 P.M. Pacific Time.